Honey Pie

ALSO BY BESTSELLING AUTHOR DONNA KAUFFMAN

Honey Pie

DONNA KAUFFMAN

BRAVA

KENSINGTON PUBLISHING CORP.
www.kensingtonbooks.com

They say it takes a village. I am fortunate to have several.
(Or maybe it just takes many villages in my case!)
This one is for my Farm-to-Florida family villagers,
my Happy Stamper crafting villagers,
my wonderful Reader villagers,
and the most amazing Kensington Publishing
villagers evah!
You mean so much to me, each and every one of you.

Chapter 1

Never underestimate the power of cupcakes. Or the women who bake them.

Honey D'Amourvell pondered that truth as she sat on the wooden bench behind Ross & Sons auto repair, trying to get comfortable. She'd long since passed any hope of civilized perspiration and had moved straight into actual sweating, so comfort of any kind was a stretch. She curled her fingers around the plastic water bottle and debated the merits of simply yanking her blouse open and rolling the cold bottle directly over her chest. Could anyone blame her? How did people live in heat like this? Much less feel like baking cupcakes? And yet, it didn't seem to be affecting the cupcake ladies in the least.

She watched the action across the narrow back alley, as the happy baker bunch piled out of their cars and trooped through the service entrance into Cakes by the Cup, the local Sugarberry Island cupcakery. They were smiling, laughing, and boisterously chatting with each other as they carted in all manner of baking supplies and tools of the cupcake trade.

Honey knew from her stroll around the small town square earlier that the shop had closed to the public a half hour ago, so she wasn't sure what, exactly, they were up to, but she doubted it was baking cupcakes for the next day's trade. According to the sign in the front window of the shop, the owner prided herself on offering only freshly baked cupcakes. A bit of quick research on Honey's phone had revealed the owner of the cupcakery to be Leilani Dunne. Wife to television star, Chef Hot Cakes himself, Baxter Dunne. Honey had even discovered a whole website devoted to their newest enterprise, Babycakes—a mail order and catering adjunct to the main bakery, located right next door.

Her gaze shifted to the narrow, whitewashed building that shared a common wall with the cupcake shop and she instinctively pressed the cold water bottle to the front of her blouse. It was a vain attempt to soothe the heat . . . and the twinge in her heart. It didn't do much for either.

She'd already noted that a covered walkway had been erected between the rear doors of both shops. She supposed she should be thankful. The covered walkway likely meant they hadn't busted through the common wall.

So, there was that.

Her gaze drifted upward to the two sets of windows on the second floor above the shop, and she pressed the water bottle harder as the twinge became a clutch. *Oh, Aunt Beavis . . . what did you do?*

Whatever her aunt had done, or had not done, it was going to take more than a few random internet searches to figure out how things had gone so horribly wrong.

I should go on over there right now, Honey thought. *Just head on in, introduce myself, explain who I am, and why I'm here.*

Yeah . . . that wasn't such a great idea. Not right this second, anyway.

She was going to have to cross paths with the cupcake crew at some point, given the surprising set of circumstances she'd discovered upon her arrival on the island. But, whenever that meeting happened, it wasn't likely to leave them wanting to welcome her with cheerful cupcakes and party sprinkles. So why rush things? She'd only been on Sugarberry for forty-five minutes, and already she had more immediate concerns. Like getting her car back up and running.

But they all looked friendly enough, and were certainly a joyful, peppy group. Maybe they were on a giddy sugar buzz high and wouldn't hold against her personally the news she had to share. It wasn't like it was her fault. Someone on Sugarberry, or at the law offices in Savannah, had clearly screwed up. Big time.

On the other hand, Honey had been on the wrong side of pack mentality types her entire life. She knew better than most not to take on a pack leader, especially when said leader was on her own turf, surrounded by her dedicated and loyal packettes. *Don't let the cheerful cupcakes fool you!*

Honey plucked uselessly at the front of her damp blouse. During their frequent phone chats, her dearly departed aunt had often mentioned the lovely island breeze and how moderate the temperatures were all year round. Since Sugarberry Island was off the coast of Georgia, Honey had expected the summers would be on the warm side. But Bea hadn't mentioned it turned into a veritable steam bath as early as April.

Not for the first time since packing up her entire life and hitting the road, Honey wondered if she should have stayed in Oregon. It had been silly, not to mention completely irrational, to think things would be different on the island, no matter how many times Bea had insisted they would be.

Honey missed her aunt terribly and would forever regret not getting to spend more time with her, face-to-face. Bea was the only other person on the planet who'd understood. The only person Honey had been able to relax with and completely let down her guard. Be herself. Along with all the lovely eccentricities that entailed.

Eccentricities. Honey smiled faintly, hearing her mother's voice echoing in her mind, as that was the term she and Honey's father had taken to using for their only daughter's odd little "differences."

Of course, growing up in the Pacific Northwest, being different should have meant she'd fit right in. After all, her own parents—God rest their unconditionally loving souls—hadn't exactly been mainstream. Her father had grown up on a commune in northern California and become an herb farmer and wood carver, while her mother was a rug weaver who spun her own wool, straight from her own personal little herd of llamas. Her parents' circle of friends had been equally . . . interesting. If anything, growing up, Honey had always felt like the normal one.

As it turned out, there was a limit on just how different one was allowed to be. And if she'd failed that litmus test in Juniper Hollow, Oregon, why on earth would she expect anywhere else to be more welcoming? Even though Bea had sworn she'd found just that place on Sugarberry.

Of course, Bea had always considered those same eccentricities to be a gift, rather than the curse Honey felt they were. But Honey was working on gaining a new perspective, or trying to, anyway. She was on the island, wasn't she?

"And yet, the joke? Is still on me." She finished her second bottle of water, staring at the building across the alley. "That's a stunner."

Honey was still there an hour and a half later, working on water bottle number four and starting to feel like a camel, when the same women exited Cakes by the Cup, boxed up goodies tucked under their arms. The rich scents of freshly baked cake, warm, buttery, and delicious, followed them into the little lot behind the shop, then wafted through the thick air, making her stomach grumble in appreciation.

She watched them pile into their cars, continuing to toss comments back and forth, still laughing and chatting, until they finally pulled out of the tiny lot in their various vehicles and drove off, leaving only the scent of buttery, sugary goodness in their wake. None of them had noticed her, sitting across the way. Maybe they were used to customers hanging out behind the repair shop, waiting for their cars to be ready. Or maybe she was as invisible as she'd been in Oregon.

She pushed up her prescription glasses—again—and scratched at the mosquito bite on her neck. She couldn't imagine ever getting used to such humidity. Or the bugs. The sun dipping behind the row of shops had only seemed to increase that particular carnivorous hoard. And, again, it had to be said . . . it was only April.

At the moment, she was praying her poor old Volkswagen Beetle would be ready soon so she could stop thinking about the happy, peppy cupcake bakers and start figuring out how she was going to inform the Queen Bee of Cake about her inheritance.

Honey decided she was okay with not being noticed, thankful for it, in fact. She'd had no real idea how she'd planned on introducing herself to her new community, but was well aware how crucial first impressions could be. She'd figured she'd settle in, get the lay of the land, start with plotting and planning out her new enterprise, then see where that might lead. Gradually integrate herself. Given her personal demons, it would be best to take folks on a few at a time, rather than en masse. At least until she felt comfortable, after such a long time spent . . . well, hiding.

Confronting the owner of what appeared to be a very popular island establishment with news that was definitely not going to go over well wasn't exactly the best way to kick things off.

For a very long time, Honey had convinced herself that being a social pariah was a blessing. If she didn't deal with folks, then folks didn't have to deal with her and her "eccentricities."

But as life marched onward for everyone else, while she hung out, safely tucked away on the perimeter, watching . . . she'd finally been forced to admit what she'd known all along: no matter how rich or fulfilling a life she'd built for herself out on the fringes, not being around people pretty much sucked.

Otherwise, she'd still be working in her barn out in Middle of Nowhere, Oregon, and not sitting on a hard wooden bench in Georgia, swatting bugs, watching the cupcake ladies . . . and allowing herself to wonder what it would be like to be one of them. To just . . . hang out, to chat, laugh, and share.

It wasn't hard to imagine how much she'd enjoy it. She wasn't awkward, socially or otherwise, or even particularly dorky. Sure, she wasn't a stunner in the looks department, but she didn't make babies cry, either. Her body might not turn heads, but it was functional and didn't let her down. She'd always been a fairly confident, self aware, decently sharp-witted person. But being confident and self-assured didn't automatically equal fitting in.

Not when all she had to do was touch someone to suddenly know all sorts of things about what was going to happen or what had already happened, good or bad, to that person. Unfortunately, the bad often far outweighed the good. Neither the party in question, nor Honey herself particularly wanted her to know about those kinds of things, but once she did know, she couldn't exactly ignore them. To her, it was sort of like a moral imperative. If you knew bad things were going to happen to someone, you had to warn them. Right? You had to at least give them a chance to change the outcome.

Otherwise, what was the point in having the stupid "gift" in the first place?

To top it off, folks were rarely grateful for her warnings. Like the bad news was somehow her fault. But she couldn't just sit there and watch the otherwise inevitable thing happen and not say anything. She'd tried that, but couldn't live with the guilt of not saying anything, and then watching something horrible, even tragic, befall the person. Who could live with that? It left her . . . where, exactly?

"The equivalent of Juniper Hollows' Fifth Horse of the Apocalypse, forced to hide out in the family barn, that's where." She'd spent her time carving from wood and creating from clay whimsical, happy little garden and woodland critters that filled her personal world, as well as the charming and amusing mail-order catalog that had turned a childhood hobby she'd started with her father into her livelihood as an adult. It was easy to pretend everything was fine when she was surrounded by whimsy, cuteness, and the always adorable. Easy to believe she was happy enough and blessed to be doing something she loved.

As long as I don't get close to anyone. Ever again.

She *was* happy. She was. In all the limited ways she could be, anyway. She loved her work, enjoyed her customers, and had built a successful, fulfilling, if very secluded life for herself. It was a lot more fun making people happy than sending them running, hiding from the very sight of her. She simply wanted the same things everyone else did—friends, acceptance, a sense of belonging. She'd actually found a way to have that, too. Just . . . at a carefully controlled distance.

With the launch of the new year—the last one before she turned the big three-oh—coupled with the loss of her last remaining family member, and a newly acquired inheritance, Honey had found herself unable to shut out the niggling thoughts and desires she'd tried to talk herself out of.

The real truth was, she wanted what the cupcake ladies had—community, partnership, family, and friends. The up close and personal kind. Watching them, knowing she was finally going to reach for what they had, the desire had become almost a physical ache. God, but she was lonely. Thriving business or no, communicating all day long with people via the phone or e-mail was a far cry from laughing, chatting, and baking in the same kitchen . . . together.

Bea's letter she'd received from the lawyer after her aunt's death, along with the packet detailing the rest of her inheritance, had been, in the end, what had dissolved her carefully constructed defenses. Honey held that letter in her heart as her real inheritance. Of far more value than the physical possessions Bea had left to her only niece had been her words of wisdom. One part, in particular, stayed with Honey always.

> *Don't ever settle for less when there could be so much*
> *more. Life is not meant to be lived in the shadows.*
> *Don't assume there is no welcome mat out there for*
> *you. I know there is one right here, Honey Pie,*
> *waiting for you. Trust me enough to come to my island,*
> *to my home, and find out for yourself. Love yourself*
> *enough to give it a true and honest chance. I love you,*
> *child of my heart. Twin to my soul.*

Honey heard her Aunt Beavis as clearly as if she were sitting beside her.

"Well," she murmured, pushing her glasses up and wiping at the corners of her eyes. "I'm here. So . . . now what?"

Bea had been right about one thing; Honey couldn't reinvent herself or turn over a new leaf in Juniper Hollow. So she'd set out for the east coast.

Bea would be proud of her. Hell, she was proud of herself. She'd made it all the way to Georgia. To Sugarberry Island. Albeit barely. Her car had started coughing and spitting—more like gasping its final death rattle—as soon as she'd crossed the causeway to the island. A sign? She didn't know. Her curse didn't include knowing things that would happen to herself—which she'd long since determined was a definite blessing.

She'd barely managed to get her car to the garage before it sputtered and died right in front of the island's only repair shop. She prayed it would survive this latest bout of operational ennui. A new car wasn't in her tightly detailed budget. Nor was an old one, for that matter. She needed the one she already had to hang in there.

Fortunately, the mechanic—Dylan Ross of Ross & Sons—hadn't seemed to think her car was a complete lost cause, though that might have been wishful thinking on her part. It had been somewhat hard to tell what he'd been thinking, actually. He gave new meaning to tall, dark, and brooding. James Dean could have taken lessons from that guy. Truth be told, Dylan Ross had it all over the movie icon in the looks department, too. He was the poster boy for every broad-shouldered, narrow-hipped, six-pack toting, pouty-lipped hunk of modeling clay who'd ever slid a pair of perfectly faded jeans over muscular thighs and very fine ass to pose, all smoldering intensity, in front of a camera lens.

Only hotter. He wasn't some smug, young dude. More like . . . well, it was hard to tell how old he was, but he was no kid. He was all man, and . . . seasoned. Experienced. Grooves at the corners of his eyes and a pouty-lipped mouth lent character to the chiseled jaw and sharp cheekbones. His gray eyes had that wise-beyond-his-years look as if they'd seen far too much already and would be perfectly happy to tune out what came next. It made her wonder what the story was behind the attitude . . . although she quite honestly hoped she never had the opportunity to find out.

He was the polar opposite of the cheerful young man— Dell, he'd said his name was—who'd greeted her at the desk and taken her keys and information, before taking off on his motor bike to run an errand. Conversely, Mr. Ross had been rather abrupt, almost bordering on rude, while asking a few more questions to help determine her situation. She'd been thankful for that, though. Mostly. A little less curt wouldn't have killed the guy. Or her.

She'd heard so many stories from Bea about the goodwill of the island denizens that she'd spent the last two states of the drive bracing herself for the physical onslaught that could quite possibly envelop her upon her arrival. Dell had certainly lived up to those standards, although thankfully without the hugging, but it was only after Mr. Ross had been so abrupt, with minimal conversation and little or no eye contact, that she'd realized how grateful she was for his brevity. And his distance.

She would handle whatever was coming at her, but she wasn't ashamed to admit it would help enormously if she could get a good night's sleep first

Unfortunately, nothing was going according to plan. She'd anticipated curling up in Bea's old apartment, which, as emotional as that was likely to be, would also be a haven of sorts. She hadn't realized how much she'd been counting on that safe and secure landing pad . . . until it had been quite unexpectedly yanked out from under her.

"Miz D'Amourvell?"

Her head jerked up at the sound of her name. Spoken the way he said it, in that deep, southern drawl . . . well, it did surprising things to her insides. She pushed her glasses up again, tugged on her sticky blouse, and shoved the strap of her satchel up over her shoulder, all while trying not to look directly at him. Or his chest. Or his hips. Or his mouth, for that matter. And definitely not those eyes. Oh boy.

"Is it ready?" she asked, making a big show of checking and double checking that she wasn't leaving anything behind. Though she'd never taken anything out of her satchel other than her phone.

"Afraid not. Needs a few parts, amongst other things. There's more wrong with it than right with it. You stayin' on the island?"

She nodded, trying not to feel more defeated. "I'm . . . not sure where."

"Barbara Hughes has a B&B a couple blocks off the square, heading toward the docks. I imagine she probably has a room."

"Okay. Thanks. Is it walking distance? I have a lot of stuff." She thought about the suitcases—none of them on wheels—and all the tools and supply boxes presently crammed into her car. Not that she needed much for the night, but some of her work things wouldn't do well sitting in this kind of heat overnight. Much less however many days it might be until her car was fixed.

"Shop's locked up at night," he said, apparently reading her concerns from her expression. "Not that anyone around here would take anything." His voice was deep, gravelly, and oh so sexily Southern. The kind of voice that vibrated along the skin. Hot, slick skin.

She shook that image off—could her thoughts be more inappropriate?—and tried to relax. Terse or not, he was trying to help her out. Yet it was almost impossible to ignore the tension that seemed to emanate from him. That, combined with the heat, the fatigue, the massive screw up she hadn't even begun to figure out how to fix, and her suddenly perky hormones made her feel jumpy . . . and restless.

"It was more the heat I was worried about. Some of the things in my car probably shouldn't be left—never mind. I can deal with that tomorrow." She sent another pensive look in the direction of the work bay. "How long will it take to get it fixed, do you think?"

She hitched the satchel strap up again—even her shoulders were sweaty—and resisted the urge to scratch her neck. Not that she cared how she looked—good thing— but she was a woman, after all. Standing in front of a guy who looked like . . . well, who looked like Dylan Ross, she imagined any woman would want to feel at least marginally not disastrous. She was pretty sure she fell short of even that low bar.

"Two or three days. Could be a week. Parts for your car don't run in stock anywhere local. Have to order them, then get them sent over from Savannah." He turned around and headed back inside, leaving her to follow him or . . . walk down the alley and out into the square, presumably to find the Hughes's place on her own. He didn't seem to much care either way. Of course, he had her car and a goodly part of her worldly possessions, so it wasn't like he had to worry she'd take off and not pay him.

She sent another look across the back alley at the cupcakery, her gaze lingering on the whitewashed brick building next to it.

It was every bit as perfect as Bea had claimed it would be. She couldn't deny she'd felt a buzz of excitement when she'd taken that short walk around the square after her car had been pushed into the service bay. It had been something of a thrill, more than she'd anticipated feeling, spying the tiny shop on the corner for the first time.

Honey had assumed Bea had romanticized the little

town, the island, but Sugarberry was exactly as she'd described it. It had all the charms of every Southern town she'd ever read about . . . along with the added twist of a more bohemian island vibe, which was just eccentric enough to appeal to her Aunt Bea . . . and to her. Enormously, in fact. Despite the swelter. And the bugs.

Don't ever settle for less when there could be so much more. Life is not meant to be lived in the shadows. Bea's words had been on her mind as she'd crossed the square.

Don't assume there is no welcome mat out there for you. There is one right here . . . waiting for you. Honey had embraced that benediction, had allowed herself to truly believe that maybe, just maybe, Bea had been right and this was her very real chance at the life she'd wanted so very badly, but had been too afraid to reach for.

It had made the blow that much worse as she'd gotten close enough to see the GRAND OPENING sign in the window of her newly inherited, supposedly empty building. The same whitewashed brick building that had once housed Aunt Beavis's tailoring shop and the apartment she'd lived in above it. The building Honey had planned to transform into her very own, very real, storefront business where customers could come in and browse, to see and touch her work firsthand. More important, to see and talk to the owner and artist firsthand. No more hiding behind her mail-order catalog and computer screen. The same building was now Babycakes, the mail-order and catering adjunct to Cakes by the Cup, right next door.

Yeah. It had been such a special day. Oh so very . . . special.

She clamped down on the fresh wave of frustration and anxiety that had started a vicious little whirl in her gut. She still had the farm. It hadn't sold yet. She could simply turn around and go home.

Home.

Instead of feeling reassured, the idea of driving all the way back to Oregon and out to Juniper Hollow, to the old farmhouse and the barn . . . felt like, well . . . it felt like failure.

She glanced one last time over her shoulder before following Dylan into the building that housed Ross & Sons.

She found him in the small office tucked in the front of the shop. It was surprisingly tidy and clean for an old time, family-owned auto repair business. In fact, the whole place had a rather . . . fresh feel to it. The bench out back had been brand new, too. But Dylan Ross was too young to have sons working for him so she assumed he was one of the sons.

"Want to get anything?" he asked, head bent over a clipboard on his desk, not bothering to look up. "From your car," he elaborated, when she didn't respond.

She'd gotten kind of caught up looking at his hands. Broad, strong, capable. Beat up a bit, but given his profession, no more so than could be expected.

"Yes? No?" he asked, finally looking up.

She jerked her gaze to his, then realized that for the mistake it was, and immediately looked toward the front of the shop, anywhere, really, but into those eyes. Eyes that met hers quite directly. Unflinchingly. With a gaze that probed, assessed, and summed up, without even trying.

She could feel the . . . beginnings of things. Stirrings. And not just *those* kinds of stirrings. Skittering around the edges of her consciousness were the kinds of things she'd spent many long years suppressing. Feeling them rattled her, adding to the jumpiness she already felt around him. Though she knew by leaving her barn and Oregon, and coming out into the world, she'd given those stirrings carte blanche to resurface—but she wasn't going to allow them to do so now. And, God help her, not with him.

Danger, danger, Honey Pie. Look away. Look away fast.

"Just . . . a suitcase," she managed when he lifted an eyebrow. "I'll . . . figure out the rest tomorrow."

He shoved back his chair and stood, and she realized too late that she was far too close to him, almost crowding him in the small office space, standing between him, his desk, and the only door out.

He was tall, towering over her as he looked down with an expression that clearly asked if she was going to move out of his way sometime in the next millennium.

"Sorry," she said, moving at the same time, in the same direction he did, which had the unfortunate consequence of brushing her up against him, which had the even more unfortunate consequence of making her gasp.

His eyes widened momentarily; then he gave a short shake of his head. When she remained standing there, frozen, staring, he bodily—if gently—took her by the arms with those broad, strong hands of his, and set her aside.

She locked up at his direct touch and had to clench her jaw to keep from screaming. It had been a very—very— long time since anyone had put their hands on her. She'd made damn sure of that. And though he probably already thought her a bit of a fruit loop, she didn't much care at the moment. "Let me go," she said—begged—almost strangling on the words.

He looked momentarily stunned, then scowled and lifted his hands away, palms out. "Just trying to get out of my own office so I can go home." He gestured to the open doorway. "After you."

"I'm sorry," she said, mortification and resignation filling her in equal measures. Apparently time hadn't healed anything. Nor had it diminished her curse. At all. *Here we go. Again.*

Dammit.

Suddenly Oregon wasn't looking so much like failure as it was the smarter option. "I—"

She realized even as she opened her mouth that there was no explanation that could possibly repair the moment, none that she was willing to give, anyway, or that he'd believe, much less understand. "Sorry," she repeated, and ducked out in front of him, careful not to come into so much as a speck of contact.

She walked back to her car, realized she didn't have the keys and turned back around, almost bumping right back into him. He held up the keys between them, his tight expression somewhere between *what the hell is your problem* and *please, dear God, just let me get out of here.*

She'd seen it before. Many times.

So, it shouldn't have felt so . . . disappointing. She snatched the keys from his fingertips and turned quickly toward the car, feeling an irrational surge of anger. At him, herself, or a little of both, she couldn't take time to figure out, but it got her through the motions necessary to dig into her car and drag out her father's old leather suitcase. She manhandled it to the cement floor of the garage, then took one last look inside the car, and immediately decided she'd dealt with all she was going to deal with at the moment.

She gripped the hard, camel leather handle and started to heave it up . . . to go where, she really had no idea, but she'd figure that out as soon as she got herself out of the garage and away from the intense gaze of Mr. Ross. How a gray-eyed gaze could be so piercing, she wasn't quite sure, but his was. Piercing and penetrating. As if he'd figure out all of her secrets without even trying, much less meaning to.

Of course, he hadn't. No one could.

"I'll just get this outside, and you can lock up for the night."

He stepped in and reached for her bag, making her leap backward as if he'd scalded her. She banged her elbow against the car, swore under her breath, and gave him a heated look before thinking better of it. "Please. Just . . . don't do that."

His jaw tightened slightly, but he managed to keep his gaze level. "I'm only trying to help with your bag. I was going to offer you a lift over to the B&B, but, you know what? My day has been long enough already, thanks. I don't know what your problem is, darlin', but I'm really not tryin' to be part of it, okay? We clear?"

"Very," she said, well past mortification and operating solely on auto-pilot. She had to get out of there. Had to get somewhere away. Alone. Immediately. Everything that could go wrong had, and then there was the heat, and now this. She didn't have anything left to deal with it. She wasn't ready. How in the hell had she thought she'd ever be ready?

She felt the tears well, which only served to undo whatever reserve she had left. When things got tough, laughter had always been her default reaction. Because crying wasn't an option. Ever. Tears lowered way, way too many guards. But . . . at this point, what the hell difference did it make what she did? The mechanic already suspected she was some kind of a nut job, and, if small town Sugarberry was anything like small town Juniper Hollow, word would spread on that little piece of news before the dinner hour was over.

He was in front of her again, but had stopped a clear foot or two away. He didn't look belligerent—exactly— but he didn't look compassionate, either. "Put the suitcase down," he said in what she assumed was as close to a gentle tone as he could manage. "I'll take it out to my truck. I'll put it in the back. You can get in the back, too, if that helps. I'll have you at the Hughes's place in two minutes. And I'll call you when your car is done."

He was trying to be kind, or his version of it, anyway. But he was talking to her like she was a crazy chick with a good chance of doing bodily harm—to him or herself. She couldn't exactly blame him, but damn, it made her feel tired. So very, very . . . tired.

And she hadn't even started her new life yet.

"Thank you," was all she said as evenly as she could manage. She let go of the suitcase and walked past him, frowning the threatening tears into submission. Straight through the back door, she didn't stop until she stood by the passenger door of the only pickup truck parked behind his garage.

A moment later, she heard the bay doors being rolled down, then the back door slap shut. From the corner of her eye, she saw him load her suitcase in the open flatbed.

"Door's unlocked," he said, walking around to the driver's side and climbing in.

She got in, closed the door, pulled on the seat belt, rolled the window all the way down, and very carefully kept her gaze straight out the front window.

He didn't say a word as he drove her the half mile or so to the front of a tidy little island bungalow with a sign out front, announcing it was THE HUGHES'S B&B. He put the truck in PARK, left the engine running, and got out.

By the time she climbed out and closed the door, her suitcase sat on the low curb by the side of the road.

"Tell Miz Barbara I've got your car, that you're stuck for a night or two. She'll give you a good deal on the room."

Honey nodded, feeling nothing but numb. And foolish. So ridiculously foolish.

Apparently happy to make his escape, and not requiring

or expecting any further conversational niceties, Dylan headed back around the front of the truck, leaving her and her suitcase parked on the curb.

"Thank you," she said, finding her voice, if not her courage. She kept her gaze averted.

"No problem."

She wasn't sure what prompted her, or where the words came from, or why on earth it mattered, but when she heard the truck door creak open, she looked up, looked at him. "I'm not crazy."

He glanced over at her and she held his gaze, almost defiantly.

"I'm not." Immediately, she wished the words back. Pathetic and pitiable were two things she refused to be. Ever.

Rather than look at her with either of those emotions flickering in his gray eyes, he did something that shook her hard-won control in a way she'd least expected. He grinned. Broadly.

"Sugar, we all have a little bit of crazy in us. It's what keeps us interesting." Then he climbed in his truck and drove off.

Honey stood there and watched until his taillights disappeared around the corner. Then she did something that only five seconds earlier she thought she no longer had in her to do again, possibly ever. She laughed.

Danger. Danger, indeed.

Chapter 2

Dylan had known she'd be some kind of trouble from the moment he'd read her name on the service order. *Honey D'Amourvell.* Sounded like very old, deep pockets Southern money. Or a stripper. Either way, she wasn't something the fine citizens of Sugarberry—well, one particular citizen, anyway—needed to deal with. Then he'd gone out to look at the car: a powder blue '72 Volkswagen Beetle.

Definitely not old money . . . unless it was eccentric old money.

So, he'd been assuming stripper, while looking over the initial list Dell had compiled of what needed to be done to get her junker up and running again. Vintage parts like she was going to need were going to take some tracking down. And likely cost a king's ransom.

Given the condition the car had been in even before it had broken down and the equally ancient suitcase she'd lugged out of the car, he'd bet his own bottom dollar she didn't have such a tidy sum. Maybe it was a sentimental junker and she had a sweet little hot rod stashed somewhere across the causeway on the mainland.

I could only be so lucky, he'd thought as he'd pushed through the door to the bench out back of the shop. He'd glanced up from the work order on the clipboard to tell

Ms. D'Amourvell the sad and sorry news, only to have the words jam right up in his throat.

Honey was no stripper. Neither tall nor short, large or particularly small, she was just . . . well, average. She had brown hair that was probably about shoulder length, pulled back in a single ponytail, and didn't wear any makeup that he could tell. Even in this heat, she'd covered herself pretty much head to toe. Definitely not a stripper.

But he hadn't actually been thinking about that. He'd been caught off guard by what she *was* revealing, inadvertent though it had been.

The one truly memorable thing about Honey D'Amourvell was her eyes. Not so much because they were an interesting shade of green, although they were so light in color they were almost spooky. Probably just an effect created by the black horn rim glasses she wore. It was what was in those spooky eyes that had made him feel incredibly stupid for assuming anything based on a name. He, of all people, knew better.

She'd been staring across the back alley at the buildings that fronted the corner of the town square. Normally, the thought of the cupcake bakery brought a pleasant smile to his face. He wasn't one for sweets, so had never been through the front door of either part of the establishment, but in the short time his garage had been in its new location, he'd done the neighborly thing, nodded when waved to, observed the comings and goings, had even jumped a dead battery for one of the cupcake ladies, and fixed a flat for another.

Small communities usually bred far more familiarity, but he wasn't a chatty sort and didn't much care to air his personal business. Several generations of the Ross family had contributed more than enough personal business to the community grapevine. The recent loss of the original garage buildings due to a fire down by the docks had stirred up the old gossip all over again. But the cupcake ladies didn't pry—much—so he'd accepted the occasional baked treat and tolerated a little friendly chitchat.

Yesterday, however, thinking of them hadn't brought an automatic smile to his face . . . because they surely hadn't brought a smile to his newest customer's face. Nor had they brought a frown. The look on her face had been . . . wistful.

Generally, Dylan stayed in the service bay and let Dell handle the people part of the business. The kid was a natural with any and all movable parts and could probably assemble an engine blindfolded, but he was equally good with the people side of things, which suited Dylan just fine. He could keep his focus on the work at hand. As he saw it, his job was to deliver reliable, dependable service, fixing what needed to be fixed for as reasonable a price as possible. It meant something to him that he'd kept afloat the family business that had been launched sixty-five years ago by his late grandfather and great-uncle, later joined by his father, then briefly by his older brother, and now operated solely by him.

He considered himself a rather observant man. Like any good mechanic, he put a lot of stock in the senses he'd been born with. Oftentimes he could decipher the problem with a car just by the sound it made, the feel of a certain vibration, or the smell it gave off. Observation skills also came in handy when judging his customers, figuring how best to deal with them. So it wasn't altogether surprising that he'd noticed her look of unfettered yearning. What did surprise him was that he'd reacted so viscerally to it.

He prided himself on his powers of observation, yes, but they were second only to his ability to maintain his objectivity in any and all situations. He didn't let things get personal, because . . . well, because he never let things get personal. And Miss Honey D'Amourvell was anything but personal to him. He'd never laid eyes on the woman before.

So why that look on her face yanked a knot in his gut, he couldn't have said. Likely, it had been his inability to figure that out that had him clearing his throat a bit too forcefully, and doling out the bad news to her a bit more gruffly than absolutely necessary. Mostly, he just wanted to get her taken care of and out of his shop so he could go back to being impersonal, private, and unaffected.

And yet, a day later, he still couldn't get her off his mind. Pushing back the heavy hank of hair that insisted on falling forward and plastering itself to his sweaty forehead, he made a mental note to visit Ollie's and get the barber to just shave his head. "Damn, it's hot."

He dropped one socket wrench into his tool box, grabbed another, then bent back over the VW's ancient engine, which some German rocket scientist had decided to cram in the trunk . . . and found himself thinking about what she'd been wearing. *Not stripper clothes, that's for damn sure.*

Not even particularly feminine ones, for that matter. She'd had on loose fitting Army green khakis that had been artfully decorated with stitching or patchwork and what looked like beads—he wasn't much for crafts—along with well-worn, combat-worthy hiking books, and some kind of white gauzy blousy thing that looked more like mosquito netting with some elastic here and there. With the stitched-on beads and gauzy shirt, she was more artsy-gypsy than stripper . . . if gypsies wore horn rim glasses. Oddly enough, those had turned him on. Just a little. Something about mystical green eyes being framed with all that serious, no nonsense black.

"Of course, she's also batshit crazy," he muttered, glowering at the clamp he was trying to wrench loose.

So . . . why was he still thinking about her?

More to the point, why couldn't he stop thinking about her? It wasn't a surprise that he'd thought about her initially. It wasn't every day—or any day—that someone freaked out all over the inside of his garage like she had. A woman like that was memorable. Just not for the right reasons.

But he hadn't been thinking about that when he'd come in this morning to go over her engine after doing some research to track down the list of parts he was going to need, and he wasn't thinking about it seven hours later as he stared at an engine that was more museum piece than part of a functioning form of transportation.

What he couldn't stop thinking about—then and now—was that one moment when he'd first laid eyes on her. Despite all the crazy chick stuff that had happened later, that moment stuck with him. It had been that vulnerable look, and maybe that moment when she'd paused with her back to him, bracing herself on the open door of her car, when he'd noticed her hand wasn't steady. And her shoulders were too rigidly held.

That raw yearning from earlier had echoed through his mind, and had him wondering what had made her react to him as she had. He'd tried to be a bit more . . . well, maybe *compassionate* wasn't exactly the right word. Ultimately, he'd just wanted her the hell out of his shop. The only problems he was comfortable tackling were the ones that could be rolled into his service bay . . . then rolled right back out again.

But she'd looked . . . fragile . . . so he'd put on kid gloves as best he knew how and delivered her to the Hughes's place then tried to turn his attention to the only aspect of her existence that he could let himself care about. Her ancient car. Because he definitely didn't need crazy in his life.

He'd had about all of that he could take growing up. Mercifully, just the one son was left of Ross & Sons—him.

He was the only one he had to deal with on a regular basis, and fortunately, he wasn't batshit crazy, which made life kind of nice for a change. Quiet, too. Maybe too quiet at times. But he'd take too quiet over the alternative every single minute of every day he had left on this earth and be damn grateful for it.

He channeled his frustration with himself into a little more elbow grease, determined to wrench the half-rotted hose and clamp loose or—

A wince-inducing squeal of metal on metal shrieked through the humid shop air, followed by a shrill snap . . . and the tinny sound of a piece of Honey D'Amourvell's Jurassic-era engine pinging off parts of the motor before clattering to the cement floor under her car.

"Well, shit." *What the hell kind of name is Honey D'Amourvell for a woman who looks like she does, anyway?* He grunted as he hunkered down and reached for the busted clamp.

So, she wasn't a stripper, or old money, but that name conjured up all kinds of sultry, breathy *Cat on a Hot Tin Roof* type images. One that came packaged with a deep Southern drawl, a throaty laugh, and a smile that promised all kinds of heartache. The kind a man would willingly suffer through, just to get more of the rest.

The Honey who drove that godforsaken pile of rust was none of those things. What she was, already, was a pain in his ass.

He crawled half under the car to reach the snapped ring, giving in to the need to vent a few of the more colorful words in his vocabulary when it skittered just beyond his reach.

"My, my, it sounds like someone is having a challenging day."

Dylan closed his eyes briefly, found a calming breath from somewhere, stretched and snagged the damn busted part, then slowly crawled out, got to his feet and turned around. "Afternoon, Miz Alva. Pardon my language. What brings you around today? Problem with the Lincoln?"

Alva Liles was one of the oldest residents of the island, somewhere north of eighty, but with the sharp mind of someone half her age. She stood just inside the bay door, decked out in one of a seemingly endless array of skirt, blouse, and sweater ensembles she always wore—today in varying shades of blue—and always with that strand of pearls around her neck. She had to be sweltering in all those layers, but she looked, as always, fresh as a spring daisy. Probably something to do with the helmet of lacquered curls perched ever so precisely on top of her head that wouldn't dare wilt, even in the heat. She was the tiniest thing, barely hitting five feet, even in her sensible, matronly pumps.

"Oh, goodness no," she reassured him. "That car wouldn't dare malfunction now that you've got her all tuned up and purring like a cat napping in a sunbeam."

Despite his momentary frustration, he felt the corners of his mouth twitch. She was a character, Miss Alva was. He wiped his hands on the shop rag he'd tucked in his back pocket. "Then what brings you by? Now, if this is about the poker game, I'm flattered to be asked to buy in, but I haven't changed my mind. I—"

"Now, now. I'm not here to strong arm you into playing in my Spring Fling tournament, even if we both know you could use a bit of socializing."

His lips did curve a little then. She made him sound like a poorly trained dog who needed a turn at obedience school. He supposed she wasn't far from wrong on that score, but he'd made it this far off the leash; he wasn't about to strap one on now. "I appreciate the leniency."

She lowered a perfectly penciled brow at the amusement in his tone, but spared him the lecture—which he also appreciated, because when Alva Liles put her mind to something, she usually prevailed.

"I dropped by because we had our little cupcake club yesterday and I still have a jelly roll left after we made our rounds of the hospital wards over in Savannah today. I thought you might enjoy something a little sweet, what with all this heat and you working right out in it. A bite of this and a pitcher of lemonade would be just the thing." She beamed. "It's cherry. Your favorite."

He accepted the neatly plastic-wrapped bundle she handed to him. "Now, how do you know cherry is my favorite?"

She smiled and those faded blue eyes of hers twinkled. "Because when you taste my cherry jelly roll, it will be."

He couldn't help it; he smiled right back. "You're probably right. I appreciate the thought. Good of you to stop by."

He crossed the cement floor and ducked into his office long enough to pop the package on top of the microwave. When he reentered the service bay, she was looking under the hood of the Volkswagen. "Careful there, Miz Alva. Shouldn't get too close."

"I remember these cars," she said, not budging, a wistful note in her voice. "I wanted one, but my dear, departed Harold thought they were impractical. His sister, June, had one when we were dating. It was 1949, or thereabouts. They were just becoming popular. We borrowed it once." She glanced up at Dylan, that twinkle magnified now. "He was right. Couldn't do a damn thing without that stick shift getting in the way."

It was a good thing Dylan hadn't given in to the growl in his stomach and pinched a bite of the jelly roll, because he'd have surely choked on it. "Well . . . I wouldn't rightly know," he somehow managed.

She continued to look over the car. "Which is why you

need to get out and socialize more. A man your age, still single, looking like you do. You're what, thirty now, thirty-one? It's almost a crime, really, when you think about it."

Completely at a loss for words, he forced himself to swallow and tried to decide the best way to get her to head on out. He tolerated her occasional attempts to talk him into attending this event or that one, but this hard press was a first, even for her. "I . . . appreciate the thought, but I'm fine. Just fine."

She turned to him then, the twinkle replaced by a shrewd, direct gleam. "You've done your granddaddy proud, you have, Dylan Ross. I haven't mentioned it, but I knew Tommy quite well. His brother, Dick, too. A bit of a rascal that one, always into this or that."

Dylan said nothing, as that was about as kindly as she could have put it. And far more than the man deserved. "I appreciate that, too. Thanks again for—"

"And I know your Daddy would have been, too." She sighed, fluttered a hand near her heart. "God rest his soul." Her voice had wavered a bit, but her gaze did not, which had his own eyes narrowing slightly; she clearly wasn't done yet. "Now, I know it's not my place to say such things, but just because your mama wasn't there to help your poor daddy with his troubles, and your brother . . . lost his way, does not mean you have to hide—"

Dylan's scowl shut down that particular line of conversation. He couldn't quite believe she'd gone there.

"I've said too much." But Alva didn't look all that remorseful.

Nor, he noted, did she give him that pitying look so many of the older islanders did. He hated that look.

"I meant it kindly," she told him, a smile back in her voice. "I've always marveled at how well you've done for yourself. We can't choose the family we're born to, and all you've done is give yours a good name. I know it had to be heartbreaking when the shop your granddaddy started up burned to the ground in that fire, but you seem to be settling in over here. This row of old buildings hasn't seen any use in as long as I can remember. Maybe now that you're in here, others will follow your lead and spruce up the rest of the strip. I heard someone bought the space right next door." She let the sentence dangle, but he didn't pick up the bait.

He was still trying to process everything else she'd said. Besides, it was no one's business but his own that he'd been the one who had bought up the adjoining building. Insurance had paid out better than anticipated on the old place and he'd had to reinvest it somehow. Way he saw it, if folks suddenly did take an interest in revitalizing the remaining buildings that fronted the channel, he could sell it at a tidy profit to whomever would annoy him the least.

"It's good to be a bit closer to the center of things," Alva was saying. "Not tucked away down there by the fishing docks, but here in the heart of town. More social, don't you think? I'd think it'd be better for business. Better for you, too."

He'd come to stand beside her, ostensibly to find some way to escort her out that didn't require bodily removing her, but before he could figure out exactly how to go about that, she reached over and squeezed his arm, then patted his hand. "Oh, don't look so stormy. I'm not asking you out on a date. But you should think about it. Dating, I mean. I'm not the only single woman on Sugarberry."

He'd stepped into the Twilight Zone. There was no other explanation. She'd gone past flummoxing him, even pissing him off, to just, well . . . flustering him. Rallying his thoughts, he somehow found the wherewithal to force a smile. "And here I thought you were seeing Hank Shearin."

If he wasn't mistaken, her cheeks warmed right up, even under her carefully applied rouge. "Now, don't you go believing everything you hear. But it's good to know you're keeping up with the goings on around town. Shows you've got some interest. That's a good thing." She patted again. "Now, cultivate it."

"I'm an auto mechanic. One step away from a bartender. I hear things whether I want to or not."

"Well, it's still a place to start." She patted his hand one last time, then slid her arm free. "You're not so brooding and quiet as you try and make us believe. I mean, look at the two of us, having ourselves a nice little chat. See? It wasn't so hard, now, was it?"

He'd rather eat fire ants. He'd also sorely underestimated his placement on Miss Alva's to-do list. He'd have to put a stop to that before it went any further, but at the moment, he couldn't come up with a solid game plan, other than to send her on her merry way as soon as possible.

"Thanks again for the jelly roll," he said by way of responding. "I should get back to work."

She turned her attention back to the Volkswagen. "I don't recognize this one from anyone on the island."

"Not a local. Just someone passing through, having a bit of bad luck."

"Not so bad as all that if she found you." Alva looked through the side windows, then glanced at the license plate. "Oregon. Long way to be passing through. Looks like she's got a goodly part of her worldly possessions with her, too."

"How do you know it belongs to a woman?" Dylan asked, bemused despite himself.

"Not too many men I know would drive a powder blue Beetle Bug. Although, they say they're a bit odd up there in the northwest, so, who knows."

Odd, Dylan thought. *That's one way to put it.*

"Only ever knew one person from Oregon. New-comer. Beavis Chantrell." Alva smiled fondly. "She was certainly a colorful one, so perhaps there's something to it. You know, she used to do costumes in Hollywood for some of the big movie stars? Then she left there and de-signed for the show girls in those big, fancy Vegas reviews. Came out here with a fella, some young slick. Card shark if you ask me. Never did trust him. Pretty sure he cheated the time or two we played poker, though I couldn't catch him red-handed at it.

"I was so happy when she stayed after he moved on, opened up her little shop. We were fortunate to keep her, we were." Alva sighed. "My Harold's suits never fit so well as when Bea took her hand to them. And the things she could do to spruce up an old hat, I tell you. You could al-ways count on her to let you know if there was trouble brewin', too. I miss her."

Dylan knew Miss Bea had lived on Sugarberry close to twenty years, before passing away last winter. Of course, anything less than a few generations of island occupancy labeled a person a newcomer. Bea had been a bit of an odd duck, but a beloved one, near as he could tell. He hadn't known her personally, mechanics not being in much need of tailoring shops, and she'd pedaled a bicycle around the island, never owned a car. Of course he'd heard about her being a bit . . . unusual, always knowing things she shouldn't be knowing. Everybody knew about it. Folks would go to her, trying to find out about their futures. Far as he knew, she wasn't any kind of fortune teller, or cer-tainly had never advertised herself as one, but it didn't keep folks from talking or seeking out her advice from time to time.

He supposed he had a soft spot for the misfits of the world, though she seemed to have made her way better than most. Still, he'd been sorry to hear it when she'd suffered a mild stroke a little over a year before. He knew it had left her unable to run her shop. Last he'd heard, she'd moved to a senior care center over on the mainland, where she'd remained until her passing.

The shop had sat empty until the cupcake crew had taken over the space to add on to their existing business. The island had been buzzing about the grand opening of the new place for months. Some were happy about it and the increased interest it might bring to the island, some were grousing that increased traffic and tourists were not something Sugarberry should be courting, that it was doing just fine on its own. Of course, that was the same argument the old-timers had made about almost every new business establishment, probably even back when Tommy and Dick Ross had opened their auto repair business.

Dylan took advantage of Alva's hand on his arm and steered her toward the open bay door at the rear of the shop, where she'd come in. She'd probably headed over straight from the cupcake bakery, jelly roll in hand. An excuse to pry and nudge, he saw now. He really was going to have to nip that in the bud.

"Well, looks like we have another newcomer from Oregon," Alva was saying. "Hope she's as delightful as the last one."

"I didn't get the feeling she was here to stay." But that look on Honey's face, in her eyes, as she'd looked across the alley, jumped to Dylan's mind again.

"Well," Alva said, clearly dismayed not to get more gossip out of him. "I'm glad you were here to help out. If you change your mind about the poker game, we always have a seat for a handsome, eligible man." The twinkle had come right back in her eyes.

"Thanks again for the jelly roll" was all he said. "Careful now, crossing the alley."

"And a gentleman, too," she said, then waved before

making her way across the alley to the rear door of Cakes by the Cup.

He watched until she waved once more before slipping into the back entrance. He hadn't realized he'd been holding his breath until he let it out in one heavy huff as the door slapped shut behind her. What the hell had that been all about? And how was he going to shut it down?

The phone ringing in the office snapped his attention back to business. He stalked over and snatched the cordless from where it was mounted to the wall, and listened as the parts shop in Savannah gave him the bad news. "Thanks," he said, before hanging up. "For nothing," he added darkly.

First Miss Alva and her nosey fruit roll, and now he had to deal with the fruitcake. And tell her it was going to be a week, at minimum, before her car was ready. He also had to give her the full repair estimate. He couldn't imagine either of those things would come as good news.

He turned toward the office, intent on grabbing the clipboard with her service order and cell phone number on it, but was once again brought to a complete and utter stop by the woman herself. Honey D'Amourvell was presently pedaling down the alley toward the rear entrance to his shop on an old townie bicycle with a white basket attached between the front handles. But it wasn't the vintage bike, or even the mode of transportation, that had caught his attention. Plenty of island residents favored bicycles over cars. It was the woman. Yesterday it had been combat boots, khakis, and a no nonsense ponytail.

Today she wore flat white sandals, a sunny yellow, short-sleeved shirt, and a flowy, billowy skirt patterned with bright spring flowers. Her hair was down, streaming behind her. It was longer than it had looked up in that ponytail. Thicker, too. But what nailed it for him, was all that flouncy femininity paired with those super serious, dark rimmed glasses. There was absolutely nothing re-motely sexy about them . . . and yet, his body stirred.

She rolled in behind the shop, then braked a little harder than was necessary when she saw him just inside the bay door, standing in the shadows. Watching her.

The short stop had her teetering dangerously and her sandals did little to steady her as they slid over the hot pavement. Without thinking, Dylan instinctively stepped into the sunlight, intent on steadying the bike to keep her from falling over, when her quick jerk back reminded him. Batshit crazy. Right.

Still, he wasn't going to let her fall over. He put his hands firmly on the handlebars, taking care not to touch her, keeping the bike upright until she got her feet under her. "Careful, there, darlin'."

"I'm fine. You just . . . startled me. I didn't see you there."

He scowled, when just moments before, watching her, all flowery clothes and serious glasses, he'd found himself wanting to smile. "The only thing I plan on touching is your car, okay?"

She met his gaze with her own. "I know. Really, it's . . . not you. Or . . . or that. It's just—" She broke off, and he could see frustration, and something else, warring in her expression. But she was right, he didn't think either was directed at him so much as herself.

Problems, he thought. She had plenty of them, the least of which, apparently, was her piece of junk car. That was the only one he had any interest in fixing.

He lifted his hands off the handlebars, palms out. "You're safe with me," he said more dismissively than was perhaps necessary, thinking *first nosey fruit roll, now fruity customer.* Was it too much to ask for a man to just work in peace, without interruption? He turned to head back into the shop. She could follow him or not.

"I'm not safe with anyone," she muttered, or that's what he thought he heard, but when he looked back, she'd climbed off the bike and was propping it against the back of the building, next to the bench.

He went in and grabbed the clipboard with her service order on it, made a few notes from the phone conversation he'd had with the parts guy while they were still fresh in his mind, then headed back to the service bay, only to find the second woman of the day poking her nose under the hood of the Beetle. "Might want to be careful there."

Honey straightened and turned to look at him. Despite what had just happened in the alley, she seemed steadier than the day before. He wasn't sure if it was the brightly colored shirt or the bicycle ride over that had lent some color to her face, but she didn't look as . . . well, as haunted as she had. She placed a protective hand on the side panel of the car. "Can she be fixed?"

He nodded. "But it's going to take the better part of a week just to get the parts here. And it's not going to come cheap."

She merely nodded.

He'd expected more of a reaction than that. Shoulders slumping, disappointment in those still-spooky, pale green eyes of hers, something.

"So . . . how long until it's done? And how much?"

"Ten days, give or take parts delivery." He quoted her the price.

He saw her throat work, then her gaze shift toward the back bay door. He thought, for a second, she was contemplating taking off, but realized almost immediately she was looking once again at the bakery shops across the alley, on the corner.

"This was a mistake," she said more to herself than to him.

Yep. She was trouble. And quite possibly *in* trouble.

He sighed. "Is there someone who can come get you? Were you . . . visiting somebody? Over on the mainland? Traveling?" He glanced at her tags and the packed contents of her car, then back at her.

"No. I mean, no, I'm on my own. I'm—I was . . ." Her chin dropped, just for a moment; then she briefly closed her eyes and seemed to gather herself up. When she lifted her gaze back to his, it was resolute and resigned. "I was planning to stay here. Move here, actually. I'm . . . not so sure now. But I guess I'll be here at least until my car is done, so that'll give me time to figure the rest out."

"We can work something out with the cost, if—"

"Oh, no, that's not it. I can take care of that." He must have looked somewhat dubious, because she added, "I know the car isn't much, but I haven't needed much. And it's . . . sentimental. It belonged to my Aunt Bea."

He'd glanced back at his clipboard, intending to see where he might be able to cut a corner or two, but his gaze snapped back up at that name. "Bea Chantrell?"

Her entire face relaxed, and the smile that naturally followed transformed her features from wary and guarded, to open and . . . well, attractive. Very attractive.

"Yes. Did you know her?"

"Not personally, but it's a small island. She was well liked here. Ran the little tailor—" He broke off . . . and looked across the alley at the buildings on the corner. Where her aunt's shop had once been. And a brand new, about-to-open bakery business now stood. That raw, wistful look he'd seen on her face the day before took on a whole new meaning. He looked back at Honey. "Oh."

Her smile shifted to one of dry humor, reaching those eyes of hers . . . and changing everything.

That did something to his insides, too.

"Right"—she held his gaze easily for the first time—"oh."

Chapter 3

Honey started to lift the bike from its resting spot against the wall behind the auto repair shop, then decided there was no point in rolling it across the alley. She'd come back for it once she was done. Besides, she wanted to get a few small things from her belongings to take back to the B&B . . . and, now that she knew how long her car would be here, she should probably see if she could work something out to get the rest of her stuff taken over later on. She didn't want it all sitting inside her closed up car for that long.

At the moment, however, she had more important things to attend to. The first of which was to stop thinking about Dylan Ross. Even on a full night's sleep and after a stern self lecture on keeping her focus on the important things, he still made her jumpy. And twitchy. Mostly, in that can't-keep-her-eyes-off-his-shoulders-and-biceps kind of way. Just because he wore a grease stained white T-shirt that the heat and humidity had long since caused to cling damply to his very nicely defined torso, did not mean she had to stare at it. Or want to touch it. Nor did she need to be paying quite so much attention to the way his jeans hung low on his lean hips or hugged a backside that gave swagger a whole new meaning.

"Why look if you can't touch," she muttered. She

pushed her hair from her face and her glasses up the bridge of her nose, and set off across the alley, wishing the elastic band she'd pulled her hair back with hadn't slid down and blown away on the way to the garage. She'd wanted to look friendly, well put together, and open to discussion when she met with Leilani Dunne. And if, perhaps, she happened to show Dylan Ross that she wasn't some deranged hippie chick, well . . . all the better.

Instead, she felt sweaty, wind blown, and . . . well . . . twitchy. She could still see Dylan's broad, very capable hands gripping the handlebars of her bike. If she hadn't jerked back the way she had, he might have put those broad, capable hands on her.

"And left grease marks on your blouse." And permanent marks on her overly-active imagination. Logic and common sense clearly weren't enough to deter her body's determination to respond to him like a hothouse flower would to a steam bath.

Enough already. Time to talk cupcakes. And lease agreements.

Honey had called her aunt's estate lawyer first thing that morning, only to be told he was away at a family wedding and wouldn't be back until the following week. The other partner in the small firm had taken her call. He hadn't known her aunt well, nor was he familiar with the particulars of her estate planning, but he'd said he would look through the file as it pertained to the Sugarberry property and get back to her. Honey had finally gotten the call from him an hour ago, and he'd said he found nothing untoward or mishandled from his end. According to the will, the property rightly belonged to Honey. If that ownership was being contested, she'd have to go to the county offices over the causeway, and get a copy of the deed, along with the papers she'd filed, claiming the property.

Except . . . no one had explained the part about her

needing to fill out paperwork to claim anything. She'd thought that had been handled by Bea's lawyer. And, perhaps it had. His partner couldn't say one way or the other. So, she'd called the county to see if they could verify any of the information over the phone, only to be told she had to bring ID and show up in person to access any of her aunt's deed information. She'd considered hiring a taxi and heading straight over, but decided perhaps going directly to the source on the Sugarberry end of things might be just as informative. Besides, it would eventually all come out anyway, so they were going to have to talk at some point. If she wanted to know who on Sugarberry thought they had the right to lease Bea's shop to Leilani Dunne, who better to ask than the Cupcake Queen herself?

Honey debated walking around the row of buildings and entering through the front of the shop, as it was still during business hours, but the back door to the alley was open, and the rich scents of butter and baked goods wafted through the screen door. Also wafting out was the pulsing sound of a tune she couldn't quite make out, which meant someone was in the kitchen baking. Hopefully, that someone was the owner, and Honey could at least begin the conversation between them in private.

She crossed the alley and found herself smiling as she recognized the music—it was the soundtrack to the Broadway musical, *Wicked*—and she realized someone was singing along. *Not too shabby, either,* she thought. Certainly a far cry from her own less-than-stage-ready voice. Not that that had stopped her from bopping and singing loudly to the music she'd always had pumping inside the barn as she worked. After all, the garden gnomes and fairy sprites she created weren't likely to be too offended when she went off key.

Her smile turned wry as she recognized the specific tune from the show. *"Popular."* "Oh, the irony," she murmured as she stepped under the awning and up to the screen door just as the final strains echoed, and the kitchen singer ended with her own flourish.

Honey took a moment to smooth her hair, straighten her blouse, shake the wrinkles from her recently unpacked skirt. The hottest part of the day had passed, but tell that to her sweat glands. Nerves weren't helping the situation, either.

The opening strains of *South Pacific* faded as someone inside turned the music down. Honey let out a long, shaky sigh, then took a steadying breath, pasted on a smile, and knocked on the door. Only no one came. Instead, she heard someone call out, "Alva, I've got to run these next door to Kit. I'll be right back!"

If there was a response, Honey didn't hear it. She was too busy leaping back as the screen door was suddenly shoved open by someone backing out of the bakery with a huge tray of cupcakes in her hands.

Honey caught the low heel of her sandal on the edge of the stone walkway that had been put in between the back doors of the side-by-side shops, sending her wheeling into the small parking lot. "Oh!"

The woman with the cupcakes spun around, sending a few of the cupcakes tottering dangerously close to the edge of the rack she held. "Oh, no! I didn't see—crap!" Two of the cupcakes took the death plunge off the side and landed, icing down, between the stone pavers.

Honey banged up against the front bumper of somebody's red Jeep, and finally managed to stop by bracing her hands on the hood—the sun-burnished, blazing hot hood. She swore and leaped away as the woman in front of her did a quick step to keep any more cupcakes from taking a dive.

"I'm . . . I'm so sorry!" Honey managed as she pressed her throbbing palms to the sides of her skirt. "I knocked on the door, but . . ."

"No, no, it's my fault. I had the music on too loud. Baxter's always telling me I'm going to boogie myself straight into—" The woman broke off, and rearranged her grip on the tray, then grinned at Honey. "Straight into a cupcake Armageddon. I hate it when he's right."

Honey found herself smiling back. It was impossible not to, really. She looked down at the smashed cupcakes and the creamy pink icing presently oozing in between the walkway bricks. "Let me at least pay for damages."

The dark-haired woman shook her head, her expression open, naturally friendly. "I make extras, and it's really not your fault. Were you looking for me? I'm Leilani Dunne, the shop owner. Everyone just calls me Lani."

Honey's gaze went from Lani's warm eyes and cheerful smile to the apron she wore, which had only now caught her attention. It featured poster art from the movie *Chocolat,* with Johnny Depp's handsome face smiling beside the title.

Lani tracked her gaze. "I know, right? Show tunes and wacky aprons are us, what can I say?"

"There's nothing wacky about wanting to wrap yourself in Johnny Depp." It was only when Lani laughed that Honey realized she'd spoken out loud.

"I like you already. What can I do for you?"

This was so not how Honey had planned the conversation to go, so she was a little bit flummoxed. "Did you— do you want to go ahead and deliver those?" She inclined her head toward the cupcakes. "I can wait. I just needed a few moments of your time." *To start.*

"Um, sure, yes. Probably a good idea." Lani didn't bother to hide her curiosity, but her smile never wavered. "Go ahead on into the kitchen. I'll be back in a flash.

Careful not to step in the cupcake carnage!" she warned, then bopped on over to the back door with a sign that said BABYCAKES, balancing her oversized tray as if it were nothing more weighty than a dinner plate.

Honey stood there for another second before heading to the screen door to the Cakes by the Cup kitchen and letting herself inside.

"Miss Lani Mae, I've locked up out front for you, but wasn't sure if you wanted me to count the till—oh! Sorry. I heard the door and thought Lani had come back. Can I help you?"

Honey stood just inside the door, hands folded in front of her, careful not to touch anything lest she inadvertently create another disaster, and smiled at the tiny, white-haired woman who'd just come from the front of the shop. "I'm waiting for Lani. She knows I'm here." Honey's gaze strayed to the apron the diminutive senior wore. This one featured Channing Tatum on the movie poster for *Dear John*. A very fine looking Channing Tatum. What was it with the cupcake ladies and the hot guy aprons? The older woman looked down at her apron, then beamed a twinkly-eyed smile back at Honey. "I liked him better in that stripper movie, but Miss Lani thought he might be too distracting to the customers without his shirt on."

Honey tried to stifle the laugh that bubbled up in her throat. Maybe it was all the sugar, or maybe they were just crazy, but all Honey could think was, *My God, Bea, you were right. I'd fit right in here.* Not because Honey was crazy, but because she was already half convinced between the sugar buzz, the hot guys, and the show tunes, the cupcake ladies might not even notice her occasional "unexplainable insights."

If only she didn't have to ruin everything with the real reason she was here.

"I, uh . . ."—Honey had to clear the laughter from her

throat—"think he's distracting at all times, but in a really good way."

"I'm Alva Liles," the other woman said with an approving smile.

"Hello, I'm Honey. Honey D'Amourvell."

And just like that, the twinkle dimmed.

News traveled fast in small towns. She wondered exactly what Mr. Ross had said about her. Had to be him. The only other person she'd met was Barbara Hughes, and a nicer woman Honey had never known. She'd even loaned Honey her bike until Honey's car was fixed. Besides, they'd only spoken a handful of words to each other, all pleasant. No odd or awkward moments. Honey had already had all of those with Mr. Ross.

Well, it wasn't like the happy cupcake vibe would have lasted much longer, anyway. As soon as she told them she was the owner of the building they'd illegally turned into a cupcake mail-order business, all the happy happy joy joy would have come to an abrupt end.

And to think she'd been worried about being ostracized because she was clairvoyant.

"Why, my goodness gracious," Alva was saying. "If it isn't little Miss Honey Pie. The sweet, sweet child my dear friend, Miss Bea Chantrell spoke so fondly of, every chance she had."

Honey's mouth dropped open. She hadn't thought—hadn't figured that folks might know her by name. But of course Aunt Bea would have talked about her family.

Before Honey could respond, Alva finished with, "That same sweet child who never managed to make it out here to visit her only kin before she passed." She was still smiling, but there was no mistaking the flinty edge to her words.

Oh yeah. Fun time was officially over.

Not that it was any of this woman's business, but Honey

made a stab at explaining. "Yes, I'm Bea's niece. We were very close. I miss her terribly. I would have spent every minute with her if I could have."

The grudging look didn't entirely leave Alva's eyes, but her tone was a bit less frosty when she spoke. "We all miss her terribly, too. She was a wonderful addition to our little island. You have a bit of the look of her. Same eyes."

Bea had been short and built like a fireplug, but, it was true, they did have the same clear green eyes. They ran in the Chantrell family. As did the curse. "Thank you."

"What brings you to Sugarberry? Here to pay your respects? She wasn't buried here, you know, her—"

"Her ashes were sent to me," Honey finished evenly. "I've just driven across the country, spreading them everywhere she asked me to." Honey also had a container from her own catalog—one Bea had chosen herself, in fact—to put the remainder in, for Honey's keeping. She smiled, thinking of the whimsical female garden gnome Bea had chosen. Short and stout, much like her aunt, with a basket of fabric scraps over one arm, and a fairy wand in the other.

Alva's expression softened then, as did her tone. "Well then, you've paid your respects quite handsomely it would seem. I'm glad to hear you were able to do that for her and for yourself. My condolences on your loss."

"Thank you. And condolences to you as well. She told me many wonderful stories about Sugarberry and all of her friends here. You all meant more to her than you'll ever know." It was comforting to learn that her aunt's passing had been noted, and that she was missed. Honey'd had the stray thought that, other than her customers, there really wasn't anyone left who would miss her when she was gone. And that was a rather chilling idea, when she thought about it like that.

"I suppose that's your car over at Mr. Dylan's garage then," Alva said. "I noticed the Oregon plates," she added, when Honey looked surprised. "I know Bea hailed from there, way back."

Very way back. Honey's mother had loved Juniper Hollow, but her baby sister, Bea, had escaped it as soon as she was able. "Yes. I'm afraid the old car has a few issues. More than a few. I was lucky to have made it all the way here, I guess."

"Well, it's seen a few years."

Honey smiled sincerely. "It was Bea's. She left it with my mom before heading off on one of her jaunts, and never quite made it back to pick it up. She handed it down to me when I was old enough to drive and I've had it ever since. I know it's seen better days, but I haven't had much need for a car, and I don't want to give it up if I don't have to." She glanced through the screen door and across the alley, only she wasn't seeing the VW in her mind's eye. She was seeing Dylan Ross. Steamy, jean clad, broad shouldered, brooding Dylan Ross. She blinked that image away and turned back to Alva. "I'm afraid the cross-country drive was its final bow, too."

"Well, I can't think of a more fitting way to go, but I wouldn't count her out just yet. If anyone can get your car up and running again, it's our Mr. Dylan. Looked to me like you brought a fair bit more than your aunt's ashes with you. Planning on staying a spell?"

Honey was saved from answering that particular probing question, or asking just how Alva knew what Honey had packed in her car, when Lani returned to the kitchen by the back door.

"Does Kit think the new packaging will work well with that size cupcake?" Alva asked her.

"I don't know, but we're going to find out," Lani said, sounding excited. "I see you two have met." She smiled as she turned to Honey. "But we haven't, not formally anyway."

"I'm Honey D'Amourvell."

"Bea Chantrell's niece," Alva offered, ever-so-helpfully.

Lani's face brightened. "You're Honey Pie? Oh, Bea told us so many stories." She reached out quite naturally to take Honey's hands, and, acting purely on instinct, Honey jerked them behind her back.

Even as Honey's face flushed in mortification, Lani was laughing. "I washed the frosting carnage off my hands, honest!"

Honey wished she was fast enough to pretend that was her concern, but her cheeks were too pink, her smile too forced. "No, it's not—I spend my days elbow deep in clay, so I'm the last one to . . ." She trailed off, wondering how in the world this had gone so far off her planned track. The women of Sugarberry—and the men, for that matter—were nothing like the folks back in Juniper Hollow, who were quite happy to let a person be if that's how the person wanted it. Here, according to Bea, they lived inside each other's pockets. Honey hadn't realized how smoothly and swiftly—and happily—they'd work their way into hers.

Alva stepped forward with a very determined look on her face until Honey was forced by the sheer pull of it to look back. "You've got it, too, haven't you?" Alva tilted her head and squinted a little as her sharp gaze probed Honey's face. "Bea had a knack for knowin' things."

Honey swallowed against a suddenly dry throat, and had absolutely no idea what to say to that. If Bea had been telling them stories about her niece, she apparently hadn't included that little tidbit.

"Bea Chantrell was a toucher, she was," Alva went on, still looking straight into Honey's eyes like she could see all her inner workings.

And, maybe she could. It was unnerving, to say the least. Especially since Alva didn't seem too disturbed by the idea. More . . . inquisitive, hopeful, even, which was a first for Honey. A shocking first.

"She always had a smile," Alva added, "a pat on the arm, and a way of lettin' folks know that perhaps they needed to keep an eye on this going on, or that."

Honey merely nodded, then forced words past the knot in her throat. "She . . . she was, yes. A toucher." She left it at that.

"You're not so comfortable with it, though, are you?"

"No, I wasn't . . . am not." Honey shook her head, still in complete disbelief they were even having this conversation . . . and that she was the only one who seemed freaked out by it. She'd come into the bakery to talk only about her inheritance. She hadn't been prepared to deal with her "knack for knowing things" as Alva had called it. She hadn't been prepared for *anything* that had happened to her since she'd crossed the causeway. "And neither was anyone else where I came from."

To Honey's continued shock and awe, Alva's face split into a wide smile, and she laughed, delight in her eyes. "Well, Honey Pie, that'll change here in Sugarberry, you can bet on it. We all came to depend on Bea, and, I've a feeling, once folks know about you, they'll find their way to talking to you as well."

Honey didn't know whether to be terrified by the idea, or just—

No, she was terrified.

Lani had been a silent bystander to the conversation, but spoke up now. "Honey, don't let her talk get you worried. We know how to respect a person's privacy, the same as anywhere else."

Alva simply snorted at that, but at Lani's warning glance, said nothing else. Her expression, however, remained lively . . . and interested.

"What was it you came to talk to me about?" Lani asked

Honey. "Why don't you come back to my office and we'll sit, have something cold to drink, and chat."

I'm well down the rabbit hole now, was all Honey could think.

Somehow, she had landed square in her own little Sugarberry Wonderland. Only it didn't feel all that wonderful. It felt scary, unknown, and completely out of her control.

"Have a cupcake," Lani called out as she led the way to what Honey assumed was her office, motioning to the rack of richly frosted chocolate cupcakes on one of the metal topped work tables. "New flavor I'm testing. Ginger chocolate fudge. I'd love to get your opinion. I'll brew us some coffee."

Not wanting to be rude, Honey picked one up as she followed the leader, then had to bite down a semi-hysterical urge to laugh when she found herself wondering if one bite would make her taller . . . or possibly make her disappear all together. She wasn't quite sure which one she wished it would be.

Chapter 4

"I have all the lease documents if you need to see them," Lani said, seated calmly behind her desk, still smiling. She seemed completely unruffled by the huge announcement Honey had just made.

"The file isn't here, though," Lani added. "At the moment, it's with Kit's boy—well, with our lawyer."

Honey frowned. "For any particular reason?"

"No, no, we're just tying up the final little threads before our grand opening, getting the permits documented and filed. Morgan—lawyer—has been helping with that, so he has the folder with all that paperwork in it. You're saying Bea left the shop to you?"

"I'm her only living heir. Who did you—well, not necessarily you, but whoever you leased it from—think owned it?"

"To be honest, I didn't ask. I worked through the management company Bea had set up to take care of the building after her stroke."

Honey was frowning and completely confused. "Wait, what do you mean? Management company?"

Lani's face flashed with momentary guilt. "Did you not know about her stroke? I'm so sorry, I thought you two were pretty close. I—"

"No, no. I mean, yes, I knew about her stroke, but not that she'd turned over the shop to a management company. I know she was closed for a time afterward, until she got through therapy and could use her sewing machines again, but she made it out to be a pretty mild thing, over-all. I thought . . ." Honey trailed off, her thoughts scattering in a dozen different directions, trying to replay conversations she'd had with Bea in the months after her stroke.

"I'm really sorry. When the management company took over the shop after she moved into senior care over on the mainland, we just assumed it was being handled as the family wanted it to be handled. I mean . . . I didn't know. None of us did."

Honey held up her hands, as much to shield herself from news she really didn't want to hear, as to slow down the volume of it. "I—wait, wait. She . . . when did she move to the care facility?"

Lani's mouth dropped open, then closed again. "Oh, I . . ." She trailed off, clearly uncomfortable, not prepared to be the one to tell a loved one difficult news about a family member. "It's probably not—maybe you should talk about all of this with her lawyer."

"I tried. He's away at a family wedding, somewhere in the Caribbean, and won't be back for another week. The other partner didn't really know Bea or anything about her estate. He looked into it for me and just told me it all appeared to be in good order." Honey didn't mention the paperwork snafu because she wasn't sure there had been one. Clearly, there was a whole pile of other information that needed to be waded through first. How could Bea not have told her any of this? And how could Honey not have known it, sensed it, anyway?

One of the oddities of the curse was that the closer she was to someone, the more deeply she cared about them, the more it clouded her ability to sense, feel, or know anything. She thought that was a blessing, knowing the sheer terror she'd have felt every time one of her parents hugged or kissed her. Bea claimed Honey's powers were stunted with her loved ones because her subconscious had blocked it out, knowing she couldn't handle those kinds of truths.

Bea, on the other hand, always knew everything. And she'd so willingly immersed herself in her special abilities that she didn't always need to touch someone to know things. In fact, her aunt had always called Honey just when she'd needed to hear from her most. Bea had known about Honey's father passing even before Honey had, and was the one calling to console Honey when her mother—Bea's sister—had passed, two years later.

Honey, on the other hand, had buried herself as deeply away from the curse as she possibly could. And what had that cost her? She wasn't even thinking about her inheritance, but about what her aunt had apparently been through in her final days. Honey had had no idea.

"How"—she paused to clear the ache from her throat—"long was she in senior care?" She immediately lifted her hand to stall Lani's reply. "I'm sorry, I shouldn't put you in this position, but I just . . . I don't have anyone else to ask. All I knew was that she'd been recovering very well after her stroke, and was happy to be back 'in the swing' as she put it."

Honey shook her head, then dipped her chin to frown the threatening tears into submission. *Oh, Bea, why didn't you tell me?*

Honey thought she knew why. Bea knew Honey would have caught the first plane out. And Bea also would have known that for Honey, being on a plane with a few hundred people in close proximity would have been terrifying. No way could she have withstood that kind of sudden onslaught. Driving cross country, seeing the countryside—

and the people in it—from the safe little pod of her car had been difficult enough.

Bea should have told her anyway. "She should have given me more credit. I'd have found a way."

Lani pushed a Kleenex box closer to the edge of the desk. Honey pulled several free . . . then just crumpled them in her palms, trying to get herself under control.

"I'm so sorry," Lani said.

"I am, too. I—we talked all the time. She sounded shaky, a little slurred, but she told me that was just a side effect from the stroke that would take longer to clear up. We used to—" Honey stopped as a sob rose in her throat. "We used to Skype, but after the stroke, we didn't. We just talked over the phone. I missed seeing her, but she said— she didn't like how the stroke had made her face a bit droopy on one side. I was surprised because she was the least egocentric person I know, but . . . now I realize she was keeping me from not only seeing her, but from seeing that she wasn't in her apartment any longer."

A tearful laugh escaped her. "She had to teach me to Skype, can you believe it? I operate my entire business on-line, but that was something I'd never done. I was kind of afraid, I guess, that if I could see the person live like that, I might . . . know things, and then I just got used to com-municating other ways."

She broke off, realizing she was babbling. To a complete stranger. And about things she had only ever spoken about with Bea. Just because Alva had seemed unfazed by it all. Honey knew better. She scooted her chair back and wiped at her face, embarrassed and feeling more than a little out of her element. "I should probably go. Let you get back to—" She snagged her purse from the arm of the chair. "I'm so sorry to have barged in, not knowing all the facts. I should—I'll take a cab over tomorrow, and . . . and fig-ure it all out."

Lani rose and scuttled around the desk so fast, Honey had to jerk back to keep from colliding with her. "Wait. Just . . ." Lani took a moment, pressed her hand to her chest and wiped at the corners of her own eyes. "I really don't mind talking. And I'm so very sorry you found out this way. I'm sure she was just protecting you. I know it's got to piss you off and hurt like hell, all at the same time."

Honey looked at Lani, surprised by the emotion in her voice, wondering how she'd nailed it so perfectly.

"My mom . . . when she passed away, I was in New York, so focused on my career and on what I wanted, and my dad tried to do the same thing. Later on, when he had a heart attack, oh, he was all 'things are great, I'm fine, don't bother yourself,' but I knew. He almost died. I almost lost him. I had to—" Lani broke off at the stricken look on Honey's face. She started to reach out a comforting hand, but pulled back at the last second, remembering. The look on her face was as good as a pat on the arm.

"Just because I knew he was in trouble doesn't mean you should have known," she told Honey. "My dad and I have a long history of him not asking for help and me giving it to him anyway. I didn't know Bea that well, or for very long. I've only been here a few years. But I do know the whole island loved her, and everyone mourned her passing. What I'm trying to say is, she had people. She wasn't alone. Not when she was here, and not when she was in senior care. There was nothing you could have done to stop what happened, you couldn't have prevented the aneurysm, no one could have."

"I still should have been there."

"But you were there for her. You said you talked all the time. She still had you, just as she always did."

"I know, but—"

"Honey—God, it's killing me not to hug you. And I'm

not a hugger!" Lani sounded so out of sorts when she said it, then a laugh spluttered out, surprising them both.

Honey couldn't help herself, she snorted. The tears in her throat made it end on a hiccup, which put Lani over the edge. And somehow, Honey was laughing along with her, only it was cathartic and emotional; the tears that streamed down her cheeks were a release of grief.

"God, I'm such a basket case," she said, still half laughing, half crying, as she tried to get herself back under control. "I was so worried, first about being here, and dealing with . . . well, with my thing, and then the shop I thought had been sitting empty was occupied and all decked out for a grand opening of someone else's business, and my car broke down . . ."

Lani motioned her back toward the seat. When Honey wavered, she said, "Don't make me hug you."

Which made the laughter threaten all over again. Honey sat. "You have no idea, but this is so not how I pictured this going."

"Is it going worse, or better?" Lani said, amusement in her words.

"Better. I think." Both smiled at that, and Honey finally got her tears to stop trickling and her heart to stop racing.

Lani refreshed her coffee and pushed the chocolate cupcake toward her. "Have a bite. Everything makes more sense with cupcakes. Especially ones filled with dark chocolate. And the sugar buzz doesn't hurt, either."

Honey peeled off the paper more for something to do than because she really wanted a bite. But peeling off the paper released the rich, decadent scents of chocolate and spicy ginger, so she gave in and took a bite. Her eyes widened, even as her body hummed. When she swallowed, she looked at Lani with a whole new level of understanding. "It's no wonder you all are so ridiculously happy. God, these are like . . . what do you put in them?"

"Love," Lani said simply. "Works every time." She handed Honey another Kleenex to catch the crumbs. "What did you mean, 'you all'? Have you met more of the crew?"

Honey's cheeks warmed, but she was so far past mortification at this point, she honestly couldn't let herself care. "I was sitting over behind the auto repair shop yesterday, and I saw you all come in for some after hours baking."

"Ah, Cupcake Club. You should have come over, introduced yourself."

Maybe I should have, she thought. "Cupcake Club?"

Lani grinned. "You know, like having a book club. Some women bitch and knit, or bitch and read, we bitch and bake."

Honey found herself smiling again. "I like it."

"You'll have to come next week. It would be a good way to get to know folks here. We're a good bunch. A little eccentric, maybe."

"Well, I think it goes without saying, I have you all beat on that score."

Lani laughed again and Honey found herself laughing with her. *Seriously in Wonderland,* she thought.

Any minute she'd wake up and this wacky dream would all be just that. Except, she realized, she didn't want to wake up. Because, as dreams went, this one was a little odd, okay a lot odd, but had the potential to be pretty awesome.

"Besides, if you really do own half the place, I could hardly keep you out," Lani said on another laugh.

Honey's smile faded, as, true to form, cold, harsh reality crept right back in. "Yes, that. I still don't know about, well . . . any of it, I guess."

"Do you want to go next door and see it?"

Then some other realization struck Lani because her face paled, just a little. "Oh my God. If you thought Bea still lived upstairs over the shop when she passed, then, did you—? Were you planning on living there?"

"Kind of."

"Oh, shit."

"That, too."

Lani's mouth quirked at that. "You can't know this yet, but I promise you're going to fit in here just fine. I can't wait to introduce you to Charlotte. And Kit. You've already met Alva."

Lani picked up a pencil, tapped it on her desk, her expression growing serious. "We'll figure something out. We will. I mean, we have to get it all sorted out legally, of course, but—" She stopped and looked up at Honey as another thought apparently struck her. "Double shit. Were you planning on reopening her shop? Are you a tailor, too? I thought Bea said you were an artist."

"I am an artist. But about the shop space, yes, I was planning to use it. Bea wanted me to open up a storefront. I've had a mail-order business for years, but she knew it was time to get out of the barn and into a real life, and she was right." Honey stopped, knowing it was pointless to explain further. The bakery adjunct was built and ready to open for business. Even if she had the legal right to take the space back, she didn't have the funds to reconstruct it from a kitchen to her little artisan shop. It wouldn't have taken much to shift it from the way Bea had had it to meet her basic needs; then, as the shop progressed, she would have made further improvements until she had it the way she wanted it.

And kicking the cupcake ladies out wouldn't exactly be the way to endear herself to her new customer base or her new neighbors. Not that she wanted to kick them out.

"Listen, I don't know what will happen," Honey said, not wanting to think abut the shop she'd finally let herself envision, only to lose it before it even began. "Obviously,

I need to talk to Bea's lawyers. I didn't come here to make trouble. I came here—"

"To make yourself a home," Lani finished, and it was only because she was smiling so sincerely, without an ounce of pity in her voice or on her face, that Honey took it as the kind gesture it was intended to be. "I know something about that, too. A lot of something, actually. As does my husband, and a few of my closest friends. Trust me, you couldn't be surrounded by more understanding people. We know what you're going through." She grinned again. "Well, the starting over part, anyway. As for the rest . . . you just tell us what you're comfortable with and what makes you uncomfortable, and we'll work around it."

She said it so simply. As if that was all there was to it. But . . . it wasn't that simple. Couldn't be. Honey knew otherwise. Didn't she?

"Okay, so maybe Franco won't." Lani laughed and rolled her eyes. "Oh my god, he'll love you. But he's a bit like a big, untamed French poodle, so we'll have to work on him."

"Franco?"

"One of the cupcake crew. You'll love him, trust me. A better friend and a more staunch ally, you couldn't hope to have. Plus he's very tall and can reach the high things. Win-win, really. So, I'm sorry, I don't remember. What kind of art? It's sculpting or something, right?"

Honey felt . . . dazed. She sat there, trying to keep up and regroup at the same time, wanting to step away from her own spinning head and thundering heart long enough to take stock of this moment, of what was happening, so she could understand how things could simultaneously be so horribly wrong, and yet feel almost magically right.

"Oh," she said, when she saw Lani's expectant face and realized she'd lost the thread of the conversation. "Yes, I work with clay; I'm also a wood carver. Not a serious one.

I mean, I'm serious about my work, but my eye lends itself more to the whimsical than the thought-provoking. As a kid, I learned to whittle from my dad and started making little fantasy creatures and woodland critters." *My own circle of friends,* she thought. "My mom would tuck them here and there in her gardens and around the property. Then I discovered clay and . . . well, it kind of mushroomed, as my dad loved to say, into a business."

"I'm sorry to say I've never checked out your catalog, but I will now. Do you have somewhere to stay? Oh, right, you were here yesterday if you saw us at bake club—and your car's in the shop. Wow, welcome to Sugarberry, huh?"

"It's been . . . memorable." Despite all the incredible things that had happened in the past hour, the first thing that came to mind when Honey thought of memorable welcomes was Dylan Ross. And his hands on her arms. And his grin when he told her a little crazy was a good thing. And that he didn't plan on touching her again.

And how much she really wished he would. And that she could let him.

"So, where are you staying now?"

Honey snapped out of thoughts she had no business thinking about. "At the Hughes's place. My car is going to take a while. Barbara—Mrs. Hughes, lent me her bicycle to use. Is it always this hot in the spring?"

"No, this is unusual, even for the South. Listen, why don't we do this? Let me get someone to cover the shop tomorrow morning, and I can take you over the causeway to get the papers and whatever copies you need from the county, and then we can come back over here and see Morgan—our lawyer and Kit's significant other as it happens. Kit is the manager next door. At least we can get that part settled. I don't know what to tell you about your plans and about the shop itself. I'm pretty sure my lease is valid and—"

"You're right. I need to get up to speed on, well, on a lot of things, it seems. I appreciate your willingness to drive me, but please don't go to the trouble. I can get a cab and—to be honest," she added, when Lani started to reassure her, "I'd like to handle it on my own."

"I completely understand. I am really sorry. I wish it wasn't happening like this, but, trust me, between me and Char, and Kit, and Morgan, Baxter, everyone . . . we'll find a solution that works."

"Honestly, I don't know if I'll stay, but—" Honey was surprised by how stricken Lani looked at the news. They'd just met, after all.

"Bea wanted you here. And you wanted to be here, or you wouldn't have uprooted your whole life to come all this way to start over. Don't let this—well, it's not a small thing. It's a huge, giant pain in the ass thing, I know, but don't give up on us, okay? I wanted to run back to New York a hundred times, a thousand, when I was getting ready to open my bakery, but thank God I didn't. You'll be happy you stayed."

Honey didn't mention that getting the shop situation figured out was only part of her problems with relocating. In fact, it might end up being the least of her worries. Alva's and Lani's easy breezy acceptance of her little "eccentricity" notwithstanding, if what Alva said was true and the islanders actually thought she would put out some kind of fortune teller shingle, they were going to be sadly disappointed.

She wanted a normal life. Or as normal a life as she could have. She'd deal with her stuff, figure out how she was going to handle it as things happened. She'd been a much younger person the last time she'd allowed her curse free reign. She hoped a bit of life wisdom and maturity would help her to deal with it better this time around. She sort of had to, if she was ever going to get the life she really wanted.

She was beyond gratified—amazed and stunned was more like it—that the locals she'd met so far seemed so unfazed by her curse. Or the idea of it, anyway. They hadn't had to deal with it yet. Bea had been open to her gift, had nurtured it, strengthened it, utilized it. Honey's "abilities," however, were significantly stronger than Bea's. When Honey let go and opened up the portals again, allowing people in . . . well, the good, kind folks of Sugarberry really might not want to know what she'd find out about them.

Chapter 5

Dylan signed the deliveryman's invoice, grunted his thanks, then used a utility knife to slice through the tape on the box he'd just been handed. He lifted out the vintage teak dorade box with a bronze cowl vent and carefully removed the packing material. "Damn, but you're pretty." He turned it so the sunlight glinted off the sleek, shiny finish, then smiled as he walked back up the crushed shell driveway.

His sailboat sat on its trailer at the far end, closest to the house. "Look what I bought for you," he said as he skirted the work bench, stepped over an assortment of tools, an overturned bucket, and Lolly, who lifted her head, sniffed once, realized whatever he had wasn't edible, and plopped back down in the shade to snooze.

"Not for you," he told the dog, then climbed up the ladder and stepped onto the back of the boat. "For you." He lifted the antique ventilator in a toast to the carved mermaid mounted above the cabin door.

Two years he'd been looking for just the right piece, combing online auctions and sale listings on several boating sites he frequented. So, naturally he hadn't found it on any of those. He'd found it on an ad for an old junker of a sailboat. In its original form, the junker had sported gorgeous hand-carved woodwork, the kind of craftsmanship rarely seen in the modern times of sleeker, faster, shinier. The owner had wanted to sell the boat "as is," all or nothing. It had taken Dylan the better part of the past six months to wear him down. Well, that and the fact that no one else had put any kind of offer on the old thing.

Of course, he'd also advised the old man that the boat was beyond salvaging. He'd advised the owner to consider putting it up for parts as he'd likely make more money (any money) on it that way, and had been gratified to see that very ad posted just last week.

Ross & Sons had still been down near the docks when he'd first discovered the little teak beauty. His boat had been parked right out back, in easy reach to work on when there weren't any cars in for servicing. And simply to look at when the frustrations of the job got the better of him. Someday he'd get her out on the water, but he was perfectly content to keep tinkering on the boat until he had her restored to the vision he'd pictured in his mind the day he'd laid eyes on her.

He could still recall his brother Mickey sneering at his decision to blow all the money he'd saved up for an old Mustang on a boat instead. Too drunk to hold his tongue, his old man had stood up for him, and had paid the price for it. Mickey had stopped accepting parental feedback the day he'd figured out he was bigger, stronger, and faster with his fists than the old man. Since their dad was usually on his way to passing out drunk, or already passed out, even Dylan, who was six years Mickey's junior, could hold his own against the old man by the time he hit puberty.

Of course, Donny Ross hadn't always been a drunk. There'd been a time when he'd been a pretty damn good mechanic and a decent man to boot. Better than his own old man or his uncle. Dylan's grandfather, Tommy, had been proud of his son . . . but of his own brother, Uncle Dick, not so much. Then again, Dick usually had a beer in one hand and a nasty observation at the ready, so it wasn't a surprise that he'd felt threatened by the father-son duo. Dick was a mean son of a bitch who'd never married, much less procreated—a fact that Dylan, in the short time he'd known the man, had thought was perhaps the only fortunate thing that had ever happened to the guy. In fact, the story went that Dylan's father had been proud of the fact that he hadn't followed the Ross family tradition, in which at least one member of every generation lost the battle with the bottle.

Unfortunately, that had changed after the sudden death of Donny's father, followed by his wife—Dylan's and Mickey's mother—abandoning them, and Dick landing himself in jail for shooting a jealous husband who'd come after him when he'd found out Dick was the guy who'd banged and banged up his wife. Fortunately Dick hadn't killed the guy.

With his dad dead, Dick in jail, and his wife gone without looking back, unable to deal with Mickey's temperamental outbursts and having another small one underfoot, Donny had cracked.

By the time Dick had gotten out of jail, Donny had claimed a permanent place on the Ross Family Drunk roster. He wasn't a mean drunk, just a sad, sorry, pitiable one.

And Dick was back to drinking again before his first parole meeting.

Mickey was fourteen when Uncle Dick wrapped his car around a tree . . . and he rose up to become the man of the house. Young Dylan had quickly learned that life could, in fact, get worse. He used to dream of the day he could run away from home.

When that day came, he'd stayed. Someone had to protect their dad from Mickey's rages. With or without alcohol, Mickey made Dick look like a choir boy when it came to getting himself into trouble.

For years, the islanders thought it was Donny abusing Dylan, and that Mickey was just a chip off the Ross family block, brawling with his old man. There had been no point in explaining that Donny was as much a victim as Dylan was, and Mickey was the current tyrant in residence. When Dylan wasn't feeling guilty for wishing his brother would do something bad enough to end up in jail like Uncle Dick had, he was feeling guilty for being so damn angry with his father. He couldn't forgive his dad for not being strong enough to handle life, to handle Mickey. To love and take care of Dylan.

"And why in the hell I'm thinking about any of that mess, I have no idea," Dylan said, scrubbing a hand over his face. What he did know was that fifteen years ago, this boat had been his salvation. If he couldn't leave home and leave his dad behind, he could, at least, run away to work on the boat. Many a night he'd slept on board, behind the repair shop, lying on his back on the deck, looking at the stars, listening to the gulls, the sound of the water, and imagining what kind of life he'd have if he could do anything he wanted.

Turned out what he wanted to do was fix cars. He was good at it. Even better than his father and his grandfather. Plus, cars didn't drink, they didn't punch, kick, scream, or shout. They didn't make his life a living hell. Instead they'd been the one thing that made his life tolerable. They made sense. If they were broken, it was just a matter of figuring out what was wrong and fixing it. And it felt damn good to know he could fix something. Because he sure as hell couldn't fix his family.

Dylan had been running the shop pretty much by himself by the time he was sixteen. Mickey was never around, and only came by when he needed to take money from the office safe or steal parts he could sell for booze or drug money. He'd never had any real interest or inclination to work on cars . . . or to work at all.

Their father had passed away from a heart attack right after Dylan's twenty-first birthday, and Mickey had finally landed himself in prison eleven months later. Only then had Dylan felt like his life was his own, to do with as he pleased. Unlike Dick, Mickey wasn't ever getting out. Dylan had tried to see him, see if maybe hitting bottom, losing their dad, and being the only family they each had left had finally shaken some sense into his brother. Mickey had refused to see him. And, family or not . . . Dylan hadn't tried again. What was done was done. Mickey had lasted twenty-two months inside before getting himself killed.

So, for a peaceful ten years now, it had been Dylan, the shop, and the sailboat. Well, and Lolly. Dylan hadn't wanted the damn dog, but she'd been hanging around the docks all last summer, and as the fall had turned into winter, she ended up crawling under his bay door to sleep in the garage at night. And if, after a while, Dylan left some scraps from his lunch or dinner behind, who was to say if she helped herself to them, too?

Then the fire had happened. An electrical fire in a neighboring building got out of hand. It had been a chilly, windy night, and sparks had flown, burning bits of the engulfed building had landed on the old roof of the garage, and it had gone up, like so much tinder.

That same night Dylan had learned a thing or two about himself. The only thing he'd about killed himself to save before the building went completely to ash, was the damn dog. Even the boat, fortunately under tarp for the winter, hadn't been the first thing on his mind when the call from the fire chief had woken him up. Just the damn dog.

Part black and white border collie, part who the hell knew what, she wasn't the standard of canine beauty by any stretch, but that didn't matter to Dylan. Almost five months later, her fur was coming back in where it had been singed off on her side and left hind quarter where the burning beam had fallen on her. She still limped a little and even though the vet said she likely wasn't more than a few years old, she slept more than she used to. The vet bills had been staggering, but old Doc Jensen had asked Dylan only one time if he wanted to put the homeless mongrel down. Apparently something in Dylan's expression had the old doctor nodding . . . and seeing to the dog's needs.

When asked her name, Dylan had answered on the spur of the moment. He'd always given the dog a hard time, complaining that she was always lollygagging about. And *Lolly* had just popped out. He hadn't even been aware that he'd already been thinking of her by a name until that moment. If anyone asked, he'd referred to her as the thousand dollar mutt—because that's what it had cost him to fix her up. He'd figured she owed him companionship after that, so it was only fair he keep her with him so she could fulfill her end of the deal.

He glanced over at the peacefully sleeping mutt. "You're sleeping on the job," he called down to the dog, but he smiled as he turned back to the boat and his prized new piece of equipment. He could already envision how it would look, mounted on the—

Movement on the road caught his eye. "Well, holy hell. What's she doing here?"

Lolly didn't seem to have an answer for that, either, but she was a damn sight more interested in finding out than Dylan. She hauled herself up and trotted crookedly down the driveway with her tail wagging to greet their guest.

"Look, but don't touch," he muttered after the dog, finding himself somewhat curious about how Miss Skittish would respond to the friendly canine overture. Dylan hadn't been a pet owner long, but he already put a lot of stock in how people responded to Lolly. Of course, she had never met an enemy. So it was all on Honey.

Honey Pie, he recalled Alva calling her, a nickname bestowed by her aunt Bea. Sounded like something you'd call a happy, free-spirited little youngster. Turned out he didn't have any part of that right.

He watched as she rolled her bicycle to a stop—controlled this time—and immediately held the back of her hand down for Lolly to sniff. Lolly being Lolly, she simply licked Honey's palm and barked once in happy greeting. Unlike Dylan, the dog loved company. He figured the only reason she hung out with him was to use his garage as a means to get attention from his customers. It worked, too.

Honey laughed and gave the dog's head a good scratch. "Well, aren't you a good girl?" she crooned. "Coming out to meet your guests."

Lolly barked again, then trot-limped back up the drive, tongue hanging out, looking proudly at Dylan as if to say "look what I found!"

Dylan was only half paying attention to the dog. He was still hung up on the sound of Honey's laugh. The woman he'd first met in his garage hadn't seemed capable of such a sound, and their meeting earlier hadn't changed his mind all that much. It was possible he'd been too busy noticing how that filmy, flowery skirt had clung to her legs when the steady island breeze picked up, making him wonder if perhaps he hadn't been too quick to pass judgment on her body as average. Now she was wearing a green T-shirt and some kind of rolled up jean shorts, proving he hadn't been wrong about those legs being noteworthy. "You changed your clothes."

Her smile didn't fade, but it did turn wry.

Damn if he didn't like that, too.

"Yes. Seemed to make more sense in this heat. You're working on your boat."

He tried not to let his lips quirk, but he had to work at it. "If I want to sail it someday, I have to do that." He set the dorade down, but didn't climb down off the boat. "Now that we've stated the obvious, are you here for a reason, or were you just pedaling by?"

"For a reason," she said, not bothering to climb off her bike. Since she had to look up to talk to him, she shaded her eyes with a hand to her forehead, which only served to make those eyes of hers even spookier looking.

It annoyed him that he was noticing that . . . or anything else about her. Batshit crazy didn't simply change with the change of an outfit. "And that would be?"

"I went by the garage after talking with Lani, but it took longer than I'd realized, and you'd closed up for the day. Alva told me where you lived and that you wouldn't mind if I stopped by. Said you'd most likely be working on your boat."

He sighed. Miss Alva was going to have to make a lot more than jelly rolls if she wanted to get back on his good side.

"Since my car is going to take a while, I was hoping to get more of my things out of it. All of them, actually, if I could."

"I open again at seven in the morning."

"I'm taking a cab over to the county offices in the morning."

"Courthouse doesn't open till nine."

She didn't ask him how he knew that.

Just as well. If she stayed on the island much longer, she'd know all about his family past anyway, and just how often he'd had to deal with the county courthouse. And why.

"Well, okay. Would it be possible to meet you a few minutes before you open, like six forty-five, and maybe get some help driving the stuff over to the B&B? I'll be happy to pay you for your time." When he didn't respond right away, she added, "Actually, I'd be happy to ask anyone other than you, but you're the only person I know with a truck."

He had to work not to smile then, too. "If it will all fit in your little car, it will fit in someone else's car."

"With some planning, sure. An open bed truck would just be a lot faster and easier. My car is in your shop. Where your truck is. Every day." She waved her hand. "You know what? Never mind. I've only met a few folks at this point, and just thought . . . but that's okay. I get it. I'll figure something out." She bent down and stuck her hand out. Lolly happily obliged and trotted right back over.

Traitor. To Dylan's surprise, the dog slowly sat, favoring her hip, then lifted her paw, something she hadn't done since the fire.

Honey, clearly delighted, took Lolly's paw and gently shook it. "Well, at least someone has that nice island hospitality my aunt was always telling me about. What a sweet girl you are." She gave Lolly another scratch behind the ears. "Go work your charms on that guy, will ya," she said, voice lowered, but still loud enough for him to hear—which wasn't by accident.

Lolly barked as if in complete understanding. And, knowing the dog, Dylan wasn't too sure she didn't.

"I'll try to get Mr. or Mrs. Hughes to come over with me first thing in the morning. If it wouldn't be too much of an imposition." She put one foot back on a pedal to turn around, which was when he noticed she was wearing beat-up red Chucks.

He recognized the classic high-top basketball sneakers because he still had his own ratty old pair.

Lolly barked once at her retreating form, then again, up at Dylan. "Oh, for Chrissake." He braced a hand on the side of the boat and jumped down, wincing as he bent his knees to absorb the impact. "Hold on. Just—hold on."

She skidded briefly on the crushed shells, but stopped and stayed upright, then looked back over her shoulder at him, and he felt that . . . thing again in his chest. For the life of him, he couldn't rightly say there was a single thing about her that should stir anything in him except a great deal of wariness. Her shorts were baggy, and rolled up the way they were, as if recently hacked off, wasn't the most attractive thing. Her legs were, well, they weren't hard to look at, but they were almost translucent in their whiteness. Her dark green T-shirt, also baggy, bore some colorful company logo that, from where he stood, looked like a gnome . . . or something. Her hair was in a single ponytail, again. No makeup. No sunglasses, either. Just the big, clunky horn rims. Her eyes were an attention getter, but her face was as fair as her legs. He hoped to hell she was wearing sunscreen.

"Let's just get it done now," he said, snagging his keys from the makeshift tool bench. He slapped his thigh. "Come on, Lolly."

More active than he could recall seeing her in months, the dog all but high stepped it over to the truck, prancing back and forth in her uneven gait.

"Lolly," Honey said. "I like it. Suits her." She climbed off her bike, then took a quick two steps back as he reached for it.

That was all it took to shake off the odd moment of awareness and get him right back to reality. "Just putting it in the truck bed." Why it pissed him off that she got all freaky again he couldn't have said, but it did. He got that it apparently wasn't personal, but it felt insulting as hell, all the same.

"Right, thanks. And, listen . . . I do appreciate this. I

meant what I said, about paying you for your time. I really didn't just mean for you to drop everything and—"

"Get in." He put the bike on its side in the truck bed so it wouldn't slide. Then he bent down, scooped up Lolly as she wasn't up to jumping yet, and set her down in the open area between the bike and the cab of the truck. "Be a good girl," he told her and got a bark in response; then he climbed on the driver's seat.

Honey paused for a moment, then the engine gunned to life and she leaped toward the passenger door and climbed in. "I really do appreciate this," she said again, but one look from him and she snapped her mouth shut and put her seatbelt on. At least she understood when not to press her luck.

They drove the short distance in silence, which gave him way too much time to think about how she could go from . . . well, ravaged, the first time he'd laid eyes on her, to jumpy and nuts in his office, to essentially normal and sociable today. *Essentially* normal. She was still jumpy. *What's that about, anyway?*

He recalled, far too easily for his liking, the way she'd looked at the bakery shops, and the way she'd trembled as she'd looked at all her worldly possessions packed in her ancient car. Maybe it had just been the fatigue of driving cross-country.

He resisted the urge to slide a sideways glance at her. He knew Bea had talked about her niece being an artist of some kind, but he'd never paid any real attention to the chatter. Just folks bragging on family, which . . . well, it was understandable why he didn't follow that much. Her artsy side might explain her rather off-the-wall wardrobe choices. Artists were often eccentrics, weren't they? Hell, maybe that explained all of it. What it didn't explain was why he gave a crap.

He turned off the town square toward the channel road, then into the alley that ran between the shops. He shut off the engine, got out, and scooped up Lolly from the back. She trotted over to the back door and waited for Dylan to unlock it.

"She seems right at home here," Honey said as she came up behind them.

"She usually comes to work with me, but it's been too hot lately."

"What happened to her back leg?

"I noticed the limp," she added when Dylan glanced at her. "And the fur growing back. Is she okay?"

Given the speedy island grapevine and the fact she was stuck on Sugarberry for at least the next week, Dylan knew there was no point in changing the subject. "The old repair shop burned down about six months ago. She got caught in the fire. Beam fell on her hind quarters."

"Oh no, that's awful." Honey immediately squatted down and gave Lolly some extra love, which, naturally, the mutt lapped up. "You poor thing." She looked up at Dylan. "How did she get out?"

Dylan unlocked the door and went inside. The sun was setting and it was still damn hot. Even hotter in the closed work bay. He went over and rolled up the bay door to let the evening breeze move the muggy air around a bit while they transferred her stuff to his truck. And managed to avoid answering her question. "I'll get the keys."

"You know, I wondered why everything looked so clean and fresh. I mean, for an auto repair shop. Given the name, I figured it wasn't likely a new business."

He stifled a sigh when he realized she was following him. "It's not." He flipped the light on and crossed to the wall next to his desk and the row of hooks used to keep the keys on the cars in for service. He didn't normally lock them up when they were locked in the service bay overnight, but since it looked like she had all her worldly possessions in hers . . . he'd figured better to be safe than sorry.

He snagged her key ring—it was easy to see with a big red and white spotted mushroom hanging from it—and turned to find her looking around the office.

"I'm guessing you're the son of Ross & Sons."

"I'm the owner, the only Ross left," he said. And hoped like hell she'd leave it at that. She'd hear all the stories at some point, but she wasn't going to hear them from him.

"Oh. I'm sorry. I lost both my parents. My dad to a heart attack when I was nineteen, and my mom in a car accident two years later."

"Sorry to hear that," he said, uncomfortable.

"Thank you. Aunt Bea was the last of my family, so her passing sort of brought it all back. Do you have other relatives on the island still?"

"Just me." He would have brushed by her, but didn't need a repeat of what had happened the other day. He jingled the keys and nodded toward the door. "Let's get to it."

"Right." She went on through to where her car sat, then stepped aside so he could unlock it. "Some of it's fragile, so—"

"Are the boxes marked?"

"Well, no. I didn't think anyone would be handling them but me. Just—here, I'll hand stuff out to you, okay?"

He backed up so she could step in, and he noticed her fragrance for the first time. It smelled like . . . sandalwood. Or something like that. Woodsy, earthy, with a bit of spice to it. Nothing flowery or feminine. He thought again about how he'd misjudged her based on a name. Seemed he was making a habit of it. He had to admit, the scent suited her. A little offbeat, a little bohemian, and unexpectedly sultry.

"Um, here?"

He snapped out of it and realized she was juggling a box from the car toward his waiting hands. He took the box.

"Not fragile," she said.

"Then stack another one on top."

She dragged out another one and carefully put it on top. Careful not to touch him, either, he noted.

"Fragile."

He said nothing, just made his way through the open bay door to the back of his truck and set both boxes in the open bed, then slid the top one off and tucked it up by the cab. He went back inside and stood behind her, ready for the next batch, trying like hell not to notice there was actually a very fine curve to her backside, where the baggy shorts had pulled snug as she reached farther into the car's interior.

He was still trying like hell not to notice when she backed out and swung around with several stacked boxes in her arms, only to smack them right into his chest. "Oh! I didn't know you'd come back. I didn't hear you." The boxes bobbled wildly. "Fragile!"

He had no choice but to grab her arm with one hand and use the other to trap the boxes between their bodies until she steadied herself.

Her eyes shot wide as his hand wrapped around her arm, and her mouth opened on a silent gasp.

"I've got them," he told her, keeping his gaze level on hers, hoping to keep her from going into . . . whatever the hell state she'd gone into the last time he'd touched her. "It's okay." He heard the edge to his words and tempered his annoyance, which was really just a cover for concern. He didn't want to deal with another one of her episodes, but didn't want to see her deal with one, either. "I got it," he repeated calmly and quietly when she simply stared at him, seemingly frozen in place.

"I'm sorry." The words sounded strangled. She didn't move or let go of the boxes.

So he didn't—couldn't—let go of her, though he was sorely tempted. If he'd thought her eyes were spooky before, something in them now downright gave him the chills.

"Let me go," she said, the words tight, almost forced, but with an edge of desperation.

"Can't do that, sugar, until you let go of the boxes. I've got 'em."

She continued to stare at him, her gaze boring straight into his.

"How 'bout on the count of three," he said, wishing like hell whatever it was she was suffering from didn't tug at him. But damn it all, it did. "One . . . two—"

She started trembling, then abruptly jerked her arm free.

If he hadn't been paying such close attention, he'd have dropped the boxes. He almost did, anyway. With his other hand under them, he managed to steady them, but his attention wasn't on the boxes. It was on her sheet-white face, her eyes wide with terror or horror as she stepped back, only to bang up against the car. He couldn't have said why, but he was pretty damn certain if the car hadn't been there to block her retreat, she'd have turned and taken off at a dead run.

Operating on instinct or his own brand of sudden onset insanity, he shoved the boxes on top of her car and shifted his body—without touching her—so she was boxed in. Not with the intent of scaring her, but with the intent of making her feel secure.

"All right, darlin'. It's okay. You're fine. It's all good, sugar, you'll be just fine." He talked to her much the same way he'd talked to Lolly when she'd been anxious and scared coming out of the anesthetic after her first surgery.

Gently, but firmly. "Nothing bad is happening. Nothing bad is going to happen."

He wished he understood why she went from normal chick to crazy chick like she did. It obviously had something to do with coming into contact with people. Not dogs, apparently. She'd spoken quite naturally and calmly about meeting Lani, Alva, and Barbara Hughes, too. Maybe it was just men—which meant, he belatedly realized, it was highly likely at least one of his gender had done some not-so-nice things to her. In the recent past perhaps? Who the hell knew. He was an auto mechanic. He fixed engines, not people.

Still, he felt a bit bad for being so pissed off about it all. He should have figured it out sooner. He remembered the way she'd stared at him when she'd said, "I'm not crazy," as if willing him to believe she really wasn't the loony tune she'd seemed back in his garage.

"I-I'm . . . s-so . . . s-sorry," she said, stuttering the words, trembling even harder, jerking his complete attention back to the present. "About . . . the fire. That's terrible. Who'd do that? Only . . . no, it was electrical. The storage place, next door? It was so windy. And your garage—" She gasped. "You ran in! You ran in when it was burning. Why, why would you do that? What was worth saving that you'd risk—oh no! Poor Lolly. Poor baby. Oh my God. If you hadn't gone in—"

She was talking and looking right at him, though it was as if she could see straight through him. Or straight into him. She clearly wasn't in the here and now, anyway, nor was he quite sure she even knew what she was saying. It was as if she was a million miles away in some other reality only she could see. Except the things she was talking about were very real and specifically about him. She had the details exactly right.

"It's okay. Lolly is okay." He thought if he responded rationally, calmly, maybe it would calm her. He wanted nothing more than for her to snap out of it. He honestly didn't know what the hell was happening or what might have happened to her in the past, but at the moment, all he wanted to do was get back to the business of moving her things over to the B&B and getting her out of his personal space. Permanently. He'd pay to expedite the parts for her car, whatever, but this was way more than he wanted to deal with. "It was an electrical fire," he told her, firmly, if gently. "Wiring shorted out in one of the storage units, and yes, wind carried the sparks and set my garage on fire. It was an accident."

"Everyone is okay? Lolly—she's trapped!"

"Honey," he said, a bit more sharply than intended, but he had to snap her out of this . . . trance, or whatever the hell she was in, and he wasn't about to risk touching her to do it. "I got Lolly out. We're both fine. You know that, you've seen it with your own eyes. Remember?"

Her gaze sharpened on his. "You almost weren't. You could have died." Her voice was a hushed whisper, laced with trembling horror as if she were there, in the moment, watching it all happen. "That beam, the second one, caught the back of your shirt. If you'd been one second later, getting to Lolly—oh, Dylan, you'd have both been lost!"

Okay, that stopped him dead. He gaped at her, stunned, and not a little freaked out. No one knew about the second beam. Not the fireman, not the local EMT, not the vet. He'd never told anyone about the burns on his back. He'd spent the night at the vet's with the dog, had shrugged off—rather firmly—suggestions that he should be looked at for smoke inhalation, at the very least. He'd been fine. The dog had not.

He also knew, in retrospect, that it had been a lot easier to focus on what the dog needed than to think about the total loss of the business his grandfather had started, and the wildly varying emotional responses he was likely to have about that once reality began to sink in. So he'd put off thinking, as long as he could, anyway, and focused his attention where it could do some good.

He wished he could do the same with whatever the hell was happening right that very moment.

"Honey." He barked it this time. "Look at me, dammit. Look. At. Me." Sometimes when Dylan's father had gotten really wasted, he'd have these waking nightmares about losing his dad, his wife, about Mickey. The only way Dylan could get him out of it was to jerk his attention in a clean snap. A slap to the face would have done it, but nothing would ever provoke Dylan to raise his hand to anyone, ever. So he'd used his voice like a verbal slap then, as he did now. "Focus," he ordered, redirecting her. "We need to unpack your car. Lolly is in the truck, waiting."

"Lolly." Honey's head jerked, but her eyes looked a little less wild, and her voice was somewhat calmer. She finally glanced from him to the open bay door and the truck sitting just beyond it. "She's in the truck."

It was the first rational thing she'd said, and his relief was profound. He focused on that, and simply shoved the rest aside. For the time being.

"Yes," he said, still forcefully, but evenly. "She needs us to unpack this car. Do you understand?"

"Lolly needs us." Honey looked back to Dylan. Her trembling had stopped and color was seeping back into her cheeks. "She's really okay?"

"She's fine. She great. You've seen her. Petted her. Do you want to go out and see her now?"

He expected Honey to nod and maybe stumble off toward the truck. At least she'd calmed down and wasn't freaking out any longer. Instead, she was freaking him out. She reached up and very purposefully put her hands on his face. He went rigid, his heart skipping multiple beats as he waited to see if the trance would start all over again. He was a breath away from jerking back from her touch when she spoke.

"Are you okay?" She asked it softly, quietly. Her gaze probed his deeply.

He could still see some kind of disconnect as if she was looking, but seeing something only she could see.

"Your back . . . it healed, too?"

"It did, yes," he said, not sure why the touch of her hands should be soothing to him. He should be the one trembling or shuddering.

As she splayed her fingers out so her fingertips brushed along his temples as if trying to deepen the connection, he felt a kind of . . . calm seep into him. "I'm fine," he said quietly, matching her tone, keeping his gaze intently on hers.

Then she slid her hands to his chest, and his body leaped into awareness so fast, so hard, it almost left him breathless. It definitely left him speechless.

"Only not here," she said, still searching his eyes. She pressed her palm against his heart. "Not here."

He had absolutely no idea what to say to that. Or how to explain the way she was making him feel. She was crazy one second, disturbing the next. Then soothing, then . . . arousing him so swiftly he ached to the point of pain with the need to pull her against him, to cover that mouth, and dear God please, make her close those all-seeing, all-knowing eyes. The compulsion made no sense, but it took every last bit of restraint and control he had not to give in to it.

She lifted her gaze to his, and those clear green eyes were swimming in tears. It was like a punch to the gut, and hurt him in ways that made no sense. He didn't even know her. But it about killed him to see it. What the *hell* was going on?

His resolve began to crumble, and he lifted his hands to

cover hers, still pressed to his chest. "I'm fine, Honey," he assured her. "Just fine."

Her hands were cold, which surprised him. They had infused him with so much warmth, with comfort. He felt a fine trembling in her fingers, and noticed the same with her lips. But she didn't say anything; the crazy didn't come back. And, defenses eroding more rapidly than he could restore them, he took a step in, lifting one hand from hers, intent on cupping her cheek, on wiping away the tear there . . . but she slid her hands free, and broke eye contact before he could.

She looked somehow smaller, seemed more fragile, than she had at any point since he'd first laid eyes on her. And he had no earthly clue what to do about it . . . or why the hell it mattered so much.

Something had obviously just happened. To her. To him. Between them. A whole lot of something. As much as he'd like to just walk away and pretend it hadn't, he didn't. Couldn't.

Batshit crazy? Maybe. Okay, certainly. But she'd gotten under his skin. And inside his head. And into a part of his past only he knew about.

The stunning intensity of his physical response to her was part of it, too. Not just because he wanted to act on it, but because it scared the living hell out of him. Crazy had no part in his life, not for a bizarre moment in his garage, and sure as hell not for a one night stand . . . or anything more. It was not his path, not any longer, and never again. But tell that to his still thrumming body, and his hammering heart.

He needed to figure it out. Figure her out. If he understood what was going on, then he could deal with it. With her. Then he'd get as far away from her as possible. And stay there. Because crazy had no place in his life. He had to believe that. Or go crazy himself.

Chapter 6

Honey kept her gaze averted, trying to come back to full awareness. It was a challenge. Part of her was being pulled toward Dylan and the exceedingly vibrant aura that continued to hover all around him, while another part was silently freaking out at the enormity and complexity of what she'd just experienced. Still another part of her was struggling mightily to shove all of it aside and simply get a grip on the here and now—which meant not looking at him. And praying he kept his hands to himself, at least for another moment or two. Or forever.

A parade of heart pounding, terrifying images kept playing through her mind, everything she'd seen, felt . . . known. All of it about Dylan, and how close he'd come to dying in that fire. The other part of it was his sharply spoken commands, contrasting with the gentleness of his touch, knowing, even as she was still trapped in the vortex, that he was trying to be there for her. Even as she knew he couldn't possibly do anything to help her, much less fix what was wrong with her. It was what it was. It lasted as long as it lasted.

But it had never, not ever, been like that. Past events, current emotions, all twisted and tangled. She'd seen one thing, and felt another, felt him the entire time. Her visions had never had that kind of scope or such vivid detail.

The disconnect with what was going on around her was usually absolute, but this time she'd known he was with her, even as she watched every horrifying detail, how close he'd come to losing his life. Maybe that's why it had affected her so viscerally. So . . . personally.

"I . . ." Her voice was little more than a rasp, and she realized her throat ached from suppressing the funnel of emotions she'd just been shoved through at warp speed.

"Shh," he said. "You don't have to—"

"Thank you." She had to get at least that much out. "For trying. To help. Nothing does." She rubbed her damp palms on the sides of her shorts, more to soothe away the last of her shakiness than to dry her suddenly sweaty palms.

"Honey—"

"I can't look at you, at the moment." She lifted her hands, palms out, dismayed that they still trembled ever so slightly. "Please—"

"I'm not going to touch you." But he didn't step back.

For some reason, that helped to calm her. He was like a barricade, or . . . or something. Against what, she didn't know, since he'd been the trigger. But . . . having him close helped, so she didn't question it.

"Okay. Good . . . okay." She tried to take slow, steady breaths, but it was a struggle. Images still hovered, so closing her eyes wasn't an option. She stared at her feet, at the grease stain under her toes. Anything innocuous.

"What happened?" he asked quietly, with more gentleness than she'd have thought him capable of exhibiting. "What happens to you?"

She shook her head. "Maybe . . . another time."

"Okay. Does it happen often?"

She shook her head again. "It's been . . . eight years . . . ten months . . . um, two weeks, and . . ." She trailed off, not wanting to think about the last time she'd let someone touch her, let someone trigger the curse. It had been in the distant and disconnected past. She'd built a whole life for herself since then. It had been in another lifetime, a different one, and as if it had happened to some other person.

Now it felt like it had been only yesterday. Except what happened with Dylan was far, far worse than that last time. Maybe burying the curse for so long had made it come out more strongly. Maybe it was because she was older, no longer a naïve kid who thought leaving Juniper Hollow to go off to art school would somehow make the curse go away . . . or diminish it. As if subjecting herself to so many people, all at once would simply short circuit the whole thing. Only it hadn't exactly turned out like that then.

And it certainly hadn't now.

"I know . . . you think I'm crazy—" She held up her hand to stall any reply, took a deep breath, and forced herself to look at him, almost nauseous with the fear that she'd go rocketing back to that place. It balled her still shaky stomach up in a queasy knot. Only, she didn't spin back. She stayed right where she was, fully in the present.

To her stunned shock, he smiled, though concern for her was still clear in his gray eyes. "Well, sugar, when I said a little crazy was a good thing, maybe I wasn't talking about this."

To her complete and utter amazement, she spluttered out a choked laugh. "Yeah, well . . ." She started to tremble again, but in overwhelming relief. She was okay. She'd made it through. It had passed. And Dylan didn't seem any the worse for wear. Well, other than he surely wanted her gone as quickly as possible, but that she could deal with. She wanted to be gone, too.

"Honey," he began, and lifted his hands, palms out, to reassure her he wasn't going to invade any more of her personal space than he already occupied. "I get that, whatever it is, you can't control it."

She shook her head, and then felt the surprising sting of tears, again. It was a reflex from the sudden release of stress.

"No, no. No more tears," he said.

Maybe it was the slightly panicky edge to those words, the realization that this big, bad wolf of a guy could handle her total out-of-body experience with barely a blink, only to be shaken by the threat of weepy girly tears, that somehow gave her that added edge she needed to take another step toward regaining control.

"Trust me," she said, with an inelegant sniffle. "I'd really rather not, either." She took another deep, shuddering breath, looked away from him once again, and gathered in the ragged edges. "Honestly," she said, as she grew steadier and the threat of tears finally dimmed, "I do thank you. For trying. For wanting to help. I know you don't get it, and you're probably thinking thank God for that."

She scrubbed her face, pushed her hair back, and lifted her chin once more. "Most folks would have freaked out. Or gotten angry."

"Well, it did kind of freak me out, sugar. I won't lie. But it didn't make me mad. It's not like you were doing it on purpose."

She expected to see it then, the pity, the relief, the "thank goodness it's her and not me." Or even the "I hope it's not contagious" look of concern. But there was none of that. He didn't seem to be thinking of himself at all, but more sincerely concerned with getting her back to rights again.

"Let's finish loading your stuff," he suggested. "Better yet, why don't I take you to the B&B with what we've got, let you get some rest. I'll bring the rest of the stuff by in the morning."

He was back to sounding like the guy talking gently to the crazy chick so she wouldn't freak out again, but it was more than she deserved. She owed him, even if he'd been the one to trigger the episode in the first place. That was hardly his fault.

She should be thanking him for that, too. At least, now she knew what she was up against. And that there was no way in hell that any kind of life, or friendships, much less an intimate relationship was possible. "Thanks. But . . . just leave it in there. I–I'm not staying. I won't bother you again, so you don't have to worry about . . . you know. The crazy chick stuff. Just let me or Mrs. Hughes know when the car is ready."

She made herself look at him again, made herself smile, though she didn't think he bought it.

"All right" was all he said. He took a step back and motioned for her to go on to the truck. "Do you want anything else from the car?"

"No. Just what's on top is good. Thank you." She might have made it to the truck and gotten safely inside, buckled herself in, and coolly finished detaching herself from . . . everything, but then she saw Lolly.

Poor, sweet, Lolly was lying on her belly, chin on her paws, studying Honey with a very worried look on her canine face.

Honey's heart broke a little. Her ability to see and know things didn't extend to animals or any living beings other than humans, but she did have a heightened awareness of general feelings and mood when it came to any species. Her little . . . event back there, had scared Lolly. Badly.

Without thinking, Honey knelt down in front of the dog and put her face right in front of Lolly's, who kept her chin on her paws, but her unblinking gaze unwaveringly on Honey's. "You were a very brave girl, you know that?" she said softly. "Being surrounded by fire like that, but you didn't panic. You couldn't get out, so you barked, so he could find you. And you tried to get straight to him when he did. You did so good."

Lolly didn't so much as blink, and Honey could still feel her concern.

"You're a very lucky girl, you know that? Because you have someone looking out for you. Someone who'll stand by you, no matter what."

Lolly's chin lifted just slightly then and her gaze grew more alert, less somber.

"I know you'll stay true to him, too," Honey assured. "You keep watching over him, okay? He needs you, too. Whether he says so or not."

Lolly let out a soft little whine and thumped her tail. Her dark, liquid eyes finally shifted back to hopeful.

Honey smiled, and felt her own heart settle a bit. She might freak out the humans, but at least she could calm the fears of one dog. "Good girl." She scratched Lolly behind her ears, and when she climbed to her feet, Lolly lifted her head, let her tongue hang out in an anticipatory pant.

"Okay, come on. Time to get in the truck. I think we're both ready to go."

Lolly pushed to her feet, then butted her head against Honey's leg, making her laugh and ruffle the dog's fur before Lolly trotted around to the back of the truck, tail wagging.

Honey took a breath, relieved to find that she felt much steadier. Lolly had returned the favor, it seemed. No more shakiness, no more trembling. The episode was well and truly over. She just had to make sure that was the last one she ever had.

It was only when Honey turned around that she realized Dylan had been standing right behind her the entire time, arms full of boxes . . . listening to every word.

"Ever owned a dog?" He asked the question off-handedly, but Honey had already figured out that Dylan didn't do anything off-handedly. She imagined he was usually a man of very few words, and none at all when he could get away with it. His gaze was sharply on hers. To the point that it felt almost like a physical touch. She wasn't so sure if it was comforting or disconcerting.

"I grew up on a farm," she said. "We had a wide variety of critters, but never had a dog, no. No house pets."

"Your . . . thing. It doesn't happen with animals." He didn't make it a question so much as a summation.

"No." She really didn't want to get into it. But before she could scoot past him to the passenger door, he continued the conversation.

"Women?"

"What about women?" she asked, truly confused.

"Do they trigger . . . it?"

"Anybody can. Well, not people I'm really close to . . . emotionally, I mean. That seems to block it out. And there's no rhyme or reason to when or with whom. Other than they have something going on that reaches out and grabs me. I just never know who that's going to be, or when."

"So, it's been easier to avoid people all together."

"That's been the operating assumption, yes."

"For eight years, ten months, two weeks and some number of days."

Her gaze narrowed, and she had to resist the urge to fold her arms protectively around her waist. No one had ever just . . . talked to her about the curse. Like this. So calmly, so . . . conversationally. No one who wasn't family, anyway.

She also doubted Dylan Ross ever made idle conversation. Of course, her little *event* back there in the garage had been specifically about things that had happened to him. It was natural for him to want to understand how she knew things. Quite possibly things that no one else knew.

"You didn't tell anyone, did you?" she asked as she realized at least a part of it. "About your back. About being burned."

"What happened eight years, ten months and two weeks ago?" he asked in lieu of a response.

She had no plan to tell him anything, but something about his stance, about the way he was looking at her, like he was going to be the one to figure this out . . . provoked her. Maybe if she revealed something personal, he'd consider them even, given she knew things about him no one else did. And then he'd stop digging. "I went to art school. I thought maybe mass exposure to the human element would shock it out of me. Either kill me or cure me. At that point, either might have been a blessing."

"But?"

"I was wrong. Apparently my capacity to withstand a constant bombardment of . . . knowledge, is boundless."

"Did you drop out?"

"Eventually."

"But not until whatever happened eight years—"

"Yes," she said, hating that she'd snapped the word out. She didn't want to let him get to her. God knows, hadn't he already gotten to her enough? First with his hormone stirring looks, and then with his surly attitude, topped off with an aura onslaught she hadn't been remotely ready to handle. And yet, it just came spilling out, rapid fire, more like an accusation than a confession. "I was a virgin, okay? And I knew when I left school and went back to Juniper Hollow, I'd stay that way. So . . . I made sure I wasn't."

To her utter shock, his lips curved. "Bad idea, I take it?"

She should be pissed off that he found any part of her confession amusing, so no one was more surprised than Honey when she had to fight to keep her own lips from twitching. Damn him for making it seem like some private joke that only the two of them understood. He understood exactly nothing about her. "You might say that," she said, trying for a grudging, flippant tone, but his knowing smile told her she'd failed miserably.

"So, what then? Back home, hiding out all this time?"

"I started my own business," she said, trying not to sound defiant. "I've stayed focused on that." Before he could ask the obvious, she added, "Mail order. I'm surprised with Bea's stories about me, that everyone didn't already know all of this."

"I'm not much for island gossip."

"And yet . . ."

He frowned, and she had to stifle the urge to smirk.

"All right, I might have heard that your aunt talked about your talent as an artist, and how much she admired you. That she loved you was clear; she was proud, too. She was . . . sketchier . . . about the rest."

"If you knew my Aunt Bea, then you knew that she— it seems like it was common knowledge that she also could . . ." Honey trailed off, not wanting to put words to it. There were no words to explain the curse.

"Either your aunt had a great deal more control over this . . . thing . . . you two have, or yours is out-of-this-world more intense."

"Bea thought of it as a gift. I . . . don't."

"There's more to it than that." He didn't make it a question.

Honey wanted to tell him he didn't have the first clue what he thought he knew, but then he was talking again about Bea. The way he did caught at her heart and made her throat tight all over again.

"She was like the kindly old grandma who had a way of knowing things. Everyone went to her, asked her about things, trusted her if she told them they needed to take care on this matter or that . . . but it was never—"

"Threatening? Scary? Intense?"

He didn't answer that, just . . . studied her in that way

she was coming to know. All focused and intent like she didn't scare him, and he knew if he looked long enough, like looking at a broken engine, he'd figure her out, too.

"Why did you expect me to get angry?" he asked.

"People aren't generally open to what they don't understand. Less so when you tell them things they don't want to hear."

That damnable hint of a smile returned. "Why, sugar? You revealin' their dirty laundry? Tellin' secrets they wanted to keep hidden?"

Honey shook her head. "I only tell people if it's something bad, something they can prevent. Otherwise . . ."

"Otherwise, you have to live with knowin' a whole lot about folks, things you'd rather not know. Things you know they'd really rather you not know. I'm guessing you don't pick up on stuff that's minor or unimportant. Must be uncomfortable."

"You could say that."

"So . . . why the fire?" His expression remained open, but there was nothing casual about the way he looked at her.

Honey merely lifted her shoulders in a shrug. "Because it was a recent traumatic thing? I don't know." As the adrenaline started to seep away, she felt the fatigue settle in. She'd forgotten how much the events took out of her. Well, not so much forgotten as blocked out. This one had been far more powerful than usual, so the weariness seemed to come on more swiftly. Either that or it was still the lingering fatigue from her trip. Perhaps both. "I don't ever know why."

"So, it's not always a warning."

"Not always. Usually, it's something powerfully affecting the person. I'm not surprised, in this case. The fire didn't happen that long ago, and . . . you almost died.

Even if you think you've dealt with that . . ." She let her words trail off.

"I'm guessin' it's not generally happy stuff that triggers your reaction, either."

"Not generally, no."

He did it again. He smiled. It was slow, almost lazy.

But she knew that his mind and manner were anything but slow and lazy, despite his laconic drawl. For the first time, she saw a glimmer of what she thought looked like . . . appreciation in his eyes—which couldn't be right. Maybe she was more wiped out than she'd thought.

"Well, sugar, you must have been real fun at parties."

"A laugh riot," she shot back, annoyed with his amusement because there was absolutely nothing funny about the curse. And yet . . . he was taking it all so calmly in stride as if it were nothing more than a cheesy parlor trick—which was annoying . . . and annoyingly reassuring. She kind of liked that he felt comfortable to not only talk calmly about it . . . but tease her about it. She might even like that a lot. Because it was Dylan, and he got it . . . so it was weirdly okay. *Dammit.*

He walked toward her then, and it was like her brain stuttered. She was still trying to process the strength and scope of what had happened, while also dealing with the immensely conflicting feelings she was having about him. The last thing she needed was him back in her personal space.

She went utterly still, debating if flight stood a better chance than fight, but he walked past her and set the two boxes he'd had in his arms the whole time into the back of his truck.

Feeling ridiculous and even more tired, she watched him scoop Lolly up and put her in the back, too. Honey really needed some quiet time alone to regroup, shake off the jumpiness, and settle her nerves. She breathed a sigh of relief, and, assuming he'd gone around to the driver's side door now that he'd satisfied his curiosity about her "gift," she took one final moment to gather herself before she had to ride in the close confines of the cab with him.

So she wasn't at all prepared, when he turned toward her and neatly boxed her in between him and his truck. He didn't touch her, and, for some reason, she trusted that he wouldn't, but she shrank back nonetheless. Out of habit more than any real alarm. He'd demonstrated he understood how easily triggered she was.

"I don't need crazy in my life," he said, looking into her eyes with such focused intensity she could only stare back. He wasn't frowning, he wasn't smiling. He was . . . invading. "I've had more than my share."

He wasn't touching her, but it was as if he was reaching inside of her, down deep, by the sheer intensity of his gaze, and willing her to understand him.

"I'm not trying to be in your—"

"Shh," he said, a mere whisper. "You might not want to be, but ever since you've gotten here, you've done nothing but. That thing you got inside you is pure crazy. And I don't need it."

After his earlier understanding, his insouciance even, regarding her abilities, the sudden callousness stung badly, surprising her with how much power he had to hurt her and proving she'd already let him get too far into her head. She'd even begun to foolishly think of him as an ally. "Lucky for you then, you don't have it," she snapped.

It only made him grin, annoying her further. *Why is he so damn confounding?*

"See, that right there? That's what you do, sugar. You don't give a damn."

"About what you think of me? No," she lied, hating that it was one. "I don't."

"Which is why I find myself wishing you didn't have the crazy. Because the rest of you . . ."

She shook her head, the hurt rapidly fading, quickly replaced by a spurt of panic. She might not have seen that particular look in his eyes before, but she understood what it meant. Desire.

"No, you're wrong. The rest of me is just boring. Beyond boring. Nobody wants that." Even with her limited experience, that much she knew for fact. "Guys say they don't want the crazy, but they secretly find it all kinds of compelling. Maybe it's the element of danger, the mystery. It didn't take me long to figure out I'm infinitely more fascinating because of the curse. I just don't care too much to suffer through it to give someone his kicks. Especially since once you've tasted the crazy, you realize that it's not as exciting and cool as it's cracked up to be. It's just cracked. And what's left after cracked doesn't add up to much. Certainly not up to the look I see in your eyes right now. Trust me."

There. That had shocked him. *Good.*

When he could lower his eyebrows again, he laughed. Laughed! "You're not kidding, are you?"

"No, sir."

"Aw, sugar. Dammit."

She raised her own brows in question, and his smile faded slowly, though a residual twinkle remained in his eyes, even as he went back into intent study mode. His gaze left her eyes and drifted down toward her mouth.

Her body reacted so swiftly, she had to shut her eyes—as if that would block out the memory. What it did, instead, was forever imprint it in her mind's eye.

"You can close those intriguing, spooky eyes of yours, but you can't hide. Your pupils just went big as dark moons. Makes it even more of a damn shame. About the crazy, I mean. I sure as hell don't have a thing for danger or mystery. I'd much rather do without than take any woman who comes with a side of drama. But you make it really damn hard to walk away, Honey Pie. Damn hard. The crazy I could do without, but the rest . . . just reaches out and grabs me by the throat. And maybe a few other places. It's a hell of a thing."

Honey trembled again, only it had absolutely nothing to do with her gift or his aura, and had everything to do with her hormones and how he'd just triggered every last damn one of them and a whole bunch more she hadn't even known she'd had. Holy . . . shit.

"As much as I'd really like for that fascination to let go, it doesn't. Won't." He moved closer.

She could feel the heat emanating from his body, his skin, and her eyes flew open. "Dylan, whatever you're thinking, stop. Don't. You—I can't go through—I . . . I can't."

He didn't even pause. "When you decided you didn't want to be a virgin anymore, you didn't have feelings for the guy, did you?"

"No, but, I—"

"Did you want him? Did he make your pupils shoot wide like that?" Dylan's gaze drifted to her mouth. "Did he make your lips part, make you sigh like that?"

He tilted his head, let his gaze drift along the slim column of her neck. "Did he make your pulse leap?"

Then, before she could even swallow, his eyes leaped back to hers. "Did you want him, sugar? So badly your teeth ached?"

Her throat had gone so dry she couldn't form a single word. She also couldn't look away from those eyes of his . . . so all-seeing, so all-knowing.

"Did you try more than one? Just to make sure?"

Her throat might be dry but her cheeks bloomed with heat.

His grin was a slow, sexy slide, and it shivered straight down her spine, then pooled, all hot and heavy right where he made her ache.

"You said when the emotions matter, it clouds your ability to . . . go there. Is wanting the same as mattering?" He moved in so close that a single deep breath would have caused his chest to brush against hers. He put his hands on either side of the truck. "Wanting so badly . . ." he murmured, slowly lowering his head. "Just to taste. To know. To find out."

She made a sound half gasp, and half . . . moan. But she didn't move. And she didn't try to stop him.

"You're thinking about tasting, too, aren't you? Knowing? Finding out?" His breath was a warm caress across her lips. "Let's find out if we can keep all your thoughts on what I make you feel . . . and not what I make that crazy mind of yours want to know." He brushed his lips across hers in a tease of a kiss. "If putting my mouth on you goes well, then we'll worry about my hands."

She should be in full panic mode, shoving him away, kneeing him if necessary. She had no idea what in the world had come over him. She wasn't the type of woman to inspire a man like him to want . . . well, to simply want.

He brushed his lips along the side of her jaw, then her temple, and what she *should* do got all tangled up with what she *wanted* to do. And what she wanted *him* to do. All thought fled entirely when he leaned in and kissed the throbbing pulse on the side of her neck. She sighed, and her eyes started to flutter shut again.

"Oh no, sugar. You keep those eyes on me."

She blinked them open and looked into his gray eyes, so steady, so true. He wanted her, desired her, she had no doubt of that and no longer questioned why. The way he captured her gaze with such certainty held her every bit as tightly as if he'd pulled her into his arms.

That smile was back, and her gaze drifted, just for a moment, to his mouth. She did wonder. She did want to know . . . how he tasted . . . and what it would feel like to have him, with all his controlled certainty, take her. Any part of her. All parts of her. She wanted to know so much she ached with it.

His lips teased the sensitive skin just below her ear. "It goes without saying"—he whispered intimately—"if at any time, you want to put more than your mouth on me, sugar . . . well then, please do."

Then his mouth was on hers.

And any chance she had to flee or fight was gone.

Chapter 7

He'd gone and lost his mind. There was no other explanation. Even without the crazy, she was hardly his
type. And yet he'd never felt so compelled to kiss anyone
in his life. Maybe she'd done some kind of mind trick on
him while she'd been inside his head, inside his past . . .
except he was fairly certain she didn't want to want this
any more than he did.

But want it she did. Her eyes were a veritable green sea
of want. Her soft sigh when he brushed his lips over hers,
and that little moan deep in her throat when he finally
took her mouth confirmed it. As did the hammering of his
heart . . . and every rigid inch of his body.

He'd planned to take her, hard, fast, and deep with an
onslaught of new, current information, obliterating any
chance of her going back inside his head or his past and
making certain to overwhelm any chance for her mind to
trip away to something—or someone—else. He'd wanted
to prove to himself that this reaction he was having to her
was a bizarre fluke, that it came out of the moment back
in the garage. And especially that there was nothing to
what he was feeling. This would confirm it, decisively, so
there would be no more questions.

Yet, the instant he took her mouth, tasted those lips, felt
the warmth and softness of them, and the utter sweetness

of them . . . he also felt the fine trembling in them. And he gentled the kiss immediately.

He'd wanted her to feel helpless against the sudden onset of insanity as he did . . . but her raw edge of vulnerability had him pulling back, urging her to respond, rather than simply demanding it. He wanted her to open her mouth under his willingly and willfully.

"Feeling cloudy yet?" he asked between slow, coaxing kisses.

"Dylan, we need—"

"Not yet, then," he said, smiling against her lips, and took the next kiss even more slowly, inviting her along. His grip on the side of the truck tightened against the urge to put his hands on her, to pull her against him. But . . . one step at a time.

"Honey," he murmured. "Open up, sugar. Let me in."

He felt another longer, lower moan vibrate deep in her throat, followed by the sigh as her lips parted under his. He hadn't believed his body could be any harder, ache more deeply, or want to take anything as badly as he wanted to take her, but at the first tentative touch of her tongue to his, he thought his knees might buckle from the sheer force of want that shot straight through him.

He danced along with her, a teasing, feather-light duel, then finally, slowly, took her fully into his mouth, reveling in the deep groan it earned him. When he withdrew, she stunned him by sliding in and taking his mouth. His groan became a low growl, partly of want, partly of frustration. He was surprised he didn't leave permanent dents in the side of his truck, he was gripping the metal so tightly.

She had a fragile, raw air about her that had worked its way under his skin from the first time he'd laid eyes on her. But in every other way, she'd had no problem challenging him, facing him head on. She didn't crumple, she didn't back down. Not from him. But she'd allowed her own . . . issues to all but cripple her.

Kissing her, he discovered, brought out the exact same confounding, compelling combination. She trembled at the idea of his seducing her, but when presented with the challenge, she rose to it, giving as good as she got. And yet . . . her hands remained at her sides. Even though she wanted this—him—with the same apparent desperation he wanted her, she allowed her gift-curse-whatever to ultimately control the situation.

If he wasn't as unwilling to have her dive into his head as she was unwilling to go there, he'd push that boundary, just to see what it would take to keep her from spinning away into whatever other place she went.

He left her mouth, trailing kisses along her jaw, thinking he could wean himself away from the want and swamping lust, the underlying concern and care . . . none of which he wanted to be feeling. Then she tipped her head back, allowing him access to the soft sweetness of the side of her neck and the pulse he found there and traced . . . with his tongue. His grip on the truck relaxed, along with his resolve. His hands slid along the rim of the truck bed, closer to her. He found the soft lobe of her ear . . . with his teeth. "Sugar, you've got about five seconds to tell me to keep my hands—"

Lolly erupted from the bed of the truck with a loud volley of barks, which had the same effect as a cold bucket of water on Dylan. He jerked his head up to see what had caused the commotion, even as Honey's eyes flew open and she, too, swiveled around to look.

Instinctively, he kept his arms braced on either side of her, so she essentially turned into the circle of his arms, with the back of her body brushing up against the front of his.

So much for the douse of cold water.

He flexed his renewed grip on the rim of the truck. Intrusion or not, what he wanted to do was wrap her up against him, push her hair to the side, and find out if the nape of her neck tasted as sweet as the rest.

He turned to look at the dog. "Lolly, hush girl. It's okay."

The sun had fully set at some point, but he'd been completely unaware of it. Security lights by the rear exits of the shops on either side of the alley put out only a small, focused glow. Clouds had come in and obscured any moonlight, so where they stood had become quite dark.

Dylan squinted into the dusk as he heard footsteps approaching. "Something I can do for you?"

Lolly let out a low whine and came to sit closer to Honey and Dylan. Honey moved forward just enough to reach out and give the dog a reassuring rub between the ears. Dylan noted that she didn't try to move out of the protective circle of his braced arms. He'd figure out later why the need to protect her was so instant and so strong. From what he'd pieced together so far, she'd been doing a pretty good job of protecting herself for some time, and had no trouble whatsoever telling him where to step off.

Morgan Westlake stepped into the dim yellow glow emanating from the security light behind Dylan. "Sorry, didn't mean to cause such a ruckus." If he was at all surprised to find the two of them in what had to look like . . . well, pretty much exactly what it was, his expression didn't so much as flicker.

Morgan was a new transplant to Sugarberry, only on the island for about seven or eight months. He'd moved so his niece Lilly, who was in his sole custody following the death of her parents, would be closer to her maternal grandmother, who also lived on the island. He was also a lawyer, environmental stuff, as far as Dylan knew, and had hooked up with another new Sugarberry resident, Kit Bellamy, who was set to run the new bakery adjunct.

"What can I do for you?" Dylan asked.

"I was over at Babycakes, talking to Kit. When I left, I saw your truck was still in the alley, so thought I'd—oh." He'd walked closer, and could clearly see the woman standing in front of Dylan. "Are you—"

"Honey D'Amourvell," she said, then cleared a little lingering roughness from her throat. "Bea Chantrell's niece. Yes."

Dylan didn't smile at the sound of that telltale roughness . . . but his body did the physical equivalent of one.

"Lani forgot to get your contact information when you spoke to her earlier today, so I was going to ask Mr. Ross here if he wouldn't mind giving me your number. But as you're here . . . I—"

"You're the lawyer," Honey said. "Kit's . . ."

"Significant other," Morgan finished easily, his smile more relaxed. He was a tall man, with dark hair and the kind of polished good looks that spoke of the wealthy family he came from. He was the kind of man women showed off to their girlfriends and took home to their mamas.

Whereas Dylan knew he was the one women came to after dark, when they wanted that walk on the wild side their mamas would never know about.

"I don't really practice business law, but I'm trying to help them get their *i*'s dotted and *t*'s crossed before the opening. Lani tells me you inherited the building she's leased for Babycakes?"

"Yes," Honey said, pushing her glasses up. "I'm going over to the county courthouse in the morning to get the rest of the legal paperwork and . . . figure things out."

Morgan walked around the back of the truck and fished his wallet from the back of his pants. He pulled out a business card, which Dylan reached out to take, so Honey wouldn't have to come into direct contact.

Morgan's gaze did take a split second pause between the two, but his smile remained even, smooth. "Why don't you call me when you get back and we'll figure out a time to sit down and go over everything. I'm sure we can get it all sorted out."

Dylan felt Honey stiffen.

"Thank you," she said. "Lani also said as much. I appreciate that. I'll—call you tomorrow then."

"Good, great. You folks have a good night." Morgan turned and walked back toward Babycakes. He was quickly swallowed up in the dense gloom, but there was the sound of a car door being opened and closed a few moments later, followed by the engine starting. The brake lights sent red strobes across the alley as he backed out, then drove away.

Honey hadn't moved. Neither had Dylan, but he knew she'd fully retreated, mentally, if not physically. No doubt the result of a douse of real world problems and dealing with yet another new person.

"Thank you," she said quietly, but steadily.

"For?"

"Sticking by me. You didn't need to take his card for me. But I appreciate that you thought to. Thank you."

He dropped his other hand away from the truck, reached past her to ruffle Lolly's ears, then stepped away, giving Honey back her space.

He'd be certain to play the entire day's events through his mind a dozen or a hundred times later, trying to figure out how and why he'd gotten himself tangled up in the first place, but, fact of the matter was . . . he was tangled.

"We should get you over to the B&B," he said, stepping over to open the passenger side door to the truck.

"Yes. I appreciate the help. Sorry I cost you the evening of work on your boat."

Dylan didn't respond to that. He was pissed off that they'd somehow gone from sharing kisses that burned a man alive to this quasi-polite, let's-be-friends bullshit. Admittedly, he'd shifted them to it with his nonresponse to her comments and his let's-hurry-up-and-go reaction. If he had a rational thought in his head, *friends* are exactly what they should be. What he wanted them to be, anyway. The rest of it, he wanted to chalk up to momentary insanity, and only because he couldn't quite get away with blaming her for instigating the whole thing with her voodoo crazy mind meld crap. One thing he knew for certain was that she didn't want what had happened to have happened, either.

Since she looked relieved and not at all pissed off, he'd evidently made the right move in stepping back. Done the right thing, for once. So why was he so damn angry about it? Because she was being all rational and he felt anything but?

He rolled down the bay door with a jerk and went about locking up, trying to quash his unreasonable temper and get them out of there. A good night's sleep, another hot day's work, and he'd put the whole episode behind him. She was officially Lani, Morgan, and Kit's problem.

He jangled the shop keys from his pocket and locked the back door. *"Thank you for sticking by me."* He swore under his breath as her words replayed through his mind. He didn't want to stick by her. Or anyone else. He was done sticking to people. These days, he stuck to tangible things, dependable things, things he could replace; his business, his home, his boat, and, okay, a damn dog . . . but that was it.

He paused, just for a moment, took a short breath and

gathered himself. He was going to climb in the truck, get her to the B&B, go home. Then he was going to fix her car, hand it off . . . and they were done. She was leaving, anyway. Going back, he supposed, to Oregon. Couldn't say as he blamed her. It's what he'd have done.

You mean hide? his little voice prodded him.

I'm not hiding, dammit. I'm simply living my life on my own terms. And no one else's. End of story.

Tired of his own thoughts, he checked the bay door, then turned to his truck. Only to discover she was still standing beside it.

He was tempted to walk past her, bark an order for her to get in, and get the night the hell over with.

But then she went and said, "Why did you kiss me?"

He stopped dead in his tracks—mostly because the parts of his body that had finally calmed down surged right back to life again, hearing her say the word.

"Was it some kind of test?" she asked, her tone sincere rather than defensive, as if she was honestly trying to figure it out.

He walked over to the truck, stopped just beside the open passenger door. "I kissed you for all the reasons a man wants to kiss a woman."

"You're not attracted to me," she said simply, matter-of-factly.

He surprised himself by smiling at that. "Tell that to my body." He couldn't quite believe he'd said that out loud. He might not come from a spiffy family tree like Westlake, but he generally was capable of not being crude.

Thankfully, she was lady enough to keep her gaze pinned on his face, though, even in the dull glow of the yellow security bulb, he could see her face flush.

"That's a physiological response. What I meant was, you're not attracted to me as a person. You don't just *think*

I'm crazy, you *know* I am. At least it's got to seem that way to you. You strike me as the kind of guy who keeps to himself, and I imagine you like your partners to be colorful, but not . . . you know."

He stepped closer then, and stopped even trying to rationalize the why of it. She was hardly a flame and he was hardly a moth, and yet . . .

"You put the *crazy* label on in big bold letters before others can do it for you. Only, the first thing you told me was that you weren't. Crazy. It bothered you that I thought you might be. Why?"

"I—" She broke off, then surprised him by smiling briefly. "For all the reasons a woman doesn't want to look like a total freak show in front of an incredibly good-looking guy. Don't let that go to your head, by the way."

"See, right there. That's the thing. You put on this big show of being self-deprecating and casting yourself in the shadows, the poor little misunderstood crazy chick . . . but that's not who you are at all. You're no shadow dweller. You're up front, direct."

"Maybe I'm both," she said, but her expression had turned considering. "I don't want to need your help. But I appreciate that you tried to give it."

"You thanked me for sticking by you. What did you expect me to do?"

"It's been so long since I've been involved with anyone, I guess I only have very outdated data to use as a guide. Most—no, any guy who might have wanted to get to know me, despite it being common knowledge that I was the crazy, misunderstood chick, would only have done so in private. In public? They'd have pretended they didn't know me, or worse, that they wouldn't be caught dead wanting to know me."

"Small towns can breed small minds."

"Well, this is a small town, too."

He grinned at that. "Nice to know I'm not small-minded, then."

"Mr. Westlake," she countered. "I don't know him, but I'm guessing he understood we weren't just standing here having an evening chat. I'm also guessing he'll mention as much to Kit or Lani. After which it will be—"

"I've never given a flat damn what folks think of me," Dylan said. "And, trust me, sugar, their opinions of me couldn't possibly get any worse than they already are."

Honey surprised him by smiling again. "So . . . maybe I'm the one who should be worried about being seen with you then?" Her smile spread to a grin. "Go, me!"

Dylan couldn't help it, he grinned along with her. "You are the damndest woman."

"So I've been told. Only with slightly more emphasis on the damned part."

Dylan shook his head and started to step around her.

She stepped forward, lifted her hand, but stopped just shy of placing it on his arm. "Kidding aside, I meant what I said. About appreciating the help. Not just with Mr. Westlake, but also before."

Dylan's grin was slow and lazy. "Sugar, most women don't thank me for taking advantage of their kindness."

"Not the kiss," she said, though that incredibly endearing flush climbed into her cheeks again. "All along, you've tried to figure out what my deal is, and you've also tried not to make it harder on me, and to . . . I don't know . . . provide a barrier, or a shield, I guess. It—nothing can do that, but that you tried, that it mattered, that—" She stopped, dipped her chin. "Never mind. I'm babbling, it's late, and you've already been kinder than—"

"See, that's the part that makes me nuts," he said quietly. "Don't do that."

She looked up, her expression one of honest confusion. "Do what?"

"You get the least bit emotional about something and you duck it, start makin' excuses. Sugar, what does it matter if the person you're thanking doesn't appreciate your gratitude, or why it meant something to you. You felt it enough to want to say it . . . so say it. Then stand by it."

"You are the damndest man," she said, and though she wasn't smiling— in fact, she looked a bit poleaxed—there was the tiniest twinkle glimmering in her eyes.

"So I've been told," he said. "Emphasis on the damned part."

She smiled up at him then, honest, open, and sincere.

His body leaped once again in response. Even more disturbing, so did that clutch in his chest. His gaze drifted from her eyes to her mouth, and he knew they were standing far closer than was wise. "Sugar, you might want to get in the truck before I kiss you again."

He lifted his gaze back to hers, and grew harder when he saw her pupils expanding, swallowing up her eyes and him in the process. "I might have been testing you a little before. But now I think I'm testing myself. And it's a test I'm going to fail."

"What do you mean?" she asked, and that breathy hint was back, undoing him and his resolve.

"I barely managed to keep my hands off of you last time. You think I'm some kind of protector, but I'm no Superman, Honey."

"Right," she said, but her gaze was all caught up in his. "That wouldn't be a good idea, then."

"Not even close." His gaze drifted to her lips, which parted on a soft sigh. "Aw, sugar, you're killin' me."

"I think I have some idea," she managed.

He inched closer or she did, or both did. She was right

inside his personal space, as close as she could be without touching him.

"Get in the truck." His mouth hovered just above hers.

She tipped her head back to look into his eyes, baring all that lovely soft skin along the side of her neck. "I will," she said, breathless indeed now. "Any second now."

"This wouldn't be a good idea for either of us," he said, hard to the point of pain.

"For you, maybe," she murmured, her sweet breath warm against his cheek. "Me, I'm feeling a bit . . . cloudy. And, I have to say, it feels pretty damn good."

For a split second, maybe a few more, he allowed himself to imagine what it would be like to put his hands on her, mold her mouth to his, and slide his hands down her body . . . to take her home, and . . . take her to bed. Because there was absolutely nothing about that scenario that made him want to move off, he forced his thoughts back to when they were standing beside her car and she was trembling in shock in some altered state of mind. He forced his thoughts even farther back to that first moment he'd laid eyes on her, when she'd looked across the alley with raw, naked yearning at what he now knew was her inheritance.

He took an unsteady step backward, clenching his hands into fists by his sides. The need to touch her hadn't diminished with his thoughts. It had grown. And not only were his thoughts sexual in nature . . . they'd become personal.

It wasn't his job to protect her. Not against what might happen to her on Sugarberry, not against her own desires, much less against something or someone triggering her . . . thing. The only thing he would—should—protect her from, was himself.

So, that's what he did. "We should get going."

"Okay." To her credit, she didn't look away, didn't look

remorseful, or chastised for being bold enough to ask for what she wanted only to be turned down. In fact, she didn't look . . . anything.

He didn't know how that made him feel. "Okay." He stepped back, allowed her to climb in the truck on her own, then closed the door for her. Their eyes met through the window and she smiled briefly, simply, before turning away to deal with the seatbelt.

He stood there a second longer, then turned to walk around the back of the truck, tucking the boxes in more securely. Lolly was up, tail thumping, as he approached the driver's side. He gave her head a good rub. "Good job there, earlier. Thanks for the warning."

She butted her head against his hand, then looked to-ward the rear cab window and Honey. Tail still wagging, Lolly whined.

"Don't you start," he told her. "I'm droppin' her off. Fixin' that heap of hers, and that's going to be that."

Lolly turned those big, liquid eyes of hers on him.

"She'll be fine," he assured the dog. But as he climbed in the truck and pulled his own seatbelt on, he wished he could say the same about himself.

Chapter 8

"**Y**our ride is here, dear."

Honey opened her bedroom door to a smiling Barbara Hughes. "Thank you. And thanks again for not minding that I took my meal up here this morning."

Barbara's tanned and age-spotted skin crinkled as she gave Honey a commiserating smile. "I've been married for more than forty years, happily so, but there are mornings when I don't want to bear witness to canoodling newly-weds, either."

From what Honey had seen of Mrs. Hughes around the young honeymooners who had checked in the evening before while Honey had been at the garage, it was pretty clear the senior B&B owner adored young love in all forms. But Honey appreciated her trying to make things easier for her single guest.

Barbara's warm brown eyes twinkled a bit as she added, "You have a safe drive over the causeway. I hope you can get things straightened out okay."

Barbara had chatted up Honey first thing that morning when she'd come down to grab coffee and some biscuits with gravy, which was when Honey learned it was already common knowledge that Bea Chantrell's niece had come to claim her inheritance, only to find it leased out to the much beloved cupcake baker—who also happened to be the daughter of the very well respected island sheriff—and her equally adored television star, British pastry chef husband.

The realization of how much Lani and Baxter Dunne had come to mean to the islanders, as people and as respected business partners who'd helped boost the island's flagging economy with their joint enterprises, cemented Honey's decision that moving herself lock, stock, and carving tools to a wonderful new life on Sugarberry had been a nice dream, but not a particularly practical one. With the farm in Oregon still on the market, and not a single offer on the place as yet, her miserly budget didn't extend to securing housing, leasing a new space, and funneling money into renovating it. Which left her with . . . a farm. And a barn to work in. All paid for . . . and empty. Just waiting for her to return.

"I just want to get it sorted out so things are all in order going forward" was all Honey said.

"Well, Miss Lani and Miss Kit are good folks. As is Morgan Westlake, though I'll admit that came as a surprise to those of us who knew his mama. What she did to Birdie Wiggins, not to mention her dear, sweet little granddaughter Lilly, depriving them of a life together . . . well, I won't tell tales out of school."

No, of course not, Honey thought, stifling an amused smile.

Barbara reached out to pat Honey's arm, but fortunately Honey had her empty plate and coffee cup in hand, so she neatly intercepted the movement without appearing rude. "Oh, thank you," she said, handing over her dishes. "I was just going to take these downstairs. Breakfast was delicious. I've never had that kind of gravy before, but it was really good."

Barbara beamed as she took the dishes, balancing the cup on top of the plate. "Scrapple gravy. My mama's recipe. Won many a contest with it, she did."

Honey smiled. "Not surprising. I'll follow you down."

She shuffled them from the room, closing the door behind her. So far, except with Dylan, she'd been able to maneuver pretty well with the folks she'd met. Of course, Alva and Lani knew she'd inherited the Chantrell's "special abilities," but if Barbara knew, she hadn't mentioned it.

Mrs. Hughes hadn't known Bea all that well, as she'd explained to Honey that morning, being as Mr. Hughes had always taken his tailoring to Bea's shop himself. Honey suspected Barbara well knew of the other "service" Bea had provided to many of the islanders, but the older woman didn't bring it up, much less query Honey on whether she planned to carry on with the family tradition, for which Honey was eternally grateful. After her run in with Alva the day before, Honey found it hard to believe the topic hadn't been covered by the island grapevine, as she'd imagine it would be among the juicier tidbits about the island's newest resident. But maybe the property battle involving the Sugarberry's pastry chefs had trumped that bit of business. At least for now. She didn't care why the reprieve, but was just thankful for it.

Barbara set the breakfast dishes down on the small foyer entry table so she could open the front door for Honey. "Will you be coming straight back? I'm making cobbler today." She leaned closer and added in a whisper, as if it were a secret of some importance, "Rhubarb. Another of my mama's favorites. We'll be serving it with iced tea and lemonade this afternoon." She beamed. "We Southerners deal with this ungodly heat by being unbearably civilized. I hope you'll be back in time to join us."

Honey smiled. She really did like Barbara Hughes. "I hope so, too."

Barbara stepped back from the open doorway so Honey could usher herself through. "And please feel free to invite your driver in as well."

Honey didn't note the merry twinkle in the older

woman's eyes right off as she'd been too busy thinking that inviting random taxi cab drivers in for tea was taking Southern hospitality to surprising extremes. So, she wasn't at all prepared to step out onto the front porch . . . and spy Dylan's pickup truck idling at the curb. Dylan was behind the wheel with a very happy Lolly in the open truck bed.

"He called this morning to let Frank—Mr. Hughes—know he was going to pick up that part for our old lawnmower when he was over in Savannah today," Barbara explained, clearly happy with herself. "I knew you were headed that way and thought I could at least spare you taxi fare one way."

A whole lot of things were going through Honey's mind at the moment, but what came out of her mouth was "Dylan repairs lawnmowers?"

"Why, not as a usual thing, no. But Mortimer Smart, who runs our little appliance repair shop on the square? Well, he's taken to being closed more than he's open of late. He's got the gout, you know. Poor dear. Dylan happened to be passing by when Frank was swearing up a storm at our ancient mower. I keep telling him to just get a new one, but he's determined this one will outlive both of us. Men. Anyway, Dylan stopped by, took a look, and said he just needed some new thingamajig or other."

"That was very nice of him," Honey said, still wrestling with the fact that she hadn't exactly gotten over yesterday's . . . everything, and she really wasn't prepared to sit in a truck cab next to the cause of most of it, quite yet. Maybe ever. But there was no way out of it that she could see. She wondered how Dylan felt about being corralled into providing ferry service. She couldn't make out his expression, but she doubted he was happy about it, either—leaving Lolly as the only excited party in this endeavor.

"Well, folks may say about him what they want," Barbara went on, "but the way I see it, just because there are some bad apples on a family tree doesn't make the whole tree rotten to the core."

Honey pulled herself from her thoughts. "I'm sorry, what?"

"Why, I have a second cousin on my mother's side who was about as bad an apple as they come. Certainly on par with Mickey Ross, that good for nothing brother of Dylan's. My lord, the trouble he put that family through. Lettin' us all believe it was their daddy whuppin' on Dylan all that time when all along, it was Mickey himself. Never did like the look of that boy, but I felt sorry for him just the same. Bless their souls. What with their mama runnin' off the way she did, leavin' Donny to care for them. Not that their daddy was a prize, of course. Leavin' those boys to all but fend for themselves while he drank himself to death. I understand grieving a broken heart, but when you've got children to care for, you find a way to pull it together."

Honey blinked, trying and failing to keep up with the flood of information. "Dylan has a brother?" She thought he'd said he was the only Ross left.

"Had. Died in prison. Was a better end for him than he deserved, I'll tell you that much. I know it doesn't sound very forgiving of me, and I like to think I'm a better person than that, but that boy . . ." She trailed off, shook her head. "Well, listen to me tellin' tales, anyway."

Honey was still staring out at the truck by the curb, as Mrs. Hughes's words and the images Honey had seen the day before all collided together in a huge jumble. Add to that all the things Dylan had said and done, not the least of which was kissing Honey completely and utterly senseless, and she couldn't have rightly said which way was up had anyone asked her at that exact moment—which was why she didn't notice Barbara coming to stand beside her.

The older woman slid her hand through Honey's arm and gave it a good, solid squeeze. "Don't you listen to this old woman, now. You go and have yourself a good morning. I say you play your cards right, perhaps there might be a nice lunch in the day for you. Don't let the dark looks and that serious air put you off. There's a decent man in there, mark my words."

Barbara's reassurances had faded to a distant hum. Honey had already been sent spinning off into that other place of fragmented visions, snippets of words, overwhelming emotions as she not only observed glimpses of future events, but felt them as if they were happening to herself. Mrs. Hughes—Barbara—was running . . . somewhere. Honey felt her own heart pound in fear, her breath coming in short gasps. Where was she running? Not across a yard . . . Honey couldn't see exactly. It was foggy, but there were docks, boats. Fishing boats, the big kind. The commercial kind. Barbara was screaming . . . something, or trying to, but she was too out of breath and it came out as a rasp. Her chest hurt, it squeezed so tightly. Frank? Frank!

Something had happened to Mr. Hughes. The skies were very dark. Wind was whipping. Raining . . . it was raining. Hard. And then Honey saw the boat. A . . . trawler or something like it. Big, with huge nets, and a loud, thrumming engine. Mr. Hughes—Frank—had gone out on one with his . . . grandson? Nephew? Someone . . . family? . . . owned the boat, or captained it. He'd been helping out. The storm had come on fast, too fast. They hadn't beaten it in. Frank had been thrown hard against the holding tanks. Cleaning knife . . . no, some kind of big hook, used to pull in fish, embedded in his thigh. Lots of blood. Too much blood.

"Honey? Dear? Oh my, I shouldn't have said those things. It wasn't my place. Oh dear, are you okay?"

"That's okay, Miss Barbara. I've got her."

Dylan? Why was he on the boat? No, wait . . . not the boat.

"Hey sugar, time to come back. Come on now." His voice was a low, deep purr in her ear, but she could barely hear him. Why didn't he help Frank? There was so much blood.

The pressure on her arm lessened—someone's hand?—then let her go.

"Honey." Dylan spoke again, sharper, his voice still low, but clear. Like an order.

She blinked, and the images and all that blood faded away. The wind and the storm receded, but her heart still pounded. The air was warm. Hot, even. And very sunny. She blinked again, and realized she was standing on the front porch of the B&B. Even as she shook off the vestiges of the vision, and tried to quell her racing pulse, mortification made her face go hot. "Oh God."

"Dear, are you okay? It's this heat, I tell you." Barbara fluttered around them, but Dylan shielded her from making any direct contact with Honey. "Why, you're white as a sheet. Dylan, you have her sit down in the rocker on the porch there and I'm going to grab some water and some ice."

"Thank you, Miss Barbara," Dylan answered her. "That's a good idea."

"Thank goodness you were here and saw her starting to fade like that. There I am, going on and on, and not paying one whit of attention. Serves me right for talking like that. Poor dear, coming from the northwest, of course she isn't used to this humidity."

"Ice water?" Dylan prompted.

"Yes, yes, of course." She bustled away and Honey heard the front screen door slap shut behind her.

Dylan shifted so he was directly in front of Honey, angling so he could look into her eyes. "You okay now, sugar?"

Honey blinked again and focused on Dylan's face. "You keep trying to rescue me."

"I'm no white knight, darlin'. Just didn't want you collapsing in a heap on top of Miss Barbara. Then you'd have both gone down the porch steps."

The more he talked, the easier it was for her to focus on him and let the vision slip entirely away. The after-effects took a little longer, but she was far, far steadier than she'd been yesterday. Of course, for all the intensity of the vision itself, it hadn't come close to dealing her the emotional blow the vision of Dylan almost dying in that fire had. Why that was, when she didn't know Dylan any more than she did Barbara and Frank Hughes, she couldn't have said. And thinking about it made her head ache.

As her panic settled, she realized there were more important things to deal with at the moment. "Has Mr. Hughes been in some kind of fishing accident recently? A serious one."

"No," Dylan said. "Come on, sit down. Miss Barbara will be out in a minute and you should get your bearings back before she does."

"How did you realize what was happening?"

"I saw it up close and personal yesterday. It's not something a man's likely to forget."

"And you could tell, all the way from the curb?"

"Man doesn't forget that look," he muttered under his breath. "You need to sit down or I'm going to have to help you, and we both could probably do without touching each other right now."

That had her glancing sharply in his direction. She didn't know if he meant because it might trigger one of her visions . . . or because of the kind of touching they'd been doing last night. Either way, she sat down. And her head began to ache in earnest. It was all too much.

One thing was clear. "We have to tell her," Honey said. "Warn her."

"Now why don't we just wait on that, okay?"

"Just . . . find out if he's gone fishing today. Please." It looked like Dylan was going to shut her down again, so she spoke before he could. "I can't head off to Savannah and not say something if it's going to happen today. Do you understand that? I can't do that and just let it happen. Not without at least saying something."

He crouched down in front of her. "What, exactly, do you think is going to happen?"

"Don't do that." She frowned, hating that she felt stung by his gently spoken dismissal.

"Do what, sugar? I'm just tryin' to sort things out and give you a few minutes to do the same before you go scarin' the bejesus out of Miss Barbara."

"I don't *think* it's going to happen, okay? I *know* it will."

"Never been wrong?"

She held his gaze steadily. "About my visions? No. Never."

Dylan blew out a long, steady breath. "Well. Okay then."

Her gaze narrowed. "Okay then, what?"

"We'll have to tell her. But you can't go sayin' something like that, looking all . . . like you do."

Her frown turned to one of confusion, and she found herself lifting a hand, smoothing her hair, even as she smoothed the skirt she was wearing. "Looking like what?"

"Sugar, it's not your hair or your clothes. It's those eyes."

She felt "those eyes" widen. "I can hardly help how my eyes look, but what's wrong with them?"

"They're damn spooky at the best of times, but at the moment, they look downright—"

"Stop." She lifted a hand. "I get it. So, fine then. You

tell her. Tell her that Frank can't go fishing with his nephew or grandson—"

"Nephew? You mean John John?"

"Does John John run a fishing trawler? Or captain one?"

"Owns and captains, yes."

"Then yes. John John is going to hit an unexpected storm, and Frank is going to end up with a huge gaffing hook in his thigh . . . unless we stop him from going."

Dylan held her gaze for a long moment. "Okay."

"That's it? Okay?"

Dylan scowled. "What is it you want from me? You get mad if I don't want to help, and now you're pissed that I do?"

"I wasn't—I'm not mad. I just—I want to make sure you understand how serious this is. A moment ago, I felt like you were coddling me. You do believe me, right?"

"I do."

"Just like that?"

Dylan sighed, and Honey knew she was trying his patience, but she wanted so badly to trust him, and it was such a new idea to her, that she could trust someone other than family. She needed to make sure it was well placed.

"Sugar, after yesterday, it seems clear to me that whatever it is you've got, you've got. I don't waste time wondering why something is what it is. Someone brings me something that's obviously not working right, I don't ask how it got that way—"

"You just fix it," Honey finished. "Dylan . . . you can't fix this. Fix me."

He surprised her by smiling. "Who said I was tryin'?"

Barbara came bustling out the front door with a covered basket and two big drinks in capped bottles. "Well, you look a mite better. Got some color back in your cheeks. Gave me a good start, you did." She turned to Dylan and handed over the stash. "I know Honey's got an important appointment, so I filled up these drinks, one with ice water, one with lemonade. And a basket of some goodies to go with." She turned to Honey. "You sure you'll be all right to travel, dear?"

Honey nodded, touched by the trouble Barbara had gone to for her. "I'm fine." She glanced up at Dylan and started to speak, only to have Dylan speak up first.

"Miss Barbara, how's that nephew of yours doin' with his trawler this season?"

Barbara looked momentarily surprised by the change of subject—or maybe it was just surprise that Dylan would willingly ask after someone's family. Honey doubted that was something he did all that often. Or ever.

Barbara's surprise changed swiftly to pleasure, as it was clear she welcomed the chance to talk up one of her favorite people. "Well, we had such a mild winter, things weren't as bad off in the early season as they usually are, so it's been going fine. Could do without this heat so early on, of course," she added, then smiled, "but men have to complain about something or it wouldn't feel right."

Dylan nodded. "Mr. Hughes helping out like he did last season?"

"You know, his hip has been bothering him something fierce of late, but will he let that slow him down? Of course not." Barbara harrumphed. "I've been trying to get him to see Doc Sievers about it, but he's a stubborn one."

"Probably good to keep him off the boat then, till he's a bit steadier. Wouldn't do John John any good to have him fall and hurt something when the boat takes a hard rock."

"I've made that same argument till I'm blue in the face, trust me. Turns a deaf ear when he doesn't want to hear something."

Dylan nodded, paused, then said, "You want me to

mention it to him when I bring the lawnmower part back? Maybe comin' from someone other than—"

"A nagging wife?" Barbara laughed when Dylan's neck got a little red. "Might as well call it like it is. And I'll take any help I can get. Don't be surprised though, if he acts like he hasn't a clue what you're talking about."

Dylan nodded. "I won't." He tipped his head and lifted the basket. "Thanks for the supply rations. We should probably get on the road."

"Happy to do it." Barbara beamed and started to turn to help Honey up, but Dylan deftly shifted between the two as Honey stood on her own.

"You all have a safe trip, now. I'll save some cobbler for you. Oh! I left water on to boil!"

"You best get to that then," Dylan said, already following Honey down the steps.

"Thank you, Mrs. Hughes," Honey called out.

The older woman merely tossed a quick wave over her head as she hustled back inside.

Honey turned to Dylan. "Thank you for doing that. I'm sure the last thing you want to be doing is talking to Mr. Hughes about his bum hip. But if we can keep him off that boat—"

Dylan glanced at her. "Don't worry, all right?"

Honey met his gaze, her mouth curving in a dry smile. "Easy for you to say."

He stowed the basket in a bin container in the bed of his truck, gave Lolly a head scratch, and opened the passenger door for Honey so she could climb inside.

He closed the door after she was settled, then surprised her by leaning in the open window. His smile was slow, sexy as all hell, and made her heart pound all over again . . . for entirely different reasons.

"Sugar . . . nothin' about you is easy."

Chapter 9

Somehow, in the span of a short forty-eight hours, Dylan's life had been tossed up in the air, twisted inside out, and had come flopping back down in a completely unrecognizable form. At least, that's how it felt.

He'd been perfectly happy to work in his garage, fixing what was broken, then head home, work on his boat, have a glass of something cold, maybe a steak, and a decent view of the sunset. It was a peaceful, contented life, and one he was damn grateful for. Hell, adding a dog to that equation had been enough of an adjustment. More than enough.

Between the fire last year, starting over with the new garage location, and taking on the care and feeding of a four-legged companion, he'd had about all the upheaval and change he could stand. He was all set to keep things status quo well into the foreseeable future.

Then Honey D'Amourvell had shown up and shot his peaceful, easy existence all to hell and back. And he wasn't happy about it. Not one bit.

So why on God's green earth was he whistling—whistling, for Godsake—as he drove back to the county courthouse complex to pick her up for the drive back to Sugarberry? It certainly wasn't because he was looking forward to the torture that surely awaited when she climbed in next to him with that odd exotic scent of hers, and those soul-exposing eyes. He'd be perfectly willing to keep his hands to himself if that's all it was, but then she'd say something or he'd see that look on her face, and his protective instincts would get all riled up, which was bad enough, but no doubt they'd be shot down again when she gave him that dry smile and smarter mouth if he so much as tried to help.

Somehow, that ended up leaving him frustrated with her, annoyed at himself . . . and dying to kiss her again until she kissed him back. He couldn't stop thinking about those soft little moans she made as want overcame worry, how, by turns, she'd be guarded, needing him to guide the way . . . and other times be bold and leading the charge. Kissing Honey twisted him up and wrung him out until he felt like the world would end if he didn't have every last inch of her for as long as he wanted.

And, dear Lord help him, he wanted.

"Yeah, and I really don't need this shit," he muttered, then pressed his lips together in case the urge to whistle came over him again.

He'd gotten a call while picking up Frank's lawnmower part that a junk car dealer he'd contacted about Honey's car parts had actually managed to put his hands on a bunch of them, and at a substantially lower price than Dylan would have paid through his regular parts dealer. So he'd swung by to check them out, more than satisfied to discover they were in surprisingly good condition. He cancelled his other order and booked time with the junker to come back and look at a few of his other old wrecks to do a deal on some parts salvage, as well. The way it was looking, he'd not only be able to get Honey's car done sooner, but for about a third the price he'd quoted her.

All good news. Hence, possibly, the whistling. At least that's what he wanted to believe. The faster he got her car done, the faster she'd be out of Dodge and headed west again . . . and his life would go back to the way it had been—which was exactly the way he liked it. He could happily not get involved with the fine folks of Sugarberry's personal business and they could stay out of his. And if he wanted to sink himself into a willing woman, he'd find one on this side of the causeway, a woman who didn't want more than that. He'd make sure they both had a good time, then retreat back to his island. The more he'd thought about it, the more relieved he'd felt.

Then he'd stopped in at the farmers co-op to pick up a parts package for Bucky Werther's tractor, get some dog food and milk bones for Lolly, and maybe flirt a little with Sally Jo, the good looking blonde who'd just started working the parts department counter. She'd made it clear on his last visit that she might be interested in more than idle chitchat and, at the time, Dylan had been thinking that might be just the thing to end the dry spell he'd been in since the fire.

Perky Sally Jo hadn't changed her mind. She'd made it clear the minute she'd spied Dylan in the dog supply aisle. The problem was, he hadn't found himself all that interested in responding to her playful, suggestive banter. In fact, by the time he'd finished his business and paid his bill, she'd been none too pleased with his businesslike responses and had let him know it. Apparently men didn't say no to Sally Jo too often.

Clearly he'd dodged a bullet there, he'd told himself as he'd given Lolly some break time in the grassy field next to the shop. A demanding, temperamental woman he didn't need, even for one night. Obviously he'd sensed that in her and that had accounted for the sudden shift in his interest. He did have a knack for that, after all. What with his amazing powers of observation and intuition and all. He'd given the dog some water and a biscuit before putting her back in the truck bed, and had managed to make it all the way over to the courthouse believing just that . . . until he realized he'd been whistling.

And thinking not about a sexy blonde with killer blue eyes and a body that would stop traffic, but a quirky brunette who wore utterly unsexy horn rim glasses, weird clothes, had spooky, scary visions, a sardonic smile that put him in his place . . . and kissed him like he was the only man in the world.

He couldn't stop thinking about wanting to kiss her again, when what he should be thinking about was that, according to her, he quite truthfully was the only man in her world as there hadn't been another for quite some time.

"Yeah. And I really, *really* don't need that." Idling at the curb in front of the courthouse complex, he squeezed his eyes shut and massaged the bridge of his nose, opening them again when he heard Lolly give a few happy yips. Honey would be gone soon enough, he reminded himself, and all this craziness would be over. After which he'd come back over to Savannah and find himself some other pretty blonde, or maybe a redhead who knew what was what without all the drama, and forget all about this crazy week in his life.

He looked up to see Honey walking up to the truck. She smiled at Lolly, paused to give her a good scratch and talk a little nonsense to her, before climbing in next to him. It didn't take any superpower to notice that, despite her smiles for the dog, whatever she'd found out at the courthouse hadn't been good news.

They hadn't talked much during the thirty minute ride over the causeway and into the historic southern city. Honey had seemed caught up in her thoughts, probably still dealing with her little moment on the porch with Miss Barbara, and Dylan had been happy to leave her to sort things out. Bad enough that he had to find some way to talk to Frank Hughes about his damn hip and keep him from fishing with his own goddamn nephew. The last thing Dylan wanted or needed was to get more involved. Forty-eight hours in, he reminded himself, and he was already being rooked into providing taxi service, playing watch dog, and running interference, all because of the woman sitting next to him. Two more days and who the hell knew what else she'd drag him into. Damn good thing he could tell her she'd be on the road back to Oregon sooner rather than later.

He was all set to explain it to her, only he screwed up and glanced over at her first. She looked so damned . . . controlled, again. All boxed up and isolated, without a friend in the world. If he so much as mentioned *that,* he could well imagine she'd be happy to set him straight, inform him she was perfectly fine. More than fine. Never had he met a woman so at ease with her self-enforced seclusion—except she wasn't as at ease with it as she wanted to be, or she wouldn't have come all the way to Sugarberry, looking to end her isolation, and she sure as hell wouldn't have put herself on a collision course with those visions of hers, again. Having witnessed them twice, he damn sure couldn't blame her for wanting to head straight back into her cave. Hell, he'd chosen to lead a pretty secluded life himself, and that was just because he wanted to steer clear of people in general. If he had to deal with what she had to deal with, he'd live on the dark side of the moon if he could.

Problem was, he'd been perfectly fine living his life. Honey, however, wanted people in hers. She wanted to stop being so alone and apart.

Dylan shifted in his seat as those protective instincts showed up again. *Dammit.*

"Things get sorted out?" he asked, still with every intention of telling her she could get back on the road a lot sooner than she'd hoped . . . but not feeling so damn righteous and relieved about it any longer.

She'd been lost in her own thoughts and looked up in surprise, whether provoked by the question or his interest, he couldn't have said.

"Somewhat," she said, looking at him guardedly.

That pissed him off all over again. She didn't have to want his help, but she didn't have to look so damn wary. Pretty much the only person on the planet she didn't have to be guarded with, was him. "Anywhere else you need to go before we head back across the channel?"

She frowned a little, surprised by the grit in his tone.

But he wasn't about to apologize for it. Just as well for both of them if he stayed pissed off. The sooner he distanced himself from her, the better.

She shook her head. "No. Thank you for waiting for me and driving me back."

So damn polite. Already in hiding, carefully tucking it all away. No one understood the need and desire to do that more than he did, but it still bugged the hell out of him that she did it with him. And it shouldn't. He shouldn't give a good goddamn how he made her feel or what she thought about him. "Turned out I had another errand to run, so it worked out. No big deal."

Her frown smoothed at his curt reply and her expression shuttered completely. She shifted her gaze to the front, again. "Well, I appreciate it all the same."

He had to fight the urge to floor the gas and peel away from the curb like some kind of pissed-off teenager— which made him feel like an idiot. He'd asked after her business, then made it clear he wasn't in the mood for chitchat. She seemed fine with that. Problem solved. So it made no sense whatsoever that he was disappointed she hadn't tossed his attitude right back in his face, or at the very least had the decency to look hurt or a little miffed. But no, no. She was apparently just as ready and willing to write him off as he was her. Happy for the shuttle service, and see ya later.

He started the engine, proud of himself for not gunning it. Small triumph, but at the moment, he'd take any edge he could get. He didn't pull away from the curb, though. "I met up with a guy who found some parts for your car from one of his salvage yards."

That roused her attention, which he realized was exactly why he'd said it. One step forward . . . one step back. He was busy watching her expression, so he'd have to kick himself later.

She turned and looked at him, her eyes a little brighter.

Naturally, since he was telling her she could leave Sugarberry sooner.

"Really?" She sounded a little more like the Honey he'd gotten to know and less like the Honey who'd shown up on the doorstep of his garage two days ago, looking like a nervous, wounded bird. "That is good news." Her shoulders softened a little, and she pushed up her glasses.

He wondered if she realized that she wouldn't have to do that so much if she didn't keep her gaze half averted all the time.

"It'll cut the estimate I gave you by a third, maybe more," he said a little gruffly still, but trying harder not to sound like such a dick—despite knowing he was acting like one. "It'll cut the time frame down, too." He wished he didn't care so much what her reaction was to that little piece of news, but he was holding his breath as he waited for her response.

She didn't smile in relief as he'd half expected her to. In fact, she went right back to looking torn and pensive again.

"I really appreciate all the trouble you're going to," she said, looking down at the fingers she'd twisted together in her lap. "Both with the car and with . . . the other—"

"It's fine," he said, cutting her off in a tone that clearly said it was anything but.

She looked at him, her expression unreadable. "Is something else wrong?"

"I wish to hell I knew," he retorted, raking a hand through his hair and swearing again because he'd meant to get it cut that day. It was easier to be frustrated by his long hair than it was by the woman seated next to him, who shouldn't have that much power over how his day went. Any power, for that matter.

"Is it the truck?" she asked, apparently assuming as much since he hadn't pulled out onto the road yet.

"No, it's not the truck." He took a moment to get a grip, then turned to look at her. "It's the people in the truck."

"People in the—me?" Her eyes went wide. "What did I do? I mean, I know what I did, but I apologized that Barbara asked you to play taxi driver, and I can talk to Mr. Hughes about the boat trip—"

"Just . . . stop, will you? Stop apologizing, stop thinking you know me, or know what pisses me off. That's what pisses me off, okay?"

She sat back and folded her arms over her middle. "Okay. Not a problem."

His breath whistled out through his teeth. He'd pissed her off, too. Finally. He shouldn't be happy about that, but the fact was, she was sharper when she was riled up, more direct with him, more honest with him. Not so damn controlled. And not so damn absent. And not so damn . . . raw.

"You know what? I can get a ride back. I've troubled

you enough for one day." She gathered the small piece of luggage she regarded as a purse and reached for the door handle.

"See? You're doing it again."

She whirled back to him. "Doing *what?* Trying to be considerate?"

"Trying to smooth everything out, like that will make everything okay. Everything's not okay. I meet you and suddenly I'm worried about accidentally touching you so you don't go headlong to some tortured place. I get roped into playing shuttle driver, and having to make sure Frank Hughes doesn't lose his damn leg or worse. I'm spending time I don't have tracking down salvage parts for a car that's already nothing more than a welded pile of salvage parts to begin with, pissing off the blonde at the co-op—"

Her jaw dropped at the last one. "How is that my fault?"

He just glared at her and she raised her hands, palms out. "Fine, fine. Continue with your rant."

"I'm not ranting, I'm—" At her lifted brow, he blew out another breath and swore under the next one. "I don't know what the hell I am."

"You're frustrated because you've been dragged, kicking and screaming, into a world full of living, breathing people, and you're not real happy about it. I get it. Trust me, I get it. I want to be in a world filled with living, breathing people, only I can't be unless I want to spend every second of every day worrying about being shot off into Never Never Land at the slightest incidental contact, and I'm not real happy about that. Am I the only one who sees the irony here? Though I still don't know what I did to piss off the co-op chick."

She raised a hand to stall his rebuttal. "And, you know what? I'm sorry. For all of it. Utterly, sincerely, abjectly sorry. I don't know what else I can say to you. I, better than anyone, understand the desire to stay out of the loop, out of everyone's business, and just mind my own. I didn't come here to wreak havoc or upset anyone's life but my own, but, clearly, that's not the way it's turned out."

She took a breath, and when she spoke again, her voice was quieter, but she wasn't in that controlled, safe place she'd been before.

And damn it if he didn't already feel better. Much better.

"I just want to get my aunt's estate sorted out so things are square and being handled correctly and legally moving forward. Then I'll get in my salvage-yard piece-of-crap car and drive, push, or have it towed all the way back to Oregon so we can both go back to our respective caves and leave the world to its business, okay?"

"That's just it," he told her, leaving his controlled, safe place, too. Fair was fair, after all. "I don't know if that's okay or not."

She frowned. "What do you mean?"

He shifted in his seat, and met her gaze directly. It rocked him a little, every time he stared directly into those eyes of hers. Partly because he knew they saw far more than anyone else did or could . . . even when she wasn't having one of her little events. And partly because he was getting better at seeing *her* inside of them, too. What he saw tugged at him—much as he wished it wouldn't. On impulse, he reached over and slid her glasses off, careful to touch only the rims and not make contact with her.

"What are you—"

"Can you see without these things?"

She frowned again and looked confused. But she didn't demand he hand them back. "Let's just say the edges of the world get a lot softer without them."

"Ever wear contacts?"

"Now you're judging my appearance?"

He actually felt his mouth twitch and knew he was well and truly screwed. No matter how foul a mood he managed to put himself into, she managed to flip the switch. And damn if he didn't like it when she got out of that self-imposed cave of hers, let her guard down, and was simply herself—smart mouth and all. Maybe especially that part. He turned the glasses around and looked through them. "Damn, sugar. You're blind."

"It's not like I asked to be."

He looked up at her, and felt his heart beat that strange tattoo again. He wished he was better equipped to handle that part. "Doesn't matter anyway, as it turns out."

"What doesn't matter?" she asked, sounding a little grumpy.

Perversely, that made his lips curve despite himself. "My opinion on your glasses shouldn't, for one. But I was thinking maybe if those eyes of yours weren't so magnified, they wouldn't have such a strong impact on me every time I looked at them." He waited until she lifted her gaze to his again. Yep. *Thump, skip, thump.* It was enough to make a grown man nervous. "Turns out, glasses or no glasses, it doesn't matter."

Her frown had faded as he'd spoken, and her mouth dropped open a little.

It had the unfortunate effect of drawing his attention there, and led to him noticing how her throat worked a bit as she tried to swallow.

Suddenly it seemed like the temperature inside the cab of the truck had gone up a few dozen degrees. And it wasn't the heat of the sun doing it.

He leaned forward, feeling like that proverbial moth drawn to the flame, knowing damn well he was facing the same risk, but not caring much at the moment. He was going to get burned either way.

Her eyes widened. "Dylan—"

"Shh."

She started to shrink back.

Mostly out of habit, he thought. Her eyes were telling him a different story. They were big and wide, allowing him to clearly see the desire as it punched into her pupils. He stopped her by lifting his hands and carefully sliding her glasses back on. "I'm not going to touch you, sugar."

But he stayed in her personal space, looking into those magnified, unearthly, beautiful eyes. And let a slow, lazy smile curve his lips as the last of his self-directed anger and most of his frustration dissolved away . . . replaced by a different kind of frustration all together.

Oddly, he was having no problem feeling the urge to flirt and seduce. "Don't let this go to your head," he said, the grit still there in his voice, along with heat and drawl, "but I think those glasses are sort of sexy . . . in a hot-for-schoolmarm kind of way."

Her eyes were big, her pupils wide, and he knew she was thinking about the kisses they'd shared, maybe wanting another one. Or two. He sure as hell did. So, it surprised him when she barked out a laugh at his comment.

"Well, that's certainly a first," she said dryly, but a most becoming blush rose to her cheeks.

One thing was for sure, he'd never have to worry about his ego getting too big around her. For some reason, that only served to deepen his smile. "Given you don't spend a whole lot of time with anyone, that's not sayin' all that much."

She smiled then, too. "Too true. Of course, maybe it's because you happily spend most of your time with your head under the hood of a car that you could possibly find these attractive to begin with. Maybe we both need to get out more."

Or stay in, he thought, and his mind went straight back to what it would be like to have her completely stripped bare, literally and figuratively. What would she be like as a lover? Would the tentative, self-conscious, worried side take over? Or would the part of her that didn't give a rat's ass dominate and allow her to take what she wanted, how she wanted?

Of course, all of that was pretty much moot, given the whole crazy vision thing. Talk about a mood killer.

He realized he was staring at her mouth again when she swallowed, hard, and wet her lips.

"Aw, sugar, don't go temptin'—"

"I—" She had to clear her throat. "Trust me, I'm not trying to." She tried for a laugh. "I mean, it's not usually a problem I have. Oddly, men aren't generally lining up to get in my personal space. You're the only one who actually seems turned on by the Magoo glasses."

"You're not giving yourself enough credit."

She glanced up at him, her lips still twisted in a dry smile, but with a genuine twinkle of friendliness in her eyes. "And you've been sucking down too much car exhaust."

He chuckled at that. She really was just the damndest thing. "You may have a point, but that doesn't change things, here and now, does it." He said it as more statement than question, but her gaze shifted away again, breaking eye contact completely.

"I . . . don't know what I want, to be honest." She kept her gaze in her lap, where she was back to twisting her fingers together. "I know what I wanted when I came here, but nothing has gone like I thought it would. Not a single thing."

The wry humor was gone, replaced by a quiet sincerity. She was no longer the wary, reclusive cave girl, but wasn't the bold, say-it-like-it-is girl, either. This was a new side of her, maybe more vulnerable . . . but definitely honest. He'd wanted that trust from her earlier, had been miffed that she didn't just offer it up to him. Now that she was . . . he didn't know how he felt.

More disconcerted than he thought he'd be, for one. He knew this wasn't the kind of thing she did often, if ever . . . and he didn't want to do anything, say anything, to abuse or ruin the trust she was placing in him. But he had no idea what to say . . . or, possibly more important, what not to say. So he did the one thing he knew how to do . . . he listened.

"I didn't expect to be homeless," she said without a trace of self-pity, but rather bluntly . . . baldly.

That tugged on him far more strongly than any woe-is-me story would have.

"I didn't count on losing my business before I even got it started, didn't count on being trapped with no mode of transportation. I've been truly terrified of letting the visions come back, of making direct contact with anyone, and then folks here didn't seem to be all that freaked out by the idea. Apparently, Bea had been giving them the benefit of her second sight all along.

"Except they have no idea how different mine is from hers. I don't know what to make of the fact that the first vision I had was far stronger and more detailed than any I've had before, or why it affected me so deeply, so . . . personally." She paused for a long moment before finally lifting her gaze to his. "And I definitely don't know what to make of you. Any part of you."

"Well, that makes us even, Honey Pie."

Her lips quirked the tiniest bit at his use of her nickname, but her eyes were still so unguarded, and he wanted nothing more than to taste that mouth of hers one more time. Take away that uncertainty and replace it with . . . something stronger, something more stable, something just . . . more.

"Part of me still wants what I came here for, a chance

at a normal life, or as close to one as I can have." She glanced away again, looking through the front windshield, though he doubted she saw anything beyond the dashboard. Her viewpoint was entirely internal now. "And then things happen, like what happened on the porch this morning, or I find out that my inheritance is quite legally leased out for the next three and a half years and out of my reach for at least that long."

She was finger twisting in earnest now, her tone agitated as she spoke faster, like she had to get it all out before running out of time.

He was prepared to give her all the time she needed.

"Not that I'd kick the cupcake ladies out at this point, anyway. That would guarantee my own business would be a failure before it even started. Plus, I like them, or the ones I've met, anyway, and I'd like to think we might become friends. Lani even invited me to come bake cupcakes with their baking club, and, you know what . . . I'd like that. No, I'd love that." She broke off, took a breath. "I know I've lived under the proverbial rock for far too long, and I'm willing to work—hard—to get the life I want, but that life doesn't seem to want me back."

She stopped then, seeming more pissed than sad or lost, and he thought she might swear at the injustice of it. He sure as hell would have. Instead, she got that resigned, squared shoulder look back, which made him want to swear at her.

"It would be easier," she said evenly, flatly, and worse, unemotionally, "and definitely smarter, to just go back to what I know I can make work."

"Only?" His question seemed to surprise her, jerking her gaze back to his.

She held it for such a long moment, he fully expected her to continue her retreat, scrambling rapidly back into

her cave. So it surprised him when she answered truthfully, openly.

"Only I don't want to go back." She paused, blew out
another breath. "Wow. Just saying it out loud makes it a
lot more real. But it's the honest truth. I don't know what
I could have here, but . . . I don't want to go back."

"Then make Sugarberry work."

"How?"

He liked that she'd asked honestly, sincerely, with no
sarcasm, no wry note. No whine or wail. If he'd doubted
how much she wanted to find a way to make her plans
work, that answered it for him. And he was smiling again.
"Well, darlin', you're a pretty smart girl. You started up
and have run a successful business, after all."

That seemed to surprise her. "What do you know about
my business?"

"You told me you ran a mail-order business, said you
wanted a shop front. I assumed that means it's a successful
one." He didn't have to tell her that he'd done a little research on it—on her—the night before. Damn computers.
He usually tied himself to one only when he was searching online for boat parts. Somehow he'd found himself
typing in her name and up popped her website, complete
with a note saying she was relocating and would post an
update when she was up and running again. He'd wondered what it was costing her, suspending operations like
that. From the list of happy customer quotes she had on
the site, it looked like she was doing quite well.

She was also a very talented artist. He might not personally be in the market for her array of little fantasy
woodland creatures and garden critters, but he'd been
around enough wood carving while looking at boat pieces
like his mermaid to know real quality and craftsmanship
when he saw it.

"Thank you," she said. "It is . . . or it has been. It was a huge risk, taking a hiatus in order to move lock, stock, and garden gnome across the country, but that was part of the budget in making this decision. It's also why I have no wiggle room when it comes to spending money I don't have to lease new property."

"Your budget assumed you already had a location."

"And the living quarters above it."

"You do it all yourself? Making the products, shipping, all of it?"

She nodded. "A one woman show."

"You plan on keeping it that way with a shop?"

"Well, my hope, I guess, when I allow myself to think that far ahead—dream that far ahead—is to get to know my customers, put a more personal face on both sides of the transaction. I want to be engaged in the world around me, and I want to engage my customers in my world at the same time. What I'd really like to do is to invite them to be part of the process, see the work, how I work. Maybe even teach wood carving and clay building and sculpting classes. I know the interaction would inspire my work as well." She lifted a shoulder, looking a bit abashed now that she'd blurted out her most personal dream. "I don't know. I figured I'd work my way into it. There was so much to overcome first, so . . ." She offered him a half smile, shrugged again. "Now there's way more to overcome to even get to the original obstacles I was worried about."

What it was about her that made him want to move mountains, slay dragons, he couldn't rightly have said. He'd been the downtrodden, so he identified, even helped out now and again, in his own low key way. A tractor part here, a lawnmower part there. Things he could do, small scale, to help out someone in need. But that impetus had never inspired him to want to leap over tall buildings in a single bound and save the day for anyone.

"If you really want it, don't turn tail and run," he told her. "Nothing happens if you don't try."

"If I keep my online business on hold too long, I may not have much to go back to."

"See, that's the problem right there, sugar. You already don't have much to go back to. Not in the way that matters to you. Otherwise, you wouldn't be here in the first place. Seems to me you've got every reason to try, and a long list of reasons not to give up. Instead of thinking about your farm as your backup plan, use it as motivation. The farm is not your backup plan, darlin', it's your give up plan. That's not the same thing."

She considered him for several long moments. "How'd you get so smart?"

"Life is long. You learn from things. If you pay attention, then you make better choices next time, and you don't have to learn them all over again."

She let out a soft laugh at that. "I hear what you're preaching . . . and I agree with the philosophy. Wholeheartedly. I just don't know exactly what to do about it." She held his gaze for several long moments, her expression bemused. In the end, it was the spark of hope his words had put in her eyes that told the story. She was going to stay. She was going to try.

And damn if that didn't make him feel like he'd leaped over a building or two. Small ones, to be sure, but he'd be lying if he said it didn't make him feel a might smug. Of course, what he should be, was scared spitless. Not thirty minutes ago, before she'd climbed back into his truck, he'd been quite relieved and happy at the prospect of her getting back in her old rattletrap car and driving out of Sugarberry forever. He should remember that, and likely would . . . later . . . when he wasn't in the middle of the hormone-induced fog he seemed to descend into every time she got within five feet of him.

"You know what I think?" he asked.

Her lips twisted in a wry grin. "Only when you grab me when I'm off guard."

It was his turn to bark out a surprised laugh. "Okay, maybe not quite that literally. What I think is that you don't give yourself enough credit. You say you hide out, and maybe you have, but it wasn't from being weak. It was an honest attempt to preserve your own mental well-being. Nothing unhealthy or weak about that."

"So say you."

"So I do say. We have different demons, sugar, but we've both chosen a path of least resistance, rather than one that constantly forces us to grapple with and over-come obstacles that don't benefit anybody by being tack-led. There's a lot to be said for peaceful living."

"So why are you trying to talk me into staying? You've been up close and personal with both of my 'events' since coming here. Nothing peaceful about them, obviously. And I don't know what it's going to take to figure out how to lease shop space with no operating capital, but I doubt it's going to be smooth sailing, either."

Hormone fog or not, Dylan was quite aware, without a single doubt in his mind, that very moment was the time to pull back, step out of her business once and for all, clear his head—and his body—and get back to his own business, his own life. He'd been her cheerleader for five whole minutes. If it helped to get her on the path to where she wanted to be, power to them both. But that needed to be the beginning and the end of it. Even Superman had his kryptonite and he was pretty damn sure she could be his.

He told himself to put the truck in gear and drive them back to Sugarberry, whereupon he would return to his life and leave her to hers, whatever course she decided to chart. So, naturally, he sat right there and asked, "If you could get the business space, think you could figure out how to handle the rest?"

"You mean like a place to live?"

He shook his head. "That's not the hard part in all this, darlin'. Folks here'd find a way to help you out until you got on your feet. Lani Dunne might have a lease on your property, but I'm betting she feels pretty damn bad about leaving you homeless, unintentionally or not."

"I don't want anyone to house me out of pity or misplaced guilt."

He stared at her, a little annoyed because he knew that would have been his exact response had the tables been turned, so he could hardly hold it against her. But what he said was, "A hand up isn't the same as a hand out."

"Easy to say, harder to accept."

"Don't I know it." Most of the folks on Sugarberry had next to nothing good to say about the other members of the Ross family, and only pity for him for being born into it. But that hadn't stopped them from trying to help him. Help he'd mostly turned down, but that was arrogance, pride, and stupidity on his part. Something he didn't learn until much later. Maybe he could save Honey the same hard learning curve.

"Okay, say that gets worked out," she said. "What did you mean then? The visions and being back around people?"

He nodded. "Including people who knew your aunt Bea and, once they learn you're a chip off the old visionary block, aren't likely going to leave you to go about your business without tryin' to get you tangled up in their own, same as she was."

Honey surprised him by smiling that crooked smile and her voice was good and dry as she seemed to have found her footing again. "One minute you're telling me to follow my dreams, the next you're trying to warn me off?"

"I'm just walking through the paces, getting you to think it through. You can't fix things until you know what things most need fixing."

"Can I ask you something? Does it matter to you if I stay or go? I know it shouldn't matter, you barely know me. But I know I have turned some parts of your life upside down, and now you've been dragged into the whole Frank thing. I could promise that from now on I'll do my best to leave you out of it, to leave you alone . . ."

"But?" His heart was pounding and he didn't want to examine the reasons behind it.

"But only if you want me to." She smiled at him. "Don't let this go to your head, but it turns out you're a pretty good kisser. I realize I say that with little experience to back up my opinion, but I'd be lying if I said that I haven't given some thought to trying it out again."

He had no idea what he'd thought she was going to say, but that wouldn't have even made the top ten list. His heart kept right on pounding, with a healthy punch of heat added to the mix. He should have run while he had the chance . . . because, foolish or not, it didn't look like he was going any-damn-where.

His grin was slow, wide . . . and he took great pleasure in watching her pupils swallow up that all-seeing, all-knowing sea glass green. "Would this be for personal or scientific reasons?"

She tried to pretend he wasn't having an effect on her, that she could say something and keep the conversation focused on her relocation woes. But the way her throat worked told him differently . . . as did the bit of roughness in her own voice when she asked, "You mean to test whether or not I'd have a vision the next time you make, um . . . personal contact with me?"

"I'm not a lab rat, sugar."

"No, you're definitely not that. Although I won't lie and say I'm not curious . . . trepidatious, even, about the scientific part, as you call it."

"Don't go using big words and wearing those glasses at the same time, schoolmarm."

Honey's cheeks bloomed with color and her pupils bloomed with something else entirely. "I . . . might be a bit personally curious as well."

"Only a bit?"

"Okay, at the risk of feeding your ego, a lot."

"Sugar, the last thing you need to worry about is feeding my ego. You set me in my place often enough."

"Do I?"

His grin deepened. "Handily."

"Is that a problem?"

"Let's just say I'm a little trepidatious."

She giggled at that, something he hadn't heard from her, and it did funny things to his insides. He leaned in closer.

"Dylan—"

"Just a little scientific discovery." His gaze dropped to her mouth, and his own voice grew just a little gruffer. "To help you make your very important decision."

"You're incredibly generous," she said wryly, but her gaze dropped to his mouth, too.

"That, too." He leaned in and brushed his lips across hers. "Anything shaking, earth trembling?"

She sighed and her eyes drifted shut. "Only in a really good way."

He chuckled at that, even as his body went rock hard. "Well then, the scientific part is over."

He laughed outright at the way her lips formed a little pout, instantly.

"Aw sugar, if you only knew what that does to me, you'd use it on me every chance you got."

Her eyes flew open, surprise in them, and he marveled at how he never knew which part of her would react to any one thing.

"Let's try out the personal part, then," she said, shocking him by leaning in and taking charge of the situation and him, kissing him like she'd been waiting for the green light. It was no teasing of lips, no tentative brush of her mouth on his. She laid claim.

He had to dig his fingers into his thighs to keep from reaching for her, to keep the contact to their mouths only. It about killed him.

She made that little moaning sound that already drove him crazy, and he might have been a little insistent at urging her to open up for him and let him inside, but that sigh, and the way her shoulders softened, and her body moved toward his, absolved him of any guilt. And then her tongue was sliding in, dueling with his, and his body ramped straight past rock hard to begging for release. Her gasps turned to groans of want and he knew that nothing short of nailing his hands to his thighs was going to keep them there much longer.

He eased out of the kiss and lifted his head slowly, leaning back and away. When he spoke, even he heard the strain in his voice. His fingers were curled into fists on his knees. "I think that ends the personal discovery portion of today's little experiment."

Honey let out a sigh of disappointment and closed her eyes, but nodded as she eased back more fully into her seat.

Dylan took another minute or two to get his body somewhat under his control, then with far more reluctance than he'd have thought possible even ten minutes earlier, he shifted the gear into drive. He took another moment to look over at her, surprised to find her watching him. "Fair warning."

"Warning of what?"

"If we ever try another experiment like that, we're going to find out what happens when I put my hands on you. No way I can do that again and keep them to myself."

To his continued surprised, rather than go wide-eyed . . . she smiled . . . very much like a cat who'd just spied a particularly plump canary.

"Okay, that scares me a little, sugar."

"What does?"

"That smile. It's kind of . . . predatory. You sure you didn't leave a string of broken hearts back in Oregon?"

"Very sure." The dry note in her voice had crept right back in, which settled him a lot more than the smile had.

He held her gaze for another extended moment as an idea popped into his head. A half hour earlier, he'd have thought himself crazy for even considering it. Not that it wasn't still crazy . . . he simply didn't care.

"Buckle up." Before he could change his mind, he leaped another tall building. "I want you to see something."

"Oh, really," she responded suggestively, even as she wiggled her eyebrows over those ridiculously unsexy glasses that made him hard all over again.

He found himself chuckling. "I'm finding it harder and harder to believe you're tellin' me the truth about those broken hearts."

"Oh, that part is true enough."

Just don't break mine, sugar, he thought, then shifted uncomfortably because it had even entered his mind.

"Where are we going?"

Dylan tightened his grip on the wheel, keeping his eyes on the road. Superman or utter fool, he supposed he was going to find out. "To look at your new shop space."

Chapter 10

That was pretty much the last thing she'd have ever expected him to say. "My . . . what? I already told you my farm hasn't sold, so I don't have the money for a lease."

"What about the lease payments on your aunt's place? That's rightfully your income now, isn't it? Wouldn't that cover all this?"

"Yes, well, that's the other thing I looked into today. Turns out Lani and Baxter paid the full five years up front with some cookbook advance they got. They didn't even do anything with the place for the first year, but Lani knew she wanted to expand when the time came, so when Bea put it up for rent, she jumped on it." Honey waved a dismissive hand. "Anyway, it's all moot. The lease payment went to the management company Bea had hired, as it should have, who deposited it into the account they'd set up for her, as they were supposed to do. That money, along with her savings, took care of her senior care living expenses and medical bills. Anything left over and her life insurance paid for her funeral and any outstanding bills. I am just thankful the Dunnes paid what they did, when they did, because if not, I'd be responsible for that debt, too."

"At least everything was handled properly. But wouldn't your aunt have known then that her property wasn't available for occupancy when she left it to you?"

Honey sighed. "To be honest, I'm not sure what her thoughts were or how sound. That she kept so much from me, which was really uncharacteristic of her, has me wondering just what her state of mind was. I think the stroke did more damage than she knew. It was certainly more than she allowed me to know."

"You were in contact with her?"

"Oh, all the time. I wanted to come out here, spend time with her, help after the stroke, but she wouldn't hear of it. She knew that flying would have been a nightmare for me, putting myself on a plane with so many people." Honey still shivered a little just imagining the horror show that would have been. "She led me to believe she was doing really well, that with physical therapy she'd recovered most of her abilities, and was doing far better than expected. I should have known when she wouldn't Skype with me that something more was up."

"Wouldn't . . . what?"

Honey laughed. "We used to chat via our computer monitors so we could see each other while we talked. It was as close to being together as we could get. Only she stopped doing that after her stroke. She told me it was because it had left her face droopy from muscle loss on one side, and she didn't want to worry me. Normally, she'd have just made a joke about it and we'd have dealt with it, but . . . I was trying to be sensitive and, given how scary the whole thing was, who knew, maybe it did really bother her."

Honey lifted a shoulder, then sighed. "That's how she got away with moving to the senior care facility without me knowing, and putting her shop up for lease. Of course, when she wrote her will, I'm sure she didn't think she'd be gone so soon. I spoke with the care facility today, too. They said she'd been doing much, much better and was in good health, just limited by the recovery far more than she'd let on to me, but needed continued assistance. The aneurysm . . ." Honey trailed off, closed her eyes for a moment, willed the threat of tears back, then continued. "She probably hadn't thought that far ahead about the shop. She should have lived for a much longer time, so maybe she just hadn't finished putting her plans into place."

"You knew she wanted the shop for you?"

Honey nodded. "She left me a letter with her will, but it was written before the stroke. She hadn't updated her will, either."

"So, it was written assuming she'd be living there and operating the business up until the time she passed it on to you?"

"Yes—which is exactly what I thought had happened. Her lawyers didn't advise me differently because they didn't know, either. Bea never planned on retiring. She loved her work, loved her customers, who were also her friends. Her business was what gave her purpose and kept her engaged with life. I had no doubts that she'd gotten back to it so quickly after her stroke. That was exactly what would have motivated her to get better."

"You weren't surprised she left the business to you, then? Even though she discouraged you from coming to see her?"

"Oh, she'd urged me to move here over the years, but I wouldn't even consider it. I told myself I was happy, successful—which I was, as much as I could be—so why mess with that? It was a lot more than some people had. It was only after I read her letter that I"—she paused again and swallowed hard—"really took stock and allowed myself to admit what I'd buried for so long, which was that I wanted a chance at a more normal life. I simply hadn't had the courage to reach for it. Bea leaving me her shop space and her apartment was . . . I don't know, like a sign. Or certainly a tantalizing prospect. One, in the end, I couldn't ignore."

"Just because it's not panning out as you'd thought it would doesn't mean it can't work."

"When the lease is up and they renew—and I'm assuming they will, given the popularity of the cupcake shop and Lani and Baxter—then it will be income for me, but that's years off. As it is now, technically, it's just an additional burden. As the landlord, I'm responsible if anything goes wrong with the place. I mean, the management company is still on the lease agreement, so that's who Lani would call to come fix whatever . . . but then they'll call me for payment."

"There are ways around that, but that's not the main thing at the moment."

She looked at him. "Ways around it how?"

"Your aunt was infirm and had no choice but to sign on with a management company. You're not in the same position—that's all I'm saying."

"I don't know the first thing about doing building repair or whatnot."

"True, but you're on a small island where if you ask pretty much anybody how to fix something, they will tell you who to call. I think if you handled whatever came up on a case by case basis, you could cut out the middleman."

"Because the management company will charge a fee on top of the repair fee."

"Exactly. When you lived out in that barn of yours, surely things came up that you had to deal with."

"True, but—" She blew out a breath. "Actually, there are no buts. I didn't always fix the things that needed fixing, but when I had to, I did. So, you're right. One less thing to worry about. Maybe."

He grinned over at her. "Don't borrow trouble."

She couldn't help it—when he grinned like that, she grinned, too. "Yeah, I have enough actual trouble already."

"I didn't say that."

She laughed. "You didn't have to."

It surprised her that she wasn't more spun up at the moment, given the avalanche of crap she had to figure out and the healthy dose of terror that went along with the idea she was going to try to open a shop, anyway. In fact, though there were a hundred different thoughts fighting for first place on the worry list, she was a lot more relaxed than she'd imagined was possible. And she knew she owed that to the man sitting beside her.

She scrunched up her nose. That was funny, because the very last thing he made her feel was relaxed. Maybe it was just having someone to talk things through with again. It helped. A lot. She knew she'd missed her aunt a great deal, but she was realizing the loss ran even deeper than she'd known.

She turned toward him. "Thank you."

He glanced at her as he took the turn toward the causeway, a lifted brow his only response.

"For . . . well, for all of it, but mostly for the ear. And the shoulder."

"Everyone needs one now and again."

"I'm thinking you don't."

"Just because I don't bend someone's ear or cry on their shoulder doesn't mean I don't have my fair share of frustrations. Just ask Lolly. Good thing she's a dog and not a kid, because she's heard some very naughty words."

Honey snickered.

He slid a glance her way again, accompanied by that slow, sexy grin that did shivery, tingling things to her insides. Now that she knew she hadn't imagined how good that mouth of his tasted, it also made everything that could ache . . . ache that much harder.

She pressed her thighs together and tried like hell to keep her thoughts on the more important business at hand. And tried not to remember the look on his face when he'd lifted his head from that last kiss. Like maybe she wasn't the only one who'd been completely and utterly poleaxed by it. There'd be time for endless analysis later. And probably one or two very heated dreams as well.

"For the record," she said, "I might have whined a little, but I didn't cry."

"Oh, those eyes of yours were swimmin' yesterday. How soon you forget."

"That doesn't count. I can't help things like that when I'm . . . seeing stuff. It's . . . emotional."

Dylan slowed the truck as he bumped over the grids at the island end of the causeway and looked at her. "How does that work, anyway? Do you just see things, like you're watching a movie, or—"

Honey shook her head. "I see things like I'm actually there. Sometimes I'm an observer and I want to rush in and help. It's very frustrating, because it's like I'm running through mud and what I see is always out in front of me. I can never catch up, never change what's going to happen. Other times, it's like I'm the person it's happening to. Or I'm in their head, seeing what they see. It's not linear. Images flash, then shift, then other information comes in. It can be a swirl. Sometimes it's clear and easy to understand; other times it's like operating in a jumbled up fog. It doesn't always make sense to me, but if I tell whoever I'm seeing, it almost always makes sense to them."

"Sounds frustrating and exhausting."

"You have no idea."

He idled the truck at the stop sign at the end of the ramp leading onto the island. "You said you see bad things more than good things. Is it because the more dramatic stuff sends out stronger signals? Have you ever wondered if maybe it's because you attract it?"

"What is that supposed to mean?"

He grinned. "Now, don't go getting all offended, sugar. I just meant that maybe you're more emotional yourself, more worried about folks, about things, so you, I don't know, draw that stuff to you. Bea was less . . . deep than you are, and I don't mean that unkindly. Maybe she only got the more superficial stuff. Or maybe you just get what you can handle."

"I couldn't handle any of it." She snorted. "That's how I ended up living in the barn."

He made the turn toward the town square, but didn't comment, leaving her to her thoughts.

No one had ever just come out and asked about her second sight so directly and matter-of-factly. Her parents had known how uncomfortable it made her, how stigmatized she felt by it, so they went out of their way to pretend it was no big deal and dealt with it only if she brought it up—usually because something bad had happened at school and she was being picked on. Her mother would focus on the bullying itself to help Honey find ways to deal with it, but largely left alone the reasons behind it, not wanting to make her daughter feel more like the freak she was.

Of course, her parents were hardly mainstream themselves, so they were used to being a bit ostracized or looked at a little funny. They'd laugh about it, try to get her to see it from their perspective—that being just like everyone else wasn't the be all and end all. But then, they'd never dealt with the things she had.

Bea had talked to her about it, of course. But the real irony was that because they both had the ability, they didn't have to talk about it. It freed Honey up to talk about any- and everything else like a normal person, without feeling self-conscious, worrying about being ridiculed, or, later, when she was away at school, that her secret would get out. She'd hoped she'd grow out of it, that if she ignored it and didn't engage with it, her powers would diminish like muscles not being used.

Her time at college had proven that assumption very

wrong. So she'd pretty much shut everything else down when she'd left school and gone back home.

Her father, bless his heart, had gotten a few local shops to sell her work, saying it was his, so they wouldn't think the freak girl was putting her weird magic into the pieces. It had been enough to give her something of an income, which had been her father's hope, and a direction to follow. Honey had been so blown away by the idea that folks liked and wanted her work, she'd begun looking for other outlets to sell it, where she could build something in her own name. The internet seemed the obvious direction, and once she'd really started selling her pieces, the business more or less grew itself from there. Since then, with her folks both gone, other than Bea . . . there hadn't been anyone to ask simple questions, nor anyone who was curious about her.

She wasn't sure how it made her feel, that Dylan was asking questions and was curious. She did know . . . she was more intrigued by it than nervous. After all, her secret was out already with him. And he was still asking questions—sincerely, it seemed—and wanting to know more.

"I can almost hear the wheels grindin', darlin'. I didn't mean to upset you."

"You didn't." She looked over at him again and smiled. "That's why the wheels are grinding. I can't remember the last time anyone just came out and asked me about . . . those things. Made it seem almost . . . normal. Or at least, not like the freak show folks used to treat it as."

"Did you ever consider that you were a lot younger the last time you outed yourself, so to speak? So maybe your perspective was a little young then, too."

"Immature, you mean? Yes. Maybe it was because I got grief from people of all ages that I felt age wasn't the issue."

"I'm not sayin' that folks here will just shrug it off. It's some pretty unusual stuff you got going on." He grinned when her mouth dropped open. "I'm just sayin' that you might not be so quick to assume how we'll react, until we do. Stand up a bit for yourself."

She closed her mouth, then laughed at herself. "Own it, you mean? Like Bea did?"

"Might not be the worst thing. Could be a good thing."

Honey looked back out the window, a furrow between her brows as she realized they were heading toward the town square. "Where, exactly, are we going?"

He glanced briefly her way, then back to the road. "Have a little faith, sugar. You're killing me with the schoolmarm thing, again. So serious."

She felt the heat bloom, only it wasn't embarrassment so much as it was a kick of heightened awareness. Like she needed to be any more aware of him. "You realize you're fixing things, again."

"Well, I may not be able to fix your second sight, or whatever you call it, but I might be able to help with the other parts of your Honey Gets a Life program."

She laughed at that, not at all offended by the label, mostly because that was exactly what she'd come here to try to do. "You're not even denying it."

He shot her a fast grin that made her heart skip all over the place. "Sugar, fixing things is what I do. It's the one thing I've always known how to do. Humor me."

She lifted her hands, palm out, in a motion of surrender. "Lead on."

She glanced at Dylan again as they turned off the square, then went past the alley that led behind his garage and the cupcakery, and turned on the old channel road, stopping the truck in front of the empty building next to the garage. Actually, except for his garage, all the commercial space on this road appeared to be empty and looked like it had been that way for a very long time. She hadn't paid much attention when she'd first brought her car in, more worried about her problems and thankful she'd seen the sign advertising the repair shop.

"Do you need something from the garage?" she asked.

He didn't answer as he turned off the engine and dug a set of keys out of the console wedged on the floorboard between the seat and the dashboard. Then he looked at her. "You took a big chance, coming all this way, sight unseen, hauling your life with you."

She still had no idea where he was going with this. "Well, technically, most of my life is still packed up in crates and boxes back in Oregon, waiting to be shipped here. I only hauled the part of my life that could be crammed into a Volkswagen Beetle."

He lifted an eyebrow. "My point is, you took a big risk, which proves you can. They might not get easier to take, but at least you know you can take them. So . . . keep an open mind."

Oh, he's opened my mind all right. She had to force herself not to let her gaze drift down to his mouth. Much less think about, even for a second, kissing that mouth—which she'd done repeatedly. And that that mouth had kissed her back.

"Sugar, you keep looking at me like that and we're going to end up finding out about what happens when I put my hands on you right out here on the street in broad daylight." His voice was a deep, drawling promise.

And oh, for just a moment, she was tempted to collect on it. She cleared her own throat to dispel the sudden dryness there. "Right. So . . . risks. Open mind. I get it. But that doesn't explain what we're doing here."

He clicked off his seatbelt, then hers, shot her a wink, and climbed out of the truck. Before he could play Southern gentleman and come around to offer assistance in helping her down, she scrambled out her side and closed the door behind her.

Dylan let Lolly out of the truck bed so she could trot across the road to use the grass on the far side. The grassy strip ran down a short incline and stopped in front of the fence between the road and the wide stretch of the Timu-cua River and the Wassaw Channel that separated island from mainland. As there were no other active businesses along this short stretch of road, there was no traffic, but Honey walked over after Lolly anyway, watching out for her and taking a much needed moment or two to gather her thoughts.

"You comin'?"

Honey looked up and saw Dylan standing in front of the door to the empty space next to the garage. Her heart sank. Not that she'd held any realistic hope that Dylan actually had a workable solution for her, but he clearly didn't understand that when she said she didn't have the money to lease a space, she really meant it. Not even some rundown place.

Honey and Lolly crossed the road together to the narrow sidewalk that ran along the street in front of the closed up shops. "I know you're trying to help, and I appreciate it more than you know, but unless they're giving away leases, this isn't going to fix anything."

"It's not as bad as it looks."

"Oh, I'm not being picky about location. My previous work space was a barn, remember? I'm saying that I imagine the owners want actual money for the space, which would be a problem for me."

Dylan gave her a hint of a smile, then used the keys he'd snagged in the truck to unlock the door to the place. "Take a look anyway."

He pulled the door open and gestured for her to go inside first. She wondered why he had keys to the place, but the question was forgotten as she stepped inside. The air was thick and still from the heat, and dank from being closed up for so long. The front windows had been covered by white paper, long since yellowed and torn around the edges, but still allowing in enough light to see the space fairly clearly. It was narrow, but deep, and bigger than it had appeared from the outside. The center area opened up all the way to the peaked roof, with a second level balcony that ran around all four sides of the building, narrow on the sides and front, then deeper across the back.

"Oh, how beautiful is that?" She walked over to the wrought iron circular stairs set into one corner, which led up to the balcony. She put her foot on the bottom stair, grabbed the hand rail, and gave it a sturdy shake. Not so much as a groan or squeak.

"I still don't know if I'd trust that," Dylan said. "Or the flooring up there."

She paused, then stepped back a few feet to look up at the second level, trying to see into the shadows up there. "Are those shelves?" She turned around, standing in the same spot, gazing upward. "Oh, they go around all three sides. Wow."

"Used to be a bookstore," Dylan said, his voice coming from right behind her.

She started slightly, still not used to having people suddenly in her space when caught unawares.

He didn't move closer, but nor did he move away. She glanced at him, but his gaze was on the second level. "Came here a few times as a kid. There's not much room up there. On the two sides it's pretty narrow, just the walkway and shelves built right into the walls. Across the front, there are windows up there, bench seating built in. Used to be more chairs in the alcove."

"Like a recessed reading area," Honey said, charmed, easily picturing how it must have looked. "What's in the back section?"

"More shelves. On the left side, in the corner, is a small office space."

Honey looked back at him. "Really? A little office up there?"

"If I recall. Mr. Beaumont owned the shop back then, and he used to keep the door open so he could keep an eye on the kids. The kids' section was down here and he didn't approve of us coming to the upper level." A smile touched the corners of his mouth. "Come to think of it, he didn't really approve of us at all."

"A bookseller who doesn't like kids? Where does he think his customer base originates from?"

"Children who look and don't touch and mind their parents. Not heathens with no supervision runnin' wild through the place." Smiling, Dylan looked at her. "I'd imagine you'd feel the same if the business was yours. I didn't take it personally." He glanced back up again, and the smile might have curved more fully. "I took it as a challenge."

Honey smiled then, too. "Yes, perhaps you have a point. Good thing you're a responsible adult now."

He slid a gaze to hers that curled her toes. "Oh, I wouldn't say that, sugar."

Just as her breath caught and held in her throat, and she braced herself for him to make a move . . . he did, but it was only to walk off toward the back of the building.

She didn't realize until she let the breath go that her sigh was in disappointment, not relief.

"There's a storage space back through here, another office, I think, or more storage. Bathroom. Small kitchen, it looks like," he said, opening doors and poking his head in. "Gutted, but that's what it once was, anyway, going by the wiring and cabinets. Maybe it was a break room or lounge." He turned around and looked back at her. "What do you think? Would it work?"

It's perfect, she thought. Charming, different, if a good bit bigger than she'd imagined when thinking about her own shop. Of course, she'd always thought small because Bea's shop wasn't very big, but this . . . this was more like her work space—open, open, with the soaring ceiling in the middle. It felt right to her, creatively. Her mind was already buzzing with ideas of how to turn this into her own magical little forest workshop. Well, her forest-meets-island workshop. She smiled, just picturing the possibilities.

She could envision making use of those built in shelves on the balcony level, renovating them to display her garden and forest creatures, creating little scenic tableaus inside the deeper, recessed shelving areas. If the storage room in the back of the building was big enough, she could make that her private studio. The other space a small classroom, maybe. Office upstairs for business purposes. She could even have a big work table right out here in the retail space, so customers could watch as she did finishing work on pieces, or started a new one. It was . . . truly . . . perfect.

"Maybe" was what she said out loud, though, already trying to temper her soaring heart. No point in letting herself dream, even for a moment. "It would take a lot of work to clean it out, get it up to code, I imagine. Among a laundry list of other things. It looks like it's been empty a long time."

"Twelve years. Give or take."

Her mouth dropped open. "Twelve *years*?"

"Island economy, especially one that doesn't have a tourist draw, is shaky at best. Beaumont Senior opened the place back in the fifties, then Junior took it over before I was born and ran it another twenty or so years, but the island dynamic changed over the years. Skewed older and older, not so many children as before, though that's changing again. The recession in the eighties put most businesses here in serious hardship. This place made it through, but never fully recovered. Beaumont shuttered the place just after the turn of the century. It was the last business on the block to close up shop. The town square had taken a pretty big hit as well, so when things finally turned around, it was those spaces that folks snapped up first. Had to if they had any hope of getting the kind of traffic they needed to stay afloat. The docks brought in the fishing trade, so the warehouses down there did okay, which is where our garage was, but the shops back here along the channel road fell further and further into neglect until no one really even came around here, anymore. Too much work to turn it around, I guess."

"Until you took over the building next door."

He nodded. "Back in the fifties and sixties, that place was run by two guys who'd gone to school together and built a business restoring old cars and fixing up old wrecks. They did some pretty amazing paint and body work. It was the only other auto shop on the island."

"Competition for your family garage?"

Dylan shook his head. "No, different services. In fact, having both shops here helped. Folks could get their repairs at Ross & Sons and body work done over here at Shellings & Rack. Worked out pretty well—till Bart Shelling got himself killed in Vietnam. Jimmy Rack held on another fifteen, eighteen years or so, till the early nineties, anyway. Heard he moved west somewhere. Not entirely sure. He turned it over to some cousin or other who ran it right into the ground, didn't have half the talent of either Bart or Jimmy, much less the business sense. Then the recession hit and he took off, and it's stood empty since then."

"Wow," Honey breathed. "Well, at least you had a garage type space to move to, which had to be easier in terms of getting up and running again, but the location can't have helped any."

"Hasn't been bad at all, as it's turned out. It was more industrial down by the docks, which allowed us to have a much bigger space than this, almost twice the size. But being right off the town square has been a boost, actually. Folks just pull in the alley and park out back, so it's convenient. Besides, it's a small island and Ross & Sons has been part of it for longer than most here remember."

"And I'm sure they're loyal. I guess it didn't really matter where you relocated then."

He shrugged. "Unless I wanted to move over the causeway for a bigger space, this was pretty much it. But yes, I do have a steady local customer base."

"Has that worked out okay? Since the space is so much smaller?" Suddenly she remembered some of the things Barbara Hughes had been saying about Dylan's family, and turned her back to him, pretending to look at the interior again. She was afraid he'd see something in her expression and didn't want to shift the mood. Not that she could name the mood, exactly, but it was . . . comfortable. And conversational. The most he'd ever been, in fact. She liked the sound of his voice, deep and with that rich, sexy twang. She liked listening to him talk, and could picture how things might have been back in the day as he'd described them.

"Well enough," he replied. "It's a one man show now, more or less, so the size suits me. Economic recovery has been slow this time around, but the cupcake shop has brought some pretty good national exposure with that feature on Chef Dunne's television show. Having a celebrity chef living on the island hasn't hurt things any, either. Stays steady enough for me, anyway."

"Plus, you're probably a bit more economy-proof than some businesses. When somebody needs work done on their car, they kind of need to get it done." She smiled over her shoulder at him. "She says from personal experience."

He flickered a smile in return, but his eyes were a bit more hooded and she regretted bringing his family into it. She was curious to know more of his story directly from him, but she'd made it a lifetime habit not to be curious about anyone, so the fact that she was curious about this man was enough to keep her quiet. Recalling Barbara's comments merely sealed the decision. If Dylan ever wanted to talk about his past, it would be up to him.

Easing away from that line of conversation and wanting to return to the more comfortable vibe between them, she went back to looking around the space. She wanted to give at least the appearance of taking his offer seriously. She didn't want to insult him, so she poked around a bit more, but stopped short of poking her head in the back rooms. The more she saw, the harder it would be to walk away. In fact, she was turning around with the intent of telling him that she sincerely appreciated the thought, but it wasn't possible, only to find him directly behind her.

She startled briefly, but fought her automatic instinct to move back, create space, and avoid contact. She held her ground and glanced up at him. "Thanks for trying to help. I mean that. But even if I had some wiggle room in the budget for a lease, I couldn't afford a space this size."

"I watched you while you were looking around. You talk a good game about codes and cleaning the place up . . . but let's pretend none of that is an issue."

"Even if it wasn't, that doesn't change—"

"Shh," he said, then lifted a finger and very deliberately placed it across her lips.

She froze, didn't even speak his name in warning for fear the added movement of her lips against his fingertip could trigger something.

"You okay?" he asked, his gaze probing hers.

She knew what he meant, and what signs he was looking for. She nodded . . . and was perversely disappointed when he let his hand drop back to his side.

"Good. Before, when I mentioned about folks giving folks a hand up? There were some folks here on Sugarberry who did that for me, tried to do even more in some cases, but I was too proud to accept most of it. Some went ahead and helped anyway. It took a while for embarrassment to turn to gratitude, longer than it should have, but I do understand now, that if you can offer to help, you do. The person being helped gains something . . . but so does the person who does the helping. Consider it giving back. Or building a community. It's what people do for one another. Or should."

"I thought you'd prefer folks to leave you alone." She didn't say it accusingly, but more because she was trying to understand him.

"I'm not one to sit around, shoot the bull, talk about other people's personal business. Never will be. And I prefer folks to keep their noses out of mine. For too many years, my family's personal business spent far too much time burning up the grapevine. But I wouldn't turn my back on a single one of them in need, if I could help them out. They stood by me. End of the day, that's what matters."

Again, his comments about his family made Barbara Hughes's comments echo through Honey's mind, but she, better than anyone, understood the desire for privacy. "I respect that."

"Good." His expression shifted then, from sober and serious to something a shade or two lighter, and an expression she hadn't seen before entered his gray eyes. The corners of his mouth turned up ever so slightly. "So . . . let me stand by you."

She'd been on the verge of smiling herself, seduced by

the almost playful look on his face. He'd teased her before, but this was something else altogether. Then his words sunk in. "Stand by . . . *me*? How? For that matter, why? I just got here. I'm not a part of anything, yet."

"Everybody has to start building a foundation somehow, make contacts, new friends if they're of a mind to, whatever it takes to weave themselves into the fabric of the community. Ours is close knit, but we have a real penchant for taking in those who come here to find a home. We're a small town, and folks here think that by taking you in, it gives them license to put their noses in where you might not want them, but we're also islanders—a different, interesting breed. None of us came here, or stayed here because we wanted a big life, but because we value setting ourselves apart, maybe a bit more than regular folk."

Honey smiled at that. "You're saying you're not regular folk?"

His lips twitched a little. "I'm saying we understand the need to be ourselves. So while we might be all up in each other's business, we will stand together against anyone who wants to come in and try to change our way of life."

"Bea always said she fit right in here, that it was a classic small Southern town and island eccentric. I'm beginning to understand that more and more. Of course, she was here for decades and was still considered the newcomer."

"Didn't stop folks from considering her one of our own."

"True. I know Bea said people pitched in right after the stroke. And Lani told me Bea wasn't alone when she was forced to move to senior care, even though it took her off the island." Honey paused, trying to tamp down, once again, the guilt at not being there and not knowing something she felt she should have known. "I'll always be grateful she had that."

"She wanted you to have that here, too."

Honey nodded. "I know. So . . . what did you mean? Stand by me? I figure, of anyone, you'd be the one wanting to run as far away as possible."

"That thought might have gone through my mind a few times." His grin unfolded slowly. "Maybe more than a few."

Her lips parted on a little huff at his blunt honesty, even as laughter rose in her throat.

"Careful, sugar, you might catch flies." He shifted just a hair closer. "Or something else entirely."

She closed her mouth, but felt the heat of his meaning seep into every pore of her body. Made her knees a bit wobbly, just thinking about what it would be like to catch what Dylan Ross was pitching.

"Bottom line is . . . you want to stay," he said, keeping that intensity right in his gaze, seemingly quite at home in her personal space, even though he was well aware of the risks. "And I know a way to help you do that."

"So . . . this is just about you fixing something you can fix?"

"Partly. If I can, then I want to, yes."

"Not about me, then. Personally, I mean."

"Shouldn't be."

She looked up into his eyes. "Shouldn't?"

He reached up and gently pushed her glasses up the bridge of her nose. His smile reached his eyes, and she was so caught up in it, she didn't realize he was trailing his finger down the side of her cheek until it was too late to worry about it.

"Shouldn't," he said again. "But I can't deny you've worked your way in, Honey Pie." His voice got softer, deeper, his drawl vibrating along the surface of her skin as he leaned down so his lips were next to her ear. "Reached right in and grabbed hold." The warmth of his breath feathered across her cheeks as he moved his mouth close to hers, still not touching her. "And I'm not sure why, but I'm not wantin' you to let go. Not just yet."

His words made her heart pound so hard she could barely hear her own thoughts, and her knees went from kind of wobbly to downright woozy. "I'm not trying to complicate your life."

He lifted his head just enough to look into her eyes. And his grin devastated any hope she had of reclaiming control. "Sugar, it was too late for that the minute I saw you sitting on that bench out back, looking across the alley like you wanted the world, if only it would want you back."

She felt . . . exposed. For the first time, she had an inkling of what others felt like when she tried to tell them what she saw, what she knew. How exposed they must have felt, how vulnerable. It was terrifying to think he could look at her, and know . . . know what was in her heart, what she'd barely admitted to herself. "I-I just wanted my car fixed."

His grin did that lazy slide into something deeper, more intimate, bringing out a devilish twinkle in his eyes. "Yes, well . . . sometimes you get more than you bargain for."

He took a step forward and she automatically shifted back, bringing her up against the door that led to the storage space.

"I'm giving you fair warning that I'm about to put my hands on you because it seems the right thing to do, but I'll admit, I'm not givin' you any time to think on it." He framed her face with the palms of his hands, so broad and strong, warm, and a little rough. Before she could even begin to process all the delicious signals that sent out, his mouth came down on hers.

She had no time to brace herself, no time to think, and then she was lost in the scents, the tastes, the feelings coursing through her. There was nothing tentative in this kiss; he took, and simply expected to be given to in return.

Give she did. Willingly, helplessly . . . and to her shock, happily. The edges of her consciousness wavered, but with the demands of lust and want and desire. Every part of her was alert, in the moment, and quite wonderfully present.

"You good, sugar?" he queried in a deep murmur against her lips.

"Very," she answered breathlessly, touched and turned on by the fact that, even in the throes of it, he was still taking care of her.

He chuckled at that. When she brought her hands up to his chest, he took hold of her wrists and pinned them gently, but firmly to the door on either side of her head. "My turn. Next time, we'll see what happens when you do the touching."

He slowly slid her hands up the door, bringing their bodies closer, making hers vibrate with the need to feel him pressed up against her. She was past worrying about what might happen. Every thought she had was on one thing, and one thing only . . . feeling him pressed up against her.

He found her mouth again and slowed things down, taking his time, taking her mouth with patient, but devastating thoroughness until she was completely focused on that and only that. Then he eased his body against hers. He was hard, muscular, warm, the heavy air making his T-shirt a bit damp, his skin a bit slick.

She moaned as he slid his tongue into her mouth, moved his body against hers . . . and everything blissfully slipped away except the blinding need to feel more, taste more, have more.

He left her mouth, and she made a brief sound of protest. The whimper turned into a groan of pleasure as his lips found the soft spot under her jaw, then traveled along the side of her neck. She moaned and let her head shift to the side to allow him greater access, reveling in the experience of discovery, of learning what it felt like to be utterly seduced . . . and the thrill of how her body responded to it. Learning where her sensitive spots were, how easily he could elicit a gasp, a moan, when he discovered and exploited them . . . much to her delight.

She had the fleeting thought that pinned against the door, all but helpless, she should have felt trapped . . . panicked, at the very least, at not having any control over how her space was being invaded. Instead, she realized she felt protected, safe. She trusted Dylan. He knew what could happen and wanted her anyway . . . and at the same time, he wasn't being cavalier or selfish about it. There was no doubt she wanted this as much as he . . . and she could certainly say no if she didn't want this to happen, which meant he trusted her, too. So, there was sort of an inner sense of calm, knowing that, no matter what happened, even if the curse was triggered again, he'd stand by her.

It was tantalizing, even a little thrilling, despite the fear, to know he'd probably keep pushing her to reach for what she wanted. He wouldn't let her run and hide.

He pressed her wrists to the wall, then slowly drew his hands along her arms to her shoulders, and she arched against him, all of her thoughts riveted on one thing, wanting his hands to keep moving, to find more of those spots that drove her wild. Two in particular would kill to have his fingertips on them.

"Sugar, you have no idea how hard it is to keep my hands off you," he murmured, his lips pressed to the base of the throat.

"I'm not . . . stopping you," she managed between short breaths. Having an episode had never been so far from her thoughts. Trying to keep her knees from going completely to Jell-O while biting her lip to keep from begging him to cup her breasts, to please, dear God, play with her nipples . . . was taking up every bit of her concentration.

"If I start, no tellin' where it'll stop," he said. "And a dusty, dank old building isn't what I had in mind."

She wanted to scream, she ached so bad. "You've . . . had this in mind?" She was trying to stay focused on the words and not the feel of his wide palms, bracketing her waist.

He lifted his head at that and grinned. "It might have occurred to me once or twice," he said, echoing his words from earlier. "Okay, maybe a few times." He lifted his hands from her waist and carefully, without so much as brushing against her almost painfully erect nipples, he plucked open one button of her blouse. "Not to say I couldn't be persuaded . . ." He plucked open another one, and that devilish twinkle was back in his eyes again.

Good Lord, she thought, *I've won the sexual lottery.* She sent up every prayer of thanks she knew and a few she improvised right on the spot. She smiled, too, despite being shaky with need. "Well, my vote would be—"

"Yoo-hoo!" A wavery, high pitched voice cut through the dank humidity and the thick fog of lust like a pickax into a block of ice. "I saw your truck out front, I hope you don't—oh my!"

Honey instinctively started to jerk away, but Dylan's hands went right back to her waist, pinning her in place. "Blouse," he whispered, then let her go and turned to face their visitor, mercifully blocking Honey from view.

"Well, hey there," he said, all relaxed Southern drawl as if they hadn't been one breath away from mating like wild animals. "Can I help you with somethin' there, Miss Alva?"

Chapter 11

"Well, I stopped by the Hughes's place to see how Honey's meeting went, and Barbara said you'd been kind enough to give her a ride in." Alva fidgeted with her ever-present pearls as she did a slow turn to take in the place, all while carefully not meeting Dylan's gaze.

Nor did she make any other comment regarding the scene she'd walked in on. Considering Alva Liles was a shoot-from-the-hip pistol on the best of days, that was something of a surprise, but Dylan was simply thankful for the unexpected blessing.

"I hope everything was resolved," she went on. "Our Miss Lani has simply been beside herself with worry about how things got so mixed up in the first place. I told her it would all work itself out, but, of course, she won't feel right until it has. When I saw your truck parked out front, I had to stop in and see for myself how it went. For Miss Lani's sake, of course."

"Of course," Dylan echoed, more concerned at the moment about the state of his body, or certain parts of it anyway, and hoping Alva continued avoiding his gaze—and the rest of him—until it finished switching gears from how tantalizingly close he'd been to discovering whether Honey's nipples were as sweet as her namesake . . . to matching wits with the wily octogenarian who always had an agenda he rarely caught on to until it was too late.

All he knew at the moment was that his body wasn't any happier than his mind was with the sudden change in *his* agenda.

"My, my," Alva went on, taking in the dimly lit, musty interior. "I can't recall the last time I set foot in here." She sighed in remembrance. "I still miss the old bookstore. A shame no one ever took it on when Beaumont finally gave up." She turned slowly, staring up at the second floor balcony level. "Imagine my surprise when Morgan mentioned you were the one who'd bought the place," she went on.

Dylan's heart stuttered. *She is a pistol. Fully loaded at all times, despite the deceptive packaging.* He really needed to keep that in mind.

"I hope you're not going to gut it and turn it into a garage," Alva said. "Seems a shame to lose all the lovely molding, all that beautiful custom carpentry with those built in shelves. The wrought iron balcony railing and stairs." She sighed. "Hard to find anyone who cares about such things these days."

Honey frowned and stepped out from behind him. "So . . . that's why you had keys to the place."

Dylan closed his eyes just briefly, then glanced over at her. "I was getting to that part."

"Well, there you are," Alva said, beaming as if Honey had just stepped in from another room, when all three of them knew better.

Honey seemed happy to play along with the charade. "Hello again, Alva. Thank you for stopping by Barbara's and asking after me. I'm still working out details, but it was a productive day."

Dylan silently applauded her for not giving Alva specifics. If Lani Dunne was as broken up by the events of the past few days as Miss Alva claimed, she could discuss the situation with Honey directly.

"Well, dear, that's good news then. I was helping out Miss Lani today and she mentioned that if our paths crossed, I should pass along that she'd love for you to stop on by and have a chat with her. She's talked with Morgan and they've got some kind of documentation for you that might help sort all this out from their end." She waved her hands in a fluttering motion. "I'm hopeless with all the legalese, but I'm thinking it will ease your mind and hers. She was planning to stop by Miss Barbara's herself after work, but when I saw the truck . . ." Alva trailed off and somehow managed to pull off an innocent little shrug.

All three of them knew her visit was no accident. The garage was the only open business on the old channel road, and since the locals parked in the alley out back, the only way she could have spied Dylan's truck in front was if she'd been . . . well . . . spying.

"I'll be sure to do that," Honey replied sincerely enough. "Thank you."

Alva gave one last glance around the space and sighed again, though there was a different expression on her carefully powdered face, one he couldn't quite read. Dylan braced himself.

"Now, Beaumont Senior, my, my, he was the one, wasn't he?" Alva sighed again.

As did Dylan. In relief. Old flames and even older gossip he could handle.

"Knew it, too," she went on. "Before your time, of course, but oh, he was a handsome devil, smooth as they come. A kind word for every customer, but especially the ladies. Always noticed if they'd done their hair up a different way, or had on a new perfume. Always had eyes for me, he did. Harold—my late husband," she added for

Honey's benefit, "never did trust me alone with him." She smiled and a particularly delighted twinkle lit up her eyes and deepened the crinkles at the corner as she added in a conspiratorial whisper, "I'll admit I might have encouraged him, just a little, you know. Perfectly harmless, of course. But it never hurts to keep your beloved on his toes."

Dylan found his lips twitching at that, and Honey was already smiling.

"I'll never understand how Beaumont Junior turned out to be such a prune. I knew Senior's wife Petula, God rest her soul, and, oh she was a delight." Alva looked at Honey. "Senior might have been something of the island ladies man, but when he met Petula Schipps, that was it for him. A late in life romance and an even more surprising late in life baby, but a happier twosome you never saw." Alva sighed one more time. "Such devoted, loving parents. Junior was the apple of their eye, he was. But then, I'm convinced some apples just blossom on the wrong tree." She gave Dylan a slightly extended glance, and he noted the twinkle had shifted to a more decided gleam.

Once again, he'd let his guard down too soon. He'd been on the receiving end of that gleam and he knew it meant trouble. He had the jelly roll to prove it.

"I knew right from the start when he took on the place that his days were numbered. He wasn't a people person, never did seem to be comfortable in the role. Of course, his father's shoes were hard to fill, especially for someone as closed off as Junior was. Never married, that one. Still, it was a shame when he had to let the place go. I might not have been a fan of his stiff, overly formal manner, but you couldn't fault him on his love of books. Why, I used to think he was more comfortable with fictional characters than he was with people." Her gaze found Dylan's again. "We all have our coping mechanisms, I suppose."

"I suppose Beaumont Junior did the best he could under challenging circumstances," Dylan said cordially enough, but with a steady gaze intended to quell further "innocent" commentary. "Thank you for stopping by," he added, starting toward the front door in the hopes of herding her straight through it, only he wasn't quite fast enough.

"Oh my," Alva gasped as if an idea had just occurred to her. The exaggerated lift of her perfectly penciled on eyebrows suggested otherwise. Never one to let things like a well established wily reputation slow her down, she clasped age spotted hands under the delicate fold of her dainty chin and gave them her best "sweet little old lady" routine. "Why, you're thinking of taking over this space for your little shop, aren't you?" she exclaimed, turning her attention squarely on Honey. The woman also knew how to pick her quarry.

It took significant will to tamp down a scowl and force a polite expression as he answered for Honey. "Well now, Miss Alva, I don't rightly know what I'll do with the space, but, as I said, I appreciate you stopping by now." He gestured toward the door and took another step in a gentlemanly attempt to see her to the door, but she smoothly sidestepped him and kept her eyes on her new target.

"What a marvelous, marvelous idea!" Alva gushed, ignoring Dylan as she swept her gaze over the space again, then focused on Honey, eyes in full twinkle. "Such charm and unique style would be perfect for your little carved creations."

"You know about my work?" Honey asked.

Alva made a token effort to look abashed. "Well, Bea was always going on and on about it, but I confess I didn't look you up until we met at the bakery when you first arrived. Quite the enterprise you've built. And such adorable little creatures. My, what an imagination you must have. Must come from the family gift, I suppose."

Dylan was surprised they couldn't hear his teeth grinding, but Honey took it all in stride with a smile.

"Why, thank you. Yes, I learned wood carving from my dad when I was little, and taught myself how to work with clay," Honey said, clearly intentionally misunderstanding which "gift" Alva was referring to. "I've always thought the world could do with a little more whimsy and I'm very, very thankful my customers agree with me."

"Well, you'd have quite the space here. Daresay more than you would have in Bea's old place. You could have your work studio and shop all in one." Alva sighed once again and pressed her still-clasped hands to her chest. "Oh, it would be so lovely to bring life to this old building. I know everyone would be thrilled. And it would build on what our Mr. Ross here has started, rejuvenating this sadly neglected stretch of town. Why, with two businesses here, perhaps others would be inclined to jump in."

She leaned closer, conspiratorial again. "And I don't have to tell you that with Miss Lani's and Baxter's joint cookbook effort about to launch, we're fast becoming something of a destination spot."

She pulled back. "Not that I want to see us go commercial, heaven forbid. We pride ourselves on maintaining our small-town spirit and making the most of what we have. But a little growth would be security for our local economy, and Lord knows we could always do with a bit more of that."

"I suppose it would," Honey said at length.

Alva's face lit up again. "Does that mean I've got it right?"

"Well . . ."

"Now, if you don't want me to pass this along, you know you can trust your little secret with me."

It took a Herculean effort on Dylan's part not to snort at that. He made some noise, however, because he caught Honey's sidelong glance from the corner of his eye. He wished like hell he knew what she was thinking right at that moment. He couldn't tell if Alva was helping or hurting his cause. Honey didn't seem particularly perturbed, but then she had her polite face on for Alva's benefit.

"Of course, if you ask me, I think you should shout it from the rooftops, straight off, get the word out, build anticipation," Alva said. "Buzz, they call it. Now, with you being Bea's flesh and blood and all, you'll already have us supporting you, but it never hurts to advertise." Her eyebrows climbed up again. "You know, I could probably help you with that! I run a little advice column in the local paper, you see—"

Dylan turned his barely suppressed choking sound into a polite cough, but there was only so much a man could swallow and he was well past his limit. Miss Alva's "advice" column was more or less a gossip column wherein she answered letters, ostensibly sent in by the locals, wanting her advice on things ranging from how to keep weevils out of their tomato plants to how to keep the mister entertained once the fire had died. Dylan had long suspected, however, that Miss Alva simply made up the letters as an excuse to spread the latest gossip, using whoever had the misfortune to be keeping the grapevine going at the time. Names changed, of course, to protect the not-so-innocent, which was ridiculous since everyone knew exactly who her anecdotal stories were about.

"—and I'd be more than happy to talk with Dwight at the Daily Islander about doing a little article on your new place. We could make it what they call a human interest story. Talk about your dear, departed aunt Bea, and how you came all the way across the country to honor her name and take up her entrepreneurial spirit, filling the void created by her absence. Maybe not with our tailoring needs, but certainly keeping our artistic needs met, as well as perhaps our more . . . shall we say spiritual ones?" Alva's thoughts clearly spun off along her new train of thought and then she clapped her hands together with surprising sharpness, making Dylan and Honey start.

"Why, you could even hold your own . . . what do they call them? Séances? Now, Bea never did such things, but she hardly had the space in her little shop, did she? Here, why, you could have groups in and—it works better in groups, doesn't it? I mean, I always see it done with every-one holding hands in a circle—"

"Alva—" Dylan began, intent on shutting this little tan-gent down before it gained even a fraction of a toehold.

Honey beat him to it, and with surprising directness. "Miss Alva, that's not something I do. Séances I mean. I think that's for contacting spirits in the afterlife. I know Bea used to help folks out with the benefit of her second sight, but as I mentioned at the bakery when we first met, that's not something I'm altogether comfortable with."

"Well, dear," Alva said, taking the disappointing news in stride, "perhaps once you get to know us better, you'll feel more comfortable. After all, if you know something that might be of help, it simply doesn't seem right not to share it, now does it?" She smiled, and Dylan shifted his weight. The gleaming twinkle was back. With a vengeance.

"Of course, I'll be happy to help introduce you around, put you at ease. And, it goes without saying that if you need any help delivering your . . . well, your news, so to speak, I can help there, too. Smooth things over, and all."

Alva leaned in closer. "Not everyone wants to hear the difficult things, of course. Why, I mentioned in my last column that perhaps it would be wiser for men who like to spend every last minute of their spare time with a fishing rod in one hand and a beer in the other, to consider filling their hands with the ripe and neglected body parts of their lonely, devoted spouses, instead. And, wouldn't you know, Bucky Hibbener got his nose all out of joint. As if he's the only one on Sugarberry who fishes like he's in some kind of lifelong tournament."

She sniffed, then beamed a particularly satisfied little smile. "Of course, Natalie Hibbener sure looks a might rosier in the cheeks of late, so . . . sometimes you just have to put the information out there and trust those who need it to take it to heart."

Dylan didn't risk a look at Honey, who had made a gargling noise indicating she was a breath away from strangling the tiny senior . . . or from giving in to a fit of hysterical laughter. Since Dylan was quite certain he would follow either path with the least bit of provocation, he kept his gaze strictly forward.

"Well," Alva said, "I'll leave you two to your . . . deliberations." She winked at Honey, who went blush pink. "Come by the bakery later. We're staying late tonight to bake for a charity event over in Savannah tomorrow. We're all contributing something from our own personal recipes. Kit taught me how to make my famous apple pies into little pot pie size miniatures. Isn't that just the most darling thing? Have you met Kit yet? She ran her family's pie empire until her brother-in-law sold it out from under her. Evil, evil man. Best peanut pie you've ever tasted."

Alva waved her hand. "Well, that's another story. Please do come. Everyone will be there. I'll introduce you to the rest of the club. You'll love them and I know they'll love you. You don't have to bake, of course, but if you'd like to join in, we'll take all the donations we can get."

"I"—Honey stopped and cleared her throat—"I'll try."

"A nod is as good as wink," Alva said cheerily, then took one last look around the place, let out a satisfied sigh that Dylan expected had very little to do with the empty building space or memories of times gone by. And before he could so much as offer an arm, she sailed out quite capably on her sturdy lavender pumps.

Dylan and Honey stared after her for a full minute without saying a word.

He cleared his throat first. "You handled her really well for a beginner."

"Good to know."

"It was smart to set her straight right off on the whole séance thing."

"You said I should just own it, so . . . I did. Begin as you mean to go on, right?"

"Exactly."

"Felt pretty good, actually. It's very different. From before, I mean."

"New place, new people, opinions yet unformed."

She let out a slow, whistling breath that let him know she'd been a lot more tense than she'd let on. "Yeah. I'm still getting used to that. But, so far . . . it's been a good thing. Well, that and the fact that in this particular place, with these particular people, I benefit from Bea somewhat paving the way."

"I thought you handled it just right. If you want the word out, the right person's ear to whisper in."

"That much, I've figured out."

Dylan smiled. "Don't let her unbridled enthusiasm about setting up shop here affect your decisions on things," he cautioned. "If we could bottle her energy, we could shut down the power grid. She means well, and her intentions are generally good ones, but don't let her railroad you."

Honey turned her gaze on him. "When were you going to tell me you owned this place? Before or after you seduced me into staying?"

His eyes went wide at that. He opened his mouth, shut it again, and ground his back teeth together.

Honey broke out laughing. "My God, you should see your face right now. I was kidding. Okay?" She tried to look sober and repentant, but the quivering corners of her mouth gave her barely suppressed giggles away.

"You totally deserved it, by the way," she added, once she got herself under control. "I think, given the events of the past day or two, the least we can do is be completely up front with each other. You should have told me straight off."

"I was going to tell you once we'd talked through whether or not the space would even work for you. You'd kind of dismissed it out of hand, if you recall."

"Because I can't afford rent on a place the size of Bea's tailor shop, much less something like this, so there was no point in getting my hopes up."

"So, are you saying that, if rent wasn't an issue . . . you think this might work?"

Whatever rational answer she thought she might give him, the fleeting look of yearning in her eyes was all the answer he needed. It was a replica of the one he'd seen in the alley the moment he'd first laid eyes on her. It was as powerful now as it had been then. More so, maybe, because he knew more of what was behind it. And, perhaps, because there was hope along with the aching vulnerability.

"I can't pay you," she said, then lifted her hand. "And no, I'm not making any wisecracks about other forms of payment. I really was just kidding. We might not know each other all that well yet, but I think I have a pretty good handle on the type of code you live by."

"Do you now?" he asked, bemused.

"I think so. Anyway, it's all moot because no money is no money."

"This place is sitting here earning me exactly nothing, whether someone is in it or not. To my way of thinking, it's better if someone is at least in it, right?"

"Fair point, and appreciated, but the renovations—"

"You had some plan for renovating Bea's place, right?"

"I did, but it's a much smaller space. I was going to focus on getting the front area set up to show off my pieces, use the back room for my work studio and her apartment upstairs to live in and as my office, then gradually upgrade as I could. I'd save the more dramatic changes for when the farm sells. Then I would get my own place to live, make the entire downstairs the showroom, keep her upstairs apartment as my office, and renovate the rest into a workshop. Maybe even a small classroom."

He could envision all of that, and she'd be good at it. It was brilliant in its own way, because she'd be instructing and demonstrating, which invited people directly into her world, allowing them to get to know her. At the same time, by keeping her students' hands on their work . . . she'd have more control in keeping them out of her immediate personal space. It was a way to immerse herself in the community, get close to people, allow them in, but still preserve that tiny bit of physical distance she needed to insure she stayed on an even keel.

He thought back to how extreme it had been for her when she'd been transported back to the garage fire, reliving that terror through his eyes. He realized what a great risk it was to put herself in any position where that might happen in a professional setting. It was one thing for it to happen between the two of them, or even on Miss Barbara's front porch. But what if she was in the middle of a class? Or ringing up a sale?

Who would help her then? Who would protect her?

The ferocity of his immediate internal response to that question floored him. There was leaping tall buildings, and then there was taking on the impossible task. No one could completely protect her . . . and more to the point, she didn't expect anyone to, much less want them to.

Her aunt had successfully offered her "advice" right along with her tailoring skills, but it sounded like Bea never had the kind of "moments" Honey had. Their familial gifts were entirely different. Bea's was much milder than her own, Honey had said. And she had come all the way across the country with the idea of trying to have a normal life, with a normal storefront business, normal friends she could actually spend time with. He didn't know if that made her courageous and brave, or a glutton for the worst kind of emotional and public punishment. But she had his admiration for trying.

"It sounds like you had it all planned out." He realized how much of a shock it must have been to arrive, only to find Bea's little shop had been renovated completely and turned into a cupcake shipping outlet. "I know this is a bigger space and it hasn't been used in a long time, but if you tried to break it down into smaller, doable chunks, the end result would put you in a much better place, right?"

"In terms of size, yes. But I owned the space in my scenario and, no offense, but now I'd be a tenant."

"A tenant who is still a property owner. I know it won't bring you income for a few years, but I'm assuming you plan to be in this business for the long haul. In a couple years, you'll have the lease income. You'll also get investment capital from selling the farm, and eventually, a profit from this place, as well. I'm assuming you plan to keep your online store going, too, so that's a good foundation to build on."

"You make it all seem so doable."

"Because it is. But only if you want it to be." He looked around again, then back at her. "You could really do something with a space like this, couldn't you?"

For all her casual dismissal earlier, her guard had been sufficiently lowered, and the poignant longing, the barely concealed, banked excitement was plain to see.

"I know it took a lot to come here, to try. More space would be a good thing for . . . the rest of it, too, right? Easier to control contact if there was less potential crowding."

"Yes, it would, but—"

"You put your farm up for sale and drove a couple thousand miles, intent on starting your own place, starting a new life. That's not something someone does who is iffy on the idea."

"Juniper Hollow, where I'm from, is a very small town in a somewhat rugged and isolated area. I didn't think a sale was going to happen right away. If ever. So, it wasn't like I absolutely couldn't go back. A risk, yes, but—"

"But, what if it had? What if the farm sells, and you're here, and it's not going as you'd hoped. Do you have a backup plan?"

She smiled then, and he liked the spark that came back into her sea green eyes as she lifted a shoulder. "Georgia is in the South, right? I figure it has a lot of barns. Probably one I could buy and move into somewhere around here." She sighed. "The truth is, whatever happened, I didn't want to go back to Oregon. Ever. I wanted . . . something new. Something else. Anything else."

He held her gaze, then let his own smile come out, as certain about his decision as she was about hers. If she could take that kind of risk and had that kind of determination, then hell, he had no choice. He wasn't leaping the tall building in this case, but the surprise was it felt every bit as good to help her leap her own.

"Then let's do this. Knowing how you feel about helping hands, we'll work out a little lease agreement that includes paying back rent for whatever time it takes to get up and running. We can get Morgan to put it in writing and make it all legal. When your farm sells, or when this place is making a profit, you can handle the lease and the back rent repayment however it works best. Like I said, I'm not making money from this place as it is."

"Dylan—" She broke off and simply stared at him, clearly torn.

"Sugar, how can you expect me to bet on you if you won't bet on yourself?"

"I do bet on myself," she said staunchly, but he could hear the quaver in her voice. She broke their gaze and slowly, as if in a dream, turned and took in the space one more time. "I just . . . I don't even know what to say. I've never . . . no one has ever . . ." Her voice drifted off, and he saw her throat work.

"What? Believed in you? Backed you up?"

"Other than my family . . . no. Not that I've let anyone in. It's just . . . a lot to take in. A whole lot."

"I've learned the only person who can get in the way of me getting what I want . . . is me. If you want it, go for it. Whether you believe I'm behind you or not doesn't matter. Are you behind you? Can you back up your dream with commitment, no matter what? That's what matters. That's what it takes."

She looked at him again. "Is that what it took for you? I mean . . . I don't know the whole story of your family history and I'm not asking for it, but you've alluded to it, and Alva has, and, if we're being open and honest, Barbara Hughes said a few things."

He frowned. "Honey—"

She lifted her hand, palm out. "I really don't mean to pry. That's not my point, anyway. I was going to say that it sounds like you've practiced what you're preaching. And that means something to me."

"We all get where we want to be on different paths, but the one thing we have in common is we have to take the path, embark on it, to get there. You won't get anywhere sitting and wondering. You already know that. So . . . keep going."

"Why did you buy this space? Don't you have plans for it?"

He shook his head. "The garage had been passed down to me. I owned it when it burned down. We'd been with the same insurance company since the day my grandfather opened. Never filed a single claim. The settlement was a good one. And, between the depressed economy and how long these properties have sat empty . . . well, to say they went for a song isn't much of a stretch. Where my shop is now was already set up as a garage, so renovation was minimal. I had more money than I needed for the garage property. It made sense to put it somewhere instead of giving it away in taxes. I have a house, so"—he shrugged—"I figured, worst case, the investment would keep me from having neighbors I didn't want. Best case, if the garage did start a trend and interest in developing the other channel road properties grew, then I could turn around and sell them at a profit. And, sugar, pretty much anything more than the plug nickel I paid would be a windfall."

She gave him a perceptive look. "You try to pass as this sort of unassuming mechanic, just getting by, running the old family business. But something tells me you're a lot shrewder than people might guess."

"Well, darlin', I'm not entirely a bad bet. Business-wise, anyway."

She grinned at that. "Yeah, I'm not buying the unassuming part anymore, either, just so you know. On any count. You forget who was almost taking my blouse off not that long ago." She gestured around her. "Not exactly the most romantic spot, so . . . you're not without skill."

"I'm not sure if my ego just got a bump, or took a hit."

She simply smiled at him. "You have your skills, I have mine. So, tell me honestly, did you have dreams of expanding the garage one day?"

He shook his head. "Expanding means growing the business, which means taking on other types of work, not to mention more employees. I've got no interest in that. I like what I've got, it suits me just right, and provides enough to meet my needs."

He let the smile come out again. "And once I have a paying tenant next door, I'll be making more money without any of the overhead or the headaches. That's more than I could have hoped for."

"It might take a long time," she warned, "a very long time, in fact, before I'm operating in the black, given the much bigger starting size of the shop. And the farm might never sell. What if—"

"Darlin', we'll deal with the *what if* when it happens. I'm not goin' anywhere. I'm right next door. Unless you get a vision in your head tellin' me it's going to burn down or blow away, I plan to still be there when I'm too old to wheel myself under a car." A smile teased the corners of his mouth. "And if you play your cards right, having good neighbors might net you some free labor now and again from me or Dell when we have the spare time."

"Oh, I wouldn't expect—"

"Shhh. For once, just say thank you. If you plan to stay in the South, you'll have to get used to folks helpin' folks. You'll get plenty of chances to pay it forward."

She smiled again. "Thank you."

He grinned. "That mean we're in business?"

She brought her hand up to cover her still smiling

mouth, then pushed up her glasses, then covered her mouth again.

"You want it, darlin', don't you?"

She lowered her hand. "More than I've ever wanted anything," she blurted in a fervent whisper that tugged at his heart. "It's perfect."

He'd purposefully ignored thinking about how it was going to affect him, so it was not the time to be thinking about what it might feel like to hear her say those same words while she was looking straight at him with that same anticipation and excitement banked in those eyes of hers . . . and not talking about an empty, musty building space.

"Then it's a done deal," he said, before either of them could change their mind.

Her eyes went wide over the fist she'd pressed against her mouth and she did a nervous little dance-in-place maneuver that had him chuckling.

He spread his arms wide. "Welcome to Honey's Next Life Adventure."

Superman, eat your heart out.

He was still grinning at her little two-step victory dance, so was completely unprepared when she impulsively launched herself right into his open arms. He caught her against his chest even as his eyes went wide with stunned surprise. He spun her around to keep from stumbling back as she whooped and laughed, which made him laugh and want to whoop right along with her. He gave her another spin and she wrapped her legs around his waist and locked her hands behind his neck as their gazes met again.

"Thank you," she said, eyes shining with emotion. "Thank you, thank you. I'll pay you back. Every penny. I'm a good bet, too, Dylan Ross."

I know you are, sugar, he thought. *I know you are.*

He was still reeling from having her wrapped around him, having her hands freely and willfully on him for the first time when she took what was left of his breath away by leaning in and kissing him soundly on the mouth. What might have been meant as a fast, hard kiss to seal the deal, quickly turned into something heated and far more intimate. She moaned first . . . or maybe he did. He was thinking about finding the nearest wall and picking up where they'd left off earlier . . . when she went oddly stiff and made a strangling noise in her throat.

"Aw, shit," he murmured.

Then he held on for dear life. Hers . . . and his.

Chapter 12

Dammit, *dammit, no! No!* But it was too late, she was already spinning away. The way he'd looked at her, encouraged her—dared her, almost—to reach out and grab what she wanted had made her feel invincible.

She should have known better.

She could still feel Dylan's arms around her holding her tightly, and he was murmuring something she couldn't make out, over and over. Surprisingly, the steadiness of his voice, the constancy of it, along with his hold on her, calmed her, and the panic she always felt at that first existential jerk sideways subsided a little.

Then things began to shift more fully into the vision and other thoughts took over. She braced herself to deal with the acrid smell of smoke, the pounding pulse, and racing heart that would soon follow. But . . . she wasn't in the burning garage, nor was she watching him race toward one. She wasn't anywhere around anything like that. She was . . . rocking. Slowly, gently. Swaying. There was a gentle pitch, then a slow dip, then another easy climb again.

A boat!

She was . . . on a boat. Oh no! *No, no, no!* Was she on the fishing trawler? Did that mean it was going to be Dylan instead of Mr. Hughes taking the gash in the leg? Or worse? Why would he take Frank's place on the fishing boat? She had to warn him not to go. But . . . wouldn't the boat be pitching wildly in the storm? She squinted, trying to make the rest of the vision come into focus, but it was just sensory, nothing visual yet. She could smell the salt water, the sting of it in the air. It was warm, humid . . . but there was heat, too. The sun! Not the storm she'd seen earlier. It was sunny, bright, hot. Oh, thank God.

So . . . where was the urgency, she wondered. Why had she been pulled in so abruptly? Usually when she was jerked in like that, it meant something big . . . something bad. Oftentimes, really bad.

She tried to focus, tried, for once, to tap in more deeply to the vision instead of backing away from it. If something was going to happen to Dylan, she wanted to know about it. But she just kept feeling the sway, the dip and roll of the water beneath . . . beneath a sailboat! Dylan's sailboat! Was something going to happen to his boat? After all his hard work, was he destined to lose it somehow? Seemed unfair for a man who'd suffered so much loss, but Honey knew all about life not being fair.

That kind of ominous vibration wasn't in the moment. Quite the opposite, actually. If she allowed herself to relax into it, she could be lulled into a very peaceful place. At least, that's how it felt.

Her breath began to steady now that the initial on-slaught was over, and she let herself relax into it more. She could feel the heat on her skin, and enjoyed the motion of the gentle swell and the slow slide down again. It felt . . . good. She tried to keep some part of herself braced for the inevitable, but the longer she stayed in the moment, the more challenging that became.

The vision formed like mists parting. Although she felt the movement of the sailboat, she was sort of watching as the scene came into focus. Out on the open water, a gor-

geous, bright, sunny day, his back was to her as he manned
the wheel. A beautifully restored, vintage wooden
wheel—or whatever they were called. He wore white
khaki board shorts that hung low on his hips, showcasing
his backside and tanned, muscular calves. His stance was
solid, his hips steady as he easily rode the pitch and roll.

He wore a faded, sky blue T-shirt and the breeze had
molded the soft fabric to his torso. Strong forearms, with
those wide palms she already knew so intimately, gripped
the wheel. His hair was longer, sun streaked, the ends
dancing in the wind as he kept watch over the waters
ahead. Something else was different about him. His shoulders were relaxed, she realized. Everything about him was
relaxed. The man she knew had an intensity about him, a
sort of banked energy that emanated from him at all times,
as if he was always braced for something. But the man on
the sailboat had not a care in the world.

Laughter was a bright punctuation to the beautiful day.
It was a rich giggle in the way that only . . . it was a child's
laughter! She didn't see a child, but she definitely heard
one. Maybe it was some kind of echo of Dylan's past, that
he was finally able to reach back and recapture the youth
he should have had? Except her visions weren't usually as
metaphysical as all that. Dylan's laughter blended with the
child's rolling giggles. Rich, deep, and completely, utterly
free. She'd heard him chuckle, heard him laugh . . . but
she'd never heard him sound like that.

He glanced over his shoulder, and there was this deep
sense of . . . connectivity. She knew that face so well.
Every scar, every line, better than she knew her own. Her
fingertips tingled with the urge to trace every one of
them, as if they had so many, many times before. Crinkles
formed at the corners of his gray eyes made almost blue by
the shirt he was wearing as he aimed that sexy, devil-may-
care grin straight at . . . her?

"Honey?"

"I'm right here," she responded, wanting to get up and go to him. Run to him. She knew his arms would open for her.

"Honey!"

She blinked her eyes open, and she was in the dusty, musty bookstore again, still in Dylan's arms, though her feet were touching the floor now.

"That's it," he was saying softly, almost crooning the words. "Come on back, darlin'. I'm right here."

She blinked again, and the sailboat was gone, the heat of the sun . . . the giggling child, and that knowing smile. So was the sense that she'd been looking into that same face, those same eyes, for a very long time.

"I'm sorry," she said automatically.

"What for?"

"I shouldn't have jumped you. I should have . . . I should have known. It was just, we've taken so many risks and it hasn't happened and I was just so excited and—"

He captured her face in his hands, held them there when she tried to pull away, and brought her gaze to his. She braced momentarily, expecting to go right back into the vision again, but nothing wavered, nothing tugged. At least not like that. She was feeling a tug of an entirely different kind as vestiges of feelings from the vision still mingled with the real feelings she was having.

"Sugar, don't ever apologize for jumping me."

That surprised a snort of laughter from her, making him smile instantly and shoot her a wink. She felt suddenly shaky, but not in a bad way. For the first time ever, she wanted to go back into the vision, to keep feeling what she'd been feeling. But she was liking where she was right now pretty damn well, too. It was so confusing. Normally visions didn't involve her so personally, but normally she didn't have visions about people she cared about, or people who were otherwise involved in her life.

"You okay? Want to talk about it?"

Yes, she thought. *I do.*

All of it, she realized. So much had happened to her since coming to Sugarberry, after years of nothing ever happening. Being around people was a huge thing, but suddenly she had people chatting with her and asking her to bake cupcakes, and . . . and . . . a man who was holding her, kissing her, seducing her. All completely normal things . . . for anybody but her. It was all happening so fast she should be completely freaking out, except the very speed of the unfolding events didn't allow time for that. The truth was . . . she didn't want it to slow down, didn't want it to stop. It was everything she wanted.

She just wanted to catch up.

"I'm fine," she said, not entirely truthful, but fine in the way he meant. "It wasn't bad. In fact . . . it was about you and your sailboat. You had it out on the water. And you were . . . you were really happy." She didn't elaborate further. She wanted time to think about what she'd experienced. There was nothing else really to tell him, anyway.

"At first, I thought I was going back to the fishing boat, and that you were taking Frank's place, but it was all peaceful and good. It was your boat. It was . . . it was good."

He grinned. "Well, that's a nice piece of news then. Now we can both celebrate."

"Celebrate," she repeated, then jerked her thoughts clean away from the vision and fully back to the moment. "Oh, right! The bookstore!"

He'd steadied her on her feet, and let his hands drop to his sides. "Your store."

A shiver raced over her. Of excitement or terror or

both. "Is it completely crazy to think I can do this? I mean, what if—"

He pressed a finger to her lips. "Remember rule number one: no what ifs. Only what's nexts. *If* things happen, then you'll figure out what to do about them."

"So . . . what's next? I guess we need to figure out what the arrangement will be. When I talk to Morgan about Bea's place, I'll let him know we want him to draw up a lease agreement for this place, too." She took a slow turn and looked at the interior, her mind's eye already seeing it as she'd want it to be. She turned back to find Dylan watching her. "What?"

He just smiled and shook his head. "You want to get on over to the bakery?"

"Oh. Right." She took a deep breath. "I guess so."

"You don't like to bake?"

"It's not that. I like Lani." She smiled wryly. "And Alva. I just . . . it's been a really wild couple days." She let out a short laugh. "I thought I was going to take it slowly, pace myself, ease in to things. Not so much, as it turns out."

"Wading in can be more torture than just jumping in and getting used to the cold water all at once."

"Maybe."

"Is it the . . . thing?" he asked, knowing she understood what he meant.

"The vision? No. It was . . . nice. Surprisingly nice . . ." She trailed off, not wanting to think about all the things she'd felt while watching Dylan at the helm of his sailboat. She smiled, and despite the still, heavy air, she rubbed her arms. "It's just . . . I have so many other things to think about right now."

"Why don't you go talk to Lani, get yourself introduced around. No one says you have to stay. Lolly and I'll go on next door and start matching up the parts I got for your car. Just come back across the alley when you're ready and I'll run you back to the B&B—"

"Oh no, I couldn't impose—"

He stopped her with a quelling look. "Rule number two: if I offer, I don't mind. Trust me. When I mind, sugar, you'll know. Besides, I have Frank's lawnmower part to drop off."

"Okay. I don't know how long I'll be, but I guess I can always come back over here and start making What's Next lists while you're working."

"There you go." He closed the distance between them and fished the keys out of his jeans pocket. "And here you go."

Honey looked at the keys, then up at him. "If this doesn't work—"

"Would you stop?" he said quietly. "Come here." He bent his head and kissed her while simultaneously pressing the keys into her hand.

Her vision was unfocused and a bit glazed by the time he lifted his head, but it was all hormone induced. She wrapped her hands around the keys, focusing on the real, the solid, the thing she could reach out and touch. For all that she could reach out and touch Dylan Ross—and had—he still felt as intangible as her visions. She couldn't let herself buy into anything more than that. Much as she might like to.

It took supreme willpower and the sound of Dylan's rules echoing through her mind to keep from wondering what would happen if or when she was no longer putting her hands on her new landlord. Or, more to the point, when he no longer wanted to put them on her.

He leaned down until he caught her gaze and smiled. "Go bake something, all right?"

She grinned, laughed. "Okay, okay. I'll uh . . . why

don't I lock the front door behind you, then let myself out the back to head across the alley to Cakes by the Cup. I didn't look in the back rooms yet, anyway."

"Okay." She thought he was going to dip his head and kiss her again. Instead, he reached up, gently bumped her glasses up the bridge of her nose, and sauntered to the front door. "Your lenses are fogged," he called over his shoulder.

"You seem to have that effect on them."

He turned and grinned. "You comin'?"

Not yet, she thought. *But Lord knows I'd like to.*

Honey poked around the storage room a bit on her way out the back and might have stayed longer, but the light was dimming as the late afternoon sun shifted to the front side of the building, casting the back room in shadows, despite the high windows and the door she'd left open to the front. Better to get on over to Lani's and have that conversation, then come back in the morning, bright and early, and start in on the mountain-sized laundry list of things she'd need to do to get to the point where she could have the rest of her things and her inventory shipped out.

She felt as if her brain was on speed, leaping off on a million different tangents as more and more ideas popped into her head of how to best utilize and lay out the space. She wanted to dive straight in, but first things first. Whether she stayed to bake or not, she did have to talk to Lani, get whatever documentation she'd put together, and, Honey supposed, make it official that she was going to take on the old bookstore space, thereby ending any conflict she and Lani might have had before it even started.

That was a huge relief. Honey needed the support of the islanders, her new neighbors and fellow business owners, if her new enterprise had a chance of succeeding.

She also couldn't deny that the very idea of making

friends with some of the happy, chatty, laughing bakers she'd spied when she'd first arrived was . . . well, icing on the cupcake.

Still, she paused at the back door and looked over her shoulder, through the open storage door into the front room . . . and felt an undeniable thrill rush through her. Truth be told, she was itching to dive in. "Well, Aunt Bea, this might not be exactly what you had in mind . . . but, if it works, I think it's going to be even better."

Honey stepped out into the waning sunlight, locked up, then allowed herself five seconds to grin like a loon. "Okay, okay, enough of that. For now." She smoothed her hair, checked her blouse again to make sure she'd buttoned it up correctly, then strolled resolutely across the alley toward the back door of Cakes by the Cup. "You wanted to be one of the cupcake crew," she murmured under her breath. "Here's your chance."

She lifted her hand to knock, but for the second time in as many attempts, the door was abruptly pushed open in her face, causing her to leap backward. It wasn't Lani with a tray full of cupcakes, but a very tall, swarthy and suave, dark-haired gentleman, who was looking over his shoulder as he exited the building, still having a chat with someone inside. *"Bonsoir, mes belle amies! Rendez-vous demain."*

Tall, good-looking . . . and French? What were the chances? Bea hadn't mentioned the island was full of eye candy.

Honey was standing well clear when he turned around, spied her, and immediately—and quite dramatically for a guy his size—clutched his chest. "Holy Jesus. Girl, you just about took five years off my life."

So . . . okay, not French. More like Brooklyn by way of Little Italy.

He paused, smoothed his hair, then struck a pose last seen in Madonna's Vogue video. "I'll deny it, of course, but I could use a five year reduction, so perhaps thanks are in order." He smoothed his shirt, then his hair again, then beamed a megawatt grin her way.

Confused by the French-cum-New York accent and his surprisingly decent runway skills, she simply waved at him and smiled. "My pleasure. I think. I'm—"

"Oh my goodness, you're Honey Pie D'Amourvell." He sketched a deep and very gallant bow. "*Mon cher,* it is my most sincere pleasure to make your acquaintance." Still in a deep bow, he glanced up at her and winked. "I'd kill for that last name of yours, by the way."

She couldn't help it, she laughed. "Well, I'll warn you, it's long, no one pronounces it right, the DMV hates me, and it hasn't really done me too many favors. What's yours? Maybe we can trade."

He straightened, chuckling; the deep, rich sound was inviting and utterly endearing. As was the twinkle in his dark eyes. He was a big, gorgeous, charismatic man, but the first word she'd used to describe him was adorable.

"I'm Franco Ricci. And I knew I was going to like you, *bellisima.*" At her raised brow, he added, "*Mais oui,* I mix in a little Italian with my French. Blame my dear, departed grandmamma. Speaking of the dearly departed, your aunt, Miz Beavis Chantrell, was a lovely, lovely woman. Also with a last name to die for," he added with a wink. "I was privileged to know her only for a short time, but she had many wonderful things to say about you. I'm so very sorry for the circumstances leading to your coming here, but welcome to Sugarberry. We're all very glad you've come."

He was a lot to take—all good—but a lot. Then she remembered Lani mentioning something about Franco, and a French poodle. She understood that now, but not remotely in the way she'd assumed she would. The best she could manage at the moment was to repeat, "All?"

"Oh, you haven't met the crew? Well, I know you met Lani and Miss Alva as they've already filled us all in."

"All?" she asked again, not brave enough to ask what constituted said "filled us all in."

"You're taking over the old bookstore, I hear?"

When her mouth dropped open, he leaned in, the accent disappearing again. "Honey, it's a small island. No secrets."

"But Alva said she'd—"

"Oh girl, no. Hmm mmm. You might as well take out a front page ad in the *National Enquirer.*"

Honey tried not to snort at that. She didn't want to appear rude, but was only marginally successful. "Right. Well . . . she's right, I'm considering it. The bookstore building, I mean. I came over to talk to Lani about . . . everything. Alva also invited me to come meet the group; she said you all were baking for charity." She winced. "Is that also something I should be skeptical about?"

"Oh, not at all, *mon amie.* You're totally welcome at Cupcake Club. We could use some new blood. Do you bake?"

"Is it a prerequisite?"

"No, not at all. Do you want to learn?"

She smiled. "Is that a prerequisite?"

He grinned. "Do you like to eat cupcakes?"

"That I can do."

"*Bienvenue en* Cupcake Club!" he said, moving in as if to wrap her up in a big bear hug.

Honey about tripped over the long cement block that fronted the nearest parking spot to avoid the contact. "Nothing personal," she hurried to add as he immediately froze, mid-arm reach. "I'm really sorry."

Begin as you mean to go on, she reminded herself. "Um . . . how well did you know my aunt?"

Franco straightened, and to his credit, didn't look offended or like he thought she was completely nuts. "I've
only been in the area for the past few years. I moved down
the same time Charlotte did. Lani's best friend," he explained. "We all worked together back in New York. I'm
mostly in Savannah—I work with Char and her fiancé
Carlo in their catering business, and as a sous chef on Baxter's television show—but I'm over here all the time. So, I
didn't know your aunt as well as most everyone who lives
here, but we spent some quality time together."

He flashed her that million dollar grin again. "You
know, we have some of the best tailors in the world back
in my neighborhood at home, but she was a magician with
a needle and thread. I've never had clothes fit me as well.
Woman could tailor a tuxedo for the Hulk if he asked." He
gestured to himself and chuckled. "And I'm a close second. Do you sew?"

"No, I'm sorry. I carve. And sculpt. Did you know
about Bea's . . . other talents?"

"Oh, you mean the—" He broke off and made a feath-
ery motion around his forehead with his hands. "Not until after I'd known her a bit. A shame, too. Lord knows she
could have saved me all kinds of heartache with that—
well, we don't need to go into that. Water under the
bridge. Bloody, hateful, cheating bastard water, but . . .
I'm not bitter."

"No, not at all. I can see that." Franco was possibly the
oddest hot guy she'd ever met. Not that her personal hot
guy—or any guy—list was long, but, still. She liked him
already. Maybe it was his very uniqueness that called to the
outcast in her. Where she might have been uncomfortable
with being different, Franco had clearly long since embraced it. Owned it with flair, one might say. "Can I ask
you something? Why the French accent? I mean, are you
part French, part—"

"I'm second generation Italian-American from the Bronx." He said it with an enunciation that would have made the entire cast of *Jersey Shore* weep with envy. (She knew about the show, so what? It was lonely, living in a barn.)

"And the French?"

He leaned slightly closer, but with clear respect for her personal space. "You ever try picking up cute guys with a Bronx accent? Trust me, French works much better." He kissed his fingertips with enthusiasm. *"Es magnifique!"*

She grinned. "I'll keep that in mind."

He grinned, completely unabashed. "You do that," he said in a dead-on Rocky Balboa.

She laughed out loud. "I bet Bea gave you a steep discount. She had to love you."

"She used to tailor clothes for Vegas showgirls and girl had an eye for sequins. It was love at first sparkle." He sighed. "I really miss her." He gave Honey a considering look. "But, I'm thinking we're going to get along just fabulously."

Honey smiled. She hoped so. "Why is that?"

"Because you have no bullshit in you. And I'm nothing but." He gave a dramatic sigh, then a wink that could only be described as saucy. "It's so nice to drop the façade every once in a while." He gave her a warning look. "Which I'll deny to my grave if you tell."

She made a cross sign over her heart. "Your inner Bronx boy is safe with me."

"Well, then, *ma chérie,* allow me to introduce you to *la dulce de la* cupcakes."

Honey laughed. Clearly he wasn't kidding about the bullshit. His French was hilariously inaccurate, but he sounded damn sexy saying it. She imagined he got away with far more than mangling an entire foreign language. "Weren't you just leaving?"

"For you, *bella,* I'd be honored to make the introductions. Consider it a favor to your aunt."

Honey grinned, feeling charmed, amused, and maybe even a little flustered—which, given he was also clearly gay, either said a lot about his bullshit skills or even more about the sad state of her only recently reborn libido.

He opened the door with a flourish, then leaned in before she could enter. "So, Bea was always a laying-on-of-the-hands type. I'm guessing you're more of a—"

"Laying-off type," she finished, nodding with him. "It's a little more intense for me than it was for Bea. Direct contact is the trigger."

"Understood," he whispered, leaning closer as the noise and music inside the kitchen came thumping out through the open doorway. "You're safe with me." He straightened and made an exaggerated doorman flourish. "Now, *entrer vous* with your bad self."

Already laughing, Honey met the cupcake ladies. And, much to her delighted surprise, that set the tone for the evening. Alva immediately came over with her official cupcake club apron for the evening. Johnny Depp as Captain Jack Sparrow.

"A pirate is a girl's best friend," she said with a penciled eyebrow wiggle.

Franco introduced Honey to Charlotte Bhandari, who had known Lani since they were in culinary school. She was striking with her beautiful, long black hair and exotic Indian accent. Honey had thought her more formal than the rest of the crew until she and Lani shared a snicker over the inadvertently phallic results of a roulade gone terribly wrong.

Honey had also been introduced to Dre, who'd been there since the start of the club along with Alva and Charlotte. She learned their get-togethers had begun a few years before when they'd stayed after hours with Lani while she worked off her brand-new bakery—and new re-lationship—stresses by, what else . . . baking. Dre was in her early twenties, a recent art school grad and dedicated foodie who had met Lani when she'd proposed a shop logo and marketing ideas as part of a school project. She'd been Lani's first part-time hire, and though she now worked full-time for a graphic art and ad agency in Savannah, she still pitched in when she could and seldom missed a "bitchy bake" as Alva called it. Honey was mostly fasci-nated by Dre's midnight blue Mohawk, eyebrow piercing, and what looked like a gorgeous fairy tattoo on the back of her neck.

Honey met Kit, of peanut pie fame and manager of the about-to-open Babycakes, and got a good look at the in-credible piece of artwork designed by Dre that was the of-ficial Babycakes shop apron. A map of Sugarberry had been turned into the most complex, delightful, fully de-tailed fairyland Honey had ever seen. "We definitely have to talk," she blurted out in awe and already in love with Dre's artistic point of view.

"Coolness," Dre said in what was her standard, under-stated demeanor—which didn't translate at all into an un-derstated passion for what she did. Immediately, she produced a sheaf of drawing paper and slid it across the worktable to Honey. "I checked out your website. Awe-some work. I had some ideas for signage, postcards, shop aprons. If you're interested."

Honey flipped open the folder, and her jaw had dropped straight to the floor as she glanced through the first few pages. "Oh my God. These are"—she looked up at Dre—"coolness."

The corner of Dre's mouth crooked into something that resembled a grin. Or it could have been the lip ring. Ei-

ther way, she seemed happy, then ducked her head and
went back to work on some elaborate chocolate structure
Honey couldn't begin to describe.

Riley was the only one missing from the festivities. She
and Quinn Brannigan—the drop-dead gorgeous, famous
Southern mystery author—had taken her houseboat down
to the Keys to meet up with some foodie friends from her
Chicago days. She'd done all the food styling for Baxter
and Lani's latest cookbook, and had done a mouth-water-
ing job. Honey knew that firsthand as Lani had gifted her
with an advanced copy, signed by all three of them.

Honey had seen Lani's hot British hubby on television,
and had met Kit's significant other Morgan briefly in the
alley behind the garage when her mind had been on other
things, but not so much that she hadn't noticed he was
also quite gorgeous. If aunt Bea hadn't already dearly departed, she'd have killed her for not mentioning the
ridiculousness that was the stunning male population on
Sugarberry.

Of course, Bea had spent her formative years in Hollywood and Vegas, so maybe good-looking men had just
been a blur of sexy grins and six-pack abs for her. Of
course, that made Honey think immediately of Dylan.
Thank you for leaving one for me, she thought with a private
grin.

"Taste test," Alva called out above the thumping bass
beat of Vicki Sue Robinson singing "Turn the Beat
Around." It was disco night at Cupcake Club.

"I'm game." Honey gladly put down the pastry bag Lani
had trusted her with. She could handle sharp carving tools
with ease, could mold a lump of clay into the cutest little
garden sprite you'd ever seen . . . but give her a bag filled
with rich, creamy Italian mascarpone and hazelnut filling
and ask her to shoot it into little carved out cupcake holes
and . . . well . . . let's just say she made a better taste tester.

"Oh, look. They are too cute!" Honey watched as Alva carefully lifted out one of the perfect little miniature apple pies and set it on a tiny plate.

"You don't have to go to all the trouble," Honey assured her. "Just give me a fork."

"Oh no, dear. This pie is meant to be eaten only one way."

Lani popped up behind Alva with a carton of vanilla ice cream and a big metal scoop. "A la mode! After this early heat wave we've been having, we're all taste testing this one."

Franco groaned. "I'm so glad you talked me into staying," he said around a mouthful of ice cream and pie. "But I'm going to hate you in the morning. Fair warning."

"It's really wonderful," Honey agreed. "Like your own individual cupcake."

"Only it's pie," Kit said, her eyes closed in bliss as she licked her spoon. "I'm sorry. I know cupcakes are my future, but Alva, this is a genius tribute to my past."

"Well, you're the one who helped figure out the recipe," Alva said, but it was clear she was loving the adoration and praise.

Lani and Honey ended up at the industrial kitchen sink at the same time with their empty tins and spoons. "I haven't had the chance to even tell you," Lani said, "but Morgan put together a folder for you. It has all the documents—copies of the lease agreement, the licenses, and inspections we went through during renovations, including the agreement signatures of the management company—okaying every change."

"Lani, I didn't think you did anything wrong—"

"I know, but I still feel like I've put you out on the curb. And as my new landlord, you'll need all of this stuff, anyway."

"I got copies of most of it this morning from the courthouse and management company, but it'll be good to have both sets in case I've missed anything."

"So . . . it's true, about the bookstore space?" Lani clasped a hand to her chest. "I have to tell you, I'm so relieved and excited for you. Is it—are you okay with it?"

"I'm a little overwhelmed, to be honest. It's bigger and in need of an undetermined amount of work because it's been empty so long." Honey couldn't stop the smile from turning up the corners of her mouth. "But I am excited. It's really the perfect space. Better than Bea's would have been, to be honest, if I can get it where I want to. I'll know more in the next few days after I get it looked over."

"Oh! I can give you a list of everyone who did work for me, renovating this place and Bea's—with notes on who to use, and who to run screaming from."

Honey laughed. "Thank you. That's a big help."

"I almost hate to ask this because things seem to be turning out decently, but . . . have you figured out where you'll be staying?"

"Staying? Oh, I'll . . ." Honey more or less froze. She'd been so focused on the should she–shouldn't she question of taking Dylan up on his offer, she hadn't even thought about that part. She couldn't afford to keep paying B&B rates for a room, so . . . huh. "I haven't figured that part out yet," she admitted. "Maybe I'll camp out at the store space, at least for the time being. It would be convenient, anyway." *Not to mention cost-effective.*

Lani frowned. "I haven't been in any of those buildings, but I know they've been closed up for at least a decade or more. I can't imagine it's livable, at least not before you do some work to it. Plumbing, lighting, air, I mean. You have no idea—"

"I know," Honey said. "Don't remind me."

"I'm sorry," Lani said, instantly contrite. "I'm not trying to rain on your parade. When I found this little place empty and made the decision to relocate here permanently to stay close to my dad, and to start something under my own name it was terrifying and thrilling all at the same time. If anyone had told me how hard it was going to be to get it up and running, I'd have hopped the next train back to New York. All I can say is, there will be those days, a lot of them, but hang in there." A smile creased her face that was nothing short of blissful. "It's all worth it, trust me. And then some."

"I hope so," Honey said, intimidated and bolstered. "Don't worry about the rest of it. I'll figure it out. I did want to ask you one thing. No one seems to know where my aunt might have stored her personal things. I found out she took most of her furniture and things like that when she moved to the senior center, but none of her personal effects—the things she gathered over a lifetime, her mementos, photo albums, that sort of thing—are at the center. Neither her attorney nor the management company have them, either. I thought she was still living over her shop, so is it possible she left anything there? Or had it stored somewhere on the island when she moved to Savannah?"

"She did!" Lani put her hand to her forehead. "I'm so sorry. I completely forgot about that. We turned the upstairs into Kit's office and storage, but yes, yes, there is a big old steamer trunk and some other boxes. I was going to ask the management company what to do with them, but never got around to it. They're tucked in a back corner and, honestly . . . I sort of forgot about them. I'm so sorry!"

"No, no, that's okay." Honey's heart squeezed and emotion choked her throat, so it took a moment before she could continue. She'd have something of her aunt's after all, and she hadn't realized how much that really meant to her. "I'll . . . I'll arrange to have it all moved over to the shop space. I'm just—"

She paused, dipped her chin, and pushed at the corners of her eyes. "Thank you," she said, smiling through the glimmer of tears. "Truly. It's all been such a shock, but that makes it more bearable, more . . . tangible. I—thank you."

"You let us know whenever you're ready and I'll have it taken over. No hurry. If you want to go up and look through it all before moving stuff, that's fine, too. Whatever is good for you. I feel so bad. If Kit wasn't still living in the apartment upstairs over this place, I'd invite you there, but with Morgan having Lilly and all, they're being a bit more careful about her staying at his place and—"

"Stop. It's fine," Honey said, realizing it really was. "Nothing may be going as I'd thought it would, but it's all going. I've got something to work toward and that's all I really wanted. Meeting you all tonight, having everyone so open, and so . . . understanding has been great. You can't know how much that means to me. You really can't."

"I can't claim to know what it's like to be that isolated, no," Lani said. "My life in pastry kitchens was the exact opposite. I might have wished I had your life then." She laughed. "And I'll have you know it's still killing me not to hug you right now. But I do know something about wanting to start over, wanting something for yourself . . . to be respected for your work, and to build something worth growing. I got so much more than I ever bargained for, coming here. If you talk to Kit or Charlotte or Riley or Franco, they'll all tell you the same thing. You came to the right place, Honey. None of us are 'normal,' you know?" She grinned as she made quotes.

"It's like the island of misfit toys, only we're bakers and stylists and . . . well . . . and carvers. I can't wait to see your work. I can't even imagine looking at a chunk of wood or a lump of clay and seeing something in it.

"I can't imagine looking at butter, eggs, flour, and sugar and whipping up the things you do. I'm lucky to scramble an egg and make a decent piece of toast."

"Well, you come to our bitchy bake nights and we'll make a baker out of you yet. Or just give you a place to bitch. Trust me . . . you're going to need it."

Honey laughed. "Gee, thanks. I mean that. And I might take you up on it. The bitching and the baking. I know I will master the first, but you have your work cut out for you with the second."

There was a knock on the back door, right next to where they were standing. Honey looked over to spy Dylan on the other side of the screen door. It was pitch black outside. She glanced at the clock on the opposite wall, shocked to discover it was after ten o'clock. She looked back and caught Dylan's gaze.

He touched two fingers to his forehead in a little salute. "Taxi service, ma'am."

Lani looked at Dylan, smiled, then looked back at Honey, then back at Dylan . . . and her smile grew wider. She leaned closer to Honey and, out of the corner of her mouth, whispered, "I know I'm totally stepping over all boundaries here and risking the start of a very good friendship, but if a guy who looked like him looked at me the way he's looking at you . . ."

From the corner of her mouth, Honey said, "You forget, I know what your husband looks like."

Lani's grin was broad and devilishly wicked. "Exactly. And I married him." She looked at Lani and winked. "Just sayin'."

"Not before he had to all but drag her by the hair into his proverbial man cave," Charlotte put in. She had come up to stand behind them. "Whereas I, on the other hand, jumped Carlo at the very earliest opportunity. And every chance I got after that. Still do, in fact.

"Yes, but you're a slut," Lani said in the way only best friends could.

"Unrepentant-until-I'm-too-tired-to-see-straight slut," Charlotte responded with that elegant accent of hers that made it much more amusing. She glanced at Honey. "And trust me, we have way more fun. Lani knows this to be true as well. Once you join the unrepentant slut club, you never go back. It's all about finding the suitable member of the opposite sex for initiation."

"And I've heard he has a very suitable . . . member," Lani murmured, then snickered, while Charlotte kept a perfect ladylike smile on her face.

Honey's mouth dropped open.

"You comin', sugar?" Dylan asked quite innocently.

All three women choked on gales of laughter. The deeper his scowl, the harder they laughed.

Alva came over and pressed a paper bag into Honey's hands. "Give him some pie and he won't be so surly. I put a few in there." She leaned closer. "Bribe as needed."

Honey took the bag, hung up her apron, and thanked everyone. "I'll come back by tomorrow to get the folder and talk about . . . everything."

"Everything?" Lani asked, and Charlotte wiggled her eyebrows.

Honey almost lost it all over again, but managed to leave through the screen door Dylan held open before he abandoned her there for the night, leaving her to walk back to the B&B. It suddenly occurred to her she probably wouldn't have had to walk back. She could have asked any number of people for a ride. Her people.

"Good night, I take it?" Dylan asked as they crossed the alley.

She looked at him and beamed. "The best. Dylan, I have friends!"

Chapter 13

For the next week and a half, it was the memory of that smile on her face that kept Dylan from wishing he'd never offered to let her move in next door. Not because she was pestering him with questions or asking for his help, quite the opposite. Her bike would be parked in the alley behind the bookstore when he arrived at his garage in the morning and would still be there when he closed up shop at night. The only way to see her or talk to her was to poke his head in and see how she was doing.

She'd always stop whatever she was doing and make time to talk with him, bring him up to date on how things were going, but he could see her mind was racing on to the million and one things she had to do—all of which were detailed on the clipboard never far from her hand. He'd managed to go thirty-one years without having her around, so why it was bugging him that she was so unavailable to him he had no idea.

"Dude, you're pouting. Not cool. You need to man up."

Dylan lifted his head from working on Honey's old Beetle to give Dell a withering glare. Of course, Dell being Dell, it didn't so much as faze him.

"Chicks don't dig it when guys get clingy."

Dylan bent back over the engine. "For your information, I don't pout and I don't cling. Never have, don't plan on starting now." He caught his knuckle on the carburetor piston valve spring and swore a blue streak, thankful for the opportunity. He sucked at the blood, spit out the grease, then pressed the gash against his T-shirt until it stopped bleeding. "Least she could do is ask about how things turned out with Frank," he muttered. "Ask someone a favor, you should follow up. That's all I'm sayin'."

"You should ask her out on a date. Get her out of the shop and away from work." Dell looked up from shelving air filters and lining up quarts of synthetic oil and grinned. "Then she can focus all her attention and make it all about you."

"I hired you, you know. I can fire you."

"Then who will be nice to your customers? Who will talk to Mrs. Bingle three times a day when she brings her car in every other week, convinced that her late husband jinxed it before he died? And who will listen to Ned Stultz tell us how he worked on Jeeps in the Army, and if anyone knows how to take apart and put together an engine, it's him? Of course, that does his Cadillac no good whatsoever. And who—"

"Okay, okay. Anyone ever tell you you're annoying as hell?"

Dell grinned. "Daily. And they're all grateful to you for offering me a job and keeping me out of their hair and off the mean streets of Sugarberry."

"Don't be a smartass."

"Too late for that."

Dylan shook his head as a smile creased the corners of his mouth, thankful the hood of the car prevented Dell from it. For all the kid talked like a seasoned veteran of dating and life, he was all of fourteen and had never been anywhere farther than Savannah. Still, he was fourteen going on forty. Too smart for his own good and twice as observant. He was some kind of kid genius who'd been doing college level schoolwork by the time he hit middle school age.

Patsy Miller, his poor mother whom Dylan had known since their own high school days, was a single mom who had tried her best to keep Dell grounded and involved with other kids his age. She'd finally given in and let him graduate early and start taking courses at the community college just over the causeway. Problem was, she worked full-time on the other side of Savannah, and had been at her wits' end, since the kid wasn't even old enough to drive yet.

Fortunately for Dylan, the kid's freakish knowledge extended to car engines. Unlike Ned Stultz, Dylan was pretty sure Dell could actually take apart and put a Jeep engine, or any engine, back together . . . probably blindfolded. The kid could look at a diagram or schematic one time and know it by heart. Same with shop manuals.

He'd hired the boy part-time right after opening up the new location. It helped Dylan out, and gave Dell a place to be when he wasn't in class. Dylan had helped find the old motorbike Dell had bought with money he'd saved up from birthdays and Christmas since he'd been ten or eleven. They'd found salvage parts and an old manual, and Dell had fixed the thing up so now he had a way to get over the bridge to class and to work.

While his constant stream of chatter might annoy Dylan no end, truth was, the customers loved it and him. Dell's winning smile and his tow-headed, brown-eyed good looks that made him seem like the poster boy for the Got Milk campaign and the Boy Scouts all rolled into one didn't hurt matters, either. The older women fawned over him like a beloved grandson and the men all thought he was a fine, upstanding young man, a role model for American youth. God help Dylan when the kid was old enough that the women started flirting with him and the guys started leaning on him to go out for a beer and shoot some pool.

Had he asked for that headache? No, he had not. He didn't want to worry about the kid, much less what kind of young man he was going to become. All he'd wanted was some part-time help. If it allowed Patsy not to worry so much about her kid, so much the better.

"So, have you asked her out? I mean, like on a real date? Because women really dig—"

"Just what is it you think you know about women, anyway? You're like, twelve."

"I'll be fifteen in five months, three weeks, four days and"—he glanced at the wall clock—"about five hours. Mom went into labor with me at three in the morning on a Tuesday, but it took her seventeen hours—"

"Spare me. Please."

Dell switched gears without even taking a breath. "Even if you just take her to Laura Jo's for lunch or something, I bet she'd really like that. She hasn't met all that many folks yet. Everyone is talking about her."

Dylan straightened and looked around the hood of the car. "Talking about her how?"

"Oh, you know, new person on the island kind of thing. I guess there's some chatter about her being Bea's niece and all. Folks are wondering if she's got Miss Bea's . . . you know . . . mad skills. Not mad as in, you know, *crazy*. It's just an expression. It means, like amazing or—"

"I know what it means."

"I was the first one to meet her, you know. When she got here, I mean. I thought she was cool. Funky glasses, sick artwork, like stitched right to her jeans. She didn't seem much like Miss Bea at all. I mean, Miss Bea was all grandmotherly and awesome, but Miss Honey, she's young and so cool."

"Too old for me, I know," he quickly added when Dylan's eyebrows rose. "I heard she, you know, knows things even more than Miss Bea did, way more. Mrs. Hughes was saying how she kept Mr. Hughes from getting himself killed, keeping him off John John Hughes's trawler last Monday before that storm came up."

"I kept Frank Hughes off John John's trawler last Monday."

"Right, yeah, but after it all worked out, Miss Honey told Mrs. Hughes she was thankful he hadn't been hurt and I guess it all came out about how she had some kind of spooky-like vision of him getting gaffed in the thigh. How awesome is that? It's like she's got a superpower."

Dylan scowled and ducked back under the hood. Drag his ass into meddling with folks and then come right on out and tell them she had a premonition. Why even bother getting him to do the dirty work for her, that's what he wanted to know. Probably just as well they weren't spending time together. Probably a sign he should get his focus back on his work and leave her to getting the shop ready for the inspectors to come check it out, see what kind of code issues she was dealing with.

That reminded him. He needed to tell her he had a guy who'd handle any electrical problems she might have for little more than cost. The guy owed him a favor for digging up a part for his '76 Mustang Cobra.

Dylan swore under his breath. It was like she'd taken up permanent residence inside his brain. He really did need to stop thinking about her, get her damn car fixed, and get back to life as usual. She was staying and she'd be working right next door. That didn't mean they had to push things between them, personally.

So he'd gotten a little caught up in it, in her. It had been a while and that was probably part of it . . . and the heat made folks do things they might not otherwise do. The storm had come, blown the heat out with it, and spring weather had returned . . . along with his sanity.

At least that's what he kept telling himself.

"Folks are wondering if she'll, you know, help them out, like Miss Bea did. You think she'll be taking appointments for that kind of thing? I read up on it a little and—"

"No, she won't be taking appointments. She's an artist, not a—she's an artist, and that's it, okay? The only thing she's going to help anyone do is add a few grins to their gardens and knickknack shelves and maybe teach them to whittle or sculpt something. Don't go bugging her about that other stuff, you hear?"

When Dell didn't respond, Dylan ducked around the hood again. "I mean it, Dell. She didn't come here for that."

Dell wasn't paying attention to him. He was looking out the open bay door, frowning. Dylan followed his gaze and saw the thin trail of smoke.

"I think it's coming from next door," Dell said.

"Shit." Dylan tossed his wrench in the tool box, grabbed the grease rag, and was still wiping his hands as he ran next door. He started to pound on the door, but decided there was no time for that and tried the knob. *Unlocked, thank God.* No smoke in the immediate storage room and the door wasn't hot to the touch, but as soon as he opened it, he could see the gray haze in the front room. "Honey?" he called out. "Honey!"

He tried not to let visions of the last time he'd run into a smoke-filled building fill his brain, but it was pretty damn impossible not to. It made his bark a bit louder than absolutely necessary; the smoke was little more than a thin haze. Maybe he'd caught it just in time.

He heard coughing coming from just past the bathroom and break room, and ran to that door. Also not hot to the touch, it led to the other ground floor back room. "Honey?" he called out as he opened the door . . . only to stop just inside, where he found her crouched on the floor.

She was hunched over a small hibachi, having just squelched what appeared to be a little grease fire. Or breakfast. A huge industrial size fan was propped up on the top of a big steamer trunk, running loudly at full force, trying to suck the smoke out and force it through the small window that had barely been cranked open.

"What in the hell are you doing?"

She let out short squeal of surprise and leaped to her feet, almost upending the hibachi and the fan in the process. Hand clutched to her chest, she turned on him. "Holy crap, I think you just took five years off my life."

"I've been shouting your name, but I guess you couldn't hear me over the vortex of fans here. What the hell happened?"

She scowled at him as she crouched back down and tried to fork off some charred black ruins that appeared permanently adhered to the grill surface. "Nothing. I just got caught up with some stuff I'm clearing out upstairs and sort of forgot I was making breakfast."

It was only then that Dylan had the presence of mind to look around the room, spying a futon, an open suitcase, a small cooler, the stack of boxes she'd retrieved from her car when she'd moved into the Hughes's place, and the rest of the stuff she'd hauled out of the car earlier in the week.

"Are you . . . living here?"

"Would that be violating some other kind of code? Never mind, don't answer that. I just got off the phone with the inspector who came by yesterday and I'm pretty sure there is no code left that I'm not already in violation of, so what's one more?"

He couldn't recall ever seeing her so out of sorts. It shouldn't have wanted to make him smile, but given he'd been out of sorts for the past week and a half, it seemed only fair. "I'll take a look at the list. Maybe I can help."

"I didn't ask for your help. I can figure it out."

Grinning, he entered the room. Fully cognizant that he was risking sending her into a vision, or possibly getting whacked upside the head with a burnt hibachi, he gently took her arm and hauled her to her feet.

She didn't jerk her arm away, neither did she bean him with anything, or go all weird in the face, so he took that as encouragement and tugged her closer. "Bad day, sugar? Week, maybe?"

She ducked her chin and let out a long breath, swore through another one, which made him chuckle. Before she could punch him, or worse, he pulled her into his arms and tipped her face up to his. "Getting a place up and going sucks. I know. More bad days than good at first. But it gets better."

"I know, but—"

"Shh. It gets better faster when you let folks who are willing to help out do just that. Like I said, you'll have ample opportunity to repay the favors down the line."

"I appreciate that, I do. It's just the inspector was—pardon my language—a real . . . jerkface."

"Jerkface, huh. Wow."

She lowered one brow and scowled. "Okay, he was a completely asinine, wholly arrogant, condescending dick-wad. There, I said it."

"Feel better?"

"Some." She said it grudgingly, and tried to shift her gaze to a point past his shoulder.

It struck him that this was the first time he'd really had her in his arms, at least, in the traditional way. He was rather enjoying how well they matched up. He shifted slightly until he caught her gaze again. "I can think of something that might take that *some* and turn it into *more*."

She turned her gaze fully back to him. "Why do men think that sex is always the answer to every problem?"

He grinned and lowered his head. "Because it often is." He brushed his lips over hers. "Or, at the very least, provides a nice break from your worries. Come here," he murmured, and took her mouth slowly as if they had all the time in the world.

She surprised him by sighing against his lips and relaxing into the kiss, into him.

Just like that, slow and languorous was the last thing he wanted. His body growled to life, pulsing hot and hard as he fought the urge to take her the way he'd imagined taking her pretty much every night for the past week and a half.

"I missed this," she said on a sigh when he finally lifted his head.

All the mad he'd built up over the past week and a half vanished. "I'm right next door, sugar. No need to miss anything." He kissed her again.

She sighed and let her forehead drop to his chest when he lifted his head again. She felt relaxed and her mad was gone, too.

"It does cure what ails you," he said.

"Don't gloat," she replied, but the dry humor was back, and she was still soft and snugged up against him.

"I'll apologize now because I've probably gotten axle grease and God knows what else on you."

She lifted her gaze to his. "I'm covered in cobwebs, dust, dirt, and reek of burnt bacon. I think we can consider it an even trade."

"Your glasses are fogged."

She smiled somewhat smugly. "I know." Then she put her cheek right back against his damp and dirty work shirt. "At least this time it's for a good reason."

He pressed a kiss to the top of her head. "Good God your hair stinks."

"Sweet talker," she murmured.

He chuckled. "Tell you what. Why don't I leave you to the fun and excitement that is your day, while I go back and try not to give in to the temptation to just push your Bug into the channel rather than working to fix the damn thing. Then, when we've had enough of that, what say we clean ourselves up and go out to eat some food together like grown-ups do."

She lifted her head, eyebrows arched above her horn rims. "Are you asking me out on a date?"

"Dell told me chicks dig stuff like that."

Honey giggled. "Dell is wise beyond his years."

"I know. It sort of bites, when you think about it. Fourteen, pretty sure he's a virgin . . . and he has more game than me."

"We all have our strengths. Hey!" she said when he pinched her behind.

"Is it a date?"

"Yes. I accept. I'd love to. Fair warning, though."

"Hey!" he said when she pinched him right back. "Sneaky."

"Like I said, we all have our strengths."

He kissed the tip of her nose. "I'd offer to clean your glasses on my shirt, but I'm pretty sure that would just make them worse."

"You smell like engine grease, and now, bacon smoke. So yeah, thanks, but, no."

Grinning, he dipped his head and stole another hard, fast kiss, risking that he'd have to wander around the block or something to let his body settle down before heading back next door. It was well worth it.

"Bring the stuff from the inspector with you and we'll look over it while we eat."

"I'm pretty sure that's in the Things Not To Do part of the dating handbook. But this chick? Yeah, she'd dig that." She tipped up on her toes and kissed him on the cheek. "Thanks. For helping. And being patient. I'm getting there."

Dylan could have told her about the very last thing he'd been feeling this past week was patient, but however he'd gotten to this moment, it had been worth the struggle. "Eight o'clock?"

"That works."

He reluctantly let her go, then went over and gave the old-fashioned louvered window handle a good yank and cranked it fully open. "I'll get the other ones in the storage room on my way out."

"My hero. Thank you."

He shot her a wink. "My pleasure, sugar."

He was back in the garage, head under the hood before he realized he was whistling again. He just grinned and put a little more effort into it.

Chapter 14

"I can't thank you enough." Honey pushed her glasses up and shifted her satchel higher onto her shoulder. "The plumber is scheduled for Friday, and then I'll be out of your hair."

Kit stopped folding the little individual cupcake boxes and smiled at her. "It's really absolutely no problem. Lani and I feel like we've kicked you out of your own home. The least we can do is let you use the bathroom and shower in the building you own. You've got a key to the separate second floor entrance, so anytime you want. Truly. I just wish there was enough room up there for you to camp out. You could have kept the trunk and boxes up there longer. They weren't in the way."

"It's okay. I've been going through them little by little, so it's easier to have them with me at the bookstore. And no more apologies. It's all going to work out for the best. Once I get a handle on what needs to be done, things should move a little faster."

Kit laughed. "Don't count on it, sister. Lani and I thought we'd have this place ready to go a lot sooner than it's taken us."

"But you only started the actual renovation last fall, right? That's actually not too bad considering how much you had to change the function of the place."

"Maybe it's just felt like five years," Kit said with a smile. She looked around at the cheerful, kitschy vintage baking décor that matched the feeling of Cakes by the Cup interior, the bright sunshiny colors, and the charming, storybook feel of the Dre-designed signage. "Even if it had taken that long, it would have been worth it. It's not mine, but it sure feels like it."

Honey studied Kit as she looked around at her little shop. She was about the same height and build as Honey, but with short red hair that provided a lively frame for captivating blue eyes. She had a quick smile and always seemed animated. Honey imagined Kit and Morgan together. With his dark good looks and easygoing demeanor, they would make quite the striking couple. "I can't even believe this was once Bea's shop. It looks like you're all set to open your doors."

"One more week. Next Sunday," Kit said, all but humming with excitement. "You have to drop in. We're giving away little mini cupcake treats." She pointed at rows of smaller boxes she'd already folded, perched on the shelves behind her. "Cutest things ever. And discount cards for our Cater Your Cupcake and Cupcakes Gone Postal services. I know you won't need the latter, but hey, you have to open your shop at some point and what better way to celebrate than with a catered cupcake party? We do custom cakes, so we could do some fun toppers to go with your adorable creations. I looked at your catalog online and I have some ideas if you're interested. I'm picturing little gnome tops, and Dre does the most amazing sugar work. She makes these stunning spun fairy wings."

Honey laughed. "Oh, you're good."

Kit beamed and curtsied. "I sold a lot of pie in my day."

"So I heard. I'm sorry, about what happened with your family's business. Alva mentioned it to me," Honey said by way of explanation. "That's brutal."

"It was," Kit replied readily. "In some ways, I can't believe it's been less than a year ago since I came here and took Lani's job offer. I feel like Atlanta was a lifetime ago. A very different lifetime." She smiled, clearly happy and content. "If you'd told me I'd come here and find not only a new career path, but a family, a community, a home—I wouldn't have believed it possible. Part of me feels like I've been here forever, but Sugarberry is like that." She gave Honey a reassuring look. "You'll understand. You'll be so glad you came here, Honey."

"I already am. At first I was ready to turn around and head back home." Honey smiled. "It was probably a good thing my car broke down, or I might have. But I already do understand what you're saying, and I am glad I'm staying. Everyone has been so . . . just so great. I wasn't expecting that. Other than my parents and Bea, I've never had people be so welcoming, much less so understanding, or . . . or open to dealing with my—

"Oh crap." She reached up and dabbed at the tears that had sprung to the corners of her eyes. "I never cry. Now I swear I do it all the time. I'm going to ruin my makeup." She laughed and hiccupped. "I never wear makeup."

Kit came bustling around the corner and handed her a few napkins with the Babycakes logo on the front. "Here, here. I'm sorry."

"No, don't be. Good tears." Honey laughed as she was forced to sniffle. "You have no idea what it's meant for me. You all have accepted me so openly and willingly. Even the parts I was fully prepared to hide at all costs."

Kit gave her an understanding smile, but her eyes sparkled. "Well, I'm not going to lie. I've been dying to ask you all about your secret talent. I didn't have the chance to know your aunt, I'm sorry to say, but I've heard so many amazing things about her. And Barbara Hughes can't stop talking about how you saved her husband's life."

"Well, I wouldn't go that far. It was—"

"It was amazing is what it was. She didn't even realize you'd had a vision, and right there on her porch. Alva is beside herself that she didn't get to break the news in her column, you know."

Honey's expression fell. "She asked to interview me, but . . . I didn't even think about that when I was talking to Barbara. I mean, I wasn't planning on telling her, I was just following up because Dylan had talked to Frank to make sure he didn't go out on the boat when that storm came, and I wanted to make sure—what?" Honey broke off when she saw Kit was obviously trying to swallow a knowing smile.

"Oh, nothing . . . except . . . we're all dying to know how you got Dylan Ross, man of few words and even fewer social appearances, to do that. I mean, he gives new meaning to tall, dark, and brooding."

Honey sniffled and sputtered out a laugh at the same time. "You know, that's exactly what I thought when I first met him, almost verbatim. And, you're right, he's not exactly the chatty type, not normally anyway. But when he does talk, it's because he's given it a lot of thought. And he means what he says. He does sincerely care about this island and the people on it. He helps out where he can, doing what he can do. I still don't know the whole story about his family history—and I don't need to. He'll tell me if he wants me to know. But I know it was a rough one and that he's had his share of being in a spotlight he never asked for. I completely understand how that feels.

"Still, it hasn't stopped him from being loyal, or from caring," Honey went on. "Do you know he spends personal time tracking down old tractor and lawnmower parts for the older men on the island who don't get around well or don't understand how to use computers to do vintage parts searches? Dell told me Dylan helped him find that

old motorbike and track down parts for it. He even took
Dell out and introduced him to the salvage guys he works
with, taught him how to search old junkyards. Dylan
might pretend that Lolly is some kind of obligation, but he
ran into a burning building to rescue her, then paid what
had to be a crazy vet bill to have her—" Honey broke off
and a little heat climbed into her cheeks as Kit stopped trying to hide a wide grin.

"It's okay. You like him. And what's not to like? He
might be tall, dark, and mysterious, but no one has anything bad to say about him. They just . . . no one here
seems to know him very well. But it sounds like you're
getting to and that he's a pretty good guy. Also sounds like
the feeling is mutual. From what I understand, he's very
protective of you."

Honey bristled a little at that. "He doesn't have to be.
I've taken care of myself all this time, and—"

"No, no, I didn't mean it like that. Well, I did, but not
because he thinks you need protecting. And . . . well, it's
kind of nice, isn't it? To have someone who wants to stand
up for you, even if you don't need him to?"

Honey heard the emotion in Kit's voice, and realized
she was talking from personal experience. "Is that how it
is with you and Morgan?"

"We have each other's back, yes, and we seemed to
have a need to do that for each other. I don't know why
or how two people connect. I never had before. But when
you do, it's natural, and instinctive. Riley and Quinn are
like that. In spades. Completely adorable together. Have
you met them yet?"

Honey shook her head, but Kit kept right on talking.
"Listening to you talk about Dylan, it's clear you two have
the same thing." She laughed. "I'm betting he'd be just as
bristly at the idea that you're protective of him. You know
he doesn't need it, but you're in his corner all the same."

Honey hadn't thought about it like that, nor had she really examined what she thought about the dynamic of her relationship with Dylan. But, maybe Kit had a point. "I really don't know what we have. I-I'll be honest, I haven't had a relationship, or tried to have one, since I was in college, so to say I'm out of practice—hell, I never even had practice, not really."

Kit nodded and lifted her hands and bowed a little. "Sister, you're talking to a woman who was married to pie for her entire life. Trust me. In this case, it's not like riding a bicycle. In fact, no previous experience is required. When the right person comes into your life, you figure it out as you go along, because you can't imagine doing anything else." Kit gestured to Honey's stitched floral skirt and rose colored, cap sleeve sweater. "Which is why you need to get out of here and go start your date. Start figuring it out." She folded her hands and braced them under her chin and batted her eyelashes. "Then come to Cupcake Club tomorrow night and tell us every last detail. Not that we're begging you. We're above that . . . except we're totally not."

Honey laughed. "I don't kiss and tell, but—"

"So, you've kissed him? I mean, Morgan thought you might have been . . . you know, when he walked up on you two in the alley that night. Seriously, is it as smoldering as we all know it has to be?"

Honey's laugh spluttered. "You're actually not kidding, are you?"

Kit shamelessly shook her head.

"You forget, I've seen Morgan," Honey said. "He's . . . well, he's stunning."

Kit beamed. "True, all true. I am the luckiest girl in the world, trust me. Plus? He's a great kisser. But Dylan is something of an island legend, an enigma, the ultimate mystery man, at least when it comes to members of the opposite sex. I'm told he never dates anyone who lives on the island. Not that it's stopped women of all ages from trying. Then you're here for five seconds and wham! I hope you'll forgive me for saying this, but we didn't peg you as his type. Not that anyone really knows what his type is. But we figured the cliché—blond, fake boobs— because we're shallow and unimaginative. But you're cool and interesting, and this kind of wild mix of ethereal with those eyes, and funky-bohemian with your clothes and awesome glasses. Honestly, don't tell me you made that skirt, because that stitch work is amazing. If you did, then why you don't sell stuff like that in your catalog, I have no idea. Anyway, everyone is curious. How did you do it?"

Honey's mouth had long since dropped open, but when Kit ran out of steam, she snapped it shut again. "I . . . well, thank you. About the skirt. I did make it, and no, I hadn't ever thought about including clothes in my catalog." She smiled. "But I might now."

"So, how did it start with you and Dylan? I mean . . . did he flirt with you? Because I can't even picture that. Not because of you," Kit rushed to add. "He just doesn't seem the type to do anything overt like that. I figure he never had to, since women probably throw themselves on him. At him, I mean. Well, probably on him, too." She laughed, even as her fair skin turned a little pink.

Honey laughed, too, mostly because from the moment she'd laid eyes on Dylan, she'd wanted to jump him. "Actually, he wasn't remotely attracted to me. In fact, I'm pretty sure he thought I was nuts. But then, when I think how I leaped out of my skin around him, it's not a surprise. I was a little bit nuts." She gave Kit a self-deprecating smile. "I hadn't been around people for a long time, and he was . . . a lot to be around. So I was kind of jumpy. I guess it started because I had a vision when he grabbed my arms to keep me from dropping stuff I was getting out of my car. And . . . I don't know, things changed after that."

"Well, I guess they would! Was the vision about him? Of course it was," Kit answered herself. "Did it freak him out?"

"No, that's just it. It didn't freak him out. In fact, he was really matter-of-fact about it, and . . . it stunned me to have someone sort of shrug and accept what had happened for what it was. I mean, he asked some questions and tried to understand it better, but then we sort of moved on as if it was just one of those things you make allowances for. Like being allergic to stuff, or . . . you know?"

"I don't," Kit admitted. "I mean, I understand it, but I can't imagine dealing with it."

Honey shrugged, feeling a little more self-conscious, but it was more a kneejerk reaction than because she felt uncomfortable. "He told me I should just own it. Put it out there as if it were just a natural part of me and expect folks to deal with it. And so . . . I have been doing that. Well, little by little. I think that's why I told Barbara Hughes."

"Normalize it. I do get that. Well, Barbara thinks you're the best thing since guardian angels. You've seen her B&B, so you know she has a thing for angels."

Honey laughed. "You know, I hadn't really thought about that, but you're right, she does have a few pillows and stitched samplers with a running theme."

"Well, I understand more now why Dylan is protective of you. He might want you to own your special skills, but after being up close and personal with what happens when you have them, it's natural he wants to make sure you're protected while you do. And the more we get to know you, the more we'll be able to take care of you, too, if it happens when he's not around." Kit lifted a hand when Honey started to respond. "I know you don't want us to take care of you, but—"

"No, I wasn't going to say that. I mean, I don't want you to have to do anything. But . . . I would be lying if I said I wasn't a little freaked out wondering what will happen when I have one in public. It's just a matter of time. I do pretty well at maintaining my personal space and it's been truly wonderful that you all have respected that. But stuff happens, visions happen. I've had three since I've been here, and he's been there for all of them. So—"

"So, he wants to take care of you." Kit smiled. "I say, let him. Men like to feel like they're taking care of their own, you know? And we want to take care of them right back. Nothing wrong with that."

"You know, you make a lot of sense."

Kit's smile grew wider. "I'm scary like that."

Honey laughed. "It is a little scary, to be honest. I'm looking at things from such wildly new perspectives. Bea tried to tell me, I guess, but with my limited experiences, I couldn't begin to dream of how things could be. I have a good imagination when it comes to creating fanciful creatures, but not so good when it comes to imagining an equally fantastical world where people might actually accept me, weird crap and all."

"Well, if you've been made to feel like an outsider your whole life, it's kind of understandable that you wouldn't be wildly enthusiastic about reaching out to anyone else. I think it's amazing you even tried. You just have to tell us what we can do to make it easier, and we will. Not that we won't screw up." Kit leaned in closer. "And not that there won't be a few who totally won't get it. But they'll be easier to deal with when you have a posse of folks who do."

"My own posse, huh?" Honey grinned. "I kind of like the sound of that."

"I do apologize for grilling you," Kit said. "When I first

got here and started seeing Morgan—who was like the black sheep of the island because of his family—I got subjected to the same thing. I hadn't dated in like, forever, and he was part of the family who'd ruined my business, so . . . I had questions, too. It was complicated."

Honey's eyes widened. "Wow. I didn't know that part."

"Well, he wasn't personally part of it, but it took some sorting out. Have you met Lilly yet?"

"That's his little niece, right? So sad about his brother and Lilly's mom, but really amazing and wonderful that he's taken on raising her."

"She's resilient and wonderful, and well—you'll love her, everyone does. Not that I'm biased or anything." Kit's smile was bright.

Honey thought Lilly was a very fortunate little girl indeed, because she clearly had two people who loved her very much.

"I can't wait for her to see your work, by the way. Alva said something about how you may be teaching classes? If you're thinking of having any clay building type things for children, or maybe children-adult combo classes, sign the two of us up right now."

Honey blinked. "I can see why Lani hired you to launch Babycakes. I'll keep that in mind, about the adult-child classes."

"Perfect! Well, anyway, I'm just trying to warn you. Sugarberry and the people on it . . . we're like the Borg. We'll assimilate you. Lani says it's like living inside the best group hug ever, and I haven't heard it described better than that. And, well . . . who doesn't need that kind of support, right?"

"Right," Honey said, slightly dazed and more than a little dazzled at the same time.

"Great! So, tomorrow night. Cupcake Club. Be there." Kit pointed at Honey. "And you're baking this time."

"I almost burned down the bookstore today just making breakfast. I really don't think you want me to—"

"Yes. We do." Kit started to reach out, take Honey by the hands, then remembered and smiled as she lifted her hands, palms out. "We want you to, okay? Any of it, all of it." She leaned in and lowered her voice slightly, even though they were the only two people in the shop. "And if you don't feel like talking about Dylan, that's fine. For now." Her blue eyes sparkled. "Instead, you can just tell us all about how this vision thing works."

"Oh, you really don't want to—"

"Yes, we do. Really."

Kit had cut her off again, and Honey began to see how she'd run an entire family empire single-handedly.

"Like it or not, Honey, you're one of us now." Kit grinned. "Be afraid. Be very afraid."

Honey was still smiling as she left the shop and headed back across the alley to the bookstore. She should probably stop thinking about it as the bookstore, she realized, and that had her shaking her head.

"What's so funny, sugar?"

She looked up to find Dylan leaning against his pickup truck. She was surprised she didn't trip over her own feet . . . or drool all over them.

Wearing black jeans and a blue polo shirt, he was freshly shaven. His hair, still a little damp, curled over his ears and against his neck. His lips quirked in that way they did, right before that sexy-as-sin grin slid across his handsome face.

Even though she'd anticipated it, it still gave her knees a bit of a wobble, and made her heart skip a beat.

"I was just realizing that I should probably stop thinking about the bookstore as the bookstore, and that led me to thinking about Sugarberry and books. I can't decide if I'm Alice, and have fallen down the rabbit hole, or heading to Oz on the yellow brick road."

"I'm afraid to ask what that would make me, in either scenario."

She stopped walking just in front of him and let her satchel slide down her arm so she could set it by her feet. "You're the Tin Man."

His eyebrows lifted. "You think I'm heartless?"

She smiled up at him. "No, silly. I think you're the one who thought he didn't have a heart, when it was right there, bigger than life, inside you all along."

He did that thing where his gaze went from casual and flirty to intense and probing. Or maybe it was always probing, but the flirty part distracted her. She felt heat climb in her cheeks, thinking perhaps she'd said too much or hit a sore spot. "I'm sorry, that was out of line. I don't even know—"

"You know me, Honey." He said it quietly, watching her from those steady gray eyes of his. "Better than you realize."

She smiled briefly. "Yeah? Well . . . ditto."

"You ready for dinner, Dorothy?"

"Oh, I'm not Dorothy." Her smile came back stronger. "I'm the Cowardly Lion, wishing for courage."

"Then we're more alike than we realized." He uncrossed his ankles and pushed away from the truck, so he stood right in her personal space. "Because I think you're one of the most courageous people I know."

Her heart beat an unsteady tattoo inside her chest and butterflies danced in her stomach. Unsettling feelings . . . and rather thrilling at the same time . . . because no one had ever looked at her the way this man did. "Fool's courage, maybe. You're talking to someone who essentially hid in a barn for the past eight years."

"You're not hiding now."

"Only because my poor, deceased seventy-two year old aunt made it her dying request. A woman who had more courage in her pinky finger than I have in my whole body."

"Whatever gets us taking that first step isn't the point. Taking the step is."

"Was that how you felt when you took over the family business? Or did you always know that was your path?"

"I didn't know much of anything when I was younger, except not to count on anything. Or anyone. I knew I was really good at fixing things. And so was my grandfather, so there was comfort in knowing I'd inherited that trait, but with it came the fear of what else I might have inherited."

Her heart clutched a little. "Dylan—"

"At first, the business was more refuge than path. Maybe something like your carving and sculpting. Your barn was my family repair shop. And, later, my sailboat." He kept his gaze straight on hers.

"You don't have to tell me—"

"Yeah, sugar. I do. You need to know who it is you're involved with."

Her heart pounded a vibrating thrum. "Are we? Getting involved?"

She thought he'd tease her with that sexy grin, but he remained more serious, more straightforward. "I think we already are."

"Dylan—"

"If I'm wrong about that, sugar, now's the time to tell me. And don't make it about the bookstore, or your car, or—"

It was her turn to get serious. "We may be involved, but we're still getting to know each other, so I'm going to pretend you didn't just insinuate that I'd ever get involved with you—or anyone—as payment for services rendered."

"No, that wasn't—" He broke off, swore under his breath. "I'm no good at this, Honey."

"At what?"

"I'm good at fixing things, but figuring out relation-
ships . . . they don't come with a user's manual."

"No, they don't. And I'm hardly an expert, given my
history." She paused, let them both gather their thoughts
for a moment, then said, "Maybe we can just figure one
of them out. This one. Together."

She thought she saw a little tension ease out of his
stance, and only then did she realize . . . he was nervous!
He was worried . . . about her? That she'd what? Turn
him down? Say no thank-you to him?

She grinned, which made him scowl, which made her
grin wider. "I think we understand each other maybe too
well. But, like you said, we just have to make sure we
don't get in our own way."

"What do you mean?"

"We're cave dwellers, you and me. You by nature and
me more from necessity, but still, we don't generally stick
our heads out much. And here we are, sticking out a
whole lot more than that. So, I think, if we want to be . . .
involved, as you say . . . then maybe when we want to pull
our heads in and hide we should realize that's when we're
supposed to do the exact opposite. At least with each
other. Talk through it, stumble through it, whatever. Just,
make sure we say something, and say what we know is
true, and not just what would make it easier."

"Great advice, but I'm not sure I follow."

"When you started to falter just now, you wanted to
make sure I didn't say I was interested in you because you've
all but given me an entire building on loan or because
you're holding my only means of transportation hostage as
a way of getting us to spend time together. If I go with what
I know about you, I know you just wanted to give me
room to feel I could be honest about what I wanted to hap-

pen with us. You didn't want me to worry about any of that if my answer wasn't the one you wanted to hear."

"That's exactly what I meant."

"But it was easier for me to take offense and assume you were questioning my moral character, because that helps me keep my guard up. I've had a lot of practice keeping that guard up, so I'm more comfortable there. So, when I feel like tucking in and taking the worst possible slant on something . . . that's when I need to take two seconds and remember who it is I'm talking to and who is talking to me. And remember that I can always talk to you. You're the first person, really, I've felt comfortable enough to say anything to."

For the first time, his lips twitched. "A point you've made abundantly clear."

"Okay, maybe I have given you a hard time," she said dryly, "but I can also talk to you about stuff that I'd only ever felt comfortable talking to Bea about, and that was because she understood. She was family. You . . . I just met you."

"You can trust me, Honey."

"I know." She smiled. "I mean, I really do know that. Do you know that? That you can trust me, too?"

"I wanted to talk to you about my past, my family . . . maybe some part of it was like you said, shoving it out there as a way to gauge things, make you duck and run if that's what you're going to do, but sooner rather than later. I don't generally need to tell anyone about that time. The past is just that, for me. It's no longer relevant—which is why I know we're involved. It might be relevant to you, so it matters to me that you know about it."

"If you think I should know, then tell me. I do want to know you, Dylan, but not so I can cut and run. I want to know you because you matter. And your past is part of you."

He smiled then, but it didn't quite reach his beautifully wise eyes. "At least you'll know who—what—you're dealing with. If it changes things, then it changes things."

She understood how hard it was for him to lower those walls. He wanted to, and that was big for her, but he was still hedging his bets. "The first time I had a vision here, it was a whopper. If anything was going to put you off, that would have done it. Instead, you shocked me by asking about it, talking about it almost casually. You were more worried if I was okay, than whether or not my head was going to keep spinning around. No one ever did that. Ever. No one looked past the spinning head to the person who was being spun. Until you.

"And then, this last time, when I spontaneously jumped into your arms that first day in the bookstore—*my* store," she corrected, smiling briefly. "And it triggered another episode, your first instinct was to hold on tight, to be there, to encourage me, calm me. You didn't let go. You knew what to do, or you followed your instincts, and that ended up being the same thing, because your instinct was to worry about me first, and what was happening to me second. That helped me. You have no idea how much."

She closed the space between them, until their bodies brushed against each other. "That I can do this, walk right up to you like this, and feel pretty much fearless, knowing that even if it triggers a vision, I can trust that you won't cut and run. That's the man you are. To me. I want to know the rest of you, Dylan. Any of it, all of it, whatever you want to share with me."

She reached up, brushed her fingertips across his cheek, watched his gaze darken, and felt her body respond to him as if he'd put out a siren call with nothing more than a look. "Because you're right. I'm already involved."

Chapter 15

She gutted him . . . effortlessly. Reached right in, wrapped her hand and all the rest of what made her so unique right around his heart, and she'd be damned if she'd let go. He'd never felt so vulnerable in front of any-one, which was saying more than he could comprehend, given how vulnerable he'd been most of his life. It wasn't because of what she could see in her mind's eye; it was what she saw every time she looked at him.

She'd meant every word she'd said. He had not a single doubt. Just as he'd meant every word he'd said. They were about to join forces, knowingly, and . . . well, the power of it scared the ever loving hell out of him.

Was that what love was supposed to feel like?

While it didn't make any sense—none of it had—he didn't know what other emotion to name this . . . feeling he had. It was the only label big enough, broad enough, deep enough, to come close. Maybe that's what scared him. Knowing this beautiful, powerful thing, was swim-ming between them, if they were brave enough to wade out into uncharted waters. Rough waters, ripping, roiling, powerful waters . . . deep waters.

Standing there, looking into those sea green eyes, so steady, so true, the past didn't matter. Not like he thought it would. Yes, he wanted her to know, but it was because he wanted her to understand him, what drove him, what mattered to him . . . and what didn't. And why. Not because he worried she'd consider him unworthy or too big a risk.

Hell, it was just like she said . . . it wasn't about the stuff spinning in orbit around them; the only thing that mattered was what was at the core of it. His throat worked, and a sensation tightened the corners of his eyes, burning with the threat of emotions he'd sworn he'd never let come to the surface again.

"Come here, sugar," he said roughly, finally feeling confident in putting his hands on her because he knew she trusted him. No matter what.

He pulled her into his arms, wrapped her up tight as he leaned back against the truck, and drew her face up to his. He looked into those eyes . . . and stepped right off into the deep water. "Come with me," he murmured, the words sounding like rough sand against smooth glass.

And she did.

He took her mouth like a man starved, who'd just been offered the feast of the gods. No holding back, no worrying about what touched where. He felt primal, like he was claiming what was his . . . and yet, when she opened her mouth, took him inside, and held him there, so tightly, so wetly, so warmly . . . it was he who'd been claimed.

If it was terrifying, opening himself up and diving in deep, the utter thrill of it made every second of sheer terror exhilaratingly, stunningly worthwhile.

He hitched her up so she could wrap her legs around his waist, and she followed, without his having to say a word. He turned, pressing her against the side of the truck, moving between her legs, the feel of her sweet softness pressed against him wrenching a guttural groan from somewhere deep inside his chest.

He knew he should pause, make sure she was with him,

but oh, she was with him. She gave when he demanded, then demanded her own in return.

"Why in sweet hell do we start these things where we can't see them through to their most amazing, rightful conclusion?" he growled against the side of her neck. Rigidly hard, it was painful to breathe, much less move.

"Because fate has a sense of humor?" she panted, sounding every bit as put out as he was, and it made him laugh. Oddly, it was the thing that tipped him completely over and in.

He lifted his head, keeping her wrapped all around him, and smiled into eyes he wanted to smile into for a very long time. "I did actually plan a real dinner. Lolly is home right now, standing guard."

"Dinner is at your place?"

"Well, sugar, I admit I've been something of a pain in the ass to deal with this week. Seems maybe I've been missing you. Some."

"Some," she repeated, and her smile was a shade smug and a shade thrilled. He loved both.

"So, I didn't want to share you with the good folks of Sugarberry. This time. But I didn't want you to think I was taking you home to show you my etchings, either."

"You have etchings?" she teased.

"Oh, darlin', you have no idea."

She giggled at that, low and throaty. Her eyes were all but drenched with want. Want of him. It was enough to drive a man to his knees.

"I set up dinner aboard."

Her face lit up. "The sailboat?"

He nodded, privately pleased beyond words with her instant reaction. "It's not seaworthy, still a work in progress, but I thought maybe a picnic with a little candlelight—"

He was cut off by a very exuberant kiss, which had him

chuckling when she finally broke off. "I take it you like candlelight?"

"I like that you thought of candlelight. Take me aboard, Cap'n."

Just like that, his body jerked so hard he winced. "Careful how you word such things, sugar," he said, his voice somewhat strained.

She batted her eyelashes and grinned. "I was."

He didn't know whether to be afraid or shout hallelujah. "I think I may have underestimated . . . oh hell"—he laughed—"pretty much everything."

"I know the feeling." Still smiling, she leaned in and kissed him again, taking his face in her hands.

It stilled something inside him, bringing peace and serenity to the center of the turmoil he didn't even know he still had locked inside of him.

Her kiss was tender, almost unbearably sweet. He wouldn't have thought himself worthy of such sweet regard, wouldn't have enjoyed it from anyone else, ever before. "Honey," he murmured, hearing the break in his voice. "You're just undoing me here, sugar."

"Shh," she said against his lips. "Kiss me back."

He'd never kissed sweetly before. Slow, easy, a comfortable slide into seduction, yes. But this wasn't anything like that. Surprisingly, when he brushed his lips against hers, dropped his guard the rest of the way, and let himself express the tumble of emotions in the form of a single sweet kiss . . . the tenderness came quite naturally.

She moaned softly against his lips, and her hold on him tightened. He responded swiftly in kind, but it wasn't that raging thing from before, though it felt a hundred times more primal. His body leaped, but he didn't let it ramp up the connection they were making with their kiss.

"Dylan," she murmured, her voice so soft he could barely hear it.

"Mmm," he managed, kissing the corners of her mouth, then tracing a line slowly along her jawline.

She groaned and dropped her head back, allowing him access to the most tender spot just below her ear. "Take me home. Please."

How a man could want to howl wildly at the moon while simultaneously suckling a woman's earlobe, he had no earthly idea, but damn if he didn't feel the urge. He finally made himself lift his head, trepidation filling him in that split second before their gazes met for the first time since they'd begun this journey. Not because he worried what he might see in her eyes, but because of what she might see in his.

But hers lit up immediately, smiling right into his own, sparking the way a woman does when she sees that thing she wants the most.

He grinned. It was that or howl. "Hold on," he said, and scooped her up tight so he could carry her around to the passenger side of his truck. He tucked her inside, fighting the urge to follow her down until they were splayed across the front seat. He closed the door before he could change his mind and walked quite uncomfortably around to the other side of his truck, almost tripping over her satchel.

He snagged it up and put it in the flat bed of the truck, then carefully slid into the driver's seat, trying not to unman himself in any way.

He pulled on his seatbelt, sucking in his breath as he worked the clutch and the brake. Damn, but he'd never been so hard in his life.

"You okay?" Her voice was deep and throaty and oh, he wanted to hear what it sounded like after she'd come apart under him.

"Yeah," he managed. "Fine."

"Liar," she said, making the word a lazy drawl filled with smug knowing.

He slid his gaze toward hers as he backed up and pulled out of the alley. She was leaning back against the seat as if it was simply too demanding a task to remain sitting upright. She'd rolled her head to the left, and was watching him.

"What makes you say that?" he asked, but he was already grinning.

Her gaze dropped straight to his crotch, and he winced audibly when his body reacted.

"That does." She sighed. "That, and the fact that I'm in much the same way. It's a sad, sorry place to be, too."

He didn't know whether to laugh at the downright forlorn look on her face, or pout right along with her. So he did a little of both . . . and drove perhaps a tad recklessly back to his house.

Lolly trotted down the drive to greet them, and Dylan reached in the console for a biscuit for her, which he tossed a few feet away for her to fetch and munch on after he carefully slid out of the truck. Lolly's hip was improving every day, and Doc Jensen told him he should see that she exercised it more and work on strengthening the muscles. That was all fine and good, but truth be told, he was just keeping the pup busy as he had other plans in mind that didn't include playing fetch.

He went around the back of the truck to the passenger side, but Honey was already sliding out of the cab. He jogged the last few steps, willing to pay the price so he could get there in time to deftly scoop her into his arms before her feet hit the ground. She let out a short squeal, and he spun her around, making her laugh. He handed her one of the biscuits he'd stashed in his pocket when Lolly came trotting up, barking playfully at their antics. They tossed the biscuits into the front yard, then smiled at each other when she trotted off.

Honey looped her arms around Dylan's neck. "Well, now that the children are busy . . . what about those etchings?"

"I thought we were having dinner?"

"Will it keep until later? Maybe as an après snack under the stars?"

"It will keep, but après what?"

She rolled her eyes, then undid the top button of his polo shirt. "Your turn."

He grinned. "Ah, that kind of après."

She batted her eyelashes. "Unless you'd rather dine first, for fortitude. I must say though, it didn't appear that stamina was going to be an issue."

He chuckled and felt a little heat climb up his neck at the same time. "You say the damndest things, sugar."

"We all have our strengths."

His chuckle was deeper, and he had the pleasure of watching her pupils slowly swallow up that sea of green. "That we do, darlin." He let his palm slide around her waist until his thumb grazed alongside the swell of her breast.

He heard her swift intake of breath, and felt her fingers reflexively dig into the back of his neck. Oh yeah. He wanted to feel her dig in, tighten up, and hold on . . . all over him. But he knew if he so much as brushed his mouth over hers, they'd never make it off the driveway, so he swung her up a little higher in his arms. "Hold on to me, sugar."

"My pleasure," she said, her voice a little throaty again as she pressed her cheek against his shoulder.

He tucked her up more tightly against him, liking the way she fit. She liked it, too, and started nuzzling the side of his neck.

He growled a little at the skittery sensations her touch

sent racing all over his skin . . . and the further tightening of the front of his jeans. He all but kicked down the front door of his beach cottage and carried her straight to the back of the sprawling structure. "Tour later," he murmured, ducking his chin to intercept her clever little tongue, capturing it in his mouth.

She was the one to moan, and even though he was mere steps away from his designated goal, they made it only to the short span of wall that separated the kitchen and breakfast nook area from the master bedroom he'd built onto the back of the house. He pinned her against the wall, and used the last shred of restraint he had left to capture her gaze. "The last time for you, it triggered a vision?"

She held his gaze, and when she realized he was talking about the last time she'd had sex, he saw emotion rise swiftly in her eyes until they grew a little glassy.

"Aw, sugar, I'm not trying to stir up bad memories—"

"No, I know. You're trying to keep me from adding to them." She slid a hand to his cheek. "Thank you."

"You sure you're ready?"

"For the risk? Or for . . . taking this step?"

"Both." He framed her face with both palms. "If something happens, it just does. I won't go anywhere, understood?" His lips twitched. "And I won't take it personally."

She let out a short, watery laugh. "That would be a nice change."

The simple little joke broke his heart. To have to go through something every time she got sent reeling off was bad enough. To have it happen during the most intimate of moments . . . he couldn't even imagine. Then to have her partner be indignant and abrasive about it? Well, he wasn't one to cling to the past, but he wouldn't have minded tracking down her past partners and spreading a little *enlightenment* their way.

"There's something else you need to know," he said, brushing his thumbs along the tender skin beneath her eyes. "I wasn't raised to play well with others. In my world, it was all about protecting your own. And I have to admit, I still don't like to share what's mine."

She surprised him by smiling, and the sheen of emotion finally shifted to one of dry amusement. "So, you're saying you wouldn't respond in a positive way if I thought I wanted to test out my new ability to take . . . certain risks with other island residents of the male persuasion? I'm pretty sure old Mr. Hanson was giving me the eye when he came by to drop off those tools you asked him to loan me. Thank you for that, by the way. Of course, it's also doubtful he'd even be aware if I was having a vision because he'd be too busy trying not to die of a heart attack—"

Dylan cut her off with a kiss. Fast, hard, deep, and absolutely intended to claim. Both were a little breathless when he lifted his head. "Do you know it's a little terrifying—maybe more than a little—and a lot humbling, that you could actually make me jealous of an eighty-six year old grandfather of nine?"

"Nine grandkids, huh?" she said, wiggling her eyebrows. "Sounds like a guy with some serious stamina."

She let out a loud squeal when he simply hauled her up over his shoulder and carried her down the short hall to the master suite. "We'll see about stamina," he said, even as her laughter trailed along behind him.

"You're way too easy, you know," she said, laughter still bubbling. "You should know better than to give me that kind of leverage."

He slid her off of his shoulder, grinning despite the fact that his desire to claim her as his own grew with every giggle, every little poke or jab. "Let's talk about leverage, sugar."

He laid her across the wide expanse of his bed, following her down and pinning her into the soft, pillowed mattress with the full length of his body.

"Oh," she sighed as she sank into the cool linens and soft, cotton-covered duvet. "This is . . . decadent."

He grinned, and pushed her glasses up on her nose. "You might be the only one who thinks of cotton as decadent."

"It's just so soft."

"Let's hope that's the only time I hear you say that, darlin'."

She laughed, and wriggled under him. "Something tells me you won't have to worry much on that score." She slid her arms around his neck. "Come here," she said softly, mimicking his Southern accent and pulling him down so she could kiss him. "Thank you," she whispered against his lips.

"For?" he asked, lifting his head just enough to brush kisses on the corner of her mouth, then along her jaw.

"All of this. Making it so easy to just be myself."

"I happen to be very interested in just yourself."

She beamed at that, and his heart did the oddest little tap dance inside his chest.

"That's really handy, because I feel the same." She surprised him by rolling him to his back. "It's a very empowering thing, you know. Mutual desire. Makes me feel like being a little"—she circled his wrists with her hands, pinned them beside his head, and grinned—"aggressive."

"I'm all yours, sugar."

She laughed, but a brief flicker of something quite . . . possessive flashed through her eyes. And rather than feel trapped—literally or figuratively—he felt triumphant.

"Good to know." She leaned in and nipped his chin, then his earlobe. "Very, very good to know."

He groaned as she continued her gentle assault. "It's a damn shame it took this long for someone to get you feeling . . . empowered." He quickly reversed their positions, laughing when she gasped. "But I'm really glad you waited so it could be me." He didn't give her time to respond. The teasing, the playing, the exploring, had pushed him past any further hope of control. Next time, he'd be gentle and tender and sweet, and only because she'd already taught him he had that in him.

But for this first time, there was only one way it was going to go. He tugged at her earlobe with his teeth. "I'm going to take those clothes off of you now, sugar. And then I'm going to find out how every last inch of you tastes on my tongue."

She shuddered under him and his body roared in response. He slowly popped open the row of tiny pearl buttons down the front of her thin sweater, parting it as he went. Her breasts were small, but full, and he teased her nipples through the thin cotton cups. Her sweater had been delicate and feminine, but something about the simple serviceability of the white cotton bra caught at him, too. It all went toward that dichotomy of hers that was handmade skirts, made more flirty and feminine with her own artistic needlework . . . and the no nonsense horn rims, the unadorned, short fingernails, and hands that bore calluses from creating her artwork.

She moaned, arching up against his mouth as he slid his hands under her and unhooked the back and slid the straps down and off her arms. Her skin was pale, soft, her nipples dark, tightly budded, begging to be licked, suckled, teased. So he did, until she was writhing beneath him and he knew if he didn't peel his jeans off sometime soon, he might become permanently damaged in some way.

As if reading his mind, she tugged at his shirt, pulling it up and over the back of his head. He took it and tossed it away. She smoothed her hands over his chest, then lifted her head and teased him the way he'd teased her. No one had ever done that, and it surprised him, the sharp tug, the aching turning to throbbing. She slid her hands down to his waistband, worked at opening his belt, and he found he rather enjoyed being both the aggressor . . . and her quarry, all at the same time. He found the thin hidden zipper on the side of her skirt, unhooked the waistband, and they unzipped each other, then slid out of their clothes.

His eyebrows climbed as he noted the hand stitched flowers and fairies on her panties. He lifted a questioning gaze to hers.

She lifted a shoulder and smiled. "I lived alone in a barn. I had time on my hands. Besides . . . I didn't think anyone would ever see them."

"You had a pretty good idea I might when you slid these on earlier."

Her cheeky grin peeked out. "I did. Better you know all my hidden secrets all at once. Besides . . . it wouldn't have mattered which ones I grabbed."

His eyebrows rose even higher. "They're all like that, are they?"

"Eight years. Alone. In a barn," she repeated. "They started my day with a smile."

"Well, sugar," he said as he pulled them off, "I'm all for starting your days with a smile. And ending them with one, too." He tossed the panties on top of her skirt and began working his way back up the curve of her ankles, the flair of her calves, the tender spot on the inside of her knee, the smooth skin of her thighs . . . with his tongue.

She let out soft little gasps, then reached down and wove her fingers into his hair, urging him to where she wanted him to be. He liked that . . . and happily complied. She arched up to meet him as he slid his tongue over her, teased her, taunted her, until she was panting as her hips pistoned beneath each stroke of his tongue. He felt her thighs trembling, and her fingers dug deeper as she gathered up tighter and tighter.

That's it, sugar, he thought. *Come for me. Come to me.*

Her short pants became little whimpers, and she bucked harder. "Dylan," she gasped. "Dylan!"

He realized, suddenly, that she might be spinning away from him and felt a moment of stupidity for not being more aware of it, being so focused on her pleasure. Then she was shattering beneath him, and he stayed right where he was, seeing it through with her, pushing her along the crest of the wave, helping her find every last ounce of pleasure there was to be had until she was trembling, her breath catching over and over.

He kissed the inside of her thigh, then the soft spot to the side of her hipbone, before sliding up and pulling her against him. "You okay?" he murmured next to her ear.

She opened her eyes to his, and they were utterly defenseless.

"Aw, sugar, I'm sorry—"

She pressed a kiss to his lips, silencing him, then kept on kissing him. There was so much emotion, sweet, tender, and passionate. All her guards were completely gone, and he worried, knowing she was at her most vulnerable.

Her eyes closed, so he let his own drift shut and went along with her gentle, but urgent demands. When she pulled him back on top of her, slid her heels up the backs of his thighs, and wrapped her legs around his waist, he slipped his hands to her hips, lifted her to him, found her, and slid steady, strong, and fully inside of her.

He might have growled . . . or it might have been her. He stayed fully inside of her, not moving, just reveling in every sensation, making sure she was okay with the size of him. Making sure she was with him. He waited for her to move, and when she did, he groaned. Long, deep, guttural groans as they slowly found their pace, the rise and fall of her hips and his body sliding into hers in as age old a rhythm as the sea under his sail. He felt like he'd known her forever even as he understood, on every level possible, that he'd never once known anything like this.

They continued to move together, and she slid her hand to the back of his neck, urging his mouth to hers again. "Dylan . . ." she breathed against his lips; then she opened her eyes, and he fell so deeply into that vast sea of green, he knew he'd drown in them and smile as he did.

She smiled back, even as she gasped when he drove into her more deeply, pulled her up against him more tightly, sinking all the way into her as she kissed him again and again, until he was the one climbing . . . and shattering.

They held on to each other, panting, gasping . . . smiling, while their heart rates slowed and their breathing returned to normal. He rolled to his side, gathering her against him. And she surprised him again, by propping her chin on his chest, and looking up with a happy gaze, eyes dancing.

"What?" he said, already grinning.

"I just . . . I didn't know. I mean, I've read about it, and I'm a modern woman and hardly a prude, so, you know, I've figured it out on my own. But . . . I honestly had no idea."

"About?" He gently rolled her to her back and pushed her hair from her face.

"How it feels, to be . . . well, to be taken like that, to climax like that. It's so incredibly . . . powerful."

He shouldn't feel so pleased with himself to discover that he was the first one to show her that kind of pleasure. But he was. Ridiculously so. And he wasn't ashamed of the pride he felt, because he knew she could share in it. No one made him feel so . . . hell, he felt *invincible* with her. "Well, sugar, I can honestly say I felt everything you did. I'm glad to know I can do that, be that, for you." He grinned. "Of course, I'm not saying there isn't always room for improvement. Practice makes perfect, after all."

"Practice just makes for perfect practicing," she said, then sighed. "And I'm all for that."

He chuckled and couldn't seem to keep his hands to himself. He touched her hair, traced her lips. "You hungry?" He reached past her and found her glasses, then slid them back on for her.

She slid them right back off again, and smiled at him as she dropped them back on the bedside table. "Not for dinner." She pushed him to his back. "My turn to do a little exploring."

He groaned and surrendered without so much as a whimper.

"My, my," she said, moments later on a giggle. "I was right. Stamina isn't going to be a problem. Eat your heart out, Mr. Hanson."

Chapter 16

Honey blinked open her eyes and took a moment to let the blur settle into a slightly more distinct fuzzy picture. She slid her hand out from under the duvet, found her glasses, and quietly slid them on, careful not to disturb the man presently in deep slumber beside her.

It was just as well. If he could see her quite decidedly Cheshire-like grin at the moment, he might be a little concerned. She was feeling rather smug, and didn't much care who knew it. If she could dance on top of the bedspread and shout to the world how happy she was, she could easily have done so.

Who knew falling in love could feel so good?

It should have been scarier, or at the very least, had her making long pro and con lists and worrying over all the tiny things that could go so disastrously wrong. While she still had lots of trepidations about her life on Sugarberry, about opening up her own business; getting back to work and wondering how all the changes were going to affect her creativity; wondering if her online customers would come back, because she'd need them to make ends meet for a long time to come and possibly forever . . . the only thing she didn't have any worries about was her feelings for the man beside her.

He hadn't left her guessing. The very best thing about Dylan Ross was that he held nothing back. Good or bad, he was entirely open with her about whatever he thought, whatever he was feeling . . . and most deliciously, whatever he was wanting.

He was far from perfect. He was demanding in wanting what he wanted, not huge on patience, and could be moody when he was worried about something or someone. She'd seen all those things in him . . . but all she had to do was look at him, smile at him, maybe poke a little, and all those walls came tumbling down. Leaving them simply open and honest, at least with each other. She felt she had the most powerful secret weapon on the planet. She had Dylan. On her side. At her back. And he'd made it quite clear he intended to stay right there unless she booted him off.

She had no intention of doing that. She wasn't perfect, either. She worried about things, had crazy visions when she least expected them, then worried about how to figure out and fix what she'd seen. She got distracted all the time and often made jokes as a way to appear more confident than she really was.

And he wanted her anyway, flaws and all. In fact, it was possible, just maybe . . . that he thought she was his best secret weapon, too. He held on to her, cared for her, yet respected her and even admired her.

She had no idea how two cave dwellers like themselves had ever stuck their heads out long enough to find each other, but she felt incredibly lucky they had. Knowing she could turn to him when she needed to was enough. She didn't need him to fix things or take care of things. Her family had been behind her, supporting her, but she'd never had anyone who'd wanted to do it willingly . . . because they cared for her.

She rolled her head to the side and watched him sleep.

Maybe, just maybe, he might be falling, too. At least as much as a man like him was able.

They had eventually made their way out to the boat and dined on cold fried chicken, the most delicious coleslaw she'd ever had, reheated biscuits along with homemade rhubarb jam, and Miss Alva's mini apple pies for dessert. They'd lain on a blanket, Lolly sprawled at their side, and watched the stars wink in and out. Dylan had held her hand and told her all about his childhood. About his mother taking off, his father sinking into deep despair, and even more deeply into the bottle. He'd told her about his abusive brother, also a substance abuser and addict, and how helpless he'd felt against the tyranny Mickey had reigned down. How angry he was at his father for not standing up and doing what fathers should do, and how equally guilty he felt because he couldn't protect his father from the abuse.

He told her how he'd felt when his brother had finally landed in prison and how, even then, he'd hoped Mickey's hitting rock bottom would change things. His father had passed by then, leaving Dylan conflicted—deeply—about his feelings on family and what it should mean. When his brother had been killed, he'd felt a flood of relief, knowing Mickey could never victimize him or anyone else again . . . and shame for feeling that relief.

He talked about the islanders thinking, for a long time, that it was his father who was abusive, and later on, when it became known what the situation really was, how he'd hated the pity they'd shown him, and how long it had taken him to realize their attempts to help him were motivated not by pity, but by honest concern. He told her how he wished he'd come to that realization sooner because he hadn't always been kind about how he'd pushed folks away, and was shamed and humbled further when they forgave him for that, too.

She understood now, the fierce loyalty he felt for his island and its people, who were, essentially, his extended family. Certainly the closest to a real one, a healthy one, he'd ever had. He'd shown her his home, which, from the front, looked like every other little beachside cottage—painted, weathered clapboard and pitched, cedar shingled roof. The dunes rising up behind it, and the waves crashing just beyond made it all the more rustic.

Behind his house, he'd developed the expanse of property that ran back to the dunes, building a U-shaped structure with short wings extending off either side of the back of the house. All one story, and almost all made of glass, it was a calm, serene oasis.

His kitchen filled one wing and was surprisingly state of the art. The man liked to cook. He'd explained that he'd had to learn to feed himself at a very young age, and when he was finally old enough to afford more than bare scraps, he'd decided there wasn't any reason not to make things he'd actually enjoy eating. So he'd taught himself, discovering a certain rhythm to preparing and cooking food that fed his soul, much as sailing and the water and fixing things did.

Two walls of his bedroom were entirely glass. Louvered vertical blinds ran floor to ceiling and could be closed against the sun or opened fully, creating the appearance that the bed he'd built was almost sitting in the dunes. He'd bartered for the custom mattress in exchange for providing service for the local manufacturer's small fleet of trucks until they were even. He still serviced the trucks, only now under contract.

She hadn't been wrong about his being far shrewder and far more successful than he gave the appearance of being. But then, he honestly didn't care what anyone thought. He lived decently and conducted himself the same way . . . and that was all that was important for anyone to know.

His home was minimally furnished with pieces that were inviting, warm, and comfortable. What little decorating he'd done had been with items that meant something to him personally. A photo of him standing next to the first car he'd ever fixed, his grandfather standing behind him. A piece of a carburetor from his first successful salvage. Nautical bits and bobs she couldn't name were from his many searches for sailboat parts. He'd found things he couldn't use on his boat, but couldn't pass up for their artistry or history. The collection was odd, eclectic, and decidedly masculine . . . and yet it all lent to the atmosphere, to the world he'd created for himself.

She understood why serenity meant so much to him. And wondered why he wanted to tangle himself up with someone who would very likely bring drama, vibrancy, and unpredictability—at the very least—to his carefully constructed world.

She'd told him about her own childhood, about her parents and their eccentric lifestyle and equally eccentric circle of friends. She talked about what dealing with what she called her curse was like, and how, even though her parents loved her unconditionally, and meant well, they never really understood the kind of alienation she felt every time she had to leave their farm and go somewhere. She told him about her aborted college attempt, and more wonderful, happy stories about learning her love of carving from her father, falling in love with sculpting, and with creating her own world of happiness. She told him about her special relationship with Bea, and her guilt and sorrow for not being with her, for not pressing her for more information about her situation, for just not knowing what had been going on.

She'd even told him about her dreams—about wanting to teach others to find their inner artist, and how she saw her shop not just as a place for folks to come and buy cute and eclectic yard and garden art pieces, but as a place where the islanders could gather and explore their own creativity. She wanted life, and noise, and people, and all the colorful things that went along with being entrenched in a community.

She smiled as she recalled the look of . . . well, not exactly horror . . . on Dylan's face . . . but certainly disconcertment. He was perfectly happy hiding under a car or on his boat, and that wasn't going to change. Nor did she want it to. He did understand her passions and why they mattered to her, just as she understood his desires. As long as they supported each other's dreams . . . she couldn't imagine a better, more fulfilling, and well-balanced partnership. It was certainly far, far beyond the scope of anything she could have ever imagined having.

Dylan mumbled something drowsily in his sleep, and shifted, reaching for her, pulling her close. But instead of seducing her—which she was more than willing to go along with—he drifted back to sleep . . . but not before sliding his hand down to find hers and linking his fingers through hers.

For all they'd come to know each other as intimately as two people could, emotionally and physically, during the past ten or eleven hours, it was that single, instinctive action, subconsciously made, that need to connect with her, palm to palm . . . that tipped her heart over the edge into the last free fall.

Smiling, she traced her fingertips over his knuckles, liking the heat and warmth of his palm against hers . . . and was unprepared for the edges of consciousness to begin shimmering, and suddenly tug and jerk her sideways. Her first instinct was still to recoil, by sheer force of will to try to prevent the vision from manifesting itself. Of course, she couldn't. Never had.

She squeezed Dylan's hand, reaching instinctively for him to help her fight it or at least to see her through it. Even as she tumbled headlong into the vision, she recognized how wild it was that in such a short period of time, after never relying on anyone, much less turning to someone, how instinctively and earnestly she turned to him.

Then she was in it, and everything else faded to the background. Her heart was pounding and she braced herself for God knew what. She wanted to scream that it wasn't fair. She'd finally found someone and the last thing she wanted was to see some sad or horrifying thing that was going to happen to him. They'd spent a significant amount of time being as physical as two people could get, without another trigger, and she'd begun to believe the feelings she had for him, the emotional connection she'd made, was going to keep her from ever having another vision about him. Like with her parents. At least, that's what she'd hoped.

So having another vision was doubly crushing. She tried to settle herself, calm herself, get in the mindset that if something was going to happen to him, then at least she could give him a fighting chance. It took a lot of focus and a lot of concentration because her heart was beating wildly and she was so afraid of what she might see.

The mists began to part . . . and she realized where she was. She was rocking again on the sailboat! Her relief was so profound she felt dizzy with it. Her racing heart began to calm, and other elements began to surface, faster and more clearly. The pitch and roll . . . the heat of the sun . . . the salty brine in the air . . . the breeze . . . a child's laughter.

The sound brought her head around, and there was Dylan at the wheel, again. She had a fleeting thought that this idyllic scene was merely the beginning of something bad happening . . . but there was not so much as a ripple of that kind of sensation teasing at the fringes of her awareness.

A cascade of infectious giggles filled the air and was joined by Dylan's deeper, resonant chuckle. Honey could feel the sun seeping into her skin, making her feel relaxed, drowsy almost, but she tried to keep her attention on the happy sounds. They did make her happy. In fact, was that . . .? That was her laughter!

In that odd purgatory of being in the moment, and observing it, she watched Dylan steer the boat, taking in his strong stance and how easy he made it look. Wait, his hands were on the wheel, but they were covering other hands. Smaller hands. Tiny hands.

Her face split wide in an exuberant grin as she realized the child she'd heard was standing in front of Dylan, his small feet propped on top of Dylan's much larger ones as they steered the boat together. She hadn't seen him before, because Dylan's body blocked her view.

She opened her mouth to call to them, the child's name right on the edge of her awareness. But then the sun was fading, the pitch and roll smoothed . . . and a moment later, she was opening her eyes back in Dylan's bed in his bedroom. She shifted her head to find him lying next to her, his head propped on a folded pillow, watching her with a steady, sober gray gaze.

He was stroking her arm and squeezed her hand still joined with his. "You okay?" His voice was gravel and grit . . . so deep.

She loved the sound of it, still sleepy from the night they'd spent together, except she didn't like the worry she heard in it. "Very okay."

"You want to talk about it?"

She shook her head. "It wasn't anything bad. I was on your sailboat again."

She debated telling him about the child. Last time, she'd thought it was an existential version of Dylan reliving his childhood. But she realized it was an actual child. Someone he knew or was going to know. They'd been happy, though, so it wasn't something she needed to get involved in. "It was more like a nice dream. A really, really wonderful dream."

He shifted his hand and stroked her cheek, then tucked her hair behind her ear. "Guess I'd better get a little more motivated to finally make her seaworthy then. Take you for a sail."

"You will," she said, then smiled. "And we will."

He tugged her close and shifted to his back so she rolled against his chest. "I like these kinds of visions, sugar."

She loved the deep rumble of his voice, the stubble on his chin, the way he couldn't go a minute without touching her hair, stroking her skin, staying in contact with her. She felt . . . tended to, desirable . . . maybe even loved, or at least deeply cared for.

"I do, too. You know, I'd thought maybe I wouldn't have them anymore . . . with you, I mean . . . now that we've gotten closer. I never did with my folks or with Bea."

"You had your guard up pretty tight all those years, though. Maybe relaxing a little, not being so worried about them, is allowing them through." He smiled and pushed her glasses up. "Maybe it's also why you're having good, positive visions along with the occasional more alarming ones."

She thought about that. "Maybe you were right about it being my own state of mind, or how I felt about them, that was attracting certain kinds of vibes from folks. Bea tried to explain that to me. Hers were almost always more positive and often minor, little things that didn't matter so much, but always made someone feel better to know.

"She had a few troublesome ones when the vibes were just too strong to ignore. Someone with an accident or a bad fight looming, a divorce maybe, or getting fired . . . and a few times when a person was going to lose someone close. But mine were never like that, never gentle, and rarely about trivial things. I know my second senses are stronger than hers were, but . . . I don't know. I'm beginning to think—hope—that being older, being more open to them, more at ease about having them . . . is changing the type of vibes I'm picking up." She leaned in and kissed him, reveling in the knowledge that she could just do that because she wanted to. And oh, she wanted to.

"I hope so, sugar." He rolled her to her back. "Maybe your spidey senses are contagious . . . because I am experiencing some vibes right now myself."

She giggled. "Are you now?"

"I'm sensing that someone might want a nice, big, stamina building breakfast before we get up and head in to work."

She pouted just a little, before she caught herself and smiled. "That would be great."

He hooted out a laugh and rolled her so she was under him. "Darlin', if you could have seen the expression on your face just now. Word of advice. Never play poker."

"I do think breakfast sounds wonderful."

"Maybe so, but you were hoping I was sensing something else entirely? Just maybe?"

"Just maybe," she admitted.

"How do you feel about water conservation?"

She frowned in confusion. "Water conservation?"

"I have this nice, big walk-in shower and oversized drenching showerhead. Seems a shame to waste all that water on just one person at a time."

"Well, now that you mention it, that does seem rather wasteful."

"Good. Come on." He rolled off the bed and tugged her with him.

"And here I thought you weren't a morning person."

"Only when I have reason to be." He reached in and turned on the showerheads. Seconds later, steam started to rise inside the glass enclosed walls. "Go ahead on in. I'm going to put coffee on. Forgot to set it last night." He grinned. "Something distracted me." He padded out into the hall, completely unself-conscious about being naked— which was when she realized he'd pulled her straight out of bed buck naked and looking like God only knew what.

The mirror was already too fogged, and she was too preoccupied poking her head out of the door to the hall-way and watching him stroll to the kitchen. Honestly, no one's butt should look that incredible. She grinned to her-self. But if anyone had to have one . . . she was happy it was him.

She heard him let Lolly in and what sounded like dog food being dumped in a bowl. Then he was coming back down the hall. That sexy, teasing grin slid across his face, looking all the more devilish with the five o'clock shadow darkening his jaw. "You peekin' at my bare ass, sugar?"

She managed a nonchalant shrug. "Might have been."

He lifted one brow. "And?"

"My, my, give a girl a string of soul shattering orgasms and you suddenly think you're hot stuff, huh?"

He moved in a sudden flash and scooped her up against his chest, making her squeal and laugh at the same time. "Soul shattering, huh?"

"You're going to be completely insufferable now, aren't you?"

He carried her straight into the shower, making her

splutter as the warm water splashed over their heads and darted off their shoulders and backs. "I was already insufferable, sugar. Weren't you payin' attention?"

He closed the shower door behind him with a flick of his foot and grabbed the bottle of scented body wash from the silver wire rack hanging over her head behind her. "Here," he said, squeezing out a pool of the creamy soap into the palm of his hands. "Let me show you some of the benefits of paying attention." He rubbed his palms together and reached for her. "Very close attention."

Chapter 17

"**H**e cooks?"

"He designed a walk-in shower?"

Honey should be ashamed of herself, she knew that. But for the first time in her life, she had honest-to-God girl-friends. Well, girlfriends and Franco, who was like a bonus girlfriend, only better. She also had herself an honest-to-God man. Could she really be blamed if she gushed about her man to her girlfriends, just a little? Just this once? It wasn't like she'd told them anything personal or intimate. That was just for her and Dylan.

"It's heavenly," she admitted. "I didn't even know they made those kind of showerhead things. It was as big as a dinner plate. It was like standing in a rainstorm."

"I saw in a magazine where you can have different nature scenes illuminate the glass enclosure like a screen, sort of like those digital picture frames," Lani said. "And speakers that play matching nature sounds."

"I already feel self-conscious in the shower," Charlotte responded. "The last thing I need is to feel like I'm standing naked in the middle of the jungle."

"I bet Carlo might think otherwise," Lani teased.

Charlotte smiled, but said nothing.

"I wonder if you could get any sort of photos to show

up on the glass," Alva mused. "I wouldn't mind taking a shower with Captain Jack Sparrow."

Honey choked on a snort of laughter. "I don't know which would make me more uncomfortable, feeling like I was showering naked in the jungle, or showering naked in front of Johnny Depp."

"I wouldn't mind it," Franco commented, "as long as Johnny was naked, too."

Everyone was still laughing when Dre came in, balancing her sugar work tool kit and several large paper bags with handles. Honey was closest to the door, so she helped her by taking the bags off her arm and closing the door.

"You can keep the white bag," Dre told her as she made her way to her regular worktable. "It's for you."

Honey followed her and set the bags on her table, then slid the white one to the edge so she could look inside. Something was folded neatly in a plastic bag.

"I thought since you liked Kit's apron, and you seemed to like some of my marketing ideas"—she shrugged— "anyway, you didn't have an apron. You could just use it here, or at your own place. It's more shop apron than baking apron."

Honey was so surprised and touched she didn't know what to say. "Dre, that's, wow . . . that's so nice of you! You didn't have to do that."

Dre continued setting out her tools and prepping her station. "Hope you like it."

"I know I will." Honey slid out the plastic bag and everyone pretty much stopped what they were doing to come closer so they could all see. She opened the bag and slid out the apron. It was of heavy cream canvas material and constructed like a shop apron with deep pockets, sturdy ties. She shook it out, then turned it around so she could see the front.

A collective "oh, wow" came from the entire group.

Tears sprang to Honey's eyes and she had to dab them away so she could marvel at every detail. "This is . . . I can't even . . . you're insanely talented."

It was a scene much like the one on Kit's apron, but instead of a map of the island with cupcakes and fairy characters representing all of the cupcake club members, this one was of a clearing in a forest filled with magical flowers, toadstools, gnomes, and fairies—all her little forest critters and creatures tucked in here and there amongst the foliage and in the trees—every one of them a design from her own catalog, stunningly reproduced in one big mural. It was like a walking billboard for her work.

She slid the strap over her neck, then hugged the apron to her chest. "I love this. It's brilliant. It's . . . I have no words. I could hug you, except—"

Dre lifted her hands, palms out. "I'm good."

Honey smiled at that, then went right back to gushing over her new prized possession. "My God, Dre, this is— well, you've got my marketing campaign, that's for sure. When I have actual money, I'd like for you to look at my print catalog and online stuff, too. I want one look for all of it. Can you do that?"

"I can."

Honey took off the apron and laid it on a clean worktable so they could all get a close-up look at every little detail. While everyone else was oohing and ahhing, Honey went back to Dre's worktable. "If you're ever interested in working with clay or carving, it would be my honor to teach you. On the house. I'd love to see what you'd come up with."

Dre looked up at that, and though she seemed not to particularly care or be all that fazed by the reaction to her work, Honey could see that telltale gleam in her eyes, that satisfied feeling, knowing something you'd created had been sincerely appreciated and acknowledged. That it had found a good home. She felt like that every time someone bought one of her pieces.

"I'd like that," Dre said, her gaze avid with sincere interest. "That's not a field of art I've done anything with and—" She stopped, seeming to realize she'd almost let herself sound excited. "Listen, I know you're trying to get up and running, so maybe we can swap classes for marketing?"

"Oh, I'd want to pay you for that," Honey responded. "You don't have to—"

"It's a good offer," Dre interrupted, the corners of her mouth curving in the closest thing to a smile Honey had ever seen her make. "I'd take it if I were you. I'm a fast learner. You'll come out ahead. Trust me."

Honey laughed, but then got a considering look on her face. "You'll do great with clay, but I think what's really going to get to you is carving. Ever done it?"

Dre shook her head. "But I'd like to."

Honey smiled. "Good. Just a word of warning. It's not a fast learning curve."

Dre bent back to her work, but Honey could see an actual smile on her face. "We'll see."

"Dre, this really is amazing," Lani said as the others remained crowded around the apron. "Honey, I can't wait to see your creatures. They're all so cute! I can put some in the cupcake shop, too. Maybe you can do some of your critters holding little cupcakes or something. They'd sell like mad."

Honey beamed, ideas already pinging in her mind. "That'd be fun. I'd love that."

"Did you get your stuff ready to ship yet?" Lani asked. "You must be dying to work. At least, that's how I felt about baking the whole time it took me to get this place set up."

"I am," Honey said. "I've been sketching some new

ideas in the evenings, and it's helped me to stop thinking about the five million things I have to do."

"Did the inspections go okay?" Charlotte asked.

"Define okay?" Honey replied dryly. "That list of five million things? Yeah, that's all just from the inspection guy."

Lani groaned. "I so remember those days."

"I'm still living them," Kit said. "We just got signed off on the final food services health inspection. Talk about cutting it close."

"Dylan is giving me a list of names of guys who can do some of the work, but Lani, if you have that list you mentioned, it would be great. I'm pretty sure I need every kind of tradesman there is for something."

"Oh, right! I forgot. I have it . . . somewhere."

"I have it," Kit said. "I kept a file on my computer. Just drop by and I'll print it out for you."

"Show-off," Lani said.

"Yeah, but I work for cupcakes," Kit shot back, and they both laughed.

Everyone wandered back to their workstations and Honey held up the apron to look at it again. "I could look for hours and keep seeing new things. I don't want to put it on; I don't want to mess it up."

"That's how I felt about mine," Kit said, gesturing to her Babycakes apron. "I've washed this a hundred times already. They hold up."

"I'm glad you said that, otherwise I might have just had to frame this." Honey slipped the loop over her head and was walking past the back door as she tied it around her waist when the door burst open and a tall, buxom blonde with hair like big corkscrews came bounding into the kitchen. "Oh! Hi!" she bubbled, stopping just short of plowing Honey down. "I'm Riley."

"I'm Honey."

Riley's eyes popped wide. "Oh, yea, I'm so glad you've joined us! Kit said you might." Before Honey knew what was going to happen, Riley enveloped her in a hug. "Welcome to Cupcake Club!"

"Riley, no!" Lani shouted.

But it was too late. Off Honey went, but it wasn't the big jerk sideways. In fact, she didn't even really leave the room. It was like she was just having a little moment. Her pulse zoomed, but there was no dread, no fear. It was more of a pleasant little buzz as if she'd just gotten a private, cerebral text message with photo attached. She had a quick visual of Riley and, well, she recognized the man as Quinn Brannigan because she knew him from his book jacket photo, but she also knew he was Riley's significant other. He was beaming, and Riley was—oh, poor thing. Riley was puking, actually. Why was he smiling? Then she saw a . . . a blue cross? A hospital? No, it was . . . on a white plastic stick. Oh, a pregnancy test!

Just like that, the vision snapped away and Honey was fully back in the kitchen.

Riley let her go, ducking down so she could look straight into Honey's eyes. "I'm so sorry. Are you okay? They told me, but I wasn't thinking. I'm a hugger, and I just . . . It was spontaneous. I was just so excited to tell everyone my news and . . . Are you sure you're okay?"

"I'm fine, really."

"Excited to tell us what?" Charlotte asked.

"Yes, what?" Lani chimed in. "How was the boat trip? We haven't heard a peep from you since you left. Was it good seeing your friends again?" She smiled. "Oh no. Did they want their boat back?"

"No, no, but something did happen with the boat."

Lani frowned. "Are you okay? Quinn? I mean, did you get caught in a storm or something?"

Riley laughed. "No, but we kind of rescued someone from a storm. Of sorts."

"A storm rescue!" Alva exclaimed. "How exciting. That would make a great article for the newspaper." She sent a short glance toward Honey, then smiled back at Riley.

"There's even more to it than that," Riley gushed on, mercifully saving Honey from Alva's continued, not-so-subtle campaign to be the one to "break" the story about Honey's "gift." "Her name is Emmaline Sweet. How awesome is that name, by the way? We brought her back with us. Well, that's not entirely true. She sailed the boat back and Quinn and I flew back up. She's an amazing cook and I got her a temporary gig working at Laura Jo's starting next week."

"Oh, sure, sure. You can call Laura Jo, but you can't call your best friends," Lani said with an exaggeratedly aggrieved air.

Riley laughed, but her cheeks were rosy and she was all but bouncing in her shoes. "There was a good reason not to call. At least it felt like a good reason at the time. I didn't want you all to be mad at me. At us."

"For rescuing someone and finding her a job?"

Riley lifted her hand and held it in front of her face, which was when Honey—and everyone else—saw the giant diamond sparkler on her ring finger.

"You got engaged? Did it have something to do with the rescue? How romantic." Alva pulled a notepad out of her apron and started writing down notes. "How did he propose?"

"Actually," Riley said, her gaze skimming the room. "He did more than propose. We eloped. We got married." She covered her mouth with her hands, but her joy was all but dancing in her eyes . . . and her bouncing curls.

The room collectively gasped, while Honey sighed in relief. So, her vision was probably—hopefully—going to be a good thing for Riley. She already knew Quinn was going to be happy. As everyone crowded around Riley, with Franco being the first one to examine the diamond ring up close, Honey watched from the fringes of the excited group.

Not that she felt at all excluded. She was certain they'd be quite happy for her to join in. But she really didn't want to know anything else about any of their futures, good or bad, at least not this evening. So she kept a little distance, and enjoyed their exuberant reaction to Riley's big news, and the good natured ribbing they directed her way for having the nerve to get married and deprive them of a big, local wedding.

It made Honey think about what life was really going to be like with these people who had so openly accepted her, pulled her into their world, and seemed to sincerely want her to be part of their lives. She wanted all of that. Badly. Everything about it, about them, already far exceeded any hopes or dreams she might have had about having a normal life.

Except it wasn't normal. She wanted to be right in the thick of the celebration, oohing and ahhing over Riley's wedding ring and romantic elopement stories. She also knew she couldn't handle a steady stream of visions like that, even the brief, essentially pleasant ones. It was still a lot to deal with, to be saddled with information about people she cared about.

In truly letting her guard down, letting people into her life, and actively participating in theirs, she wasn't going to have the one protection she'd enjoyed in the past—that of not knowing things about those closest to her. She was still having visions about Dylan and imagined she would have them about many people in her life.

That was something she had to really think about—both the energy it took to experience them . . . and the burden of knowledge they left behind. Even though it was happy news, knowing Riley was going to become pregnant in the not too distant future was something Honey didn't want to think about every time they saw each other or chatted. There was no compelling reason to tell Riley what she knew, nothing seemed wrong or dangerous in the vision she'd had, so that meant she should keep it to herself and just . . . know. That begged the questions, How much would she learn about her new friends? And when would it simply become too much?

Even worse, at what point would they realize they risked her knowing any number of things about them just by inadvertently touching her? Interesting and intriguing, it was like a cool party trick, but what happened when they realized she couldn't turn it on and off? She was going to know whatever she was going to know, and there was nothing they could do about it. Not if they wanted to stay friends, anyway. Honey knew she wouldn't want anyone knowing *her* personal business. She certainly wouldn't want to think about that every time she looked at a person and wonder . . . She'd probably steer clear of them just to avoid it. Who wouldn't?

"It's just a matter of balance," she told herself, trying to quell the surge of panic and tamp down the gut knowledge that this best life, these new friends and new community . . . couldn't stay that way. Not realistically. She simply had to learn her limits and find a way to keep from knowing things. Pacing was the key. She'd stay a little apart, give herself some space and the protection that would afford her. She wanted her new life and her new friends, so she'd simply find a way to figure out how to balance it all, and be thankful for all the good things she had and would continue to have.

"You saw something, didn't you?"

Honey jumped, startled, so lost in her thoughts she hadn't noticed Alva had come around to her side of the worktable. "Alva. Listen, I'm sorry we didn't get the chance to talk, you know, before I spoke to Barbara. That wasn't planned—"

Alva waved her hand. "Water under the bridge."

Honey glanced down at her, thinking it was obviously anything but without saying so.

Alva moved a hair closer and lowered her voice. "So, what did you see? When Riley hugged you. That girl deserves all the happiness in the world, so if you know something that might affect her newly-wedded bliss, you should tell me. We'll figure out how best to handle it. I'm good with people."

Honey didn't know whether to laugh or cry, but she understood why Alva was willing to forgive her for letting Barbara Hughes scoop her on the latest in hot gossip. Alva wanted to be her partner in extrasensory perception crime. "It's nothing to be concerned about," she told Alva. "I think Riley and Quinn can look forward to a good life."

Alva's interest only increased. "So, you did see something! Well, perhaps you should let me be the judge of what should be passed along. After all, you don't really know Riley as yet, about her past heartbreak and how truly wonderful Quinn has been for her. If it's good news, perhaps that is something we should pass along." She beamed up at Honey, who didn't miss the calculating twinkle in her eyes. "Like a wedding present, of sorts."

"I-I think we should just let Riley and Quinn be happy newlyweds and—oh look! Franco and Charlotte are already talking about catering a reception for them here on the island, and Lani's going to do cupcakes for dessert. You should—don't you want to be in on the planning?"

Alva was clearly torn between pursuing her new path as

Honey's second sight assistant and not being left out of the latest turn of events. "We'll talk more later." She bustled back over to the excited group.

"That's what I'm afraid of," Honey murmured under her breath.

It would take a little time to figure out the delicate balance of making friends and being a good friend in return, while keeping the visions separate, but she wasn't exactly sure how that was going to work. Her friends were so good, so sweet and understanding about giving her space, about not intentionally intruding or making it hard on her . . . but the fact was accidents were going to happen. Contact amongst good friends was going to happen. At least, if she really wanted to be a part of this group, this community, it would. And if she wanted to gush about the man in her life and be a part of things like Riley's big announcement it stood to reason her talent was also going to come up in conversation . . . like it just did with Alva. They were going to notice when she had visions and naturally be curious.

What would happen when it was something she did feel compelled to share? Something that did require a warning?

Honey rubbed her forehead as the mounting tension began to make her temples throb.

"You feeling poorly, *mon amie*?"

She looked up to find Franco standing on the other side of the worktable. The smile she gave him was sincere. "I'm okay. Just . . . a lot on my mind."

"We'll understand if you want to duck out." He smiled. "With Riley's big announcement and the party planning, I don't think much baking is going to happen tonight, anyway. Just promise me you'll come again next time. You are coming by the open house next Sunday, right?"

"The grand opening? Of course." She had been planning on dropping in. But she might be a little more . . . tactical about choosing her timing. Hopefully a less crowded time. She'd keep watch from across the street, pick her moment.

Franco's smile was steady, but his gaze was a bit probing. "Anything else on your mind, *chérie*?"

"I'm still getting used to this, I guess."

His smile deepened. "We can be a lot. But we mean well."

"I didn't mean that in a bad way," she hurried to add, realizing it might have sounded like an insult. "I meant for me. I haven't been around a lot of people for quite some time. I'm still . . . finding my way. It's been wonderful, really. More than I ever expected."

"Doesn't make it easy, though, does it?" He laid his hand on the table between them palm down, and she understood it for the gesture it was. A pat on the arm, a squeeze of reassurance, just without the actual contact. "Maybe, since it's more than you hoped, it also makes it more than you bargained on having to cope with?"

Honey's smile grew as well, as did the honest affection she felt for her new friend. "You're very wise, but then I hear you French-Italians are like that."

Franco snorted a laugh. "And don't you forget it, sister," he said, all pure native Bronx.

"Thank you," she said, never more sincere.

"Just remember, even when a lot feels like too much, real friends still understand, forgive when necessary, and want to be there. Our hearts are in the right place. I think yours is, too. At the end of the day that's all that matters. Right, *ma chérie*?" He winked at her, then blew a kiss, making her laugh despite the tears she felt gathering at the corners of her eyes. "I told you none of us is perfect, and this group in particular is like the band of merry misfits."

She let out a snort. "Then I'll fit right in."

He rolled his eyes, but was grinning. "That's what I'm trying to tell you. You already do. Go on. I'll cover for you."

Honey slipped off her apron, folded it carefully, and put it back in the white bag. She didn't have any baking tools of her own, so she winked at Franco, mouthed *thank-you,* and ducked out the back.

She had a lot to think about. Despite Franco's much needed and timely words of encouragement, the fact remained that she was going to have to figure out how to handle a lot. She questioned if she could. How much harder would it be when she cared more deeply, loved more deeply, only to find out that the people who were being so wonderful to her found they had their own limits as to what they could handle.

She saw Dylan walking toward her across the alley and was torn between the strong desire to run and fling herself into his arms and pour out all of her mounting fears . . . and the equally strong urge to turn around and simply run. And keep running. From all of it.

Chapter 18

"**G**ood," Dylan said when he saw Honey come out the back door of Cakes by the Cup. "You saved me from having to kidnap you from Bake Club."

"Cupcake Club," Honey corrected, smiling as he drew closer. "Why were you going to kidnap me?"

He lifted his hand and dangled a set of keys between them. "Thought there was something you might like to see."

Her eyes grew wide, but not before he'd gotten close enough to see the tension around them and that her smile was a little bit pinched.

His instinct—a rather strong one—was to pull her into his arms, kiss her until that pinched look went away, then get her to tell him what had put it there in the first place. He wasn't quite sure what kept him from following through on it . . . maybe the fact that she hadn't had that same urge.

The pinched look disappeared as she realized it was her car keys he was jangling. "My car? It's done?"

"It is." He dropped the keys in her open hand. "Come on. Take a look."

If she was at all surprised by the less than intimate greeting, considering they had spent the previous night and a good part of the morning in his bed . . . and in his shower and his kitchen and back in his bed, she didn't do or say anything to indicate it. He didn't know if that relieved him, concerned him . . . or just plain pissed him off.

But he did know until he figured that out, it was probably a good idea to keep his hands to himself.

He'd left the back bay door open so the light from the garage spilled out, adding a brighter glow to the moonlit alley. They walked around his truck and though he was a little confused by their interaction, he took great satisfaction from her gasp of delight.

"It's . . . it's actually pretty. And shiny, too." She turned to him and his heart skipped a little, seeing an equally bright and shiny light in her eyes.

He shouldn't be miffed that same light hadn't been there upon seeing him, but the truth was he was a bit put out.

He reminded himself he had no idea what had been going on inside the bakery, or what she might have been dealing with. Socializing was still very new to her, and it had to be a lot of work, learning to balance that against her second sight.

He wished she felt she could bring any or all of her problems to him, unload if she had to, or find a haven of sorts with him, but he knew she was figuring it all out. He gave her space, letting her set the pace . . . but that didn't mean he didn't feel disappointment.

"How did you get it to look so glossy like that? You couldn't have had time to paint it." She walked around the car. "I can still see all the scratches and dents, but—it looks so cute now." She smiled at him. "So Bug-like."

Dylan shook his head, wondering how he could be amused and annoyed at the same time. "You can thank Dell for that. He found some article on a new compound being developed to help seal boat hulls to keep the salt water from corroding them so quickly and thought maybe it would work on your car. The salt air here and your worn off finish were going to be a lethal combination, sugar. All my hard work would be for nothing when the body turned to rust only months after getting it back into pretty decent running condition."

She ran her hand along the roof and over the wheel hubs, and he realized he was a sick, sick man indeed, for being jealous of a damn car. But he'd already gotten a little attached to feeling those same hands stroking him. Something told him that wasn't in the cards for him again anytime soon. He was on the verge of asking her to tell him what had happened at the bakery and get her to talk about it with him, but she spoke first.

"Well, you can tell Dell he's amazing. I will thank him profusely, the first time I see him." She looked over at Dylan, eyes still shining. "Thank you, Dylan. For all of this. You put a lot of work into this poor thing. I'm not sure it deserved it. But I appreciate it. More than you know." She looked back at the car. "Now I have an escape hatch."

His smile didn't just fade, it winked directly out, right as his gut knotted up. "Thinkin' about runnin' off already?"

"What?" She looked up at him again, her tone perplexed, but a tinge of guilt in her eyes. "No. I just—I meant it will be good to be captain of my own destiny again, and not dependant on the kindness of strangers."

She'd done her best Southern drawl on that last part, but he'd seen right through it and heard the anxiety . . . and decided it was bullshit to keep his distance.

He strolled around the back of the car, half expecting her to back away as he came up to her. But she stood her ground—which was exactly how it felt—like they'd somehow entered a field of battle. For the life of him, he didn't know why. So he pushed. Not because it pissed him off, but because it hurt him. If she was going to have the power to hurt him, then the least he deserved was an explanation.

He blocked her in, between him and her car, bracing an arm on either side of her, holding her gaze. It occurred to him that this was how it had all started, standing next to her car. One bobbled stack of boxes and a freaky vision later . . . and here he was, all tangled up.

More surprising was that he didn't so much mind the tangled-up part. He understood these moments, much as the easy moments, mattered, and hoped like hell he didn't screw it up. "How was your day, sugar?"

Her brows lifted. "How was my day?"

He nodded.

"Uh, well . . . it was pretty good. I've gotten the ground floor pretty well cleared out, just need to do some industrial cleaning. Jake came by and fixed the stairs. He made sure they were stable, so they'll pass inspection now. Thanks for sending him, by the way. I was going to call him, but it saved me a lot of time. I can get started on the upper balcony and office tomorrow." She stopped, took a breath, then looked at him and held his gaze. "But that's not what you're really asking."

"Actually, it is. I know something is wrong. Or at least not entirely right. It's not how we left things this morning, anyway. But if I came out and asked you that, it would put you in a defensive position, and I didn't want that. Especially if what's not right has anything to do with me. So, I figure the safest way to find out is to ask about your day, give you a chance to tell me."

A dry smile teased the corners of her mouth. "I thought you said you weren't good at this relationship stuff."

His urge to smile came back, even if there wasn't quite the sense of relief he'd been hoping to feel along with it. "I'm trying not to screw it up."

"I'm sorry I'm not good at this. It's funny. I've been thinking a lot about how it feels, opening myself up to knowing things about people who are becoming my

friends, things I'd rather not know, things—if they knew—
that they'd rather me not know. Even if they're good
things."

"Something happened at Bake Club, huh?"

"It wasn't a big deal," she said, admitting as much. "No
one noticed except Alva. Riley came back and she hugged
me hello and . . . anyway, it wasn't that big a deal. It was a
good thing, not a bad thing."

"Like the two you've had about me, about the sailboat."

"Like that, yes."

Dylan studied her face, her eyes. "It's still a lot, isn't it?
Never knowing what you'll find out, or what to do
with it."

"Yeah," she said quietly. "I just . . . realized that being
close to people isn't going to protect me from having visions about them, maybe quite the opposite. Even good
ones come with a price, and I feel . . . well, I feel like a
whiny, ungrateful jerk. I'm getting so much more than I
expected. I'm getting *everything.* How dare I complain,
you know? Even to myself."

"You're getting a lot all at once. Cut yourself some
slack."

Honey let out a brief laugh and shook her head.
"Maybe I should have just run into your arms after all."

He lifted her chin, cupped her cheek, the first he'd
touched her after a day spent apart. "I'd have liked that,
sugar. Welcomed that. Why didn't you?"

"You're right that it's been a whole lot all at once.
Tonight, with everyone being so excited—Riley and
Quinn eloped—I just . . . after the vision, I kind of stood
apart, trying to figure out how I was going to be a part of
things the way I want to, the way they want me to, and at
the same time, deal with the fallout. And it is fallout. I
can't pretend it isn't or that it won't be. It's only going to
accumulate."

"I guess it will. I don't know what to tell you about that. I can say what anyone who cares about you would say— that you'll figure it out, that you'll find a way if it's what you want, that we support you and will help you any way we can. All of which is true. But I don't know what it's like to be you, and I don't know how you'll make it work. Frankly, if it were me, I don't know that I'd even want to try."

Her eyes widened at that.

"But you're not me, and I'm not you," he said. "I'd go deep into cave mode and be happy there, tuning it all out. You wouldn't, you won't, especially now that you know what you can have, and that it's what you really want. I'm guessing it would be harder going back to hiding again. I guess the question is . . . which is the harder of the two? Giving it all up and dealing with the loss of what you really want . . . or trying to find a way to make it work without exhausting yourself and becoming so stressed that you can't enjoy the life you finally get to have."

She didn't say anything for several long moments and he felt his own heart pound, waiting for her to speak and dreading what she was going to say. The fact was she'd opted not to run to him, and had seen a means of escape when she'd looked at her car.

"I do know one thing," she said at length, and warmth finally came back into her eyes. "You didn't screw it up."

"But?"

She ducked her head again. "I don't know, Dylan. I don't know the answer to that question. And the longer it takes me to figure it out, the harder it gets, the scarier it gets"—she lifted her gaze to his—"because I am getting attached . . . to the island, to the people here . . . to you. It's all happening so fast, and you're right, it's so much all at once. I know no one is pressuring me to do anything or figure anything out. I feel like if I could just bury myself in the bookstore—my shop—and focus on getting that up and running, it would buy me time. But it's just more hiding in the barn, you know? The only way to figure it out is to get out and live it, do it, and let it happen.

"It scares the hell out of me. I realized tonight that reality might not turn out to be what I want. We'll all get closer, we'll care more, and . . . I will know more. Our friendships will change, people will change, the more things I know. I'll change. I'll care a lot more, and it will be harder for my friends, maybe too hard, if they realize they can't handle having me around. And . . . I don't know . . . I don't think I can—" She broke off and looked straight at Dylan.

He saw the utter dread—and the absolute longing—in her eyes. And his heart broke. She was right. It was the one thing he couldn't fix . . . and the only thing he didn't think he could take, if it stayed broken.

"Come home with me," he told her. "I have a guest room," he added, before she could reply. "You can be comfortable, have some peace, a little quiet and comfort."

"I'm—thank-you, but I think I need—"

He cupped her face with both of his hands. "I want to fix this, and I know I can't. That's as hard for me as this is for you. It's the only really important thing that needs fixing, and I feel helpless. I don't want to add to your pressure, either. But don't go hide in your space, in your new barn. At least come hide in mine. Give me that much."

"Dylan," she said, the word choked with emotion.

He knew she was going to turn him down, just as he knew he shouldn't take the rejection so hard. She wanted—needed—to regroup and naturally wanted her own space to do it in. But he also knew if she had any hope of figuring things out so she ended up staying and reaching for the life she wanted, she was going to have to break some of her old habits. He knew that better than anyone.

"I've never wanted what you want." He wasn't sure how to say what needed to be said, but had to risk trying. "I've also never wanted what I want right now—which is you. This . . . thing we've started. I want that. And I don't know any more how to go about getting it and keeping it, than you do about handling the big, wide world crashing in on your carefully constructed bubble. We've both protected ourselves, and with good reason.

"But I'm stepping out of my bubble—hell, sugar, I'm busting it to pieces. If you don't think it scares me spitless, you'd be wrong. I've already asked myself my big question. Which is harder? Trying to figure out what we have, stumbling through it, terrified I'll just screw it up, and making myself vulnerable for the first time in a very long time by giving someone the power to hurt me . . . or not waking up to you like I did this morning ever again. For me, sugar, it was a no brainer."

Tears leaked out the corners of those voluminous, beautiful eyes, and he felt like the worst kind of bully. He was also a desperate one. If he didn't at least put in his claim and make her aware of what was really at stake, then she was going to make her choice without all the information she should have. Perhaps the most important information. At least, it felt that way to him.

"Just . . . come home with me, Honey. We'll create our own sanctuary. Together. Take whatever space you want. But do it with me." He reached up and dabbed at her tears. "You're breaking my heart here, darlin'. I'm not trying to make it harder."

"I know. You can't help yourself." She sniffled, letting out a choked, watery laugh at the same time. "You have to try and fix it anyway."

He pulled her into his arms and wrapped her up tight, feeling her cheek pressed against his pounding heart. Trying to will her to feel what he felt—that nothing was more right than this—he kissed the top of her head. "I don't have a choice, sugar," he whispered. *I'm falling in love with you.*

He felt her stiffen in his arms, and worried for a split second that he'd triggered another vision. Good or bad, that was the last thing she needed. She needed to be held, stroked, kissed, reassured . . . loved. And love was worth the risk.

He relaxed his hold, leaning back so he could see her face. She looked up at him, and it was misery, rather than relief he saw on her face. He was thankful that she wasn't off in Never-Never Land, but it was scant comfort to him.

"I hope it's enough for you to know that I want to," she said, and his heart fell another giant notch. "I . . . you're giving me more than I deserve."

"Honey—"

"I want it all, but I have to know I can give back, just as fully. It's just . . . it's all happening so fast. I thought I could handle it, just let it roll over me and I'd roll along with it. That I would simply be assimilated, as Kit said. It turns out it's not that easy. I wish it was." Honey reached up and cupped his cheek, and his own eyes burned. "I want to figure it out, Dylan. I just . . . need some time. And space. I have to slow it down at least a little and give myself a chance to work my way into it."

"Okay." He knew it should be. It was little enough to ask. It felt like the wrong tack to take, but it wasn't his choice to make. "Offer stays open, sugar," he said, wanting to ease the tension.

He knew if he kissed her, he would be hard pressed to stop. Easing her out of his arms, he tapped the top of her car with the flat of his palm. "Why don't you take her for a spin."

Honey looked a little lost for a moment, blinked behind those glasses of hers a few times, then turned and cleared her throat. "Yeah. Maybe I will. Get some fresh air, clear my head."

"Do I need to block the bridge?"

She shot him a dry smile, and a part of him settled a little. "I'm not running away. Not tonight anyway."

"Just don't run without saying good-bye." Well, that had kind of slipped out. So much for lessening the tension.

She blinked a few more times and he knew tears threatened again.

Even though her pain tore at his gut a little, it was also too damn bad. He wasn't going to walk on eggshells.

"I wouldn't do that" was all she said, then opened the door and climbed into the Beetle.

He let her pull her seat belt on, then closed the door for her. He felt a moment of pride when the engine started right up with nary a rattle or wheeze. He knew she understood the magnitude of that accomplishment by the way her brows rose and the quick look of wonderment she shot his way. She put it in gear and pulled out, pausing once she'd cleared the bay and lowered her window.

He walked to the edge of the open bay door.

"Thank you, Dylan."

He lifted his hand in a half wave, smiling briefly. "You'll get my bill."

She smiled, too . . . then drove off.

He watched until the taillights disappeared around the corner at the end of the alley and wondered if either one of them had believed her. "Good-bye, sugar," he murmured. Just in case.

Chapter 19

Honey used a wooden dowel to press a vent hole in the bottom of the snail body, then propped it back on her worktable and gave it a critical once over. Her favorite pieces incorporated real wood, whether it was a foundation she'd hand carved or a natural piece of wood—a small tree stump or limb. Hollowed out, then formed into a planter with either real or man-made moss, live plants, or life-like silk flowers and foliage, her clay creations were usually tucked in here or peeking out from there.

The snail she was working on would sit under a large red and white polka dot capped toadstool house she'd already completed. A series of smaller, fat little mushrooms would eventually be wedged in a great piece of dried wood limb she'd collected ages ago, but hadn't worked with yet.

She sighed and looked around at the bare basics of her new work studio. The larger rear storage room had been designated for her personal workshop. Reassembled metal racks lined the walls, all of which would eventually hold newly created product. Her kilns and small polymer ovens had been relegated to the smaller storage room. Now that she had fully functioning air-conditioning and ventilation fans in the rear workrooms, she'd moved her living space into what she privately referred to as the mezzanine level office. It was still a bit stuffy up there, so she'd supplemented with a few floor fans. She'd have to consider forced air ventilation at some point, but that wasn't anywhere in her budget at the moment.

Her stock had arrived from Oregon and was sitting in many boxes stacked in the front of the store. She wished there had been built-in shelving on the main floor like there was around the balcony level, but a few second-hand tables could display her wares in the front window. If she spent a little more on some interesting pieces she'd more or less have the bare bones to get going.

"Who are you kidding,?" she muttered. She'd painted only half the space and knew she needed professional help to reach the high central ceiling. She wanted to paper the walls and add other décor, wainscoting maybe, but until she figured out display setups, that would have to wait so she could incorporate all of it together.

Even keeping everything bare bones, and using all local labor, who had worked for as close to dirt cheap as she could have hoped for, she wasn't marginally close to opening. Without so much as a peep of interest in her farm property as yet, she knew the smartest thing to do was open up her online store again. By taking orders, working on new product, and getting that part under way again, she could use the income to finance the rest of the shop rehab. Running her online business was pretty much a full-time occupation and would leave little time for her to work on getting the shop going. While there was no actual deadline on opening, the longer it took, the longer she was taking advantage of Dylan's generosity.

If he thought she was worried about that, he'd be pissed off. Of course, he was probably none too happy with her, anyway. It had been a week since their conversation the night she'd gotten her car back. They'd exchanged greetings every morning since then, when he came to the garage—small talk, mostly updates about how the shop was going, discussions on work that needed to be done next, recommendations on who to use . . . business, essentially. He hadn't tried to so much as touch her, much less kiss her, nor had he made any effort to pick up the discussion where it had left off. He was giving her the time and space she'd asked for.

She was grateful for it, more than he knew . . . but she wasn't any closer to an answer. Her belongings had begun arriving the day after their chat, and she'd shamelessly buried herself in unpacking, and looked for solace and guidance where she'd always found it . . . in creating things from clay and finding whimsy in pieces of wood. It had helped to calm her nerves, soothe her worries. But it hadn't brought her any answers.

She knew that was why she hadn't pulled the trigger and reopened her online store or done anything more than scrape the dirt out of the shop and get all the utilities functioning. Those were things any tenant would have to do . . . without altering or putting her own stamp on it.

She was startled out of her thoughts by the jangling of the bell she'd hung on the front door. The various workers she'd hired had been told to come to the back door, but as often as not, they stood out front and banged on the door. So she'd left it unlocked and put a bell on it.

"Be right out!" she called, straightening from her work stool and stretching as she washed the clay from her hands in the industrial sink in the back corner. She was drying her hands on a towel as she stepped into the front area. "Oh, hello. I thought it was the guy coming to wire the fridge in the kitchen. I thought I could just plug it in, but I blew some circuit or other. Of course."

Morgan Westlake smiled even as the little girl with him tucked herself behind his legs.

Honey came a little closer. "Hi. I'm Honey. You must be Lilly." She glanced up at Morgan and he nodded, so she crouched down next to him. "What do you have there?"

Lilly kept her head ducked, but held out the big, stuffed binder she had clutched to her chest. "My turtle book. Miss Dre maded it for me."

Charmed by her five-year-old pronunciation, Honey sat down on the swept out and scrubbed, but otherwise bare cement floor. "Can I see it?"

Lilly finally looked up, and Honey's heart was instantly lost in those huge, luminous eyes. "Okay." She handed the book to her.

"Why don't you sit down and show me." Honey looked up at Morgan. "Do you have time?"

"I just brought by the lease agreement papers on your new space. I have to stop in and talk to Lani and Kit about some last minute things for the opening tomorrow. Is it okay if—"

"Absolutely." Honey looked at Lilly. "Would you like to see some of the things I make after we look at your book? Maybe we can figure out how to make a sea turtle."

Lilly's eyes grew wide and she looked up at Morgan. "Can I stay, Moggy?"

"If Miss Honey is sure." He waited until Lilly looked back at Honey and silently mouthed *I'll be ten minutes, tops.*

"I'm totally sure," Honey said. "I'm waiting for the repair guy and I should be setting up some accounting, but I got sidetracked making snails and toadstool houses. You know how that is."

He chuckled. "I'm raising a five-year-old. I know exactly how that is."

"You made snails?" Lilly asked. "What's a toast—toads—"

"Toadstool," Honey said more slowly. "It's a big, colorful mushroom."

Lilly made a face. "Uncle Moggy gets them on his pizza. Yuck."

"I think you'll like mine." Honey leaned closer and whispered, "Mine are actually houses where magic snails and fairies live. They're not for eating."

Lilly's eyes shone with wonder. "Magic snails?"

Honey nodded. And just like that, Lilly plopped down next to Honey and took back her binder, opening it up and laying it out on the floor. "Miss Dre drew me some fairies. See?" She opened it, quickly passing many pages of colored-in sea turtles, to another page Honey immediately recognized as Dre's immaculate and fantastic pen and ink work. That one, too, was colored all over with great enthusiasm and an amazing ability to stay inside the lines, by the little girl seated beside her.

"They're beautiful. Miss Dre made me a shop apron with fairies. You want to see it?"

Lilly scrambled to her feet, careful to close and pick up her much cherished, very dog-eared binder, and nodded.

Morgan saluted his good-bye and was grinning as he let himself out the way he had come. Honey would have told him to use the rear entrance so he could cross the alley to the bakery, but she had a very excited five-year-old claiming all of her attention. "Come on," she told Lilly.

She spent almost an hour with Lilly, and knew by the time Morgan came around the third time that she was itching to teach classes. Lilly might be young, but her imagination was wildly unrestricted and that fueled Honey's own creativity. She was excited not only by how Sugarberry and its unique wildlife and shore life might impact her work, which had been all woodland focused, but also by how the people of Sugarberry would inform her artwork through their own creative impulses.

She'd told Morgan she'd look over the agreement, and

having just signed away another chunk of the miserly re-
mains of her budget to the appliance repair guy, she finally
sat down at her worktable and slid the agreement out of
the manila envelope, thinking in her present, optimistic
mood, she'd be most prepared to deal with it.

So, she thought as she skimmed over it. There it was,
spelled out in black and white, with a nice blank space for
her to sign her name. And another for Dylan's signature.
She sighed . . . and laid the papers on top of the worktable
without reading through the fine print. Maybe she wasn't
ready yet.

When will you be? What is it going to take to decide?

She hadn't gone to Cupcake Club, begging off because
her inventory had been arriving steadily all week and she
didn't want to leave a note on the door to contact her at
the bakery. That hadn't stopped Alva, Lani, Kit, or Franco
from dropping by the shop, checking on her, seeing how
the renovation was going. Kit had dropped off the list of
tradesmen and subcontractors she and Lani had used on
Babycakes and Cakes by the Cup. Alva had invited her to
her poker tournament and tried to weasel more information out of her on what she'd seen regarding Riley. Lani
invited her to the reception they were throwing together
for Riley and Quinn, the weekend following the grand
opening. And Franco had just hung out, teased and flirted
with her, and generally been a friend. Of course, he'd also
jokingly asked if she'd put her hands on him and tell him
if the guy he was currently seeing was "the one" . . . but
it had been funny at the time. She'd been grateful for the
comic relief . . . and the friendship.

By comparison, Dylan's lack of involvement had been
pretty glaring, but she understood he had to protect himself and didn't fault him for it. But it made her feel worse
for not being able to sort her mind out faster. If she could
just stay in her shop and have people drop by to visit like

they had this week, that would be great. But the truth was, even though she dreaded certain aspects of it, she wanted to go to the grand opening, wanted to celebrate with Lani and Kit, and be part of the event, not just hear about it from people or read about it in the local gazette.

She missed Dylan. She missed his friendship, his teasing sexy grins; she wanted him naked, and wanted to be naked with him. She missed the way he looked at her and understood her. She missed talking to him, figuring things out with him, hearing his well considered thoughts. And dammit, she missed the way he took care of her, and wanted, so badly, to fix things for her so she'd be happy.

What it came down to was knowing whether or not she could make him happy. That was the reason she hadn't reinitiated things with him, which he was clearly waiting for her to do. She wanted to be all those things, do all those things for him, too. But she could only be honest about the situation, and the reality was . . . she was the one who was going to bring the issues, the drama, and the complications to any relationship she tried to have.

He'd made it clear he was perfectly happy living a life that consisted of working on cars, fixing up his boat, helping out how and where he could, but generally staying behind the scenes, uninvolved, a happy non-participant in active island life. Because he cared for her, she knew he'd try to help her by running interference, as he'd done with Frank Hughes. Dylan would try to help her find that critical balance she'd need, so people—her friends—would want to keep her in their lives, and not instinctively shut her out in order to protect their privacy.

Through all of that, his nice peaceful life would cease, and though he might initially think he was willing to make that kind of adjustment, wouldn't it wear thin in the long term? She couldn't help thinking it would. What would she bring to him? How would she be enhancing his life, in order to make that kind of sacrifice worthwhile?

Where would either of them be when he realized there was a huge imbalance in their relationship? He didn't need more heartache in his life. She didn't think she would survive living and working next door to a man who could quite possibly be the love of her life . . . if she wasn't any longer the love of his.

For the first time in her life she wished she could have a vision about herself, something to guide her and tell her which way to go. "And ain't that a kick in the pants," she muttered. She thought about her aunt Bea, and knew what she'd say. She'd tell Honey she was a damn fool for not going for it, for not sticking it out and letting herself and everyone else just find out how it would all turn out. But would even Bea agree that it was worth it, given the potential cost if it didn't? Sure, Honey could tell herself she had the consolation of knowing she'd tried, but somehow that didn't make her feel all that much better.

The bell on the front door jingled again, which surprised her because she was pretty sure she'd locked it after the repairman left. She looked up to find Dylan strolling toward the open door to the storage room.

Honey actually blinked her eyes to make sure she hadn't just conjured him up from her thoughts. Maybe she *was* having her own personal vision.

Except nothing was ephemeral about the man entering her workroom. He didn't say hello, didn't pause at the door, didn't even take a look around at all the changes that had happened since she'd turned the room into her workshop. From the looks of him, he had only one thing on his mind and she had no doubt what—or who—that was.

"Hi," he said somewhat gruffly, then without waiting for a response, he pulled her from her stool, into his arms, and kissed the absolute living daylights out of her.

She made it past the first split second of shock, past the second split second of half-expecting a vision . . . and then she sighed a soft sound of complete and utter capitulation, threw her arms around him, and kissed him right back with everything she was worth.

He groaned, maybe even growled a little as he took the kiss deeper and a lot more carnal. On the fringes of her thoughts, she worried he'd clear the worktable with a single sweep of his arm, but decided it was a small price to pay as long as he didn't stop kissing her, didn't let her think, and didn't let her worry.

She gasped and whimpered a little when he finally lifted his head.

"It's late," he said roughly, his eyes so intent, his gaze so focused on her, she wasn't too sure he wasn't having his own vision. Although maybe he was, at least about who and what he wanted. "And it's past time I did this. Come home, Honey. I'm done letting us figure this out apart. It doesn't make any sense. If we want to be together, then, dammit, we need to work it out together."

He framed her face, brushed callused thumbs gently over her cheeks. "I miss the hell out of you."

She smiled even as her eyes burned. "I miss you, too. I was just sitting here having quite the pity party for myself."

"Then what are we doing?"

"I don't want to hurt you," she said as plainly as she could.

"Well, you're already failing on that point."

Her heart skipped several beats, then dropped right to her stomach. "I'm so sorry," she said, forcing the words out past the thickness in her throat. "But it would be so much worse if I led you on, then couldn't hack it—"

"Trying to make things work when we both acknowledge the problem going in is not leading anyone on. I'm a big boy, Honey. If I get hurt, I'll survive. So will you. It's a risk we should be willing to take. We could take the leap, and one of us could get hit by that proverbial truck the next day. So . . . what? Do you just say no thank-you, something bad might happen at some point and we'll get hurt? Well, guess what? Love is like that. It can hurt like hell. It can damage, destroy, decimate. But it can build, lift, energize, motivate, inspire, and push us to greater things, things we couldn't do alone. So if that's not something you see as worth fighting for, then fine. Go, leave, run, hide. I'll even help you. But don't you dare decide this for me. Like I said from the beginning. Own who and what you are." He lowered his mouth, and she expected something intense, maybe even angry.

Instead, he shocked her straight to her core. His kiss was soft, so tender it made her heart quiver. He was gentle . . . sweet, coaxing her, wooing her, until her quivering heart filled right up and overflowed with love.

When he lifted his head, his eyes burned into hers. "I know it's fast. I know it's a lot. And I just don't give a shit. I want it fast, and I want a lot. I want you. All or nothing. I'm done being patient. That's where I stand. Figure out where you stand, Honey. And get back to me."

He let her go, and she had to grip the sides of the work-table to keep from sinking right to the floor. He stalked through the door and a moment later she heard the bell jangle, but there was no slamming door following it, just the click of the lock.

It was, she thought, the most final sound she'd ever heard.

She sank back down onto her stool. She was shaken, dazed, confused, and not a little afraid. Afraid she'd screwed up what might have been the best thing to ever happen to her. She was also pissed.

Did he really think he was just going to storm the castle, kiss her senseless, then kiss her sweet, and demand she hop to it if she wanted the bad ass prince to stick around? *Really?*

Without a thought to the clay pieces she'd been in the middle of working on, or anything else, for that matter, she snatched her keys off the rack by the back door, yanked her satchel off the floor where she'd dumped it the last time she'd come in, and slammed out the back door. His truck was gone, so she jumped in her car and tore off down the alley after him.

If he thought he was going to make demands . . . well then, she had a few of her own.

Chapter 20

"**W**ell, that was quite possibly the stupidest, most dumbass thing you've ever done in your entire life." Dylan swore under his breath all the way back to his house. He'd never, not once, manhandled a woman as he'd just done with Honey. But he'd never, not once, been pushed to his breaking point the way he had been with her. She'd looked almost fragile and lost when he'd set her away from him. Yes, she'd kissed him back, but then he'd gone and yelled at her and laid down his stupid ass law and she'd just looked poleaxed.

He'd had to do something, dammit. He was all for giving her space, but at some point, it wasn't sitting and thinking, it was hiding and avoiding. He'd watched folks troop in and out, deliverymen, locals, repairmen, subcontractors. What he hadn't seen was her come out. Not once. There was plenty to do in the place to give her an excuse to not surface until next spring, if that's what she wanted.

But it wasn't what he wanted. So, faced with going home alone, again, he'd gone next door to have a calm, rational conversation. All he'd wanted was to put his two cents in, see if that mattered at all. Get some sort of idea about how it was all going and where her mind was after playing hermit all goddamn week. He'd taken one look at her—hair pulled up in a tangle, serious glasses, clay covered shop apron, creating a scene that looked like it was something out of a Disney movie—and his resolve had snapped.

If she could sit there creating happy little cartoon characters, then she wasn't exactly wallowing in self-doubt and worry, was she? That was something a happy person did. If she was that damn happy, why hadn't she come over to tell him about it?

So he'd kissed her. He'd wanted a reaction—something, anything—to help him understand. And he'd gotten a reaction all right. Then he'd ruined it by throwing out ultimatums.

He pulled into his driveway, shut off the engine, and lowered his forehead to the hands still fisted on the wheel, wondering if maybe a few good whacks would knock some sense into him. The least she could have done was get pissed at him, God knows he'd have deserved it, but no, she'd stood there and looked . . . well, he didn't rightly know, but nothing about her reaction had made him feel remotely good about what he'd done.

He'd finally found one last brain cell she hadn't warped and gotten the hell out of there before he did anything more monumentally stupid. If that was possible.

"I told her I suck at this." He slammed out of his truck, but slowed down his stomping steps and his temper when Lolly came trotting down from the side screened-in porch, tail wagging in happy greeting. He crouched down and gave her a good scratch behind the ears. "You don't know this, but I so do not deserve a happy greeting."

"No," came a voice behind him. "You don't."

He gave Lolly one last good scratch, partly because he wanted to and partly so he could get his suddenly thumping heart and slightly wobbly legs under control. Then he straightened up and turned around. "Honey, I'm sorry."

"I'll agree with you there."

It made absolutely no sense whatsoever, but when she stepped closer and he got a good look at just how angry she was, he wanted to smile. Clearly, that was not the appropriate reaction. But a pissed off Honey was a hell of a sight better than a poleaxed, fragile looking Honey.

"Where do you get off stomping into my shop and telling me what I am and am not going to do?"

"I don't," he said simply. "I should be flogged for even considering it. Although, for the record, I didn't stomp." He walked down the driveway toward her. "I know you're mad, and you have every right to be, but I don't want to fight with you. I never want to fight with you."

"Oh no. Don't you go and get all reasonable with me now. I get to keep my mad on long enough so I get my turn to tell you where you can step right the hell off."

"And you should. And I know you will. Probably many times. I know I'll deserve it, every time."

"Don't patronize me."

"I'm not. I just . . . come here, sugar." He reached for her, but didn't grab her like before. "Please?"

The fight went out of her body. Her shoulders lost their rigid, squared off look, and she shifted out of her braced stance, but there was still a storm going on in those eyes, one he'd be well advised to heed.

"You don't fight fair," she muttered. "I get my turn."

"I don't want to fight at all." He stepped closer. "Can we kiss and not make up, then kiss some more until we both want to make up?"

She snorted, then she swore. "I really hate it that you can make me laugh right now."

"I really hate it that you came here with me, and made a permanent mark on this place . . . then left and never came back." Dylan lifted his hands out to her. "Come home, Honey. We'll figure the rest out. One way or the other. Just . . . don't go away again, okay? We need to do this together. We're better together than we are apart. That's all that really matters, right?"

She kept her arms folded tightly over her chest, looked down at her feet, and kicked a rock or two. "Have I mentioned that I also hate it—a lot—when you're always right?"

He took her elbows gently and tugged her close. She went grudgingly, arms still folded, but she went.

"You can be right next time. And the time after that. Now please, you're killing me. Come here, sugar."

She finally lifted her gaze to his and he saw that her eyes were swimming in tears. It would have been easier and less painful if someone had stuck a knife in his gut. "Aw, now don't do that."

"Trust me, I don't want to. You don't deserve tears." She sniffled, even as her expression remained stormy. "I don't want this to be so hard. I wasn't trying to hurt you. I was trying to do the exact opposite of that. I wanted to make sure. Not of you, but of me. I don't know how to do that because I don't have a lot of faith in my ability to see it through. I'm a hider, Dylan. And you're a cave dweller. If I come out of hiding and take this on, I'm going to drag you into it with me. You're already so many things to me, everything I wanted and more than I ever knew existed . . . and I'm so afraid I won't be that for you. I'm afraid that you'll start out wanting this, then you'll realize you signed on for complete and utter chaos, and you'll walk away. I wouldn't even blame you. But you were wrong about one thing. You said if anything bad happened, we'd survive. But"—her breath hitched, and the tears leaked out, making tracks down her cheeks—"if I ruined your life so badly that you had to leave, and you didn't want me . . . I don't think I would survive."

"Here I thought I was the dense one," he said, tipping her chin up, bringing her mouth close to his. "I love you."

Her breath caught at that, and she pressed her fists against his chest. "Dylan—"

"I love you, Honey Pie D'Amourvell. I know it's fast, but nothing about any of this has gone according to anything like a normal plan, and . . . I've never said those words before, to anyone. I wouldn't say them now if I didn't mean them." He hurried on before she could say anything, suddenly way out on the longest limb of his life, and scared like hell it was about to crack underneath the weight of what he'd just put on it. "Don't say it back, don't even respond. I just want that to matter. If it does, well, then we'll figure out the next step, whatever that—"

She cut him off by grabbing his face and pulling him down into a hard, fast, tear-stained kiss. "It matters," she said against his lips, then kissed him again before looking up into his eyes, her own still glassy and beseeching. "I just need to know, to believe, it will be enough."

She caressed his face with work roughened hands, and it was all he could do not to take them, and kiss those palms, her fingers, so she'd know, she'd understand. But she either would . . . or she wouldn't. He couldn't make her love him back.

"You've become so much to me, so fast," she said, and his gaze sharpened on hers.

"But?"

"No but. I've never said those words to anyone but family. You're more certain than me, more confident than me. This is all so new, and because it's happened so fast, I want to sort it out, make sure it is what I think it is, not rush into anything for fear I'm mistaking lust for love, or security for love. I have no experience, and sometimes I feel so naïve and so stupid about stuff because I've so completely cut myself off. You matter so much, more than all the rest of it. This . . . what we already have . . . it's everything. Everything. And that scares me because that can't be normal, right? Is it even healthy? Shouldn't I just pack it in and run now?"

She laughed and there was a slight edge of panic to it. "That's how my mind works because that's how I've managed to survive. While I want this new normal life more than anything, I don't really know what normal is, Dylan. I've never lived normal. *I'm* not normal. I can see it for other people, but what shape does it take on for me? No matter what, I can't fully engage in a normal life, I know that much."

"Do you trust me?" he asked when she paused to take a breath.

"More than anyone I've ever trusted, even Bea." She said it without hesitation.

And that branch under him got a little stronger. "Then that's where we start. You have to understand, I don't honestly give a shit about anyone else's idea of normal. I sure as hell don't live that way. All I care about is what works for me. So, you and I will figure out what normal is. For you. And for us. It's that simple, Honey. I know you. I know what you're dealing with, and I'm still here. It's not just a *you* thing anymore, it's an *us* thing. All that matters is what *our* normal is."

"What is your middle name?"

He frowned, completely at a loss. "What? Thomas. After my grandfather. Why?"

She smiled through the shimmer of tears, and smoothed her palms flat to his chest over his heart, then lifted one hand to his face, and wove her fingers back through his hair. "Because, Dylan Thomas Ross, it's quite possible I love you right back. I sure hope you're ready for that. I have a feeling we have absolutely no idea what's in store for us."

He took her hand and kissed her palm, curled her fingers inward to capture it, then placed it over his heart. "Well, see, that's just the thing, sugar," he said, heart thundering so loud he almost couldn't hear himself speak. "I figure if anyone's gonna find out about that, it'll be you."

Then he made her squeal by scooping her up in his arms and carrying her into the house—their house—with Lolly barking excitedly at their heels all the way.

Epilogue

Honey tipped her face up to the sun and enjoyed the warm breeze as it rushed over her skin. She couldn't believe summer was almost over. They'd gotten the sailboat in the water a few weeks ago, and already it was pretty much her favorite place in the world. Even more than her still half unpacked jumble of a studio, although that was a close second. But out on the water, it was just her, and Dylan, and the rhythms of the sea. She felt completely and utterly free. It was the one place, outside of Dylan's arms, where she could let her guard down completely.

She looked at Dylan manning the wheel, and smiled all the way down to her toes. Figuring things out hadn't been easy, and she was still unsure how she was going to balance the different parts of her life, but they were slowly learning each other's moods and their own rhythms, while blending their daily routines and opening up to each other even when it was hard, maybe especially then. But he'd been absolutely and utterly right about one thing . . . figuring it out together beat the hell out of spending a moment trying to do it alone.

She'd had the vision again this morning when he'd taken her hand in his while still asleep. He did that often, and it charmed her, touched her every single time. It had been a while since she'd had the sailboat vision, and she'd thought maybe she wouldn't have it again, so she'd been happy to sink into it. Now that she'd been on the boat for real and experienced part of that vision, she embraced it more fully. Maybe that was why she'd gotten another piece of it.

Her smile spread to a wide grin, even as her stomach did a few little cartwheels and flip-flops. She'd finally seen the child. He'd turned and looked right at her. Her child . . . with eyes of pure, clear green. They'd shared a smile, mother and son, a secret smile. Honey knew then that she had no choice but to keep figuring out how to balance her gift while living in the real world. She was going to have to if she was going to guide her son down that same path . . . because no way was he going to be a hider. She wouldn't let him.

She was very sure his daddy wouldn't, either.

She let the butterflies dance, but at her core, felt nothing but contentment. She continued to watch Dylan, so confident, so happy . . . and to her absolute and utter relief . . . also sublimely content, and wondered if she should tell him.

Her laughter danced to him over the breeze and he turned and smiled. "Come here, sugar." He winked at her. "Time for you to learn to steer this thing."

She stood up and walked over to him on her steadily improving sea legs. He tucked her easily between his body and the wheel and she reveled, as she always did, in how good and right it felt to be in the circle of his arms. She knew she'd always fit right there, no matter what. The strength she drew from that absolute knowledge was immeasurable and made the decision on tackling the rest, as he'd said, a no brainer.

He placed her hands on the wheel. "Kind of like a car.

Ten o'clock, two o'clock. But you have to get a feel for it, because this road is ever changing and it's never the same twice. Figuring it out, though, is the best part."

She smiled, thinking that was pretty much the story of her life . . . her new life.

He covered her hands with his, leaned down, and kissed the side of her neck. "Got it, sugar?"

Yes, she thought, looking up into his eyes. *I really think I do.*

Find out what's cooking from the ladies of the Cupcake Club . . .

Alva's Minced Apple Pie Minis

I adapted my Grandmother Margie's pie recipe to make these little cuties. In her pie pastry, she always used shortening. (Okay, so, early, early on, it was lard . . .) All the time I was growing up I used shortening to make my piecrusts and I have to say they were always pretty darn good! But as I've gotten more into baking while researching the Cupcake Club books, the pastry chefs I've studied have always used butter. And . . . who am I to quibble with the likes of Julia and Nigella? So I've substituted butter here and I've really liked the results. However, if, like me, you've a soft spot for doing things the old-fashioned way, you can substitute shortening and it will still be just as yummy. (And the added bonus is you don't have to wait for it to become room temperature to start baking!)

And! You won't need any special pie tins for this recipe—these mini-pies bake right in your cupcake pans. Yes, apple pie cupcakes! (I know, it's like the two best things all in one. And they look pretty darn adorable, too!)

For the crust:
2 cups flour
2 teaspoons salt
2 teaspoons sugar
1½ sticks butter (¾ cup), room temperature but not too
    soft, cut in small cubes
4–5 tablespoons ice-cold water

1. Preheat the oven to 375°F.
2. Whisk together the flour, sugar, and salt.

3. Cut the butter into small cubes and work it into the flour mixture with a fork or pastry blender. (Yes, you can use a food processor, but it can make the finished mixture granular and your crust then becomes very dense.) Work the fork or pastry blender until the dough is in small, pea-size pieces.
4. Sprinkle the cold water over the dough one tablespoon at a time, and work the dough into a ball.
5. Put the dough in the fridge until you finish making the filling.

For the filling:
5 medium-size tart apples (If you can find them, Jonagold, Cortland, or Northern Spy are great for making apple pies!)
½ cup sugar
½ cup brown sugar
2 teaspoons cinnamon
1 teaspoon nutmeg
⅛ teaspoon salt
2 tablespoons flour
2 teaspoons pure vanilla extract

6. Peel and cut up the apples to remove the core, then dice the apples into small slivers or pieces (about the size of slivered almonds, only thicker).
7. In a separate bowl, use a sturdy whisk to mix together the sugar, brown sugar, spices, salt, and flour until blended. (Break up packed brown sugar with a fork before blending to make whisking easier.)
8. Stir in the vanilla extract.
9. Add in the diced apples and stir gently with a mixing spoon until the pieces look evenly coated

and there is little of the mixture left in the bottom of the bowl.

10. When all the filling ingredients are well mixed, take the dough from the fridge. Lightly flour a rolling pin and your flat surface, then roll the dough out to a uniform ⅛-inch thickness.

11. Lightly dust the surface of the rolled dough with flour. Place a small bowl (approximately 4½–5 inches across) open side down on top of the dough and cut around the edge. Gently press the dough circle into each cup of a cupcake pan, trimming or pinching off any excess to the edge of the cup. Make sure the dough comes to the top edge all the way around, as you'll need it to put the top strips on. Repeat until all 12 cups are lined.

12. Keep all the scraps and leftovers for the top strips, and wrap them and put them in the fridge briefly to firm up while filling the cups.

13. Scoop the filling into each of the prepared pie cups, filling to the top, but not over the top edge.

14. Press fork tips into the bottom of each pie cup several times.

Making the lattice top:

15. Take out the remaining dough from the fridge, and as before, roll out to ⅛-inch thickness. Use a table knife to cut the dough into thin strips approximately ¼- to ⅜-inch wide. Lay the strips over the tops of each pie cup in a lattice. (There may be 10 or more strips in each direction. Don't separate them too much, but don't put them so close together that it will be difficult to weave the cross-strips over and under them.) Push the edges into the edge of the cup, or press lightly with the dough at the edge.

16. Bake at 375°F for 35 to 40 minutes, or until the

crust turns golden brown. Put a baking sheet on the rack under them to catch any apple mixture that might boil over. When finished baking, set the cupcake pan on a rack until cool, then carefully slide each pie from its cup. Use a table knife gently to loosen the edge, especially where apple mixture might have boiled over.

Makes approximately 12 mini-pies. (These are especially good with a scoop of ice cream on the side!)

Ginger Chocolate Fudge Cupcakes

1¼ cups all-purpose flour
½ cup Dutch-process cocoa powder, sifted
2 teaspoons ginger
1 teaspoon cinnamon
¾ teaspoon baking soda
¼ teaspoon allspice
¼ teaspoon salt
1 cup sugar
⅓ cup canola oil
1 egg
1 teaspoon pure vanilla extract
¾ cup buttermilk
½ cup semisweet chocolate chips

1. Preheat oven to 350°F. Line a cupcake pan with paper cupcake liners.
2. Whisk together flour, cocoa powder, ginger, cinnamon, baking soda, allspice, and salt.

3. In a separate bowl, mix together the sugar and oil, then blend in the egg. Do not overmix.
4. Stir in the vanilla.
5. Alternate adding in the flour mixture and the buttermilk, blending after each addition.
6. Stir in the chocolate chips.
7. Use a small ice cream scoop to distribute the batter evenly to all 12 cups, filling each about ⅔ full.
8. Bake for 20–25 minutes, using the toothpick test— when it comes out clean, they're done!
9. Cool the pan on a rack for 10–15 minutes, then remove the cupcakes and cool them completely on the rack before frosting.

For the fudge frosting:
1½ squares unsweetened chocolate (1½ ounces)
¼ cup unsalted sweet cream butter
1½ cups 10x confectioners' sugar
1 egg white
1 teaspoon pure vanilla extract
Water (if needed to adjust thickness)

1. In a small saucepan or double boiler, melt the chocolate and butter together, stirring frequently.
2. Beat in the confectioners' sugar and egg white until thickened and smooth.
3. Stir in the vanilla extract. Add water, if needed, by the teaspoon, to make the frosting the right consistency.
4. Spread on the cupcakes with a knife, or pipe from a pastry bag.

Makes 12 cupcakes.